THE CRUSADER

BY KATHRYN LE VEQUE

Kathryn Le Veque Novels

Medieval Romance:

The de Russe Legacy:
The White Lord of Wellesbourne
The Dark One: Dark Knight
Beast
Lord of War: Black Angel
The Iron Knight

The de Lohr Dynasty:
While Angels Slept (Lords of East
Anglia)
Rise of the Defender
Steelheart
Spectre of the Sword
Archangel
Unending Love
Shadowmoor
Silversword

Great Lords of le Bec:
Great Protector
To the Lady Born (House of de Royans)
Lord of Winter (Lords of de Royans)

Lords of Eire:
The Darkland (Master Knights of
Connaught)
Black Sword
Echoes of Ancient Dreams (time travel)

De Wolfe Pack Series:
The Wolfe
Serpent
Scorpion (Saxon Lords of Hage – Also
related to The Questing)
The Lion of the North
Walls of Babylon

Dark Destroyer
Nighthawk
Warwolfe
ShadowWolfe

Ancient Kings of Anglecynn:
The Whispering Night
Netherworld

Battle Lords of de Velt:
The Dark Lord
Devil's Dominion

Reign of the House of de Winter:
Lespada
Swords and Shields (also related to The
Questing, While Angels Slept)

De Reyne Domination:
Guardian of Darkness
The Fallen One (part of Dragonblade
Series)
With Dreams Only of You

Unrelated characters or family groups:
The Gorgon (Also related to Lords of
Thunder)
The Warrior Poet (St. John and de Gare)
Tender is the Knight (House of d'Vant)
Lord of Light
The Questing (related to The Dark Lord,
Scorpion)
The Legend (House of Summerlin)

**The Dragonblade Series: (Great
Marcher Lords of de Lara)**
Dragonblade
Island of Glass (House of St. Hever)
The Savage Curtain (Lords of Pembury)

The Fallen One (De Reyne Domination)
Fragments of Grace (House of St. Hever)
Lord of the Shadows
Queen of Lost Stars (House of St. Hever)

Lords of Thunder: The de Shera Brotherhood Trilogy
The Thunder Lord
The Thunder Warrior
The Thunder Knight

Highland Warriors of Munro:
The Red Lion
Deep Into Darkness

The House of Ashbourne:
Upon a Midnight Dream

The House of D'Aurilliac:
Valiant Chaos

The House of De Nerra:
The Falls of Erith
Vestiges of Valor

The House of De Dere:
Of Love and Legend

Time Travel Romance: (Saxon Lords of Hage)

The Crusader
Kingdom Come

Contemporary Romance:

Kathlyn Trent/Marcus Burton Series:
Valley of the Shadow
The Eden Factor
Canyon of the Sphinx

The American Heroes Series:
The Lucius Robe
Fires of Autumn
Evenshade
Sea of Dreams
Purgatory

Other Contemporary Romance:
Lady of Heaven
Darkling, I Listen
In the Dreaming Hour

Sons of Poseidon:
The Immortal Sea

Multi-author Collections/Anthologies:
Sirens of the Northern Seas (Viking romance)

Note: All Kathryn's novels are designed to be read as stand-alones, although many have cross-over characters or cross-over family groups. Novels that are grouped together have related characters or family groups.

Series are clearly marked. All series contain the same characters or family groups except the American Heroes Series, which is an anthology with unrelated characters.

There is NO particular chronological order for any of the novels because they can all be read as stand-alones, even the series.

For more information, find it in **A Reader's Guide to the Medieval World of Le Veque**.

TABLE OF CONTENTS

CHAPTER ONE

Year of our Lord 1192
The Holy Land

T HE MOON HAD long since disappeared behind the gathering storm clouds. Smoking torches lit the muddied street, a dank avenue smelling of urine and sweat. Shouts could be heard in the distance as a figure in the shadows turned his head in the direction of the clamor, listening intently. Staying to the recesses, he moved away from the uproar that was following him.

A heavy mist began to fall, washing the blood from his boots and leaving a clear path for his enemies to follow. As the man struggled down an alleyway and emerged onto a larger avenue, the shouts of urgency and the clink of armor seemed to be growing more distant.

A small ray of hope filled his dying heart as he succeeded in losing his adversaries for the moment. But soon enough, he knew, they would discover their folly and retrace their tracks. Tracks that would lead them in the direction of their crippled quarry.

The injured man refused to ponder the eventuality of his capture. His interest at the moment was locating the healer he knew to be located along this avenue. And considering his life was draining with each step, he knew his time was running short to find him.

His breathing was coming in heavy gasps by the time he reached the end of the street, stumbling as he veered to the right. Recapturing his balance, albeit clumsily, his fading eyesight struggled to locate the door emblazoned with a carving of a flaming candle. A door, the bleeding man had been told, identifying the finest healer in Nahariya.

By the time he reached the end of a long row of mud-brick housing with still no carving in sight, the man began to wonder if he would live long enough to find it. Had he missed the symbol? Mayhap. It would not have been difficult considering death was claiming his eyes as well as his body. Mayhap he simply hadn't seen it.

Meanwhile, the mist had turned into a steady rain. The man licked his lips, quenching his dry mouth. Stumbling over the gutter, he fell heavily against a bricked wall, grunting with pain. Slouching against the hard stone, struggling not to collapse completely, he realized that he was angry with the turn of events. He wasn't ready to die and resented the fact that he was being forced to accept his demise prematurely.

Aye, he had come to the Holy Land to fight the Muslim insurgents and was fully prepared to meet his death on the field of battle. But not here, dying like a common villein on the streets of a dirty town without his armor and weapons to verify his importance. Dying before he could complete the task he had started.

The warrior drew in a heavy breath, glancing down at the massive hand covering the wound in his torso. Noting the fingers covered with rich, red blood and the deepening crimson stain on his hose, he knew the prognosis was grim and found himself wondering why he was wasting his time in search of a physic. He was as good as dead. Still, it was not in his nature to accept defeat. He had to continue or die trying.

Sighing again, he lifted his gaze to make another attempt at locating he physic's hovel when he abruptly caught sight of a small, uneven door several yards away. And beneath the rain-soaked tarp, he could vaguely make out a crude carving of a candle.

With a renewed surge of strength, the knight pushed himself away from the wall and staggered across the street, ignoring the driving rain as he pounded on the crumbling door. Pounding again, he didn't wait to be ushered inside when the panel finally opened. Using both his strength and his weight, he propelled himself forward and collapsed heavily on the mud-packed floor.

The room was foggy, faint, and blissfully cozy. He could hear a soothing voice and then felt liquid to his lips. Tasting the sharp tang of alcohol, he drank greedily until the cup was removed.

"Rest easy, Englishman," a heavy accent met his ears and he could feel gentle hands pulling the torn, stained tunic away from his torso. "Ah, so you have been gored like a goat on a spit. Most unfortunate."

Barely conscious, although lucid enough to understand the uttered words, the knight grunted weakly. "I was told… told you could help me."

"By whom?"

"The… innkeeper named Hut. I am lodged at his hostel by the bluff overlooking the waterfront."

"I know this man. Has he a wart on his forehead?"

"The same."

The tiny old man with skin as brown as leather examined the wound carefully. It was deep, puncturing a major organ and he knew his time to save the English knight was growing scarce.

"You're dying," he commented, almost casually.

The knight struggled to open his eyes, focusing on the frail old man. "Your powers of diagnosis are as…astounding."

The healer continued to probe at the gaping wound. "Who did this to you, Englishman?"

The warrior didn't reply for a moment, swallowing hard as his strength faded. "A… man. A man I believed once to be my friend. A man with piercing brown eyes that are surely a window to his darkened soul." He tried to lift his head and failed miserably. "Can you help me or do you resign my fate to God?"

The old man stood up, moving for a cedar table flanking the wall. A table ladened with a variety of mysterious devices, potions, and medicaments. He rummaged about with urgency as he spoke.

"There is but one true God, Englishman. But Allah does not accept

English into his Heaven. Therefore, I must save you from the fires of your pagan-made Hell."

Wet and bleeding on the floor, the knight closed his eyes wearily. "I've not come to debate the differences in our religions. For what I have witnessed within the past two years, it would be quite easy to question the existence of any god, Mohammed's or Abraham's."

"But you do not question," the old man said softly, casting the English knight a long glance. "You believe fully, 'else you would not be here in an attempt to save your life."

The warrior's clear brown eyes opened, slowly, to focus on the wrinkled old man. "Why... why do you say this?"

The Muslim smiled faintly. "Because I sense your work on this earth is not yet complete."

He turned back to his table, leaving the Englishman staring after him, pondering his words. As the old man busied himself at the cluttered table, the knight slowly turned his focus to the ceiling above.

"There is much yet to do," he mumbled. "Much... yet to live for."

The healer lit a wick dipped in fish oil, heating the contents of a small, glass vial suspended on a metal frame. "A wife, Sir Knight? A lover, mayhap?"

Dark blond hair, closely cropped, dried soft and bright in the warmth of the room. The knight's breathing calmed, growing more unsteady as his physical state deteriorated. Still, his mind struggled through the cobwebs of approaching death to concentrate on the old man's question.

"Nay," he whispered, the heavy lids closing. "No lover. No wife. Only... secrets."

Hands full, the healer made his way back to the fading knight. With a sharp slap to the stubbled cheek, he managed to bring his patient around.

"No sleep, my English lord," he said quietly, with the gravity dictated by the situation. "There will be time later to sleep a-plenty."

The knight's eyes rolled open again, muddled by pain and depletion. "I... I brought no money with me. My possessions are still at the inn. You have my permission to seek my purse and collect your fee."

The healer eyed the young knight, surely handsome by English standards. In fact, he had heard the rumors of dark-skinned Muslim women fighting over the white-fleshed Christian warriors from across the sea. But for Kaleef, the war between the Christians and the Muslims was of no particular significance. His religion had always been his work and, at the moment, that work included a dying Christian knight.

"What is your name, Sir Knight?"

"Sir Kieran Hage."

"How many years have you seen?"

"Thirty-two."

Kaleef nodded, swirling the heated liquid in the small, glass vial. "You understand, of course, that I must do all I am able to save your life."

Kieran nodded in understanding. "I wo... would expect so."

"Good," the healer said softly. "Just so you understand the potential consequences."

Kieran's brow furrowed slightly. "Wha...what does this mean?"

"It means that in order to save your life, I must allow your body time to heal. And you do not have any time left."

Kieran's frown deepened. "I still do not understand."

Kaleef put his hand under the knight's head, bringing his lips to the warmed vial of liquid. "Drink this and you shall."

Kieran obediently downed the contents; bitter, oddly metallic tasting. Licking his lips, he found he could scarcely move his massive body as death drew near. And the feeling was increasing with each passing moment.

"What did you give me?"

Kaleef grasped another potion, a cold concoction in a fluted, pewter flask. "A medicine to suspend your bodily functions."

The knight didn't reply for a moment. The clear brown eyes were remarkably focused for a dying man, the voice unusually strong. "What does this mean?"

Kaleef lifted a sparse eyebrow. "A medicine to suspend your bodily functions. And the potion I now hold in my hand will heal your wound internally."

Kieran stared at him. "You... you plan to give me an elixir to heal me from the inside? You do not plan to sew my wound conventionally?"

The old man smiled. "Of course not. Why would I?"

"Because you are a physic. You must sew the wound in order to halt the bleeding."

Kaleef leaned over the massive Englishman, his black eyes filled with a piercing intensity. "I am not a physic, Sir Knight. I've never sewed a wound in my life."

The knight's brown eyes widened with confusion and, Kaleef thought, horror. "You've never... then what are you?"

"An alchemist."

Kieran blinked. "An alchemist?" he repeated, the confusion in his voice evident. "Why... why did the innkeeper send me to you?"

The alchemist's expression was steady. Frighteningly sincere. "Because I am the only one who can save you."

Kieran continued to gaze into orbs as black as a moonless desert night. Not a particularly skittish man, he realized there was nothing he could do against the alchemist's attentions and he furthermore realized there was little reason to resist; clearly, he was dying. And mystic care was better than bleeding to death, alone and feeble, on the mud-hewn avenue outside.

He had no control over his fate. He hadn't since the day he boarded the ship bound for Acre. In the past three years, Kieran had found himself committed to a mission so enormous, so hazardous, that he could scarcely believe God had chosen him for such a task. A mission that had taken him on a wild ride of emotion and adventure, ending with an assassin's broadsword lodged deep in his gut.

A resulting wound that continued to ooze even as Kieran and the alchemist locked gazes, each man deliberating the other. After a moment, Kieran simply closed his eyes. He had not the strength to oppose the old man's concern. He simply wanted to be done with it all, to sleep away the pain and injury. And if the alchemist was convinced he could heal the mortal wound, then Kieran would allow him the faith of his conviction.

"Get on with it then." The English accent was scarcely a whisper.

Sensing resigned faith, Kaleef resumed his actions with an increasing measure of urgency. As the fire in the hearth crackled and spit, the old man leaned over the dying warrior and dispensed two more potions. The alchemist poured, Kieran drank, and the rain outside grew more violent as if to disapprove of the men attempting to cheat death.

In truth, Kaleef wasn't attempting to cheat death, merely delay the final judgment for a time. As long as the English knight was willing to submit, the old man would administer the correct potions in the correct sequence. A recipe he had spent the better part of his life developing, never tested on a mortal man until this very moment. But the Englishman need not be made aware of that small, insignificant detail.

"Wh...what are you giving me?" Kieran's voice was weaker.

Kaleef lifted the Englishman's head one final time, pouring the last of the bitter-tasting liquid down his throat. "'Tis the Recipe."

Kieran was too frail to open his eyes, lest he would have cast the man a dubious glance. "R...Recipe?"

The last of the Recipe administered, Kaleef collected a series of linen rags, unclean, to press them against the oozing wound. "A mixture you would not understand, Sir Knight. Succotrine aloes, zedoary gentian, saffron, rhubarb and agaric have I placed within your wounded body. The Recipe will suspend your mortal functions while a healing potion mends your injury."

Kieran could feel the old man as he wrapped his torso in linen strips. "This... this healing potion. What does it contain?"

"Ram's blood, owl's flesh, snakeskin, various roots and plants."

Had Kieran not been so ill, he would have reacted with disgust. Instead, he found himself unconcerned with the vile elixir so long as it bore the promise of restoration. "How long will it take?"

Kaleef's movements slowed, gazing down at the ashen face. For the first time that eve, his confidence and determination seemed to falter. "The healing will take place in nominal time." His voice was quiet. "There is another matter, however. The matter of reviving you."

Kieran heard the odd words, his mind floating on a hazy mist of herbs and elements and mystical powers. Oddly enough, the pain was gone only to be replaced by a numbing lethargy. He could no longer feel his legs and his torso was growing dull as well.

"Re…revive..?"

Kaleef retrieved a coarse woolen blanket from his bed, wrapping it about the dying Englishman. There was nothing left to do now but wait. If the injury had drained too much of his life away, then the potions would do nothing. But if the dying process had been intercepted in time, then the English knight would have a chance of survival.

As the fire in the hearth died and the pounding rain seemed to quiet, Kaleef lowered himself beside the supine warrior. Gazing into the pallid face of even features and square jaw, he patted the man on the arm in a comforting gesture.

"There is only one method I have been able to discover that will revive you from the endless sleep of the Recipe," he said quietly. "You must understand, Sir Knight, it has been my life's dream to discover an elixir to Immortality, in which I am positive gold is a primary ingredient. The Recipe is a failed result of one such endeavor; although it is quite sufficient in putting one to sleep, never aging, revival is another matter."

Kieran heard him, too weak to respond. In fact, at that very moment, he almost didn't care if he ever awoke or not. The pain was gone, the apprehension and exhaustion had vanished. He was finally at peace and grateful for such a miracle. God only knew, he hadn't been at peace in nearly three years.

Kaleef knew the knight was listening, even if he hadn't responded. With a long sigh, his black gaze moved to the glowing embers of the hearth.

"I had a pet monkey when I was young, a monkey who grew ill with age until I finally administered the Recipe to prolong his life. The little beast slept for forty years until I unknowingly awakened him with an affectionate kiss. An accidental discovery, I assure you."

Kieran was fading fast, the fog of darkness descending on his drug-entrapped mind. Kaleef turned his gaze to the dying warrior, knowing that time was growing short. Within a few short moments, the man would be entering a timeless limbo and the alchemist hastened to inform him of the final aspect of his journey.

"A kiss, Sir Knight, by the one who loves you best is the only catalyst for the Recipe." The foreign accent was soft in Kieran's ear. "When the kiss is given, you shall awaken complete and whole. I apologize that I cannot be more precise than that. For certain, alchemy is not an accurate science. It is the way of men who dare to explore the realm beyond conventional knowledge."

Kieran heard the words at the exact moment darkness claimed him. A kiss, Sir Knight, from the one who loves you best. There was no one who loved him best, except for God. Mayhap God would rouse him personally, welcoming him with open arms into Heaven. And it was thoughts of Paradise that accompanied Sir Kieran Hage into the dominion beyond the pain of mortal existence.

Paradise and visions of his secret.

C3

THE NEXT DAY dawned remarkably bright as the populace of Nahariya went about their business. Almost no one noticed the alchemist and the innkeeper, digging a hole in the floor of an ancient Greek temple. Once dedicated to the Wine God Bacchus, it was now dilapidated with age.

No one cared that two men were out to bury their rubbish within the confines of the pagan sanctuary, a large bundle of castoffs that they could hardly maneuver between them. Not even the collection of worshippers entering the mosque several hundred paces to the south noticed the activity. Certainly, it was quite normal.

"Did you collect all of his possessions?" the alchemist asked over the dust and insects.

"Everything he left in his room. I did not want a trace of the man to linger. He's being hunted, you know."

"I know. I saw the knight with the piercing brown eyes earlier today, apparently following the trail left by our English friend." The old man sighed heavily, unused to such physical exertion. "Although I do not want to bury the man, there is little choice if we are to hide him from his enemy. Why do you suppose his fellow Englishman would want to kill him?"

The fat man with the shovel huffed and sweated over the half-filled grave. It was a moment before he answered. "Last night, while collecting the English knight's property, I came across his journal. Naturally, I was curious and read the contents. And if what he says is true…"

The alchemist looked at him strangely. "If what is true?"

The last shovels of earth filled the hole. Perspiring heavily, the innkeeper focused on the alchemist. "Amazing things, Kaleef. Perhaps I will tell you someday when there is no risk of our conversation being overheard," he groaned, leaning on his trowel. "I have written of the discovery in my own chronicle so that if something should ever happen to me before the truth is known, someone will know the amazing devotion of this English knight. Someone will read my words and pass the information to a person with as much devotion to the Christian cause as the man we have buried."

Kaleef watched his friend collect his digging instruments and trudge down the hill. Glancing to the fresh grave, he seriously pondered Hut's words. A secret, had Sir Kieran said? A secret worth subjecting himself to an alchemist's treatment in the hope that, someday, he could awaken to relive a secret that was valuable enough for one man to kill for and another to die for?

Kaleef wondered; what was this secret? Perhaps he would never know.

He wasn't sure he wanted to.

CHAPTER TWO

Nahariya, Israel
Present Day

BENEATH THE INTENSE rays of the Middle Eastern sun, clouds of dust rose from a hillside covered with ropes secured into grid patterns. A small army of swarthy-skinned workers passed baskets of earth from the area of excavation to a pile that would be sifted through at a later time. The singsong chant to help pass the time was as repetitious as the work, but the native laborers welcomed the tedium. Such were the perils of the archaeological dig that kept them employed.

A bright blue tarp shielded the heart of the activity, pretending to offer some relief from the blazing sun. Deep in a protected trench, a Caucasian man with a sunburned nose carefully swept away clods of earth from what appeared to be a flat, well-worn surface. Around him, the workers continued to clear the earth away and made a cautious effort not to disturb him.

"Well? What do you think? Did we hit the floor?"

The man in the hole heard the question, brushing his fine-bristled brush across the flat surface a few more times before straightening. Glancing over his shoulder, he caught sight of tanned, shapely legs.

"It sure looks like it," he said. "I guess you were right."

"Of course I was." Knees popped as the figure crouched at the edge of the hole, her shaded face beaming beneath a broad-brimmed hat.

Hazel eyes, wide and beautiful, fixed excitedly on the man in the hole. "I told you this was an ancient temple sight, Bud. Now I've finally proven it to you."

Dr. Frederick "Bud" Dietrich smiled broadly at his colleague, his perfect teeth reflecting the brilliant blue of the tarp. "So I'll kiss your feet later. Right now, I want to get a sample of this floor for carbon testing. Where's Dave?"

As if hearing his name, Dr. David Peck made a hurried appearance at the edge of the trench. In his hands, a digital camcorder was poised to begin documenting the discovery. He'd been in the very same hole not fifteen minutes earlier when it had become apparent they were on to something. The woman in the broad-brimmed hat smiled into his bespectacled brown eyes.

"We've hit floor, Dave," she said eagerly. "Didn't I tell you it was here? Didn't I?"

Dave gazed into her beautiful face, flushed with excitement and temperature. "Yeah, yeah, you were right and I'll never hear the end of it. Now, move out of the way so that I can record your auspicious find."

Smiling confidently, the woman rose and stepped aside, allowing Dr. Peck to descend into the trench. As Bud and David swarmed over a very small patch of hard-packed earth, Dr. Rory Osgrove observed the activity with the aura of a conquering Caesar. It had taken fourteen long months of sweat and labor but, finally, she knew she had found what they had been looking for. At least, she hoped so.

Dr. Peck began to record the discovery of the ancient floor, orating a blow-by-blow account as Bud resumed his brushing and proceeded to dust away centuries of dirt. Technically, Dr. Osgrove was on a break, as she had been working in this precise spot for the past seven hours until Bud demanded she take a breather. Even as her supervising archaeologist continued brushing away the loose soil where she had left off, Rory was unable to leave and certainly unable to rest.

And the idleness only grew worse. Unable to stand it any longer, Rory collected a smaller, finer brush from Bud's arsenal of instruments and descended into the trench. Finding a comfortable position, she began to delicately brush the edges of the ancient flooring as Bud watched her from the corner of his eye. Knowing how excited she was, he just didn't have the heart to scold her for disregarding his order to rest.

"Look how hard-packed this stuff is," she murmured, ignoring the dust billowing up her nose. "Once we clear away more of the debris, the size of the sanctuary ought to take shape."

"If it's even a sanctuary," offered the ever-logical Dr. Peck with his steady wisdom to offset his colleague's enthusiasm. "It could be a number of things, Rory. We've discussed this already."

Rory didn't look up from her area of concentration. "All of the data supports the fact that this should be an ancient Muslim mosque. All of the artifacts we've tested simply strengthen that claim."

Dr. Peck kept his eye to the viewfinder of the camcorder. "You're basing your reasoning on fourteenth century manuscripts as well as regional folklore. Other than a few pieces of pottery and polished stone, we've found nothing further to substantiate your theory. Show me an ancient Koran beneath this flooring and I just might believe you."

Rory paused, the smile gone from her face as she focused on her skeptical associate. "How do you think most archaeological sites are plotted and discovered, Dave? Ancient manuscripts have always been a fairly reliable source of information and I spent the better part of my post-graduate work locating this exact site. Are you telling me that I've been leading the university and its funds on a wild goose chase without good reason?"

Peck didn't reply, refusing to delve into the familiar argument. Having worked and lived with Rory Osgrove twenty-four hours a day for the past fourteen months, he was coming to feel as if he had married her. And, like any married couple, they had their share of spats. But nothing could dampen the fact that there was a good deal of professional respect between them; not even the fact that David himself believed their dig to be nothing more than an ancient trash dump, even if Rory believed it to be the site of a ruined mosque.

So he bit his tongue, unwilling to detract from the reality that they had actually come upon something substantial this day. The more Rory and Bud worked, clearing away the loose debris, the more David began to realize that, perhaps, she really was on to something. Keeping the videotape rolling, he stood back to record the unfolding of events.

High above, the sky began to take on hues of golds and pinks, signaling the approach of a Middle Eastern sunset. The usual quitting time came and went, but the workers refused to leave. Even among the laborers there was a palpable sense of discovery and they, too, were eager to see the results of their backbreaking labor.

When the sun finally dipped below the western horizon, the foreman cranked up the gasoline generator and the mercury vapor lamps hummed steadily beneath the brilliant night sky. Deep in the hole, Bud and Rory wallowed in sublevels of earth several centuries old, brushing carefully, picking, and then brushing again. It was slow, steady work as the entire camp hovered expectantly, waiting for the miraculous discovery to reveal itself.

A miraculous discovery that was hardly valuable to the untrained eye. But to the archaeologists, it was increasingly significant. By ten o'clock, several feet of flooring had been cleared, uneven and worn, and the activity continued steadily until Bud neared a particularly hard-packed section of earth. Suddenly, his careful efforts came to a halt.

"Whoa," he muttered, dropping his brush and collecting a bulb syringe. Blowing cautiously at an odd-shaped mound of mud, he set the syringe down and grasped a dental scaler. Rory, covered with dirt and sweat, watched him curiously as he picked at the chalky-white lump.

"What's wrong, Bud?" she asked softly.

Bud's brow furrowed slightly, his ice-blue eyes intense as he picked away at chunks of dirt. "I'm not sure," he replied, retrieving his brush once again. "This doesn't seem to be… hell, I don't know what this is."

Rory set her brush down, peering over Bud's shoulder. He felt her presence, inevitably distracted from his work. She had always affected him that way, ever since the first instant he'd beheld her hazel-eyed, chestnut-haired beauty almost two years ago. The very moment the head of the Archaeology and Anthropology Department of the University of California San Marcos had informed him of his new Middle East assignment and the driving force behind it.

Dr. Rory Osgrove was a new Ph. D. that had managed to convince the university's board of regents that a substantially valuable find was located in the heart of the Israeli city of Nahariya. Enthusiastic and intelligent but lacking the experience of a seasoned archaeologist, the board had been adequately convinced to pursue her petition by assigning two of the university's premier field professors to aid her efforts.

Doctors Dietrich and Peck had been called in from a minor dig in Cyprus to assist the new Dr. Osgrove at her Nahariya site. Bud had been reluctant at first, considering the very goal of her excavation was outlandish at best. But the moment he gazed at Rory's eager, beautiful face, he began to think that committing himself to a dig in the coastal town of Nahariya wasn't such a bad idea after all. And David had agreed, although far more hesitantly; where Bud went, he went, no matter how foolish the venture.

Which was why the dusty, milky mound of earth Bud continued to pick away at disturbed him so. He knew it wasn't what they had spent over a year searching for. It didn't belong in the middle of an ancient mosque, considering the holy temples of long ago were devoid of furnishings but for the few things the holy men could carry. No altars, no pews, and nothing that could be considered of any value.

Rory continued to hover over his shoulder, her gentle breath on his ear. Twice, Bud had nearly stabbed himself with his dental pick as he struggled to keep his mind on his work.

"What do you think it is?"

Her voice was breathy, soft, and an erotic chill ran down his spine. Swallowing hard, he realized his mouth had gone dry. "I really don't know," he responded steadily, rather pleased that he hadn't come across like a giddy teenager. Setting the pick down, he collected the bulb syringe once again and blew hard. "It almost seems as if the mud is caked to something. Some sort of…"

Abruptly, a large chunk of earth fell away, landing on Bud's hand and immediately drawing blood. Rory gasped, clutching at his injured fingers even as Bud himself moved to examine the wound. Their flesh touched in the hurried reaction to study his scraped knuckles and Bud suddenly realized he was inches from Rory's flushed face.

She was staring at his lacerated skin, her lips pursed with concern. "Are you all right?" she demanded. Before he could reply, she was turning to the nearest worker, politely but urgently asking the man to retrieve the first aid kit. Returning to Bud's fingers, her tender touch was enough to make him forget the stinging cut.

"I'm fine," he managed to whisper, his heart thumping madly against his ribs. Not to be too obvious that he was enjoying her attention, however, he smiled wryly when her hazel eyes focused on his face. "You worry like my mother."

She frowned. "Fine, then. Bleed to death all over the dirt and see if I care."

He laughed. "I'm sorry, I'm sorry." He was pleased when she didn't release his fingers. "I'm not ungrateful for the concern, Mom – I mean, Dr. Osgrove. Really."

As Rory and Bud traded weak insults over the top of Bud's bloodied knuckles, David handed the camcorder over to the foreman and picked up a fine-bristled brush. Brown eyes narrowed in concentration behind the thin-rimmed glasses, he began to chip away at the cavity left by the crumbling mud.

Beside him, Rory and Bud were still bickering over Bud's lack of graciousness towards Rory's concern. David knew it was a bluff on Bud's part, considering he was in love with the woman. And had he not been so concerned with what was coming to light within the caked mud of a dozen centuries, Dr. Peck would have been happy to cast Bud a series of disbelieving glances. But he couldn't spare the attention.

"Hey, Bud," he called softly, blowing gently at the ancient earth. "You'd better take a look at this."

Bud tore his gaze away from Rory's face, his features morphing from soft to serious in an instant. Peering closely at the muddied impression exposed for the first time in over a millenium, he forgot all about his injured hand. Snatching the brush from David, he continued to sweep the dirt away from the underlying relief.

"Christ," Bud hissed, watching as another hunk of mud broke loose and tumbled to the ground.

"What?" Rory was poised over Bud's left shoulder, squinting in the dim glow of the vapor lamps. After a moment, her expression slackened. "It looks like… like a…"

"A Greco relief," Dr. Peck finished for her. As Bud continued to gently loosen the dirt, David pointed to the faint outline emerging into the heated night. "Look… definitely a Greek etching. Note the rounded cheeks, the cherub influence. And these wavy lines; hell, Bud, they look like vines, don't they?"

Rory ceased to breathe as she listened to Peck reason out what was emerging from the foundation of her Muslim mosque. Certainly nothing of Greek influence should be here, a paganistic religion invading Allah's sanctuary. Her heart began to sink as Bud finished chipping away at a small panel of dried earth. When it crumbled away completely, he set his brush to the ground and blew lightly at the surface.

No one dared to move as Bud studied the ancient veneer. The senior archaeologist on the dig with more than eighteen years of experience, he clearly knew his field. After a lengthy pause, he sighed heavily.

"It's Bacchus," he said quietly, pointing at the vines encompassing the rounded face. "These are grape vines, indicative of the wine god's mantle. He always appears the same in mythology relief."

David lowered himself to sit beside Bud, studying the dirty surface. "There's no way Grecian marble would find its way into a Muslim mosque," he muttered, neglecting the fact that all of Rory's hopes were being shattered by his analytical words. "The Muslims considered the Greeks and Romans to be pagans, their ancient temples unclean. In fact, they buried their sinful dead and trash in what they considered to be unconsecrated ground."

"The grounds of an ancient Greek temple," Bud concurred.

"A trash dump," Rory said in a quiet voice. As Bud and David looked to her, varied degrees of regret in their eyes, she forced herself to stand tall and brush the dirt off her hands. No matter if her heart was breaking with the reality of the find, as undeniable as it was, she would not let on.

She would have liked nothing better than to argue the point. Fourteen months of labor and devotion demanded as much, but she realized as she gazed at the worn marble face that she could not, in good conscience, contradict Bud or David's reasoning.

She should have prepared herself for the moment of failure. But she had been so sure of herself that she realized, somewhat dazedly, that she was unprepared to accept defeat in the least. In lieu of falling apart completely, she squared her shoulders with as much courage as she could muster.

"I guess you were right, Dave. This must have been an ancient trash dump." Before Peck could reply, Rory was making her way from the trench. "I suppose I should have listened to you. When we found shards of pottery and marble, I called them Muslim artifacts and you called them ancient trash. When I indicated that fourteenth century Byzantine manuscripts pinpointed this location, you told me they were open to interpretation. I should have… listened."

She was out of the hole, moving through the cluster of workers surrounding the trench. As she marched towards the distant camp, David leapt to his feet with the intention of apologizing for her failure and his correct assumption. But Bud stopped him before he could follow her.

"No." His ice-blue eyes were riveted to the khaki shorts fading in the distance. "Let her go. We'll talk about this later."

David was genuinely remorseful, removing his gaze from the distant figure to focus on his friend and colleague. "I never meant… well, you know, to hurt her feelings. I would have been very happy to have been proven wrong about this whole dig. But what she was saying, Bud… it just never made sense to me. All of this hunting for the Crown of Thorns that Jesus Christ wore at Mount Calvary. Just what in the hell would a Christian relic be doing in a Muslim mosque?"

Bud shrugged faintly, his heart aching for the lovely young lady he was so fond of. "I don't know, Dave," he said quietly, glancing once more at the bas relief as if it contained some sort of curse. The longer he gazed at it, the more he wished he had never found it.

"The university is going to pull the funding for sure now." Peck's voice was quiet in his ear. "Rory will be lucky if she isn't given a desk somewhere in a stuffy office for wasting such a tremendous amount of money and effort. With this disaster, they'll never trust her again."

Bud's square jaw ticked. "But they trust me and she'll go where I go. I'll resign my fellowship if they put her behind a desk somewhere, cataloguing trivial items that a monkey could take care of."

Peck sighed, his gaze finding hazy, white marble covered with filth. Sensing their employers' disappointment in what had apparently been uncovered, the crowd surrounding the site began to disband as David knelt beside the faded relief.

"What made her think we'd find a biblical relic in Nahariya, of all places?" he muttered softly, more to himself than to Bud. "I saw her data and, although I admit it was powerful, it just wasn't convincing enough. Certainly not convincing enough to warrant university funds for a complete dig."

Bud glanced down at his associate, his mind a jumble of thoughts as he pondered the immediate future. When the university was informed of their failure, the site would be dissolved. "She's a biblical archaeologist, Dave. She delves into areas that most classical archaeologists scoff at." Brushing off his hands, he leaned wearily against the side of the ditch. "I don't have to tell you that the university has powerful backing from both the Lutheran and Presbyterian leagues. Not to mention the fact that three ordained ministers sit on the board of regents. It was never surprising to me that she obtained approval for this dig. Besides, she can be really convincing."

Still staring at the impression of Bacchus, Peck slowly shook his head before rising to his feet. Even if he had never truly believed in the purpose of the dig, still, it was disappointing that he had been proven right and Rory had been proven wrong. One year and two months of sweat and effort down the drain.

"Well, I've had enough for one night," he said quietly, climbing from the trench. "I suppose we should call Dr. Becker and make a report."

"I'll do it," Bud said quickly; too quickly. When David looked as if he didn't believe the man's word, Bud merely shrugged and hoisted himself from the hole. "I want to talk to Rory first. So she understands what's going to happen."

Peck emitted a long sigh. "She understands, Bud. She's understood the potential consequences from the beginning. It doesn't matter how you confirm the fact that her project is ended, it's still going to hurt. And you can't ease the pain no matter what you say."

Bud gazed into the heated night sky, a billion stars glittering wickedly against the heavens. After a moment, he clucked with regret. "I realize that." The two men began to move in the direction of the camp. "Still, I don't want her to feel like she's failed. We've still come up with some marvelous artifacts in spite of everything."

The smell of roasting pig was heavy as they drew near the encampment. David eyed the glow from the cooking fires, realizing he was going to miss the rustic atmosphere when they returned to the States. He was quite at home roughing it among the natives, which made him ideal for this profession. And the fact that he had the sensitivity of a rock, as Rory had so delicately phrased his character, made him perfect for a job that took him far away from the normal, compassionate populace.

A sensitivity, however, than was oddly intact this night. "But we didn't find her crown," he replied belatedly to Bud's statement. "To her, that constitutes failure."

Bud watched the man disappear into the clutter of canvas structures, chewing his lip in thought. No, they hadn't located their ultimate goal and, in a way, Bud blamed himself for the disappointment. Perhaps he could have worked harder. Perhaps there was something here and he was just too blind to see it. Or maybe he should have discouraged the dig from the beginning and saved them all the trouble.

The workers were eating beef and lentils as he made his way to his tent. A quick wash, a change of clothes, and then he would find Rory and try to comfort her. Try to comfort them both.

CHAPTER THREE

T HE NEXT DAY emerged dusty and uncomfortable. The howling desert winds blasted the barren hills like a furnace as Rory sat in Bud's tent, her long chestnut hair wound up on top of her head and her loose cotton shirt already soaked with sweat. They were seated around a folding table, David a few feet away and toying distractedly with a pen. His laptop computer was open and engaged. A message on the screen was waiting to be emailed to the head of the Archaeology and Anthropology Department of the university.

Bud was lingering by the open flap of the tent, conversing with the foreman in Arabic. But Rory wasn't listening to their conversation; at the moment, her thoughts were centered on the cessation of funds and the closure of her dig. Since retiring to her tent the night before in the throes of defeat, she'd pondered little else. She simply couldn't believe it had come down to this.

When the brief dialogue came to a conclusion, the foreman ducked away and Bud turned to his subdued colleagues. His eyes were riveted to Rory, his heart aching for the conversation to come. Quietly, he took a seat.

"I didn't see you at breakfast," he said softly, noting the circles under her eyes and her pale complexion in spite of the heat. "You know the rule; you've got to eat something before going out in the field. It's too easy to collapse in this heat with an empty stomach."

She sighed faintly, the hazel eyes coming up from the tabletop. "I'm not going out in the field today, Bud. None of us are, I would guess."

His gentle expression faded, feeling Peck's intense stare. But his focus remained on Rory. "I went to your tent last night after supper, but you were already asleep. I'd hoped we could talk about the situation."

Rory shrugged. "I wasn't asleep. I just didn't want to talk to anyone. Especially you. I sort of needed to come to grips with this by myself."

Bud held her gaze a moment longer, feeling the pain radiating forth from the intense hazel eyes. David had been right; there wasn't anything he could do or say to ease the ache of failure and he suddenly felt frustrated with his impotency. But facts were facts. "I just don't know what else I can do, Rory. I'm sorry. I really am. I don't think there's any doubt that we've found an ancient trash dump and there simply isn't enough, at this point, to keep us here."

He saw her swallow, struggling to maintain her composure even though she knew what his answer would be. After a moment, she nodded as if to acknowledge the fate of her precious project. "Then I suppose you should go ahead and send your report to Becker. Tell him what a fool I made out of him and the university."

"That's not true," Bud said firmly. "We found some priceless pieces that will easily compensate the funding that supported this dig. You have nothing to be ashamed about."

Rory stood up, turning away from the table. Her back was damp with perspiration, her shapely legs glistening with sheen. Bud watched her as she wandered to the edge of the tent, trying not to stare at her perfect bottom when he realized David wasn't being quite so discreet. As Rory paused at the tent flap, Bud cast his associate a withering expression, causing the man to look away in embarrassment.

"I'm not, really. It's just that I can't believe what's happened," she uttered, her gaze focused on the encampment that was still for the most part. After a lengthy pause, she sighed heavily. "Archaeology has always been my passion. When I was a kid, my mom bought this old house and I liked to dig in the backyard because a hundred years ago, that's where people buried their trash. I found all sorts of old milk bottles and broken plates, and I loved it. My mom thought I was nuts."

Dr. Peck tossed the pen he had been toying with aside. "Hell, I was even worse. I used to dig up old animal bones and my parents thought I was going to be a grave robber."

That statement brought a smile to Rory's pallid lips. "I'm not surprised, Dave. You always were a little weird." When Peck met her smile and looked away sheepishly, the hazel eyes focused on Bud. Her smile faded. "It's not like I didn't research all of my facts before going ahead with this project. I spent the majority of my graduate studies in Rome and Istanbul, studying Byzantine manuscripts that had been translated from ancient Arabic text. Particularly, several parchments that had to do with the Christian religion's influence on the Third Crusade as translated by a monk named Ottis. The guy really knew his stuff, Bud. He was so... convincing."

Bud nodded slowly; he had heard all of this before. "I saw the copies of the scripts, Rory. And you have all of the translated information here. If I thought you had been off base, I wouldn't have agreed to head this undertaking in the first place. I know you were convinced of the authenticity of the facts. I was, too."

Arms folded across her chest, Rory kicked at the ground in frustration before meandering back to her colleagues. Reaching the table, she suddenly slammed her palm against the peeling surface.

"Damn," she hissed, her mannerisms growing more animated as she spoke. "It's got to be here. I know it is. But we're not looking in the right place!"

"Where else are we going to look?" Peck was always the voice to contradict her theories and Bud cast him a warning glance. Now was not the time to say I told you so. "We followed your leads, the information provided. Rory, do you realize what we were looking for in the first place? You're talking about a biblical relic to end all biblical relics; the actual Crown of Thorns that Jesus Christ wore on Mount Calvary. And the fact that we were looking for a Christian artifact on the grounds of a Muslim mosque just never added up."

Rory stared at him, the warmth from not a moment before vanished. "I told you why, Dave. The transcripts stated that the crown had been buried secretly, but I don't know why. It wasn't very clear." She was struggling to keep calm. "Look, I never entered this field with the intention of finding Christ's bones. Although my degree is in Biblical Sciences, my emphasis is the Crusades. But when I came across an obscure reference to the Crown of Thorns while studying for my doctoral thesis, I just couldn't let it go. It was like an addiction, one that I had to pursue or regret the rest of my life."

David shook his head, lowering his gaze. Watching his grim expression, Rory was seized with the familiar anger she quite often felt as a result of Peck's cynicism. Since the moment the project began, she'd been defending her ideas to him almost daily. "You never did believe in what we were doing here," she said, her voice was uncharacteristically cold. "God only knows why you agreed to this assignment, because your heart certainly wasn't in it. The harder I tried to prove my theories, the harder you tried to shoot me down."

"That's not true." David rose from his chair defensively. "If I didn't have a good amount of faith in your speculations, nothing in the world could have convinced me to participate in this dig. But I'll admit, Biblical Archaeology isn't something I put a lot of trust in."

"Why not?" Rory demanded.

Peck threw up his hands. "Because you're chasing myths. To most scientists, the Bible is just a book full of folklore and stories. It's not fact!"

Rory turned away from him, growling with irritation. "Neither was the city of Troy, but Schliemann proved that it did, in fact, exist."

"The city of Troy and biblical relics are two different things." David's argument was gaining steam. "There were varied sources confirming Troy's whereabouts. You're basing all of your ideas on one single book and the writings of men who believed in the existence of God and angels and demon sorcery."

Rory paused by the edge of the tent, her cheeks mottled with heat and emotion. "Then you're telling me I'm basing my beliefs on the ignorance of religious idiots?"

"I telling you that you're willing to give the tales of Medieval monks more credit than you should. And your blind faith has cost the university a hell of a lot of money."

She continued to gaze at him, blinking slowly as her composure slipped another notch. "Did it ever occur to you that the ancient manuscripts may be correct? That, maybe, the tales Byzantine monks spent their lives putting to paper just might have some basis? Or do you just assume they're all a bunch of ignorant asses simply because they don't have a Ph.D. in Anthropology like you do?"

David let out a long sigh; it seemed like every time they delved into this subject, the exchange became increasingly bitter. But, in his opinion, his argument was valid. More so as of last night. "You'd make a hell of a theologian, Rory. But you've got a lot to learn about archae-ology."

Rory's control was dangerously close to breaking. The urge to plant her fist into David's eye was overwhelming. "And you've got a lot to learn about faith, Dr. Peck. Not everything in this world is subject to hard facts and logic. Sometimes there is more truth in the unknown than the known."

Before the verbal battle grew out of control, Bud decided to inter-vene. "Enough of this," he said in a tone that discouraged further argument. "We've been through this before and I'm sick of this constant bickering. Dave, sit down and shut up. Rory, come over here and sit. Your pacing is digging holes in my floor."

Jaw ticking, Rory reluctantly did as she was asked, refusing to look at Dr. Peck across the table. Bud watched her a moment, feeling her tension and disappointment.

"Look," he said quietly. "I'll see what I can do about extending this project another month or two. Maybe you're right… maybe we're not looking in the right place."

David let out a harsh hiss before Rory could respond. "We're looking exactly where she said to look, Bud." His voice was strained with irritation. "What will it take to convince you that the Crown of Thorns is exactly what I said it was from the beginning – a myth. It's not here; nothing is!"

Bud's expression was tight. "You're contradicting yourself. Only a minute ago you were saying that you wouldn't have agreed to come on this dig if Rory's facts hadn't been somewhat solid."

Peck held Bud's gaze a moment before looking away. "She presented a hell of an argument, Bud. Enough to make me think that maybe she was right. And you thoroughly believed her, so I guess I just went along with the general opinion." His voice was softened as he focused on Rory. "But I've got to tell you this; your ultimate goal to not only locate the crown but to match whatever DNA blood evidence might exist with similar swatches from the Shroud of Turin is about the craziest thing I've ever heard of. Just what are you trying to prove, anyway?"

Rory was staring at her hands. She should have been used to Dr. Peck's personal attacks by now but, when it came to her pet project, her skin wasn't as thick as it should have been. "I'm trying to do what all scientists have been trying to do since the beginning of modern archaeology," she replied quietly. "I'm trying to shed some truth on myths and legends. In my case, the reality of biblical fables."

"All you would succeed in proving is that both relics belonged to the same man if, in fact, you were successful in linking them. There is no way to prove that it was Jesus Christ. And there wouldn't be any way of proving he was anything other than an ordinary man."

"But I can try to give more accurate credence to his myth. You of all people should appreciate the tangibility of hard fact."

"We do," Bud interjected, casting David a stern look that indicated he dare not contradict him. "Which is why I'm going to try and buy us a little more time. We've put a lot of work into this dig to see it end on such a negative note."

Back to the subject of extending the dig; it was obvious that Peck continued to disagree and he lurched from his chair. Leaving the tent in a huff of skepticism and irritation, Bud watched the tent flap swing back and forth in the wake of his colleague's departure. Scratching his head, he sat back in his chair.

"I'm sorry about Dave," he offered weakly. "I've worked with the man for twelve years and he's always been like this."

Rory looked up from her hands, cocking an eyebrow. "Like what? A jerk?"

Bud smiled, his perfect teeth gleaming within his square, stubbled jaw. "He certainly can be. But he's one of the smartest guys I know and I wouldn't want to be without him on any project."

A faint smile on her lips in response to Bud's grin, Rory gazed steadily at the man who had become her friend and boss over the past fourteen months. A man who would have done anything in the world for her. Including risk his reputation on a dig that was clearly a waste of time.

Rory liked Bud. She always had. And she'd known from the beginning that he was in love with her, although she had tried not to encourage him. He was a good-looking guy, his masculine features and crew-cut blond hair a tremendous comfort in a land full of dark-haired strangers. But she simply didn't feel an over amount of attraction to him and she wondered, when he realized his infatuation with her had nearly ruined his reputation, if he wouldn't grow to hate her. She hoped not.

Taking a deep breath to chase away her annoyance with Peck, she put a palm on Bud's hand. "You said it yourself, Bud. There's nothing on that hill but an ancient trash dump and I doubt that a month or two or even twelve would do a whole lot of good. Maybe you should just go ahead and email Becker your report and see what he says."

Bud stared into her hazel eyes, wondering if he and Rory would ever make as good a pair as Louis S.B. and Mary Leakey. He certainly intended to spend the rest of his life pursuing that thought. "Are you sure?" he asked, his voice raspy as her touch sent bolts of electricity through him. "I mean, I can stall for time."

She smiled and he went weak. "Time for what? For Dave to become even more of a jerk and time for you and me to dig an even bigger hole into nothingness? Thanks for your support, but maybe we'd better go ahead and end this now. While we've still got our dignity."

Bud thought a moment, still fixed on her beautiful face. But visions of him kissing her luscious lips infiltrated his mind until he had to look away or risk doing something drastic. Christ, he hated to see it all end like this.

"Are you sure?"

"Yeah."

There was nothing more to say. After a moment, he nodded in agreement. "All right." He sat forward, reaching for David's laptop computer. Rory released his hand, rising from her chair as Bud began to sequence the email command.

She wandered to the canvas opening, watching Bud type with his index fingers. The more she came to grips with the cessation of her dig, the more her anguish threatened to overwhelm her. By the time she turned away from her supervising archaeologist, she could hardly breathe with the pain in her chest.

"Let me know what he says, huh?" she asked softly, exiting the tent. "I'll be around."

Bud stopped typing long enough to watch her heart-shaped bottom fade into the brilliant sunlight. With a sigh of sincere regret, he finished the last of the command and pressed enter.

Dr. Uriah Becker received the email a half-hour later.

03

THE WINDS HAD died by early afternoon but the temperature remained unbearable. As the camp lounged lazily in an attempt to seek some relief from the heat, Bud went in search of Rory to give her the just-received reply from Dr. Becker. When he failed to find her in her tent, he spent a half-hour scouring the grounds. But it was soon apparent that she was not within the camp perimeter and his concern mounted as he widened his area of search.

In triple-digit heat, he headed for the excavations on the distant rise, concerned that she was struggling in the last few hours of her project to prove her point. Sweating profusely, he was somewhat disturbed to see David coming down the hill towards him. Baseball hat stained with perspiration, Dr. Peck's expression was grim.

"She's going to kill herself, Bud," he said severely. "She's up in that damned trench again, digging as if her life depends on it. I tried to get her to come out but she won't even talk to me."

Bud sighed heavily, rolling his eyes with regret. "How long has she been there?"

David turned to follow him as Bud continued up the hill. "I don't know. Hours, at least. She's as red as a beet."

Bud winced. "That's not like her at all. She's usually so careful about sun exposure."

David agreed. "No water, either."

Bud's expression hardened. "Christ," he swore. "Like it or not, she's coming out of there if I have to carry her."

"You'll probably have to."

Reaching the top of the slope, Bud's gaze immediately fell on Rory's chestnut head bobbing in the trench. Catching a glimpse of an extremely red face, he put his hand on David's arm in an urgent gesture. "Go get some wet towels, Dave. And hurry up!"

David fled. Marching to the edge of the trench, Bud jumped to the dirt several feet below. Rory was furiously, meticulously, sectioning earth with a pickaxe, a method used to loosen sod for later removal and processing. When the pickaxe came up, Bud grabbed hold and yanked hard.

Rory almost toppled with the strength of his pull; the pickaxe tugged free, leaving splinters in her blistered hands. Her beautiful face, confused and glistening with sweat, met his angry expression.

"Just what in the hell are you doing?" he demanded. "How long have you been here?"

Dazed and ill-feeling though she might be, Rory stood her ground. "This is still my dig until we pull up stakes. And I'm going to work on it until I'm forced to leave."

He tossed the pickaxe aside in a fit of fury, grabbing her hand. "I'm forcing you to leave now. If you stay out here any longer you're going to end up in the hospital."

Resistant to his demand, Rory jerked her hand away and nearly fell on her bottom. "It's my dig, Bud. I told you, we're not looking in the right place. I… I just have to keep searching!"

His eyes glittered with rage. "Not four hours ago you told me that any more digging would be a waste of time."

She was emotionally and physically unbalanced. For the first time since he had known her, Bud saw Rory's eyes fill with tears.

"It's my dig," she repeated quietly, her lower lip trembling. "The manuscripts weren't wrong, Bud. There's something here. I know it."

His anger fled. How could he tell her that Dr. Becker had ordered an immediate cessation of all work and the complete disbandment of the camp within the next forty-eight hours? Of course, he couldn't. Not when she was so emotionally brittle. What mattered most was cooling her down, calming her down, and then talking some sense into her. Reaching out, he grasped her hand again. More gently, this time.

"I believe you, honey," he said softly, watching the tears spill down her dusty cheeks. "But now is not the time to go looking. It's far too hot and you need to rest. Let's go back to camp."

She shook her head feebly but he tugged on her arm, encouraging her to the edge of the ditch. Making sure he had a good grip on her, he climbed from the trench and practically lifted her out behind him. When she began to weave dangerously as he moved her down the hill, he swept her into his arms and made haste for her tent.

Rory's arms were wound around his neck, her scorching body sweating all over him. "I'm going back in a little while, Bud," she murmured. "After a little rest."

Her damp forehead was against his stubbled jaw. In the distance, Bud could see Peck running towards him with an armful of dripping towels. "Whatever you say, honey," he murmured, loving the feel of her in his arms but wishing the circumstances were different. "I won't argue with you."

Her tent was sweltering but it provided some shelter from the sun. As Bud lay her down on the narrow bed, David hovered over her like a mother and placed cooling towels over her face and arms. Bud bathed her legs as Rory lay still, panting softly with near-heat stroke.

"If... if we section away more of the loose earth, maybe we'll get a better view." Her voice was barely audible. When David lifted her head and ran a cold, wet towel across the back of her neck, she gasped softly. "The sod is really sandy in some places, which will make it easier to remove."

Bud didn't reply as he removed her shoes, noting the fuchsia-painted nails and delicate toes. Christ, even her feet were lovely. "Get her some water, Dave. She's really dehydrated."

Peck laid the wet towel across her forehead, gazing at his young associate with genuine concern. Regardless of their differences and the fact that he wasn't usually a compassionate person, he was nonetheless concerned for her health. Being insensitive didn't mean he had a heart of stone and, in spite of everything, he truly enjoyed the love-hate relationship they seemed to share. She was one of the only people he knew who could stand up against his arrogant nature.

"How 'bout some Gatorade, Rory?" he asked quietly, as if a louder tone would cause her to break. For some reason, he felt responsible for her condition. As if his bitter cynicism had forced her to prove her point. "My parents shipped me a whole case of it. There's lemonade flavor and cherry and..."

Rory shook her head listlessly. "No thanks, Dave. That stuff tastes like flavored sweat. Water's fine."

He smiled, glad she wasn't ill to the point of being nonresponsive.

"It's better for you than water. You should know that; you studied Pre-Med for a couple of years, didn't you?"

She nodded weakly. "Yes, but I still don't want any."

"Salt, sugar, potassium. Yum."

When she stuck her tongue at him in response, he pursed his lips wryly. But he was still smiling.

"All right, all right, don't get nasty," he said, moving for the tent opening. There were several workers huddled outside, trying to catch a glimpse of what was going on. They had all seen Bud carrying Rory down from the excavation and rumors of her ill health had spread like wildfire.

David caught sight of the gaggle of employees, scattering the majority of them with a brusque order. But he retained a couple of the women, instructing them to bring Rory a pitcher of purified water and more wet towels. As the women scurried away, David found his attention drawn to the site on the distant rise.

He didn't know why his attention was riveted to the dusty hill. After what he had seen yesterday, he shouldn't have given the site a second thought. But Rory believed there was something up there, something worth risking her health and reputation for. With a heavy sigh, David found himself trudging up the gritty slope. If only to see the same old dirt she had been so intent to risk heatstroke over.

The earth was hot enough to cook meat. David paused at the edge of the trench, observing the grids that he had constructed himself. Rory's precise digging was apparent, the pickaxe carelessly thrown to the side by Bud's fury. Stepping into the hole, David studied the newly exposed earth.

Rocks. Dried mud. Nothing of significance met his trained eye. David sighed, flicking aside bits of debris as he scanned the area Rory had been working in. He didn't even know why he was here; obviously, there was nothing to be seen. But in lieu of a verbal apology to Rory for their earlier confrontation, he was almost determined to find something. Something that would bring her joy and ease the fact that his logic had driven her to the point of illness. But the more he probed, the more he realized the futility of his search.

There really wasn't anything here.

David stood up, his gaze lingering on the piece of earth Rory had been working on when Bud had interrupted her madness. Heart sinking, he was about to turn away from the depressing sight when something caught his eye.

He wasn't even sure what it was. Truthfully, he wasn't even sure why it had snared his attention. But something made him pause and peer closely at a section of earth nearly hidden beneath the disturbed parcel of soil. Crouching on his haunches, David dusted away several square inches of dirt. With a sudden jolt of curiosity, his fingers probed the dust only to come into contact with a hard, ungiving surface.

Baffled, David sat down and began to earnestly inspect the dislodged earth. And what became evident beneath his seeking fingers sent him running for Bud.

And for Rory.

CHAPTER FOUR

T HE MERCURY LIGHTS were buzzing with intensity. Within the site that had spent the entire day silent and still, a cluster of workers labored under the night sky with their shovels and baskets. Dust rose in luminous clouds as the earth was rapidly, carefully, removed from the area of excavation. And deep in the widening trench hovered three archaeologists, more involved in their work now than they had ever been over the past fourteen months.

And no one was more involved than Rory. The wooden slats David had discovered had been carefully catalogued, videoed, sketched and numbered. As Bud and David removed the amazingly solid planks piece by piece and placed them in sterile gauze wrapping, Rory perched herself at the edge of what was revealing itself to be a shallow grave.

Hazel eyes glittered into the rock-lined hole. The Syrian foreman handed her a flashlight and she peered intently at the now-exposed bundle.

"It doesn't look like a normal grave," she murmured, noting the wrapped contents to be well over six feet in length. "It's way too big to be a body. Bud?"

Dr. Dietrich knelt on the opposite side, his trained eyes roving the parcel as David joined him. Together, the four of them, including the foreman, scrutinized the uncovered treasure.

"Do you suppose it's a sacrificial cow, buried by the Greeks as an offering?" Peck wondered aloud.

Bud's brow furrowed. "All offerings to the gods were burned. Unless this body was buried to fertilize the ground for Bacchus' grapevines to ensure a prosperous harvest."

The excitement that had seized Rory the moment David had burst into her tent sputtering words of discovery was now forcibly banked as she lay on her stomach at the edge of the trench. Barely two and a half feet deep, she was able to reach down and touch the coarse material of the wrapping.

"This has got to be indigenous material," she said. "Cheaply made, too. With some sort of water reed or flax, I'd say. Look at the wide, uneven spacing in the weaving process."

Bud and David were on their stomachs, too, noting Rory's observations. The three of them were so caught up in the discovery that they failed to notice that half the camp had come to a stop, straining to catch a glimpse of the mysterious treasure.

The Syrian foreman, entranced though he might be by the fruits of their labor, was not so stupefied that he did not realized his workers' disobedience. Shouting in Arabic, the removal of earth resumed with a frenzy as the archaeologists continued to deliberate their find.

"What if it's just more trash?" Rory asked, tearing her eyes away from the dusty mass long enough to look at Bud. "I believe yesterday proved this wasn't my Muslim mosque. What if we've simply succeeded in locating more ancient trash?"

"Wrapped in a several yards of fabric and buried in a hole lined with rocks and sealed with slats of wood?" The usually-cynical Dr. Peck seemed amazingly optimistic. "This is a grave, Rory. And we're looking at a body."

Rory knew as much. Still, she wanted to hear the group's naysayer voice his speculation before she offered her novice opinion. That way, if it turned out to be just a heap of ancient trash, she wouldn't look like a failure twice in two days. For once, she decided to show a small amount of restraint; truthfully, she didn't think she could take it if her hopes were dashed a second time around. Perhaps a little self-protection, in lieu of recent events, was a good thing.

Across from her, Bud had pushed himself to his knees to determine the best way to lower himself into the grave. Moving to the western edge of the hole, he noted that there were a few scant inches on either side of the parcel at this end. Bracing his muscular arms against the sides of the trench, he lowered himself down and straddled the bundle. Gingerly, he examined the fabric.

"Hold on, hold on," he suddenly muttered, more for his own benefit than for anyone else's. Jerking his hand away, the material seemed to dissolve beneath his touch, mingling with the dust of the ancient grave. Consequently, a small portion of the object was revealed, leaving the archaeologists straining to catch a better glimpse.

"I see… my God, Bud… is that steel?" Rory's voice reflected her shock.

"There's no way it could be steel," David hissed. "If this is Grecian, it's iron or copper or precious metal. Steel wasn't known during their period."

"I'm aware of that, Dave," Rory snapped softly. "But if it was iron, it would have rusted over a two thousand year span. And if it was copper, we would be able to see the red hues. Look at the color; I swear to you, it looks like tempered steel."

Bud crouched over the exposed metal, silent as his colleagues displayed their educated theories in a snappish exchange. After a moment, he timidly picked away at the opening, enlarging it significantly. As the foreman chattered in Arabic, demanding the Nikon camera from one of the clerks, Bud continued to break all of the rules of excavation by chipping away at the wrapping before it had been properly logged. For some reason, his curiosity had the better of him and he found he couldn't help himself.

David and Rory had quieted their debate, focused on Bud's picking fingers. The foreman collected the camera and began clicking away just as another large piece of wrapping collapsed into dust. Abruptly, a dark gray object was exposed and Bud instinctively pulled back, staring at it with disbelief.

He wasn't the only one. For a moment, no one was able to move. Even the foreman had stopped taking pictures as the yellow moon cast its sickly light on metal that had not seen the familiar glow for centuries.

"Christ," Bud swore softly.

"Of all the…" Amazingly, Peck seemed unable to finish his sentence. He simply knelt by the edge of the hole, shaking his head in wonder.

Only Rory seemed able to snap out of her trance. While the rest of the world remained paralyzed, she lowered herself into the ditch, straddling the massive bundle with cautious feet. Her wide eyes were fixed on the exposed object as if beholding the Secret of Life; certainly, to the biblical archaeologist whose specialty was the Crusades, the discovery was even better.

"It's a helm," she murmured, reaching down to brush away some of the dust from the closed visor. "Look at the style; square, lacking any detail or artwork. Very functional head protection for a warring Medieval knight."

"Time frame?" Bud was so surprised he could hardly speak.

Rory touched the steel again, the first human fingers to handle the metal in centuries. "Offhand, it looks to be eleventh or twelfth century. Before the suits of armor grew particularly bulky and before the helm became more of an ornamental object." Suddenly, the hazel eyes were focused on Bud. And he swore, at that moment, he'd never seen such naked joy.

Joy, indeed. Rory could barely control herself. She knew her history and she knew her field, and the dirty object at her feet was something she had spent the past ten years studying. Even if she was a fledgling archaeologist chasing myths, as Peck had so tactfully phrased her pursuits, she was no idiot. She was well-versed in her specialty.

It was difficult to keep the elation from her voice as she spoke. "I'd say we've found ourselves a crusader, Dr. Dietrich." Slowly, her attention moved to the ever-skeptical Dr. Peck and an arched eyebrow lifted. "And you, Dave? Do I sense concurrence in my opinion or would you prefer to debate the obvious?"

Peck stared at the exposed helm a moment longer. Meeting Rory's challenging gaze, he shook his head. "Absolutely not, Dr. Osgrove. You're the religious expert and you ought to know."

Her smile was genuine. "Thank you for your kind words, Dr. Peck. At least you're willing to admit that I'm not a complete idiot." Her gaze, once again, turned to the shrouded warrior. "It makes perfect sense finding him here. Nahariya was located along the Pilgrim Trail and frequented by crusading knights. If this guy died on the Quest, then there was no way he would have been buried in a mosque. Unconsecrated ground was the only possible alternative."

"I'm surprised his buddies buried him within the grounds of a Grecian temple," Peck put in softly. "They considered the Greeks and Romans to be pagans. Most crusaders were just buried in the desert, left for the jackals and elements."

Rory stared pensively at the dusty, obscure figure. "But not him. And I wonder why."

The corner of David's lips twitched as his focus moved between his awe-struck associate and the bundle at her feet. "By damn, if you weren't right, Rory. There really was something here."

Smile still on her lips, Rory gazed at the ancient head protection. Crouching low, as if to sit on the knight's chest, she let her slender fingers trace over the metal. "A crusader," she muttered, hardly daring to hope that she was actually right. "If it's true, I really can't believe it. Here I was, looking for one of the most potent biblical relics of all time and not even hoping to find anything else. I just wanted my crown."

"But this isn't your crown," David said, his manner uncharacteristically soft. "If this guy is really a crusader, then he ought to be loaded with valuable information that should more than make up for the fact that we were unsuccessful in locating our original objective. I mean, just look at the size of him for instance. He's huge!"

Rory's gaze wandered the massive bundle. "Most knights were maybe five feet seven or eight inches tall. One was considered a giant at five feet ten. But this guy… if it's really all him, he's got to be well over six feet."

"I'd say six and a half feet, at least." Bud was becoming swept up in the thrill of discovery, too. Never in his eighteen years had he come across anything so potentially awesome and he was understandably moved. Rising from his hunched position, he gestured to the foreman. "Haro! Get the clerks sketching this guy immediately! I want a full catalogue of the shroud and a detailed indexing of his grave down to every last rock. Come on, let's move!"

The Harvard-educated foreman leapt into action, snapping orders to the hovering workers. As the entire camp swung into a frenzy, Bud pulled himself from the grave and began conversing with Dr. Peck about what, exactly, to tell Becker.

With the encampment moving at a purposeful pace, Rory remained inside the grave staring at the partially-shrouded visor. Behind that closed visor lay a man, a man that Rory was wildly curious about. A crusading knight, buried on the grounds of an ancient Greek temple dedicated to the wine god Bacchus.

Intrigued, Rory realized that the disappointment in her failure to locate the Crown of Thorns was fading. True, she was still discouraged, but the exposure of a real-life crusader was enough to ease the ache of defeat. After all, the Crusades were her specialty, a specialty that had lost focus a few years back when she discovered a paper trail alluding to Christ's Crown of Thorns.

Now, gazing at the massive knight cradled in the crude grave, she found her interest in the Crusades rekindled. If she wasn't able to have her crown, maybe the man lying at her feet was the next best thing.

☙

RORY THOUGHT SHE got three or four hours of sleep that night. Maybe.

She didn't think Bud got any at all, although he had insisted she retire about three o'clock in the morning. Since the crusader had to be catalogued as originally discovered, there wasn't anything else to do but meticulously log the body and its surroundings, and Bud had an army of clerical workers to complete that task, including the ever-fastidious Dr. Peck.

Just after dawn, Bud was in Rory's tent, gently rousing her. Rory rolled out of bed with her shoes on her feet and the laces untied, a situation patiently corrected by Bud. She tried to brush her hair and put on some lip balm, but Bud had laughed at her when she couldn't seem to function properly and, irritated, she took a swing at him. Sleepy but loaded with excitement, she finally pulled her hair into a ponytail and followed him to the distant rise.

David was still there. His brown eyes were circled, his face stubbled and gray, but he wasn't about to leave in the middle of cataloguing. He heard Rory and Bud before he ever saw them, his nose still buried in a journal.

"How are we going to unwrap this guy, Rory?" he asked as his pen scratched against the paper.

Alert after her brisk walk up the hill, Rory studied the ancient bundle in the weak morning light. Somehow, in the brightness of a new day, it made the discovery seem almost surreal. Excitement filled her as she crouched next to David while he continued to write.

"I have a hunch that we're going to have to cut the material straight down the midline," she said thoughtfully. "With the condition of the shroud, there is no way we'll be able to unwrap him and keep the material intact. It'll just fall apart in our hands."

Bud stood next to them, his hands on his hips as he observed the corpse. "The condition of the wrappings makes me wonder what kind of state the body is in," he muttered. "Probably nothing but bones."

David snorted ironically, laying his pen down and looking to the swaddling in the ditch. "We'll be lucky if we find bones. I'm opting for complete dust."

Rory pondered their statements a moment before lowering herself into the hole. Bending over, not to mention offering both Bud and David a tantalizing view of her rounded rear, she gently probed the massive form from abdomen to thigh. After a moment, she straightened up and put her hands on her hips.

"I don't know, guys," she ventured. "He seems to be pretty firm for just bones."

"It's the armor," David said confidently.

Rory shook her head. "No way. This guy should be clad in mail only, with maybe a few pieces of plate armor. Remember that suits of full armor, the big heavy things, weren't widely used until the thirteenth century. And by the looks of this guy's helm, I dated him at eleventh or twelfth century. Were he to have deteriorated to dust, the mail would have simply collapsed and this bundle wouldn't be so bulky. So... solid."

"So you think the body is intact?" Bud cocked an eyebrow. "A fascinating concept if it's true. Do you think it's possible that he was mummified somehow? Preserved, even?"

Rory shrugged, once again crouching over the body and running expert hands over what should have been the thighs. "I doubt he was conventionally mummified. But it is possible that the dry desert air somehow naturally preserved most of his mass." Her gaze followed her hands as they moved down the right leg. "Good Lord, this guy was huge. One of his legs is bigger in circumference than my entire torso."

Bud smiled faintly. "I'd really hate to meet this guy on the field of battle. He must have been an imposing sight."

Rory nodded in agreement. "Six feet six inches and well over two hundred pounds. For a man of ancient times, this guy was the size of Goliath."

"What do you want to cut the material with, Rory?" David asked, handing his journal over to the ever-present foreman.

Rory looked up from the bundle, surprised. "Me?" she repeated, looking between David and Bud. "You want me to cut the shroud?"

Bud shrugged faintly. "It's your dig."

"But you're the senior archaeologist. You should do it."

"Why?" Bud yawned, scratching his head as the morning temperature began to rise. "I've never done this before, either. He's your knight, Rory. You do the honors."

Rory gazed at Bud, swallowing away her shock as a definite sense of pleasure took hold. "All right," she murmured, looking once more to the ancient parcel wedged between her ankles. "I guess I'll need a scalpel or a single-edge razor. I want something really sharp."

"This wrapping is crumbling as it is," David pointed out. "Do you really think you need something that exact?"

"Absolutely," she said. "If I run into any resistance, I don't want to wrestle with it. I don't want to damage anything inadvertently."

David looked to Bud, who merely shrugged. "You heard the good doctor. Go find her a scalpel or a razor blade."

Peck was gone, taking the foreman with him. Bud continued to watch his associate as she pondered the best place to begin cutting, her beautiful face etched in concentration. He was perfectly content to observe her in silence until David and the foreman returned bearing two scalpels they had confiscated from the first aid kit. As the foreman collected the video camera and began rolling, Rory accepted a scalpel from David and bent over the crusader's neck.

It wasn't until she hovered over the ancient bindings that she realized her hands were shaking. From his position at the edge of the grave, Bud put his hand on her head in a comforting gesture.

"Relax, honey," he comforted. "You're doing fine. Just go layer by layer like you've been taught."

Rory took a deep breath, offering the man a weak smile. "I thought I was calm until a moment ago," she said unsteadily. "But, God, Bud… this is really scary. And really, really exciting."

He met her smile. "So cut already. I can hardly stand the suspense."

She laughed at his words. "If Becker were here, you realize he would demand that you do this yourself. Leaving such an important task to a novice archaeologist is risky business."

His eyes were like blue ice; glittering and intense and potent. "I'll take my chances."

Rory caught an underlying message in his softly-uttered statement but said nothing. He did very well at keeping his emotions concealed, but there were times when the dam would crack and a sliver of sentiment would slip past. And if Rory really thought hard on it, it wouldn't be so difficult to give in to his magnetism. He was a truly handsome guy with a golden character. But at this point in her life, she wasn't interested in a relationship of any kind. For the moment, she was only interest in her dreams. Taking a deep breath for courage, she leaned over the shroud and began to cut.

As she knew they would, the bindings turned to dust in her hands. She wasn't cutting the material as much as she was simply brushing it away, revealing a sight more astonishing than she had ever dreamed possible; apparently, the knight had been buried hastily. So hastily that the helm was the only part of his armor that he wore. The rest of it, the mail and war implements including his sword, were laid on the body that was then tightly wrapped in coarse material.

As she progressed, Bud was forced to jump into the grave to assist her. The body of the knight was loaded with possessions and he began to carefully remove the items as Rory freed them, turning them over to David for cataloging. The broadsword, still in its crafted leather sheath, weighed over thirty pounds alone and both Bud and David were awed by the mighty weapon.

Rory paused in the middle of her task, looking to Bud and David as they removed the broadsword from its protective cover. Gleaming and flawless beneath the scorching Israeli sun, the timeless beauty was overwhelming.

"Christ," Bud hissed as David held up the heavy weapon, the hilt inlaid with several semi-precious stones. "Have you ever seen anything so beautiful?"

Peck, his eyes wide with wonder, shook his head. "I've never seen anything like this in my life," he muttered. "Look at the craftsmanship on the pommel. Hell, I'd hate to take this thing into battle for fear of damaging it. It's too beautiful to use as a weapon."

Rory wiped at the sweat on her brow with the back of her hand, smiling faintly. "Boys and their toys. From century to century, it never changes."

Bud grinned, running his gloved finger over the edge of the sword. "How'd you like to have this blade driven into your guts? Pretty horrible, huh?"

She turned back to the knight. "Yeah, but given the odds, you would still take the risk you were trained for. And that risk is probably what killed our friend. Here, look at this."

Bud and David looked to the source of her focus. The knight was clad in tunic and hose, fairly simple clothing for the crusaders who had preferred a somewhat lavish wardrobe. Discolored with dirt and the passage of time, the lower portion of the tunic as well as the hose were shaded a dark brown. It didn't take a genius to figure out it was a bloodstain.

"What a way to go." Bud shook his head slowly. "But why in the hell would they bury him still clothed in his bloodied tunic? It doesn't make sense."

"None of this does," Rory said, cautiously removing the last of the bindings from the man's feet. "Nothing about this guy makes any sense whatsoever."

For the first time in centuries, the body of the knight was open for the scrutiny of the modern world and David set aside the broadsword long enough to study the man with interest.

"Hell, look at this guy," he muttered, moving to gain a better view. "You were right, Rory. He's as solid as a rock."

At the knight's feet, Rory simply shook her head in wonder. "This is the most beautifully preserved corpse I've ever seen. No odor, no deterioration, no nothing. It's almost as if... as if he had died yester-day."

Bud, too, studied the ancient warrior. After a moment, he looked to the collection of property resting along a wide strip of cotton material near David's makeshift desk. The foreman was in the process of numbering and photographing each item when Bud's gaze came to rest on one particular object.

"Dave, take a look at that book," he gestured towards the far end of the collection. "It could be a diary or letters. Maybe it'll tell us this guy's name."

"Or it could be a Bible," Rory suggested as David moved to collect the leather-bound book.

The cover carefully opened, David slowly meandered back to his colleagues as he reviewed the ancient pages. Pausing by the edge of the grave, he cast Rory an odd expression.

"Can you read Medieval writing, Dr. Osgrove?"

She pursed her lips at his ridiculous question. "I should hope so. I spent most of my graduate years doing just that."

David shook his head, cautiously passing the book to her gloved hands. "Well, good luck with this stuff, anyway."

Rory accepted the volume, being extremely careful with it. The cover was opened to the first page, fine parchment that was remarkably preserved. The script was faded with time, extremely ornate, and she sighed when she realized she was dealing with an educated man who had apparently loved to write. The entire first page was some sort of lengthy poem in script she could hardly decipher.

"Whew." She leaned against the side of the grave as she studied the writing. "This is going to take some time, isn't it?"

Peck smiled wryly, turning back to his artifacts. Bud stepped over the body, moving to stand beside Rory as she examined the ancient text.

He couldn't make heads or tails of it. "Turn the page. Maybe we'll find something recognizable."

She grinned. "What's the matter, Bud? Can't read anything but ancient Greek?"

"That's easy compared to this. Turn the page before I go blind."

"You could be reading a Medieval curse and not even know it."

He cast her his best intimidating expression. "Quiet, you trouble-maker. I'm not afraid of any ancient curse. Well, not much."

With a soft laugh, Rory turned the fragile page, amazed with the resilience of the vellum. "By all rights, this stuff should be crumbling. I can't believe how well preserved it is."

Bud squinted at the faded transcript. "Maybe the grave acted like a time capsule, preserving everything in an air-tight fashion. But I suspect the condition of this book won't stay good forever; exposure to the air will speed the decaying process. It needs to be sealed."

"After we find out his name," Rory said, glancing to the helmed head at the other end of the trench. "Come on, big boy. Tell us who you are."

Being very careful, Bud turned another page. He was about to turn another when Rory suddenly stopped him.

"Here." She jabbed her finger at the bottom of the fourth page. "From what I can tell, this is the knight's journal. He's talking about his trip aboard a ship... and here he mentions the city of Acre. My God, Bud, this guy really was a crusader. Bingo!"

Bud grinned at her excitement. "You already convinced me of that last night. So what's his name?"

Hazel eyes scanned the pages. After a moment, she appeared to find a passage of particular interest.

"Right here," she murmured, struggling to read the script. "Heck, it's so faded I can hardly read it. But he is swearing the truth of his recollections by God's Holy Order and whosoever should repeat these tales... on and on and on... now where does he mention his name?"

Reseated beside the artifacts, David's cataloguing came to a halt as Rory read aloud from the chronicle. Even the foreman had paused in his duties, listening carefully. Bud had given up trying to read the stuff and now stood waiting patiently as Rory completed her analysis.

The activity grew oddly still as Rory scrutinized the unfamiliar writing. Turning a page, she seemed to go back and forth between a couple of pages before her gaze came to rest on what she apparently sought. Slowly, her face lit with a beautiful smile.

"Well?" Bud demanded. "What's his name?"

Rory sighed dreamily, gazing to the ancient knight. There was gentleness in her expression as she spoke.

"Good Doctors, meet Sir Kieran Hage of Nottingham. A crusader with Richard the Lionheart." Her smile broadened when she met Bud's gaze. "A real honest-to-goodness English knight."

Bud grinned timidly in response to her declaration. Even Peck was smiling. Hardly able to control her exhilaration, Rory impulsively threw an arm around Bud's neck and kissed him loudly on the cheek.

"I want to send a message to Becker personally," she said happily. "I told you guys there was something here. And I would say Sir Kieran is a pretty big something."

Peck scratched underneath his baseball cap. "Even if he's not your crown?"

Rory removed her arm from Bud, much to the man's disappointment. Her smile faded as she moved to the rim of the grave, holding the journal up to David.

"It's not like I'm going to give up looking for it altogether," she said, the usual defensiveness absent from her tone. "But what I've got here... it's real and it's tangible. It's not as if I'm chasing a myth. I've got some hard excavation waiting for my attention and I intend to give it my full focus."

David's brown eyes were soft, hearing his own cynical words reflected in her voice. He suddenly didn't like the idea of Rory unwilling to pursue her dreams; as outlandish as they could be and as much as he criticized her, the world would be a dismal place without people like Rory to have faith in the impossible. People willing to take the risk whereas David, deep down, was afraid to.

"But you're not going to give up?"

"Never. Just call my crusader a momentary diversion."

Peck was oddly comforted by her words. "When this is over, I'll help you go over the Byzantine manuscripts again. Maybe there is something there you missed, something an unbiased view can help clarify." He felt foolish for his hypocrisy, embarrassed that he was all but admitting his faith in her beliefs. "I've... I've invested too much time not to do all I can."

The smile returned to her tired face. "Thanks for your devotion, Dave." Noting his flush as he refused to meet her gaze, Rory nonetheless winked at him and turned back to the knight. After brief deliberation, she moved to the helmed head and hunched over it, running her fingers over the movable joints. Bud, still feeling her kiss on his cheek, edged closer to observe her actions.

"You want to remove that now?"

She nodded. "I think if we raise the visor, we won't risk damaging his facial features when we pull off the helm. The last thing we need is the visor dragging across his face and ripping his nose off."

He shrugged. If she was determined to discover everything about the man in one day, he wouldn't stand in her way. Fourteen months of frustration was about to find a release and he realized he was as eager as she was. "The joints are probably frozen." He glanced over his shoulder at David, who had returned to his cataloguing. "See if you can find some spray oil, Dave."

David sent the foreman for a can of lubricant. When the man returned, Rory allowed Peck to carefully disperse the oil on the frozen couplings.

"That's good," Rory murmured. Applying gentle pressure to the lowered visor, she was rewarded by slight movement. She and David, her friend one moment and arch-enemy the next, exchanged grins as he sprayed again.

"Careful, Dave, not too much," she admonished easily. "We don't want to get oil on the corpse."

"We won't," he said confidently, observing her gentle manner. When her fingers slipped off the metal as a result of the oil and too much pressure, he put out his hands. "Do you want me to do that?"

"No, thanks," she murmured, completely focused on her task. "I can do it."

He moved his hands away. As the small crowd watched in silent anticipation, Rory continued to loosen the faceplate of the helm, working it to the point where she could see a portion of the knight's cheek. Peering underneath to get a better look, she could see his nostrils but little else. It was still too dark.

"What can you see?" Bud asked from above.

She shook her head. "Not much. Just skin and part of his nose." She moved to the knight's right side, squeezing her booted feet into the narrow margin between the body and the side of the grave. "Come here and help me, Bud. Maybe, between the two of us, we can work this free."

As Bud leapt into the trench, David lifted an insulted brow. "Oh yeah? You'll let him help but not me?"

Rory grinned and brushed off her hands. "Rank doth have its privileges, Dr. Peck. Besides, if you and I were to do it together, it might end up a tug-of-war. You're so damned competitive."

Shrugging in agreement, David remained at his post by the edge of the grave, watching as Bud and Rory grasped the sides of the visor and attempted to work it free. Rory's fingers were red from wrestling with the metal and she finally let go, allowing Bud to work alone. Little by little, the visor gradually worked its way up until, finally, it gave a loud pop and broke free completely.

The crowd hovering around the grave gave a startled gasp, including Rory. As Bud stood, somewhat stunned, with a Medieval visor in his hand, Rory's gaze immediately fell on the ancient features. And what a face it was.

She didn't know why her entire body suddenly washed with a warm, languid feeling. But it did. And she had no idea why her heart was racing a mile a minute. But it was. The more she gazed at the discolored face bordered by the metal of a twelfth century helm, the more amazement and wonder she felt.

Slowly, so as not to break the spell of awe that had settled, Rory knelt beside the knight, reaching out to touch the ashen flesh.

"My God, Bud," she whispered. "Have you ever seen anything so marvelous in your life?"

Bud was still standing with the visor in his hand. Slowly, he shook his head. "Never. In all my years of digging."

She ran a finger down the stubbled cheek, the expression on her face one of the utmost marvel. "Look at his flesh. Hardly any deterioration whatsoever. And the stubble is enough to scratch my skin."

Peck was in jeopardy of tumbling into the grave as he leaned forward at an exaggerated angle. "Hell, he looks young. How old was he?"

"I don't know," Rory replied, her tone soft. "Late twenties. Early thirties at the very most."

Joints popped as Bud knelt beside the knight, the visor still clutched in his fingers. He'd come across a couple of graves in his career, one on Cypress of an ancient Greek soldier that had yielded quite a bit of artifacts. But he couldn't remember feeling the same awe and satisfaction he was feeling at this moment. As if somehow, this grave meant more to him than the others. It was Rory's grave.

This was her baby. Therefore, it held more significance for him as well. Gazing down at the miraculously preserved face, he smiled weakly. "Sorry, pal. I ruined your visor. Thank God your broadsword is hidden away or I might be running for my life."

Rory smiled at him before returning her attention to the knight. If Bud hadn't known better, he would have sworn her expression to be most tender. And when she touched the aged cheek again, it was with the gentleness of a lover.

"Touch his skin, Bud," she insisted. "Feel how resilient it is? Maybe you were right when you hypothesized that he had been mummified somehow. But I can't imagine what sort of ingredients would maintain the skin's elasticity as well as this."

Bud ran a calloused finger down the knight's cheek, pausing when he came to the mouth. He poked gently a moment, prodding. Rory paused to watch him, wondering what he was doing. Feeling her stare, he met her gaze.

"Even more amazing," he said with just the slightest bit of awe. "Look at his mouth."

He crooked his finger into the corner of Sir Kieran's lips, pulling slightly. They were like rubber, as normal, living lips would have been. Peeling the flesh back to reveal a perfect set of anterior teeth, he shook his head with growing incredulity.

"And the mucosa membrane is still pliable. Almost... almost as if he were still producing saliva. Christ, that's fantastic."

Rory was staring at the knight's mouth, almost startled when Bud let go of the lips and they sprang together. Her hand was still touching the ancient flesh as she realized that this find was perhaps even more precious than her Crown of Thorns. A man who lived and breathed centuries ago, buried in a shallow grave. At that moment, she'd never felt so fortunate.

"Let's get his helm off." Her voice was oddly hoarse. "I want to see all of him. Bud, do you think we could just pull it off without damaging the body? I'd hate to ruin it by trying to cut it away."

Bud was already moving to do her bidding. "It should slip off easily. This is the most remarkably intact corpse I've ever seen and I don't think removing this helm will have any ill-effect whatsoever."

He was right. The crusader's head protection slid off with amazing ease, revealing a man of the most amazing beauty. Short-cropped, dark blond hair met with the early morning light, incredibly pliant. Sir Kieran had a jaw of granite and large dimples carved deep into his cheeks. Rory stared, entranced, as the warrior became a man of flesh and bone before her very eyes.

"Oh... Bud," she murmured, touching the ancient flesh once more. "Look at him. Isn't he incredible?"

Bud smiled faintly, handing the helm and detached visor to David. "He's good-looking enough to run for Mr. America."

Curious, Rory timidly touched the hair and, although it was somewhat oily, she wasn't surprised to find it thick and soft. "He has the same crew-cut as you do, Bud."

"His barber is better than mine." Bud knelt beside the knight, looking the length of the corpse as Rory continued to caress the warrior's head. "Well, now. What do you say to tearing yourself away from this guy and taking a break, Dr. Osgrove? A good breakfast ought to do us all a world of good."

Rory removed her hand from his hair, reluctant to leave but knowing a meal was in order. In fact, she couldn't remember when she had eaten last and if she were to admit it, she was rather hungry. Elated, but hungry. "All right," she said, glancing at David. "Put a team of security guards around the site, Dave. I don't want anyone near him until I get back."

David nodded, still studying the helm. "You got it."

Dr. Peck ended up guarding Sir Kieran himself. If anyone wanted to disturb what Rory had worked so long and hard for, then they were going to have to go through him first.

CHAPTER FIVE

I T WAS WELL after sunset. The knight's possessions had been safely tucked away for the night in David's tent and Bud would not have been surprised if the man had stayed up all night admiring the treasure. The only artifact Peck didn't have was the journal. That piece of property was currently in Rory's company.

Even now, as Bud made his way to her tent, he knew exactly what she had been doing for the past several hours; poring over the ancient pages with a zealous fervor. And he could hardly blame her.

He was pleased to see he knew Rory as well as he thought he did. Ringing the little set of brass chimes outside her door, the first thing he came into contact with was her smiling, bespectacled face.

"Hi," she said jovially, pulling him into the tent. "Do have a reply from Becker?"

He nodded. "A few minutes ago. Fastest reply I've ever received from him, considering I only sent word of the find three hours ago. Seems the old man is absolutely thrilled with the discovery and we have his permission to do whatever necessary to bring our crusader home."

Rory cocked an eyebrow. "Home where? You realize that when the British get wind of our find, they're probably going to demand that he be returned to England."

Bud shrugged, lowering himself into a rickety chair. "They have no legal grounds to do it, of course. We found the body and by the laws of international salvage and domain he belongs to us. But I did give Becker the knight's name. He's going to contact the British Consul personally to inform them as a courtesy."

Rory's smile faded. Moving to the small table covered with disjointed notes, she sat heavily and removed her reading glasses. Bud watched her closely.

"Hey," he said. "Don't worry about it. Unless they're willing to start another revolution, they can't take him away from us."

She nodded vaguely, staring at her hands, the floor. "I know. But you know the British; if this guy has any living descendants, they're going to act as if we've stolen a close relative. Whether the knight died five years ago or five hundred years ago, you know how the English are about their relatives and bloodlines. Possessive as hell. They might turn this into an international incident if we refuse to turn over one of their own."

Bud pondered her words, being very careful with his reply. "And you don't think it would be acceptable if Sir Kieran was returned to Britain, to be displayed in the homeland he died for?"

Rory looked up from the floor, defiance written all over her face. "Good Lord, Bud, he isn't even out of the ground yet. Why do we even have to discuss this? He's our find and we're going to keep him!"

He maintained his calm tone. "I realize he's our find, but the idea of returning him to England will undoubtedly come up at some point. I have a feeling you're already pretty attached to the guy and it might be better if we talk about this now, while you're still rational, and not wait until I have to separate the two of you with a crowbar."

She pursed her lips wryly. "You may never get the chance. I may just run off with him and live happily ever after, far away from his selfish countrymen." She scratched her arm in a fidgety gesture, digging her heels into the dirt floor. "It's just that he's our find, Bud. Sir Kieran belongs to the university and not to a stuffy British museum."

"He'll be among his peers."

"They have enough knights. He'd get lost in the masses."

"He's part of the masses, Rory. He and twenty thousand other crusaders who came to the Holy Land to fight for the righteousness of Christianity. If it were up to me, I'd return him to the country he was born in. The one he loved enough to risk his life for."

Rory was fully prepared to defend her claim when she realized, more than likely, Bud was right. Still, it was difficult to visualize turning her precious find over to strangers who couldn't possibly give it the love and attention she could.

With a heavy sigh, her gaze trailed to the mound of papers on the small table. "Oh, hell. I suppose Sir Kieran would look out of place among the Sumerian and Dead Sea artifacts in the university's museum. We don't even really have a British section to put him in."

Bud smiled. "We could always donate him to the Huntington Library Foundation and they could display him along with their works of Chaucer and Shakespeare. That way, he'd still remain in Southern California. And close to you."

She met his smile, ironically. "But I'd be here, with you, still looking for my crown." With another sigh, she scooted her chair closer to the cluttered desk. "Besides, he's so big he'd probably scare the daylights out of the visitors who go to the Huntington Library looking for tame entertainment. Like something out of a bad horror movie."

Bud laughed softly, his ice-blue eyes moving to the pile of papers at Rory's elbow. "Well, we don't have to decide anything right this moment. Like you said, the guy isn't even out of the ground yet." He nodded his head in the direction of the clutter. "So, what have you found out from his journal so far? You've been holed up in your tent since before supper."

Momentarily distracted from the subject of the knight's destination, Rory focused on the paperwork. As Bud hoped, it was enough of a diversion to lighten her mood and she perked up as she collected a few of her notes.

"This journal has been an absolute treasure, Bud," she said enthusiastically. Holding out a couple of translated pages, she watched him scan her work. "As near as I can figure out, Sir Kieran was from a noble Saxon family who practically ruled Nottinghamshire. He came to the Holy Land a full two years before Richard the Lionheart and laid siege to Acre with Guy de Lusignan's French army. He's very poetic, actually, talking about the conditions of life during the siege of Acre. Considering it was probably one of the most hellish campaigns in history."

Bud looked up from her pages. "If I remember my facts correctly, about one in two knights died during the siege from either wounds or disease. Pretty terrible odds."

Rory nodded, gazing to the open journal. "This is the most amazing account I've ever read. An actual firsthand description of the fall of Acre is more than most scholars ever dream of." She leaned forward and put her reading glasses back on. The parchment was reflected in the lenses as she scrutinized the faded writing. "He also speaks quite frequently of a knight named Simon de Corlet and refers to the man as his brother, although I can't determine if he means literally. And he also makes it quite clear that he knew King Richard on a first-name basis."

Bud cocked an eyebrow, laying the pages back on her table. "Do you think he's being truthful?"

She paused thoughtfully, chewing on the end of her pen. "Considering the size of the man and the beauty of his sword, indicating wealth and status among other things, I would wager to say that he probably did know Richard the Lionheart personally."

Bud shook his head in wonder. "Absolutely amazing."

"I know," she grinned. "Now I remember why the Crusades fascinated me so much in the first place. With my focus on the Crown of Thorns, I'd almost forgotten the power and mystery behind the greatest quest of all."

He chuckled softly, patting her hand in a friendly gesture. "Welcome back to the real world, kiddo. A place where hard fact often proves more rewarding than chasing the improbable."

Her smile faded. "Now you're starting to sound like Dave."

"Am I?" His features twisted with exaggerated horror and Rory laughed. She couldn't help it. "Christ, I didn't mean to. I guess what I mean to say is that I've spent my entire adult life on one dig or another, dealing with the tangible evidence of archaeology. This is the first dig I've ever supervised where we've been searching for something a lot of people believe to be purely legend."

Hazel eyes glittered at him in the dim illumination of the tent. "And you?"

He met her gaze. "You're very convincing with your facts."

"That's not what I asked. Do you believe I'm searching for a myth?"

He stood up, shoving his hands in his pockets. "If I did I wouldn't be here. But I have to say that I'm a lot like Dave in some respects; an old school guy like me is partial to hard evidence over tales written by God-fearing monks."

"So you have difficulty putting faith in Ottis' manuscript. I can appreciate that. But do you disbelieve the Bible as well?"

Bud scratched his head, trying fervently not to say anything that would offend her. When discussing her passionate beliefs, it was easy to send her off into a rage with a single misspoken word.

"I was raised Protestant," he said after a moment. "I guess I've always grown up knowing that I should believe. But being a scientist… well, sometimes it's difficult. Especially when we're digging up pre-humanoids hundreds of thousands of years old. How does the Bible explain the existence of something like that?"

Rory smiled faintly. "It does if you look in the right place. For example, the book of Genesis, verse 2, lines 1 and 2; 'Thus the heavens and the earth were finished, and all the host of them. And on the seventh day God ended His work which He had made; and He rested on the seventh day from all His work which He had made.'" She leaned forward on the cluttered desk, her chin resting in her hand. "God said it took seven days to create the heavens and the earth, Bud. But he didn't say how long the days were."

"A day is a day. Twenty-four hours."

"Maybe not in God's time. Considering He believes the life of a man to be barely a breath of air before it's gone, there's no telling what God considers to be a day's length."

Bud's perfect teeth gleamed in the soft light. "Dave was right. You're one hell of a theologian. I really pity your theology professor."

She grinned, leaning more heavily on her arm as her fatigue deepened. "Old Dr. Hayworth, head of the Theology and Philosophy Department. I gave him a brain hemorrhage, I think. The guy retired right after I graduated."

"That's because poor old Louis was probably having nightmares of the beautiful student with the cunning of a barracuda." Somewhere outside of the tent, a dog bayed in the distance and Bud turned towards the canvas opening, gazing out over the encampment. He wished that he didn't have to go back to his own tent and sleep alone in his cold, hard bed.

"Tomorrow, we should figure out how to get him out of the grave," Rory said from behind him. "I'd like to do some tissue analysis if possible."

Bud turned to her. "We'll be doing an autopsy. Why do you want a preliminary analysis?"

She shrugged and stood up, moving to stand beside him as they both enjoyed the gentle breeze. "Do we really need an autopsy? I think it's pretty obvious how he died. We could simply do a physical and a few tests to determine his health and other factors."

Bud crossed his arms; he had to. It was either that or pull Rory into a crushing embrace. "It's fairly standard to do autopsies on intact corpses. I don't think there's any question that we should, for a myriad of reasons."

Rory's expression darkened as she looked out over the distant settlement. After a moment, she lifted her shoulders uneasily. "I don't know... I mean, I've never agreed with that particular aspect of excavation. So what if we cut this guy open and find out that he had heart disease and tapeworm? It's just so undignified to hack him up when he's survived all of these centuries intact."

Bud toyed with his chin, noting her sincerity as she spoke. She was so damned sensitive, concerned for all things great and small. "Autopsies have told us a lot about how ancient people lived. They're a very enlightening process."

"We know how he lived, fighting off starvation and disease when he wasn't battling Saladin. Couldn't we just x-ray him? It would be a lot less intrusive."

Bud nodded after a moment. "I suppose we could. Radiographs will tell us just as much. Maybe more."

She smiled gratefully. "Thank you, Bud. You really aren't such a bad guy, after all."

He cocked an eyebrow. "I hope you remember that."

Rory watched him stroll from her tent, his hands dug deep into the pockets of his jeans. "What is that supposed to mean?"

He cast her a long glance but continued walking. "When the time comes, you'll know. Now get back to work on that journal. I want to know every gory detail of Sir Kieran's life by morning."

Rory watched him go, smiling to herself. He really wasn't such a bad guy, after all.

CB

MIDNIGHT CAME AND went. The camp was dark, devoid of any activity except for an occasional security guard. Bud and David were long since asleep, much needed rest after a night and day of continuous digging.

Only Rory seemed to be awake, so deeply immersed in Sir Kieran's journal that she hardly realized it was the middle of the night. Once she got past the beginning of the knight's trip to the Holy Land, sailing on a ship crowded with mercenaries and horses and weapons, the true scope of his adventures came to light and, like any good book, she couldn't put it down.

Surprisingly, Kieran didn't seem to be the arrogant sort. He was frank, brutally opinionated when he had to be. But, for the most part, he seemed to be even-tempered and rational. He spoke with appalling honestly when he described heathen women, hairy wenches with a powerful smell as he had so kindly phrased them. They clung to him like leeches, he said with genuine puzzlement, wondering why they found him so attractive. With his size and alien coloring, he had expected nothing less than naked fear.

As Rory read into the night, she found herself visualizing the warrior wrapped in coarse cloth and buried in the ancient Grecian temple. He had a droll sense of humor and more than once Rory found herself chuckling over something he had commented on. But even more than the humor and vivid descriptions of deplorable life in a land under siege, she came to realize that Kieran had a good deal of modern insight to the world around him.

It was a sensitivity that ran deep as he described giving heathen orphans food from his own stores, or preventing his comrades from "doing as they so pleased" with a female captive. Rory, in fact, was amazed by his altruistic ideals; so many of the crusading knights were corrupt that she found it astonishing that Sir Kieran possessed the scruples to distinguish right from wrong. To deter a rape and feed hungry children were examples of commendable, and nearly unheard of, standards.

The Israeli evening passed in heated silence; still, Rory remained riveted to the pages of Sir Kieran's journal. The more she read of the man and his exceptional ideals, the more she found herself liking him. And the more she wished she could rouse him from his eternal sleep to ask questions until he ran out of answers. Engrossed in the man and his tales, Rory realized that Sir Kieran Hage was a knight taken straight from the pages of a fairy tale. Strong, chivalrous, and exceptionally brave.

It was close to dawn when she neared the last pages of his journal. Rory had long since stopped transcribing the text, instead, thoroughly absorbed in the stories. There would be plenty of time later for translating and she was to the point where she could actually read an entire page of Medieval script in less than five minutes.

The complete journal was no more than forty pages, but the beautiful sketches had slowed her progress down considerably. Staring at their faded quality was an invitation to daydream of a time gone by, and Rory was entrapped in their spell. In fact, she had been scrutinizing a particularly lovely drawing of a crumbling citadel when an odd notation, hastily written, caught her eye.

Acre, it said. Somewhere by the bottom of the page she caught the name of the all-mighty Saladin and another strange name she couldn't quite make out. El-Hadid or Jadid, she thought. Curious, she rubbed her eyes, trying not to grind mascara into her corneas, and tried again.

A Christian offering of peace. That much she could decipher. But she couldn't figure out if Sir Kieran meant the Christian armies offering a truce or Saladin's army offering a gesture of harmony. The writing was smeared, as if he had written in haste and failed to properly sand the ink before it could dry. El-Hadid's name came up once more, directly linked to Saladin, and Rory's interest was piqued.

Turning the page, she was distressed to note it was completely blotched, almost illegible. Squinting at the smeared writing, she picked up her pen and began to transcribe the page letter by letter, hoping to make some sense of it. In the distance, she could hear a cock crowing, announcing the onset of a bright, new day. But she ignored the rooster and everything else around her; all that mattered at the moment was the message Sir Kieran had had such difficulty writing.

Again, a mention of an offering of peace. A Christian offering. El-Hadid had offered, Kieran had accepted. But like the pieces to a puzzle that didn't quite fit, Rory put the pen down and started to read aloud, hoping she would be able to better sound out the words. A syllable here, a word there, but nothing that made a great deal of sense. Sir Kieran was trying to tell a story, a story that had been mussed and faded by the passage of time, and Rory felt her frustration mount.

And then came the name Simon again. This time, the words surrounding the name were biting and angered. She thought she came across the word "betrayed", but she could not be sure. The further she read down the page, the more she began to realize a change in Sir Kieran's attitude. No longer was he the tolerant knight she had come to know. His fury was evident, a disbelief in what had become of his glorious mission to rid the Holy Land of the Muslim insurgents.

Even with the volatile emotions Rory was sensing, still, Sir Kieran never rambled and he was very exact in what he wished to say. If only she could make sense of it. Nearing the end of the journal, she came to suspect that he had somehow been double-crossed by Simon, but the exact circumstances had yet to make themselves clear. El-Hadid was mentioned again, but almost in passing. More muddled ink, a few water stains and brown splotches she thought might be blood.

Confused with the tale to the point of frustration, Rory hunched over her collapsible desk as her tent began to warm with the first rays of a new sun. As she sounded out several more words, writing a few of them down for future reference, she came across a clear reference to Jesus Christ. Not God, as he had referred to his Lord throughout the chronicle, but Jesus Christ himself. And words pleading forgiveness from God's only son.

Rory took off her reading glasses, the hazel eyes circled with fatigue and her brow permanently furrowed as she struggled to read the final passages of the journal. The last page was completely illegible, so she focused on the bit of comprehensive text preceding it. Finishing the lines, she read them again. And again. Then she simply stared. Suddenly, as if a fire had been lit, her eyes bulged to the point of exploding and she stood up so quickly that her chair toppled.

Staring at the volume still clutched in her hands, Rory tried to read the passage again but realized she was shaking so badly that such a feat was impossible. Taking a step back, away from the table, she stumbled on her overturned chair and scrambled from the tent.

The journal remained clutched against her chest as she struggled across the sand, shoeless, striving for the grave on the crest of the hill. Blinded to all else around her, she knew she had to make it to the grave. She had to see him. Knowing he could not respond to her but, still, it was imperative that she reach the man if only to see the truth for herself.

Good Lord… was it really possible?

Bud was just emerging from his tent when he saw Rory racing up the rise. It took him less than a second to realize she was barefoot, half-dressed, and staggering unsteadily. Tossing aside the towel he had been using to dry his face, he took out after her.

The entire camp was awakening to the sounds of shouting, the workers in an uproar as Dr. Osgrove and Dr. Dietrich headed for the dig at breakneck speed. David bolted from his tent, struggling to put his glasses on as he caught sight of Bud halfway up the hill, his shirt hanging out of his pants and his boots untied. With a muttered curse, he followed.

Rory was oblivious to the cries of the workers or to the sand burning her tender feet. All that mattered was that she had to reach the grave, to demand answers from a man who was incapable of replying. But a sleepless night spent immersed in the crusader's chronicles had muddled her thought processes and after reading the last startling passage, she was hardly able to think rationally.

She was only aware of her need to discover answers. But the moment Rory laid eyes on the knight's eternally slumbering face, all thoughts of disbelief and astonishment faded. Embracing the journal to her breast, she sank to her knees as Bud raced up beside her.

"Rory!" he gasped, putting strong hands on her shoulders to steady her. "What's the matter? What hap..?"

She thrust the book at him and he had to take a step back to avoid being hit. His ice-blue eyes were wide with confusion, concern, and he could see even as she held the journal up that her hands were shaking terribly.

He took the book, eyeing David as the man came to a panting halt beside him. "Rory, what's wrong?" Bud demanded urgently. "Why were you running up here?"

Rory continued to kneel by the edge of the grave, her long hair askew, tendrils blowing in the early morning breeze. It was a moment before she was capable of answering.

"He knows where it is, Bud."

Bud was understandably baffled. "Who? Who knows where what is?"

She didn't say anything for a moment. "Second to the last page. The final passage. Read it."

Brow furrowed, Bud did as he was asked with David hanging over his shoulder. After several tries, he shook his head. "I can't read this stuff, honey. It's too muddled."

David took the book from him, hoping he could make a better attempt.

"I see the word Jesus," he said, comparing it with a more-clearly written representation of the word on the previous page. "Here, let me give this a try; 'Forgive me Lord Jesus that my... mis... mis....'"

"Mission." Rory's voice was barely audible. After a moment, her knees creaked softly as she climbed into the grave. Straddling the body, she suddenly balled her fists and brought them weakly against the chest of the knight as if to beat the truth out of him. A gesture of frustration that she could scarcely contain.

Her voice, when she finally spoke, was nearly a groan. "The passage reads like this: 'Forgive me Lord Jesus that my mission in Thou's Name hath been thwarted. The diadem of Thou's sacrifice entrusted into my hands is forever sealed, hidden so that no man can pilfer Its beauty or omnipotence. Until such time that I can safely transport It to the land of my birth, Its whereabouts shall remain my knowledge alone.'"

David was still looking at the smeared words she had so eloquently repeated. Bud stared at her, however, a disturbing twinge of recognition flickering in his eyes. A growing ember that seemed to bloom as Rory remained bent over the knight, her fists against his chest and her eyes closed.

"Rory," his voice was hoarse. "You don't think..."

"Yes, Bud, I do." She lifted her head, the hazel eyes rolling open to focus on him. She was terribly pale, ashen with defeat and exhaustion. After a moment, she simply shook her head. "Don't you see? He's speaking of the Crown of Thorns. How much more obvious can it be?"

David looked up sharply from the yellowed parchment. "What in the hell are you talking about? He's speaking of Jesus' diadem of sacrifice, not a wreath of thorny vine. His words could be purely symbolic. You can't possibly think…"

Rory removed herself from the knight, throwing herself at the edge of the grave. Reaching out, she grasped David by the ankle and nearly pulled him to the ground. Hazel eyes blazed into surprised, bespectacled brown.

"Not this time, Dr. Peck," she snarled. "I've spent fourteen months listening to you refute every theory I've ever entertained, but I refuse to allow you to reject the truth of Sir Kieran's words. He's speaking of the Crown of Thorns, for God's sake. Ottis was right all along when he pinpointed Nahariya as the crown's location because, somehow, he came into the knowledge that a crusading knight buried along the Pilgrim Trail was in possession of Christ's diadem. Don't you get it? By word of mouth or by smoke signals, somehow, Ottis heard the rumor and wrote it down!"

Dave was struggling to keep his balance. "Hell, Rory, how would he hear such a thing? What you are suggesting is so far-fetched, it's absurd even for you!"

"The world was a smaller place back then. News and rumor traveled by word of mouth and it would not have been unusual for the story to be passed along, divulged to a scholarly priest by a passing traveler."

Peck tried to pull his leg free without much success. "You're talking about a two hundred year lag between Sir Kieran's acquisition of the crown and Ottis deciding to put the information to parchment. Two hundred years for this rumor to be floating around!"

"Time and conditions didn't move as quickly as they do today. Stories were kept sacred, told and retold. If one didn't know how to write, which most people didn't, oral recitation was the only way to pass along vital information."

David shook his leg again, nearly tripping. The frustration in his voice was evident. "All right, all right, so the old priest heard the rumor and wrote it down. But that still doesn't explain or justify Sir Kieran's mysterious words. He doesn't mention the crown by name, Rory. His journal is open to interpretation, just like the rest of your holy manuscripts."

She was possessed with certainty. "He says the diadem of Thou's sacrifice, David! What else could he mean but the crown worn by Christ when he sacrificed his life for the sins of Mankind?"

Bud knelt beside the grave, prying Rory's fingers off David's leg. Holding her hands tightly, his expression was gentle and concerned at the same time. As crazy as this quest had been from the outset, it seemed to be growing in power and mystery. Bud was coming to wonder if there weren't greater forces at work around them, arranging the happening of events with appalling coincidence. He just didn't know what to believe any more.

But it was apparent that Rory had interpreted the knight's journal to suit her own failing ambition. Smiling gently, he brushed a stray piece of hair from her eyes.

"How can you be so sure your knight had the crown?" he asked. "There has got to be more to it than one solitary passage. Did he allude to it at any other time?"

She shook her head unsteadily. "No… I read the whole journal, Bud. Sir Kieran was a powerful knight with a good deal of intelligence and principle. Towards the end of his chronicle, the pages became very difficult to read, but I came to understand that he had either been entrusted with an important task, or possibly that he was a part of a group involved in a significant mission. At any rate, it had something to do with Saladin himself and one of Saladin's generals. After that, I could make out very little because the ink was so badly smeared."

Bud was caressing her hands in a comforting gesture. "So why do you think he's speaking about the Crown of Thorns?"

She shrugged, struggling to reclaim her composure. "Because he kept alluding to his sworn duty of God's choosing. How he was the only man worthy of such a task. At the conclusion of the journal, his attitude changed dramatically as I came to understand that his brother, Simon, betrayed him regarding this particular duty. I don't know the details of the treachery. But clearly, a holy relic is enough to kill a man over. Even one's own brother."

"Even if that's true, it still doesn't explain why Saladin and his general would be involved with a Christian relic," Bud pressed gently.

The madness was fading from her eyes as fatigue took its toll. "Oh, hell, I don't know," she murmured, removing her hands from Bud's warm palms and putting them to her head. "Nothing about this guy has made any sense from the beginning. In his journal, he kept talking about a Christian offering from Saladin's general, never clear as to what the offering was, but it suddenly seemed to make sense when I read the last passage of the journal. Saladin's general gave Sir Kieran a Christian offering of peace. A holy relic."

Bud cocked an eyebrow, waiting for Peck to leap into the conversation with his usual petulance. And knowing for certain that he would break the man's nose if he did. "The Crown of Thorns?"

Rory nodded faintly, the pain of years of research in her eyes evident. "Yes," she whispered. "All along, Ottis' manuscript described finding the Crown of Thorns buried within the ruins of a Muslim mosque. But what if it wasn't the actual crown, but the very man who could tell us where it was located? Maybe through the process of translation, the facts became twisted. Maybe we really were looking for Sir Kieran all along because he knows where the crown is."

Bud watched her closely as she spoke, noting how tired she was. Maybe what she needed was eight hours away from Sir Kieran and his mysterious journal to give her a fresh perspective. But from the passage she had repeated, he honestly couldn't fault her interpretation. Especially when, oddly enough, it seemed to make sense.

"It wasn't as if Sir Kieran had the power to stop the war by accepting a peace offering. But he could have been a part of a peace delegation sent to retrieve a token of truce. And when the offering was presented to King Richard, it would have undoubtedly had a powerful effect. Maybe enough to end the siege." Not surprisingly, Bud was intrigued. But he was also concerned for Rory's health as she lingered unsteadily by the edge of the shallow trench. Pushing his theory aside for the moment, he focused on her exhausted face.

"Look," he said softly. "We don't have to get into a heavy philosophical discussion right now. Why don't you get some sleep and let Dave and I hold down the fort for a while. You'll feel better when you wake up."

Rory was reluctant, looking to the knight once more. "'The diadem of Your sacrifice entrusted into my hands...'"

Bud reached down and grasped her by the arms. "Really, I love a woman with a photographic memory, but you need to sleep and Dave and I need to eat breakfast. Come out of that hole before you become physically attached to it."

He lifted her out of the grave with assistance from David. Exhausted and muddled, Rory took the journal from Peck's hands. "I'm not done yet," she mumbled, refusing to look him in the eye. "I... I'll finish when I get up."

"Sure, Rory, whatever you say." David let her take the precious artifact as Bud put his arm around her shoulders. Together, they made their way down the hill as the sun broke free of the eastern sky, signaling the start of a bright, new day.

CHAPTER SIX

R ORY SLEPT ALL day and into the night. Bud refused to continue work and the entire camp came to a standstill for nearly twenty-four hours. He and David kept checking on her, sprawled out on the bed like a rag doll and sleeping so deeply that she was scarcely breathing. Once, David sat down at her desk to read through her transcribed notes and realized that throughout the entire two hours he was there, she never moved a muscle.

It was a deep sleep indicative of exhaustion and emotion. Supper came and went and still, Rory slept. At one point, Bud tried to rouse her simply to get her to eat something, but she ignored him irritably and pulled the pillow over her head. Patting her shoulder with an affectionate smile, he left her alone for the rest of the night.

It was a short night, however. Rory awoke promptly at three-thirty and after a luxuriously long shower, a definite no-no in the middle of the desert, she emerged into the early morning loaded with determination. Rousing Bud by tickling his ear and then bouncing on his bed until the frame collapsed, their laughter had been enough to wake David and half the camp.

At four-thirty in the morning she looked absolutely lovely; mascara and lipstick and Bud even smelled perfume. Pleased her groomed appearance matched her renewed frame of mind, he felt rather slovenly accompanying her to the dig. As David cranked up the gasoline generator, Rory beheld her knight with a far more rational attitude.

"So… you're feeling better this morning?" Bud asked.

She cast him a sheepish glance. "Yeah. Sorry about my freak-out episode. I was really tired and I guess I just let everything get to me."

He smiled knowingly, his eyes puffy from lack of sleep. "Forget it. We're all allowed a freak-out episode now and then." Slowly, his smile faded. "Do you still think he knows where the crown is?"

She nodded, without hesitation. "Absolutely. I'm convinced of it."

Bud observed her a moment longer before tearing his gaze away. He didn't want her to see the doubt in his eyes. "Too bad we can't ask him. Even if we could, I don't think he'd tell us anything."

"Ah, but we have ways of making him talk," Rory said in her best pseudo-Nazi accent. "He'd never survive a round of torture with the evil and domineering Dr. Peck."

Bud laughed and Rory returned his smile, glad all was well between them and he didn't think she was bordering on insanity. But with everything that had happened over the past two days, there were times when she wondered herself. The more she lingered in the world of the knight and his journal, the more consumed she became.

Especially now, as she stood by the edge of the grave; what she wouldn't give to ask him what he knew about her crown. But even if he knew the whereabouts, it was obvious the only answers she would receive were those she discovered herself. Lowering herself into the trench, she glanced at Bud. "Did you and Dave figure out how to remove him?"

Bud scratched his head and yawned. "Fortunate for us that Dave is a whiz in physics. He's designed a fairly simply wench system that should remove him quite nicely. And I put some of the carpenters to work yesterday building a casket. It should be finished by this afternoon."

Rory nodded with satisfaction, straddling the knight with her fists on her hips. After a moment, she crouched down, touching his face and feeling a resurgence of the warm feelings he seemed to provoke. "I… I dreamed about this guy last night. I mean, after everything I read in his journal, I feel like we're on a first name basis."

Bud cocked an eyebrow. "So you're dreaming of him now? I'm sensing a good deal of infatuation, Rory."

She grinned. "And why not? He was chivalrous and moral and kind."

"And brave and clean and thrifty. An overgrown Boy Scout."

"A Boy Scout with a broadsword as big as your leg."

"Then it's a good thing he's dead and can't hear my disrespect."

Rory laughed. "Not to change the subject, but have we heard from Becker since his initial reply?

Bud sat down, swinging his legs into the trench. "No. But he's had time to make the necessary boasts and contact the British Consul. We should be hearing from him soon. In fact, I wouldn't be the least bit surprised if he showed up here personally." From the corner of his eye, he caught the appearance of the sleepy Dr. Peck as he prepared his work table for the day's events. "Dave, did we get a reply from the American Embassy regarding our request for an x-ray machine?"

Yawning, David didn't look up from his pens and files. "Not yet. I'll call them again later today. Or I can try to locate one at a local hospital."

Bud nodded, gazing at the body a moment longer before looking to Rory. She was staring dreamily at the knight, her hand still on his face, and Bud realized he would have given twenty years of his life to see the same gentle expression on her face when she looked at him. He suddenly found himself jealous of a man who had been dead for eight hundred years.

His reaction startled him. It shouldn't have, but it did nonetheless and he struggled to keep the quiver from his voice. "We should examine him completely before removing him from the grave." He noted bitterness in his tone, wondering if she heard it.

Apparently, she hadn't. She was still looking at the knight, oblivious to all else. "He's so incredibly intact that I doubt anything will snap off during the extraction. What, exactly, did Dave devise?"

The camp cock crowed, announcing the commencement of a new day. As the horizon turned shades of pink, Bud found himself struggling against the most powerful surge of jealousy he had ever experienced.

"Basically, we're going to slip him onto a backboard and lift him out with a wench," he said as steadily as he could manage. "As soon as his current state is logged, we can give it a try."

"Great." Rory continued to stare at the knight. He really was a handsome fellow. Remembering how Sir Kieran mentioned that heathen women had clung to him like "leeches", Rory found she could hardly blame them. He must have been a dazzling sight.

Knowing he had been forgotten, Bud climbed from the grave and headed towards camp. A casual glance over his shoulder showed Rory to be in the same position he had left her, hovering over the warrior as if she were incapable of focusing on anything else. Increasingly bitter, he turned away and descended the small hill.

If they had found her Crown of Thorns, at least she wouldn't be mooning over the wreath like a lovesick teenager. It was crazy for him to be jealous of a man dead eight hundred years, he knew, but he simply couldn't help it. Rory was his, or at least he intended to make her his when all of his gentle attention broke down her resistance. Until then, he had no intention of sharing her with anyone else. Period.

The Israeli dirt crunched softly beneath his boots as he made his way to the canvas shelters. He found himself hoping there would be a message from Becker on his computer, informing him that England threatened to go to war if the crusader wasn't returned home. It would give Bud an excuse to get rid of the guy without making himself look like a villain.

Feeling like a fool for his irrational thoughts, Bud shifted gears and tried to focus on the excavation report that Becker was expecting. Hoping he could refrain from using words like "bastard" and "home-wrecker" when describing the knight in the grave.

C3

THE CRUSADER EMERGED from his tomb beautifully. The carpenters had finished the box, a massive casket lined with cedar from Lebanon. Lowering the knight into the coffin had been tricky, but David and Bud had worked with precision to accomplish the task. As Rory stood by like a nervous mother, Sir Kieran Hage finally came to rest in his custom-made crypt.

It was past supper but no one seemed to care. A couple of journalists caught wind of the find through relatives working the site and had shown up to write an article for the local paper. Bud thrust Rory at them, staying out of the limelight as she used her broken Arabic to answer their questions.

Truthfully, there wasn't anyone better to handle public relations than Rory. With her beauty and poise, she naturally had the press eating out of her hand and Bud watched from a distance, pretending he was seeing to the final aspects of disengaging the wench when he was really focused on Rory. David finally pushed him away, far more efficient than his preoccupied colleague, to finish the task himself.

Bud hardly noticed he had been shoved aside. Removing his gloves, he tucked them into his back pocket and continued to watch as Rory dealt with the journalists. His jealousy fit had faded over the past several hours, leaving him feeling somewhat emotionally weak and foolish. But it threatened to surge again as he listened to Rory speak so dearly of her knight.

It didn't take Bud long to realize he had asked her to handle the publicity to keep her away from the corpse. Christ, he felt like such an adolescent being jealous of an inanimate object. But he couldn't help his feelings, not where they pertained to Rory, and in lieu of sending her away from the dig altogether he realized he had better deal with them.

And he would. Someday, when he was strong enough. But for now, there was work to be done and daylight was fading. Stooping over Sir Kieran, he was in the process of inspecting the body for damage that might have occurred during the extraction when David suddenly nudged him. Glancing up, he noticed that his associate was pointing to Rory. Bud looked casually in her direction and what he saw sent him bolting.

The journalists were gone, replaced by a fair-haired man in a suit and two soldiers in fatigues. A Land Rover sat parked just outside of the camp perimeter and Bud cursed himself for not having been alert enough to see the vehicle coming up the road. Even as he and David rushed to Rory's side, Bud knew who the men were. There simply wasn't any other alternative.

Rory was playing the perfect hostess when Bud and David marched up. The man in the suit acted as if he hadn't seen them, listening to Rory's description of the site with a leering expression that made Bud's blood boil.

"I'm Dr. Dietrich, senior archaeologist of the dig." He practically thrust himself in front of Rory. "What can I do for you?"

The younger man with the receding blond hair tore his eyes away from Rory, smiling cordially. "I'm Justin Darlow, Senior Administrative Aide at the British Embassy in Istanbul. We received an amazing phone call from our embassy in the States informing us of your miraculous find." He glanced at Rory. "Dr. Osgrove was very graciously explaining the particulars. Would it be possible to see the corpse?"

The veins in Bud's temples were pulsing furiously. "If it's all right with Dr. Osgrove, I suppose it's all right with me." It was difficult to keep his tone steady. "But just for a moment. I want to seal it up before nightfall."

Darlow's smile faded, sensing the man's guarded manner. "Thank you," he said, casting Bud a long glance. "I understand that you've also come across some valuable artifacts. Could I see them as well?"

Even though Bud had told the man he could view the corpse, it was apparent he wasn't yet willing to show him. Crossing his arms in an unfriendly gesture, Bud realized in hindsight that he had been willing to be affable when he realized the British had come to inspect the find. But the moment the young aide cast Rory an openly interested glance, all goodwill flew out the window.

Rory sensed Bud's foul mood, an odd circumstance coming from the usually-sunny man. She wondered if he was being cautious on her behalf, considering the conversation they'd had regarding the validity of the British claim. As much as she didn't want the British pushing their way onto her dig, the very last thing Bud needed was to punch out a foreign aide.

"I'd be happy to show you the artifacts," she said, putting her hand on Bud's shoulder to calm him. He was as tense as stone. Casting him a concerned glance, she tugged on his arm to get him moving. "But if you want to see the corpse, we'd better do it first. We've got to seal it before the moisture in the air grows heavy."

Holding Bud tightly for fear he might do something rash, she directed the aide up the hill. Peck followed close behind, casting cool glances at the two Marines. Darlow pretended to ignore the tension, brushing the dust off his Armani suit. By the time they reached the cedar box bearing Sir Kieran's body, the atmosphere was crackling with stress.

Darlow looked closely at the knight. "Hmm. Rather well-preserved. When did he die?"

"1192 A.D.," Rory said, her protectiveness surging as Darlow inspected Sir Kieran like a side of beef.

The aide was peering at the brown stains on the tunic and hose. "Remarkable," he said. Even the British Marines were looking over his shoulder, examining their military predecessor. "He's bigger than any knight I've seen in our museums."

"We're guessing six feet five or six," Rory said. "He weighs well over two hundred pounds now. We've estimated that during his prime he was close to two hundred and forty."

Darlow nodded, walking around the box to better study all angles. Pausing by Sir Kieran's feet, he suddenly dug into his pocket and pulled out a small camera. Peck leaped into action before Rory or Bud could respond.

"No pictures," he said firmly. "This is our find and all pictures will be printed and copyrighted through the university."

Darlow looked somewhat surprised. "I... I apologize," he said, tucking the camera away. "I didn't mean any harm. It's just that the knight's family asked that I send a photograph. You know, for a keepsake and all that."

"Family?" Rory suddenly felt as if she had been punched in the stomach. "What... what family?"

Darlow nodded his head in the direction of the corpse. "His family, of course. His descendants. Didn't your university tell you that we had succeeded in locating them?"

David looked at Bud. Bud looked at Rory. Only Bud seemed capable of answering. "No, they didn't."

Rory's breathing began to come in heavy gasps. Behind her, she could feel Bud's hands on her arms for support. "You found his family?" she repeated, her voice a whisper. "How could you do that so quickly? We only notified the university of the find three days ago."

Darlow smiled at her as if she were a moron. "Dr. Osgrove, we British consider lineage to be the very basis of our society. When your university supplied us with the knight's name and area of birth, it wasn't difficult to locate his descendants through records. The University of Sussex has a Genealogy Department that was able to determine Sir Kieran's living heirs within twelve hours of receiving the information."

Had Bud not been holding her steady, Rory knew she would have collapsed. "Oh, God," she gasped, turning away from the group. She simply had to. Darlow watched her walk away, noting her delicious figure far more than he should have with the hostile archaeologist standing within striking range.

"They're anxious to have their ancestor returned, Dr. Osgrove," he said, a sincere inflection in his tone. Knowing that, legally, the British had no claim to the man, but hoping the rightness of returning the knight to his family would weigh heavily on the situation. "He has a very large family, actually. The House of Hage is an extremely old Anglo-Saxon family said to have descended from the kings of Mercia. Naturally, they are thrilled you have found one of their ancestors and wish to have him returned to England for proper burial in the family crypt."

The dagger Darlow had driven into her heart with the first mention of Sir Kieran's family was being further twisted by his manipulative words. Rory's hands were pressed against her mouth as if to stifle the scream that threatened.

"I don't believe this," she whispered. After a moment, hazel eyes fixed on Darlow's face. "Is that why you're here? To convince me to send Sir Kieran home to his family?"

Darlow shrugged. "Not really. I was merely sent to inspect the find. But if I had dug up your grandmother, wouldn't you want her returned to you for a proper burial rather than displayed in a museum like a freak?"

"That's enough," Bud growled. "Get the hell off my dig or I'll throw you off myself."

The Marines that had accompanied Darlow tensed, preparing for a fight. But the aide merely held up his hand, calming the already-strained situation before it grew out of control.

"I didn't come here to offend, Dr. Dietrich, I assure you," he said sincerely. "My interest is genuine. Sir Kieran's family is very concerned what will become with him. They merely want him to rest in peace, not be open for scrutiny next to the dinosaur bones and Egyptian pottery of an American museum. He's a man, for Heaven's sake. Not a commercial object."

"Don't you dare to presume to tell me about this knight!" Rory exploded, the unprofessional tears falling. "I've spent the past two days reading his journal and I happen to know him far better than you, your damned government, or his haughty blue-blooded descendants. Don't ever imagine that I'm unconcerned with what becomes of him!"

Bud had to grab her to prevent her from charging the aide. "Calm down, honey," he whispered in her ear. "Everything will be fine, just calm down."

Rory struggled against him, her shock of not a moment before transforming into anger so vicious she could hardly control it. The mere suggestion that she didn't have Sir Kieran's best interest at heart sent her erupting like a madwoman. She thought her concern stemmed from the fact that he seemed to be her only link to the elusive Crown of Thorns but, just as quickly, she realized her emotions were rooted in something far deeper.

Bearing that in mind, she struggled to reclaim her control. "There is no one more concerned for the dignity and preservation of this knight that I am, Mr. Darlow." Wiping hastily at her tears, she took a deep, cleansing breath. "You go back and tell your government that whatever becomes of him, whatever we decide what's to become of him, that it will be entirely honorable. You'll just have to trust us."

Darlow wasn't happy with her response. "And you don't believe that returning him to his family would be of the utmost honor? He belongs to England's history, Dr. Osgrove. And we should like to respect him as such."

"He belongs to the world's history, Mr. Darlow." She was calming a little more now. Bud's hands were still on her and she drew strength from him. "It wasn't merely the English who went on the Crusades, although they believed themselves to be the most important of the participants. There were French knights, Teutonic knights, not to mention the Spanish and Irish mercenaries. It was a worldwide affair; not just the arrogant English."

Darlow drew in a deep breath; the meeting with the Americans was not going well at all. Rather than spend all night debating the facts with an emotional female, he decided it would be wise to retreat to the hotel and call the embassy for further instructions. The work at the site wasn't finished yet and Darlow estimated it would be some time before the body was moved. Time enough to try again to convince the

Americans that their find belonged to Britain.

After a small eternity locked in the glare of hazel eyes, Darlow looked to Bud and David. "I apologize if my actions have offended anyone. It's just that this English knight, any English knight, means a good deal to my country. This is our heritage, something America can hardly claim."

Rory let out a long sigh, an odd weakness encompassing her as her composure returned. "My family immigrated to America in the early nineteen twenties, Mr. Darlow. My mother's parents were born in Hastings, so don't patronize me with lectures of pure English blood. I could probably give you lessons on it."

Darlow's gaze lingered on her a moment longer before casting a final glance at the cedar-lined box. "He belongs with his family, Dr. Osgrove," he said quietly, turning to leave. "Put yourself in their position. You would want your relative back, too."

He strolled down the hill with his two guard dogs in tow. Bud and David stared after him, but Rory refused to linger on the man once he was gone. Instead, she moved to the reinforced casket.

"Bastards," she hissed, reaching out to finger Sir Kieran's tunic. "I knew they'd come, I just didn't think it would be this soon."

Bud let out a long sigh, frazzled by the whole situation. "What I want to know is why in the hell Becker didn't send word that they had found his relatives. He knew the British would make it to the dig site posthaste; he should have prepared us."

David went to stand beside Rory, his gaze roving over the corpse. "Maybe he didn't think they'd come this quickly. Or maybe he's already up to his eyeballs in diplomatic demands and hasn't had the time."

"With all of the assistants he employs, I can't believe that one of them couldn't have sent word if Becker was occupied." Rory was touching Sir Kieran's cheek and Bud had to look away; he couldn't stand the adoring expression on her face. "So they want you to come home, my lord? I can't say I blame them. If you could talk, somehow I think you'd want to go home too."

Bud did look at her, then. "Rory?" he asked hesitantly. "Are you actually considering…?"

She shrugged faintly, taking a deep breath to ease her nerves. "We've talked about this before, Bud. And you were right, although I wasn't going to give Mr. Embassy the satisfaction of knowing we've been considering his very proposal. But now, with a family involved… I really can't believe that they've found them."

Peck turned his back on the corpse, leaning against the casket and crossing his arms. "Believe it. And unless they get him back, I suspect the situation will never rest."

Rory laid her cheek against the edge of the box, still toying with the neck of the knight's tunic. The thought of turning him over was almost more than she could stand and, for the second time that evening, found herself fighting against tears. Her obsession with the knight was growing into something she didn't recognize and had no desire to resist. Knowing that his fate, his chance for eternal peace, rested solely in her hands was a decision she would not take lightly.

"It just wouldn't be fair to prop him up in a museum like some stuffed animal," she murmured. "The more I come to know of this man, the more I can't stand the thought of treating him like a prize. He doesn't deserve to spend eternity being gawked at by curious visitors."

David was watching her over his shoulder, knowing how hard this was for her. Her very first find destined to be taken away, never to be seen again. Bud had acted like the decision was Rory's to make; they all knew it was Bud's final decision regardless of Rory's feelings. But considering the Nahariya site had been her project, Bud had allowed her to make the final determination of Sir Kieran's destination.

The Crown of Thorns was slipping through her fingers in more ways than one. Her only link was apparently bound for England, the journal and artifacts with it. Peck couldn't imagine that she would have made any other decision; she knew that Bud was just being accommodating, too. And she wouldn't dream of taking advantage of his kindness. No matter how painful the decision, there was really no other alternative.

The knight had to go home.

"He'll be a lot happier resting in a marble crypt than a glass case," David said quietly.

Rory nodded, her eyes riveted to the corpse. "So will I."

Standing behind her, Bud sighed. "Are you sure?"

"Yeah," she whispered. "Tell Becker that Sir Kieran goes home to his family."

Bud passed a long glance at David, his comrade's face unusually impassive. "If you say so," he said, moving beside the casket. "Would it matter if I told you I think you're making the right decision?"

Rory smiled weakly. "It would matter," she murmured, her expression suddenly taking on a dreamy appearance as if she were a million miles away. Bud noticed the change in features, wondering if she was going to start crying again and wishing he could say something to ease her ache. But the tears didn't come.

"In his journal, Sir Kieran spoke about a number of incidents he had been involved in without a hint of arrogance," she said, distracting herself from her turmoil by reliving the tales from the journal. "I mean, this guy was so humble it was unbelievable. Once, fifteen of his fellow knights had been captured by a Muslim general named Al-eb-Alil. This general buried the English knights in the sand up to their necks and threatened to decapitate them if the Christian armies' most powerful warrior didn't meet him in a personal battle. Sir Kieran rode to the task while the Christian commanders were still debating the crisis and killed the general himself."

Bud glanced to the casket, his admiration for the knight somehow easing his jealousy. "And he saved the knights?"

Rory nodded, her gaze riveted to the pallid face. "All of them. Instead of bragging over his victory, though, he finished the story with these final words; 'Without danger there is no glory, and without glory there is no point in being a knight.'"

Bud watched her as she spoke, coming to realize why Rory was so infatuated with the man. She was acquainted with the stories in his journal, knowing him as Bud did not. Maybe if he read the stories, he would become infatuated, too. Clearly, there was more to the corpse than a warrior believed to have once been in possession of the Crown of Thorns.

"What else did he do?" he asked. David settled in on the other side of Rory, waiting for another tale of honor and glory like an eager child.

Rory smiled, the horrors of the British aide forgotten for the moment. As if losing herself in Sir Kieran's fame would help stave off the reality that would be upon them all too soon.

"Well…," she looked thoughtful, glancing to the corpse seriously. "Please jump in if I fail to tell this correctly, my lord. I'm sure I can't do it justice like you can."

Bud and David grinned, Peck going so far as to elbow her in the ribs to force her to proceed. Rory rubbed her side, pinching David's arm in retaliation.

"Quit annoying me or I won't continue," she told him sternly, then returned to a thoughtful expression. "As I was saying, Sir Kieran mentioned an adventure about a tavern in Joppa where several Frankish knights insulted King Richard. Well, it was just Sir Kieran and two other buddies against eight Frankish warriors and…"

"Dr. Bud!" came a shout from the camp below. "Dr. Bud, come quick!"

The archaeologists looked to the source of the cry with concern, noting the Syrian foreman approaching. The black-haired man waved urgently when he saw their attention.

"Dr. Bud!" he called again. "Email from America! Dr. Becker has sent you a message!"

Bud looked to Rory. Rory looked to Bud. David looked to both of them. The somber reality they had been so successful in forgetting for a few brief moments had suddenly returned with a vengeance. Finally, Bud waved his acknowledgement to the foreman.

"I'll be right there!"

No one had to guess what the message contained.

Cʒ

BUD WASN'T SURPRISED to find Rory seated beside the cedar-lined casket at dawn the next morning. Already, she had removed the lid, exposing Sir Kieran to the brilliance of a new Israeli day. Meandering up to the knight and his most fervent admirer, Bud shoved his hands into the pockets of his jeans and smiled weakly when Rory glanced up from the journal.

"Hi."

"Hi," she answered. "I was just doing a little more studying. I won't have this in my possession much longer and…"

Bud held up his hand, a silencing gesture. "You still don't have to do this, Rory. I haven't replied to Becker's email from last night and there's still time to change your mind."

"I thought you said I was making the right decision."

"I believe you are. But I also don't want you thinking that I forced you into making this choice."

She inhaled, drawing deep the early morning air. "I don't think that. But you're making it harder on me by acting as if I haven't yet made a decision. I thought I made it last night, Bud, quite clearly."

His gaze lingered on her a moment, his face lined with fatigue from a sleepless night. "You did," he said quietly. "But I also knew you probably spent most of the night thinking about your choice and I didn't want you to wake up this morning resenting me."

She smiled weakly, shaking her head. "Resent you for what? For thinking of Sir Kieran's best interests when I could only think with my emotions? You were right from the very beginning, before we even knew about his descendants or the political pressure involved. You knew exactly what was going to happen and you tried to prepare me."

He smiled wryly, kicking at the dirt. "I tried. I don't know what good it did in the long run, but I tried."

"You did a good job. Had you not forewarned me, I might be in even worse emotional shape than I am now. Even if I act otherwise, I know deep down that Sir Kieran deserves to go home."

Bud looked up from the hole he was digging with his heel. "We'll go visit him in England, I promise."

Rory's smile faded. "I want more than that. I want to go to whatever service his family has for him. Will you see what you can do?"

"Sure," he said. "Becker can arrange it. After all, it's the least he can do, considering we're making his job a whole lot easier by contributing to cordial international relations."

Rory nodded in agreement. "Considering what his email said, I guess he's had a pretty rough time of it. Who would have thought that Sir Kieran's family would have hired a lawyer to enact legal action if Sir Kieran wasn't returned? No wonder Becker didn't notify us immediately that the knight's family had been located; he's been dealing with more important issues. Like preventing a nasty lawsuit."

Bud pursed his lips impatiently. "There's nothing that hotshot lawyer could have done. Even with the British Government applying political pressure in support, he wouldn't have had a true claim. There's nothing he would have been able to do to dispute the law of international salvage and domain. Like the saying goes; finder's keepers."

"Maybe so. But in this case, the finder isn't keeping."

Rory's smile faded completely as she looked, once again, to the volume in her lap. Bud continued to watch her, noting that her gorgeous hair was pulled away from her face, soft waves falling down her back. He was beginning to think that she was going to be all right with this when suddenly he saw a tear fall to her hand. Another quickly followed. Disheartened, he knelt swiftly beside her chair.

"Oh, Christ," he murmured, clasping her fingers with one hand and wiping at her tears with the other. "Please don't cry, honey. I told you, you don't have to turn him over. If you want him to return to the university, then he's as good as there. I swear it."

She shook her head. "No, Bud, I've made my decision. Besides, there isn't any other choice."

"Yes, there is. If you don't want to send him home, then we won't. End of discussion."

She snorted. "It's not like I've found a stray dog. Sir Kieran isn't a possession; he's a man, just like Darlow said. What right do I have to lay claim to him over his family? Even though my mind wants to put him on display in the university's museum to announce to the world that I didn't fail at my Nahariya dig, my heart knows that he should go home. And the truth hurts."

Bud squeezed her hands sympathetically. "Honey, don't let Darlow influence you with his guilt trip and diplomatic bull. And as for failing at Nahariya, I don't ever think I've seen a more successful venture. The university will be talking about this for years to come and I'd wager to say that you'll have carte blanche with any future dig you want to pursue."

She looked at him, a weak smile on her lips. "What if I want to continue looking for my crown?"

He met her smile. "They'll let you. Becker may grumble about it, but they'll let you."

She wiped the remaining tears from her eyes. "I don't know what I would do without you, Bud. You'll always be my greatest supporter."

His smile faded, a fire suddenly igniting in the ice-blue eyes. "More than you know, Rory. I'll always be there for you."

She caught sight of the flame, his expression tender and passionate at the same time. Sensing that, somehow, the focus between them had changed dramatically, Rory struggled to acclimate herself to the shift of mood when his lips were suddenly on her, warm and insistent and gentle. Momentarily stunned, she was compelled to react when he let go of her fingers long enough to tenderly cup her face.

Jolted with surprise, she pulled away sharply and stumbled from her chair. Bud was still on his knees, his ice-blue orbs filled with the pain of a love unreturned.

"I... I'm sorry, Rory," he whispered. "I shouldn't have, but... Christ, I'm sorry. I didn't mean to frighten you."

She took a deep breath, struggling to make sense of the event. Not strangely, she wasn't the least bit repulsed nor had she been frightened. Bud was a warm, wonderful man and she liked him a great deal. And over the past three days, they had become extremely close. Still, she wasn't ready for his amorous attentions.

"It's ok, really," she said, trying not to appear unnerved. "I… I suppose I should cover Sir Kieran back up and return to camp. There's a lot to do before…"

"Rory." Bud rose to his feet, his expression beseeching. "Please don't run off. Like I said, I didn't mean to frighten you, but I couldn't help myself. I've wanted to do that since the day we met."

She was having difficulty looking him in the eye. Good Lord, she just didn't know what she was feeling. She'd never looked at Bud as a love interest, but the past few days had seen an odd change in her opinion. It wasn't as if she was ready to jump into bed with him; still, she couldn't outright shun him. Maybe he was exactly what she needed only she had been too distracted or blind to notice.

Truthfully, she simply didn't know. And she was almost angry at him for throwing yet another wrench into an already chaotic situation.

"I…" She emitted a blustery sigh, forcing herself to meet Bud's gaze. He looked so uncertain that she found herself wanting to put him at ease. "Wow, Bud. I just don't know what to say."

He seemed to relax a little, letting out a weak chuckle. "Don't say anything. I should have never… it wasn't like I planned it. It just happened."

She nodded. "I realize that. We're both kind of caught up in this and I've been pretty emotional lately. Maybe you thought kissing me would shut me up."

He shook his head, his hands finding their way back into his pockets. "Not at all. I just don't like seeing you unhappy. Maybe I hoped I could give you a little comfort." He took a deep breath, looking uncomfortable and determined all at the same time. "Look, I know this isn't the time for this, but I've already made an ass out of myself and I might as well go all the way. You see, Dr. Osgrove, I'm in love with you. The past fourteen months have been the greatest of my life and even if we walk off this dig tomorrow and never see each other again, I'll still remember them with the fondest of memories because they will always remind me of you." He took another deep breath and shrugged, like the weight of the world had finally been lifted from his shoulders. "There. Now I've said it."

He turned and walked away, leaving Rory speechless. She watched him disappear into the camp, her stunned gaze staring at the canvas tents as if she could hardly believe what she had heard. True, she had always known his feelings, but for Bud to admit them was something she thought she would never hear. The sad part was, she couldn't reciprocate his sentiment. Although she wouldn't have hurt him for the world, at the moment, she simply couldn't tell him what he wanted to hear.

Hand to her mouth in a dazed gesture, Rory found herself turning aimlessly for the knight's casket. The rising sun was bathing the corpse in a soft, golden light, giving the cold skin color as if attempting to convince the world of his life. Thoughts lingering on Bud, Rory suddenly realized she was still clutching the journal. Throughout the exchange, she'd never put it down.

And she still didn't put it down, even as she reclaimed her chair and stared absently over the camp. Her search for the crown was a failure, Sir Kieran was going home to England, and Bud had declared his undying love. If Rory had known what she was getting herself in to two years ago when she first began the petition for this project, she would have gladly thrown it all away. Bud's pain of a one-sided love and her pain of losing her knight as well as the crown just weren't worth the trouble.

Maybe none of this was.

CHAPTER SEVEN

Heathrow Airport
London, England

THE 747 SET down in fog thicker than anything Rory had ever seen. Even Bud, who had been completely silent since leaving Tel Aviv the day before, commented on the blanket of clouds to the man across the aisle. Staring into the hazy morning as the plane taxied to the terminal, Rory wasn't particularly interested in the fog. All she could ponder was the fact that this was the first time Sir Kieran had been home in over eight hundred years.

The tears threatened again, as they had been hovering near the surface for the past twenty-four hours. Leaving David to oversee the cleanup of the dig, Rory and Bud, two British embassy officials and four Israeli security guards escorted Sir Kieran and his possessions to the Tel Aviv Airport. The knight and his artifacts had been carefully loaded into the belly of the British Airways plane and personally secured by Bud. When the jumbo jet took off, she finally gave up the struggle against the tears and let them come.

Sir Kieran was going home.

Athens Airport had been a nightmare. Their layover had been over eight hours because of a bomb threat and Rory spent the time seated in the terminal next to their plane, watching gun-toting soldiers patrol the area. One of the Israeli security men told her it wasn't unusual for

Athens Airport to be swarming with men bearing AK-47 assault rifles, but Rory still found the situation unnerving. And the fact that she couldn't spend any time with Sir Kieran in the bowels of the plane only made it worse.

From Athens, the flight was direct to London. Bud sat beside her the entire time, writing in his old, leather notebook and completely silent. Ever since he had made his confession the day before, he hadn't said a word to her. Rory couldn't stand the tension between them, especially since she needed his comfort now more than ever. But in truth, she wasn't sure what to say to him. She couldn't give him any hope, any encouragement, and she suspected he knew it.

Therefore, she was resigned to the brittle silence between them and turned her attention to the brilliant skies beyond the window, pondering the coming separation between herself and Sir Kieran. She knew that she was doing the right thing by returning him home but wondered if she would ever recover from her noble, if not reluctant, sacrifice.

It was a heartache that increased when the plane landed and the captain wished everyone a pleasant stay in England. The Israeli guards were up, disembarking with the embassy officials who had already obtained clearance to proceed to the tarmac. Bud collected his carry-on, as did Rory, and they silently followed the group of men to the blacktop below.

It was a cold day. Rory was so used to scorching temperatures that she found the change refreshing. Dressed in slim-fit jeans, boots, a sweater and her camelhair coat, her long blond hair was stylishly pulled back from her face and gathered in a clip. But even if her appearance was sharp, the gleam in the hazel eyes belied the dullness of her soul; watching as the belly hatch was opened, the Israelis were into the hold before the airline employees could move a muscle.

A forklift was rolled out, removing the massive casket so loving built by the Turkish workers. The Israeli guards were all over the coffin, like an odd army of pallbearers. But Rory would not be deterred from her determination to check the body; she hadn't seen Sir Kieran since they had left the dig and she wanted to make sure he had survived his journey intact. But more than that, she was simply desperate to see him. Like an addiction, she had to feed her habit.

"Get me a crowbar," she snapped to one of the British officials, the man giving her an intolerant look before passing the order on to an airline employee.

But Rory didn't care what the British thought of her manners; all Americans were pushy and loud and she was simply verifying the stereotype. Moving for the casket, she pushed between the Israeli guards and ran her hands over the box, making sure it hadn't been damaged by the turbulence they had experienced over the Alps. Bud came up behind her, a large screwdriver in his hand.

"Here," he said quietly. "This ought to work."

It was the first thing he had said to her in nearly a day. Rory didn't reply, merely standing aside as he worked at the seal. The Israeli guards began to help, prying their fingers under the lid and pulling as Bud gained leverage. One side of the cover had been hinged, but the lid had been nailed shut for extra security during transport. Just as Bud reached the fourth and final nail, his progress was abruptly interrupted.

"Is that truly necessary?"

Rory turned, somewhat surprised, to find piercing blue eyes fixed on her. Giving the tall, pleasingly-built man the once over, she cocked a well-defined eyebrow.

"Who are you?"

The Israeli guards already had their weapons drawn as the man put up a supplicating hand. "I have security clearance, I assure you," he said, very slowly reaching into his coat pocket and withdrawing a pink piece of paper. "See? Written permission."

Rory, still wary, took the paper from his hand and unfolded it. Glancing over the official form, she handed it to one of the embassy aides. "Mr. Corbin, how can I help you?"

The man smiled faintly, a rather handsome fellow in his late thirties. "Dr. Rory Osgrove, I presume?"

"Yes."

Corbin's gaze seemed to linger on her a moment. "Dr. Becker said I'd find you here. I've come on official business. I represent the Hage family."

Rory's uncertainty of the man was fading, being replaced by a stunning dislike. "A lawyer?"

He nodded. "I've recently been in touch with Dr. Becker at the University of California San Marcos and he was gracious enough to inform me of your flight and arrival time." Glancing over Rory's head, his gaze fixed on the coffin. "Sir Kieran Hage, I presume?"

Rory could feel her defenses going up. She hated this man already. It wasn't merely that he represented the relatives determined to snatch Sir Kieran away from her, but the mere aura about him was disturbing. He made her uncomfortable. "I was just about to check him to make sure he hadn't suffered any damage in transport," she said. "It will only take a minute if you'll allow me to…"

Steven Corbin held up a hand, politely, to interrupt her. "That won't be necessary, Dr. Osgrove. I'm sure the corpse is in fine shape." He pushed past her, moving towards Bud and the half-opened lid. "Seal it back up, if you would. I will be taking Sir Kieran to the morgue at Middlesex Hospital where several professionals hired by the Hage family are eagerly awaiting his arrival."

Rory's thinly-held composure snapped. "What are you talking about?" she asked, putting herself protectively between the casket and Corbin. "We've arranged to take Sir Kieran to the University of Oxford, where he'll be x-rayed and studied for a few days before being placed in the custody of his descendants."

Corbin's piercing blue eyes were suddenly hard. "Plans have been altered, Dr. Osgrove. Sir Kieran is to be placed in immediate family custody."

Behind Rory, Bud cleared his throat and stepped forward. She wasn't surprised when she felt his warm hand go about her arm, gently, pulling her away from the confrontation.

"Look, Mr. Corbin," he began evenly. "I'm Dr. Dietrich, supervising archaeologist on the dig. Until such time as the university officially places Sir Kieran within his family's custody, he is still our property. We've already made plans for him and I have no intention of deviating."

Corbin looked at Bud as one man would size up a potential enemy; when the chips were down, Bud could be a formidable opponent and it was clear that Corbin sensed that. After a moment, he reached slowly into another pocket.

"If I may, Dr. Dietrich," he removed another piece of neatly folded paper, extending it to Bud. "From your director."

Bud's jaw ticked as he unfolded the paper and read it. Rory saw a faint flush come to his cheeks and she was seized with immediate concern.

"What does it say, Bud?"

He sighed, looking for the proper words as Rory hung over his shoulder, trying to read the message. But Bud wanted to tell her himself and attempted to move away, hoping he could relay the news in a manner that would ease her into the reality of the situation. Rory, however, refused to allow him to move; putting one arm around his waist and the other on the hand clutching the paper, she read it completely.

Bud watched her face, just inches from his own. When she had finished reading the emailed message, he was mildly surprised to note that her features held no discernable reaction. But her somewhat wild gaze had moved to the lawyer, like a cat moving for a mouse, and Bud literally reached out to prevent her from advancing on him.

"Becker gave his permission for the family to take custody of the body the moment we landed, Rory," he said, trying to stop her from taking her aggressions out on Corbin. "Remember, we did agree to return it. It was fully within Becker's right to hand it over sooner than expected, considering we had no valid excuse to delay the transfer. The family is willing to take full responsibility for all tests and research on the corpse."

Rory swallowed, hard, and Bud could see that her controlled facade was purely an act. "But... we had planned to study him ourselves, Bud. Lacking the proper facilities at Nahariya, we weren't able to do a complete study of the man and this was going to be our chance given the appropriate implements at Oxford. Good Lord, this is our find! Can't we even complete what we've started?"

"There are several professionals prepared to do just that, Dr. Osgrove," Corbin said confidently. "The Hage family has recruited a historian from the University of Sussex, a professor specializing in Medieval biology, a forensic pathologist from Middlesex Hospital, and a..."

"No!" Rory suddenly roared. "No autopsy!"

Corbin looked somewhat surprised. "What do you mean? Have you already done one?"

Before Rory could respond, Bud pulled her against him, forcefully, to shut her up. "Given Sir Kieran's perfect state, we determined an autopsy to be unnecessary. We arranged to have the body x-rayed at Oxford, a procedure considered a lot less intrusive to his fragile composition. There's no need to cut him open."

Corbin eyed Rory as she struggled with her composure. "That will be for the pathologist to decide," he said, pulling his gloves tight against the chill wind that was kicking up. "If everything is collected, then I have arranged for an armored car to carry the valuables to the University of Sussex where they will be extensively studied. The family has donated the armor to the British Museum, by the way. And the broadsword will have a place of honor in the museum's collection of Medieval swords."

Rory's face went from a mottled red to a sickly gray. "They're not going to bury him in his armor?" she whispered.

"And waste such a fantastic piece of history?" Corbin snorted as if she were an idiot. "I should say not."

The rage building within Rory's heart was vanished, replaced by disbelief. Ignoring the icy wind whipping about the tarmac, her hazel eyes were wide with untamed emotion.

"But you have to bury him in his armor," she said, her voice tight. "To a Medieval knight, his armor was a physical part of him. To be buried without it was to dishonor the knight completely."

Corbin cocked an intolerant eyebrow. "Your ideas of Medieval romance are touching, Dr. Osgrove, but they fail to encompass the reality of modern times. Sir Kieran Hage is dead, with or without his armor, and his family is being most gracious by donating the valuable pieces for the country's enrichment."

"It's not idealistic romance, Mr. Corbin," she shot back. "What I am saying is hard fact; if Sir Kieran is buried without his armor, it will be a disgrace to both him and the Hage family. And the mere suggestion that he be buried without his broadsword is ludicrous; the weapon, even more than the armor, was a part of the knight's very soul."

Piercing blue eyes studied her a moment longer before looking to Bud. "You seem to be more rational than your spirited young colleague, Dr. Dietrich. Maybe you can explain to her that it is no longer the time of King Richard the Lionheart or Frederick of Barbarossa. We are far more practical these days."

Bud's expression was intense. "I would be glad to explain, if you will kindly justify how a country that is so dedicated to its history that it would threaten an international lawsuit over an American archaeological find could then so callously treat the very object of its interest by disregarding some very basic facts. Nothing Dr. Osgrove has said is untrue or exaggerated, Mr. Corbin. I find the fact that Sir Kieran is going to be buried without his armor completely shocking."

A faint mist began to fall as Corbin looked around in dismay. He didn't have time for the hysterics of the two American archaeologists. He had a job to do and was determined to accomplish it regardless of the emotions involved. Pulling his collar tight, he turned to the embassy officials behind him.

"I've a truck waiting to take us to the armored vehicle," he said crisply. "We've a long way to go and I'd like to get moving."

So they were taking him. Just like that. Rory looked at Bud, such horror in her eyes that he felt the physical impact, reaching out to destroy his heart. But there was nothing he could do to prevent Sir Kieran from being taken away, as all channels had been legally maneuvered by the proper authorities and the crusader was no longer the property of the University of California San Marcos.

"Bud..." she whispered.

He grabbed her arms, holding them tightly. The defenses that had been up since his personal confession the day before were suddenly gone, vanished as the emotion in her face reached deep into his soul. He knew she didn't love him, but that didn't stop him from abandoning his self-protection in order to comfort her. "I know, honey. It's all right. They'll be good to him."

Directly behind them, the coffin was being loaded onto a small, flatbed truck with British Airways logos on the doors. Rory heard the forklift jerk into gear and she whirled about, pulling one arm free of Bud's grasp as he struggled to keep hold of her. Reaching out, she was only able to draw an index finger along the side of the coffin as it moved past, flanked by the Israelis. Bud was positive that if he lost his grip, she would have thrown herself on the casket as if to never let it go.

When the coffin slammed against the bed of the truck, Rory started violently. All she could think, see or feel was Sir Kieran's body being unceremoniously jerked around by men more concerned with protecting him than preserving him. Her breathing was coming in harsh gasps by the time several boxes containing the knight's possessions were loaded behind the casket, the pain in her heart finding a tangible release in the foggy puffs of air.

With a lingering glance to the two American archaeologists, Corbin climbed into the cab of the truck, followed by the two embassy aides. The Israeli guards jumped onto the bed of the rig, their weapons drawn as if they were expecting trouble. Rory watched, her mouth open and her heart in her throat, as one of the soldiers sat carelessly on the end of the casket. As if they had little respect or conscience for the magnificent man inside.

"Bud…"

"What, honey?"

"They're taking him."

"I know."

She didn't say anything for a moment, watching as the truck lurched into gear and rumbled down the tarmac. It had all happened too fast, too forcefully, and her mind was whirling with the reality of the situation. When she finally turned to Bud, her eyes were filled with an ocean of painful tears.

"I don't want to give him up!" she sobbed. "I want him back! Get him back, Bud!"

Of all the times he had quashed the urge to pull her into a powerful embrace, now was not one of them. His muscular arms went about her, pulling her tightly against him as if to forcibly chase away her sorrows. Rory's face was buried in the crook of Bud's neck, weeping as if her heart were breaking.

"I want him back," she cried softly. "Please, Bud… oh, please, go get him back."

His own eyes were stinging with tears, ignoring the mist and the cold as he cradled Rory against him on the glistening tarmac. The world around them was busy and brusque but, still, he continued to hold her.

"I can't, honey," he murmured, pulling her closer. "He belongs to his family now. There's nothing I can do."

"I've changed my mind."

"You can't."

She continued to sob pitifully, so much pain and grief evident. "But… but they don't even care. They're going to bury him without his armor. And his sword; if his body is simply dead, surely they're going to kill his soul."

He rocked her gently, listening to her gut-wrenching sobs. "He'll be properly buried, honey. We'll see to it, won't we? Becker arranged for us to attend the interment."

She suddenly pulled back, her gorgeous hair mussed and her face tense with emotion. "And I'll give that family an earful, damn them! How dare they demand Sir Kieran's return only to show such disrespect for his honor! I swear I'm going to..."

He put gloved fingers over her mouth, silencing her tirade. "You're not going to do anything. You're going to present the perfect picture of a dignified professional and if there is to be any protest of this situation, we'll do it through proper means. The last thing we need is for you to get in a fistfight over Sir Kieran's honor."

She was angry and hurt, pouting and dazed. "Somebody's got to defend him," she muttered, her head aching with jet lag as she struggled to get a handle on her tears. "I just can't believe they took him so quickly, Bud. I didn't even get a chance to say goodbye."

He sighed heavily, his eyes full of compassion. Noticing that the mist was growing heavier, he pulled her into the curve of his torso and gently led her towards the terminal doors. "I'm sorry, honey," he said gently, stooping down to pick up their carry-on bags resting on the pavement. "Let's get a good meal and some sleep and then I'll give Becker a call. I'd say he has a bit of explaining to do about recent events."

Rory was exhausted. Losing Sir Kieran was nearly more than she could handle and her emotional fatigue was growing by the minute. Laying her head wearily on Bud's shoulder, she felt as if she could sleep for a hundred years. Just long enough to wake up and realize that this entire episode had been a horrible nightmare; were she able to go back in time to the point where Sir Kieran was still in her possession, she would never let him out of her sight. Ever.

Her crown. Her knight. Everything was gone. By the time they hit the warm, stale air of the terminal, she had started crying again.

C3

IT HAD BEEN raining steadily since leaving the airport. Taking the subway, or the Underground as the British called it, Rory and Bud had taken the Piccadilly line to the Central line, disembarking at Lancaster Gate. The small hotel that the university had secured for them was right across the street, a quaint hostel that Becker's wife was very fond of. Bud had carried all of the bags except for Rory's carry-on, checking them both into the Parkwood Hotel just after noontime.

The landlady was warm and gracious, directing them up the stairs to their adjacent rooms. Rory hardly noticed the lovely room with yellow chintz wallpaper and matching bedspread, ignoring it all as Bud set her single large suitcase just inside the door. The landlady offered to bring them some tea and he agreed readily, hoping the warm drink would aid Rory's mental state. Since the moment they'd left Heathrow, she'd hardly stopped crying.

Oddly enough, he was more concerned for her when she finally stopped weeping. Her mascara was smeared, her nose red and irritated as she seemed to wander aimlessly across the room. Setting her carry-on to the bed, she proceeded to struggle from her coat. Bud pulled it off her arms and laid it across a chair, wondering if it would be entirely wise to leave her alone at this moment. His baggage was still in the open door, the key to his own room lodged in his hand.

"I should go put my stuff in my room," he said. "Are you going to be all right for a minute?"

She nodded, a weak smile coming to her pale lips. "I'm not an invalid, Bud. Go ahead and unpack. I'll be fine."

He scratched his head in an uncertain gesture, glancing to the window lined with the same beautiful yellow chintz material. Outside, the weather was gloomy to match their mood.

"All right," he finally sighed, moving for the door. "I'm just across the hall if you need me, okay?"

Rory nodded, her gaze lingering on her overstuffed tote bag. After a moment, she reached out and began fumbling with the fastens. Bud was in the process of collecting his beat-up Samsonite and his canvas carry-on, pausing in his quest to leave the room when Rory's actions caught his attention.

"What's the matter? Are you missing something?"

She shook her head, brushing a stray lock of long blond hair from her face. Suddenly, the hazel eyes were on him and the pale lips were twisted in a wicked smirk. Puzzled by the odd expression, Bud cocked a curious eyebrow.

"What's wrong?"

"Nothing," she said, her movements slowing as she refocused on the large tote bag. "Just making sure everything is here."

"What does that mean?"

She drew in a deep breath, an amazingly tranquil sound after her marathon crying jag. Bud's curiosity was growing as she sat on the bed, turning to look at him with a somewhat mischievous expression.

"You're going to be angry with me."

"For what?"

She dug into the bag, removing the object of her search. "For this."

It was Sir Kieran's journal. Bud stared at it a moment, hardly grasping what he was seeing, but truthfully not all that surprised. The Samsonite and the canvas carry-on hit the floor with a thud and the bedroom door slammed shut with heavy force.

"Rory, what in the hell are you doing with that?" he demanded, moving towards the bed.

Her expression hardened and she lowered her gaze, looking to the ancient book. "What does it look like? I kept it."

"You can't keep it," he hissed, his ice-blue eyes blazing. "Do you know what sort of trouble you could get in to? Christ, Rory, what are you thinking?"

She continued to stare at the journal, trying to maintain her calm. Even though she knew he would become angry with her, still, Bud was so mild-mannered that his fury intimidated her. But she wasn't going to back down; not yet, anyway.

"I'm thinking to keep it, at least for a little while," she said quietly.

"Remember, we were planning on spending a few more days with Sir Kieran. I kept it with me, afraid that if I put it in the inventory boxes it would become damaged. Besides, I was going to return it to the family when we were finished."

"You're going to return it now," he seethed quietly, his cheeks flushed. "I honestly can't believe you'd do something this stupid. Christ, Rory, you've stolen something that doesn't belong to you. Didn't you think that they'd discover it missing when they went over the artifact inventory?"

"If you recall, I did the inventory myself," she suddenly snapped. "And this isn't on it."

He froze, his eyes wide with disbelief. The air between them was suddenly silent and still, in sharp contrast to the raging that had been going on not a moment earlier. Hazel eyes were riveted to ice-blue, the thunder from the storm outside all but penetrating the tension in the room.

"Why?" he finally managed to rasp.

Her chest was heaving with emotion and she tore her eyes away, looking once again to the journal that had cemented her most powerful obsession. Now that the body was gone, it was her only link to the magnificent knight and the mystery he harbored. But even more than symbolizing the bond between herself and the elusive Crown of Thorns, it was the sole representation of the power Sir Kieran held over her. Knowing that for him and him alone she was willing to lie, to steal, and to jeopardize everything she had worked for just to keep him with her.

"Because," she whispered. "I was still working on some of the more illegible passages. I never meant to steal it because I honestly thought we'd have a few more days with him and I planned to use the time to transcribe more pages. And when I did the inventory from Dave's initial indexing, I left it off because it was technically still in my possession and not a part of the tally. My motives weren't covert in the least until Corbin showed up demanding Sir Kieran's body. And there was no way I was going to hand over Sir Kieran's journal to that bastard. No way in hell."

Bud stared at her, not knowing what to believe. Not knowing if she was trying to take advantage of their relationship, confident he wouldn't condemn her for her unauthorized actions because of the emotions he felt for her. After a moment, he simply shook his head.

"I wish to God that we'd never found that damned knight," he muttered, turning away from her. "Everything was fine until we came across him. Now, it's as if the entire situation is out of control and I don't like the direction it's heading."

"What you mean to say is that I'm obsessed with him."

He paused, his back to her. After a moment, he ran his fingers through his cropped blond hair. "Yeah," he whispered. "You are. I don't like what it's doing to you. It's like… like you're turning into someone I don't recognize."

Rory stared at the back of his head, pondering his words. She knew he was correct; nothing was right any longer, or normal. Ever since she had laid eyes on the swathed bundle in the shallow grave, it was as if everything had somehow changed. She had changed.

It was a change she didn't like. Sir Kieran was out of her control, in the custody of his family. There was nothing she could do for him any longer and it was important that she come to terms with the situation. Any more refusal to acknowledge the reality of events and she could very well find herself in a lot of trouble.

Trouble in the form of the journal in her hands. She had told Bud the truth, how she had kept it with her simply to finish transcribing it. But, on the other hand, she'd kept the journal with her since the moment of its discovery and the thought of relinquishing it was a painful concept. She knew Bud was having difficulty believing her and she only had herself to blame. Since the moment they had discovered the crusader, she'd become an emotional bundle with an obsession for a dead man. A dead man and his unreachable knowledge.

It didn't seem to matter any longer that Sir Kieran apparently knew the location of the Crown of Thorns. More than the ancient diadem,

Rory was consumed with the knight and his fascinating life. But her magnificent warrior was gone and that reality was like an open wound in the center of her heart. Like anything else, it would take time to heal. But she had to start somewhere.

"I'm sorry, Bud," she murmured, the tears that had so recently fled returning with a vengeance. "I... I've just never faced a situation like this. I can't help myself from getting involved."

He turned to her, feeling himself relent when he knew full well that he shouldn't. But Rory was starting to cry just when he had succeeded in calming her, and he was grieved by the return of her tears. If anyone had allowed themselves to get too involved with the situation, he was certainly one to blame. He didn't even have the good sense to be on his guard as the tears spilled down her cheeks.

"It would have been pretty hard not to have become involved," he said. "And I'm not really angry with you. But you've got to give the journal back, honey. You can't keep it."

"I know," she sniffed, looking to the aged leather volume. "Maybe my keeping it was a subconscious attempt to seek revenge against Sir Kieran's family; they kept the body, but I kept his thoughts and hopes and dreams."

Bud crossed his arms, leaning against the canopy post. "So you can still have all of that even if you return the book. We'll find a printer tomorrow and copy the pages."

She nodded in resigned agreement, wiping at the last of her tears and setting the book to the end of the bed, next to Bud. Throwing her tote bag on the floor, she fell back on the mattress with an exhausted sigh. Bud watched her snuggle into the pillows, abruptly finding himself wondering what it would be like to make love to her. He was so close he could almost taste it.

"You're tired," he said, turning away before he jumped onto the bed next to her. "The landlady was bringing up some tea. I'll tell her to hold off while you sleep."

Rory watched him move for the door, the lethargy of his movements, the fatigue in his voice. She had caused this, she knew, wreaking havoc with his emotional state with her mood swings and irrational actions. He was such a good man, always considerate of her feelings, always looking out for her. Even though she didn't want a husband, someone like Bud Dietrich would be the perfect mate; devoted, loving, kind. Maybe she wasn't being fair by not giving him a chance. Now that her knight was vanished and her dreams were quashed, maybe she needed someone like Bud to ease her out of her addiction. To bring her back to reality.

In truth, she was hurting. Maybe she just needed a little comfort at the risk of exploring her confused feelings. At the risk of encouraging Bud's devotion. Maybe it was exactly what she needed at the moment.

He was almost to the door. "Bud?" she called softly.

He paused, reaching for his bags. Outside, the thunder had commenced, rattling the windows with its intensity. She met his inquisitive gaze, reaching up a hand to turn out the brass lamp.

The room was dim, the storm outside gaining speed. Rory snuggled into the comforter, listening to the driving rain.

"I don't want to be alone," she whispered. "Please... will you stay with me?"

Bud could hear his heart pounding in his ears. The door remained closed and the luggage on the floor. "Uh... yeah," he said, moving hesitantly for the chair next to the bed. But Rory stopped him.

"No, not the chair," she said, patting the mattress behind her. "Here."

The gushing in his ears had turned to a roaring river. Bud was hardly capable of forming a rational thought as he moved to the other side of the bed, lowering his muscular frame down beside her and wondering if this was an entirely wise decision on his part. He sat up against the pillows, stiffly, feeling like a giddy teenager on the verge of losing his innocence. The emotions surging through his veins were wild and wonderful and far too powerful to believe. Far too powerful to deny.

Christ, he couldn't believe this was happening.

"Lay down, Bud," Rory rolled onto her back, gazing up at him. Her swollen eyes were half-lidded, shadowed with fatigue. "It's cold. Pull the edge of the comforter up around us."

He was actually shaking as he slid down on the bed, dutifully reaching over to pull up the fluffy comforter. Covering them both, he found himself pressed up against Rory's warm back, thinking she felt more wonderful than he had ever imagined.

Much to his surprise and disbelief, she seemed to snuggle back against him, sighing with comfort. He kept trying to figure out where to put his right arm, either tucked in between their two bodies or draped over her torso, awkwardly trying to find a position that wasn't too suggestive or intimate or just plain weird. He heard Rory laugh softly.

"You can put your arm around me, Bud. I don't mind."

He did, almost fainting with the sensation of her in his arms. But he suddenly found the need to make one thing perfectly clear before they proceeded any further. Feeling like he was choking over the mere suggestion, he swallowed hard and hoped he wasn't about to make a fool of himself. Christ, it was the hardest question he had ever had to ask. But for sanity's sake, he felt he had to.

"Rory?"

"Hmm?" she was nearly asleep.

"Are you..." swallowing hard, he tried again. "Are you trying to seduce me?"

She laughed again, moving his arm to a comfortable position around her waist. Pulling the comforter close, she sighed. "Not at the moment. I... I guess I just need a little comfort, that's all."

"Oh."

"Disappointed?"

"Well... yes."

She chuckled, listening to the storm outside and feeling quite content lying in Bud's arms. "Trust me, Bud. If I was trying to seduce you,

you wouldn't have to ask. You'd know."

The landlady came with a tray of tea and biscuits five minutes later. Dead tired and fast asleep, Rory and Bud never heard her.

CHAPTER EIGHT

RORY AWOKE TO the soft colors of sunset on the wall above the bed. The storm had vanished, leaving the sky scattered with puffy clouds. Stretching her muscles with a groan, she noticed immediately that Bud had vanished. A groggy glance around the room told her she was completely alone.

Yawning, she sat up, the jackhammer in her head reminding her of the emotional upheaval she had suffered earlier and the fact that she had always been prone to jetlag. Stomach churning, she forgot all about Bud's absence and staggered into the bathroom. Turning on the shower, she went back into the bedroom to gather a few things while the water heated up.

She lost track of time in the shower, washing her hair and shaving her legs and trying not to think of Sir Kieran. She knew that if she allowed herself to linger on him, it would only serve to upset her all over again and, at the moment, she was doing fairly well staying calm. Even with the pounding headache.

Taking time to put her makeup on, she directed her attention away from thoughts of her crusader by focusing on what had become of Bud. She had fallen asleep in his arms and she imagined that, someday, she might even grow to like it. But the fact remained that as much as she thought, perhaps, that Bud Dietrich was what she needed in a stable relationship, he simply didn't set her on fire. He was the sweetest guy in the world but, beyond that, there wasn't much of a spark. There never really had been.

She put on three coats of mascara pondering the dilemma of Dr. Dietrich. Odd that she seemed so dependent on a man she wasn't in love with. It certainly hadn't been fair to encourage him into her bed, but she was hurt and confused and needed the warmth of a human touch. And without even asking her mother, she knew what the woman would say; stop chasing dreams, Rory. Get your head out of the clouds and focus on what's real in this life.

Maybe by her willingness to explore her feelings for Bud, she was somehow proving that she was sensible. And how better to prove it than a relationship with a sensible guy? Maybe people wouldn't think she was so outlandish when they saw who she was married to; ah, yes, I know Bud Dietrich. A nice, level-headed guy. But his wife is a little eccentric; chasing after biblical relics as if they actually exist. Good thing Bud's around to keep her feet on the ground.

Rory put down the mascara tube before she put on another coat. Flipping her head upside-down, she blow-dried her hair until it was scorching, still thinking on the chaotic situation around her. Too much was happening, her thoughts drifting in several different directions. Her crown, the knight, Bud... she simply didn't know what she was thinking any more.

By the time Rory finished her hair and pulled her shoes on, there was a knock at the door. Bud was standing in the doorway, dressed in a nice, if not slightly wrinkled, pair of pants and a linen shirt. She could even smell aftershave. He smiled weakly and held out a fistful of yellow and pink flowers.

"Hi," he said.

She had to smile at him. He looked really nervous. "Hi," she said, accepting the flowers. "Wow, Bud, flowers? I'm touched."

He shrugged, shoving his hands into his pockets. He always had his hands in his pockets, as if he couldn't think of anything else to do with them. "The landlady had them and... well, I just thought you could use them."

She was genuinely warmed by the gesture. "Thank you very much, Dr. Dietrich." She went to the bathroom and put them in the sink, stopping up the drain and running some water to keep them fresh. "So where have you been, other than out buying me flowers?"

He was standing in the middle of the room, watching her as she came out of the bathroom drying her hands. "Unpacking. And looking around a little. I have a view of Hyde Park from my window."

"You do?" She had a view of buildings and a garden from hers. "I've never been to London. I think I'd like to see a little bit before we leave."

He nodded. "I was talking to the landlady and she was telling me about some tours that run through the city. Maybe if there's time tomorrow, we can look around."

The idea of sightseeing perked Rory's mood. But not entirely. Thoughts of perusing the city only made her think of the London hospital where Sir Kieran was being held and, once again, she found herself struggling against depression. She knew for a fact that if the tour bus drove past Middlesex Hospital, Bud would have a hell of a time keeping her from jumping out the window.

But she agreed with him anyway, trying to hide the fact that her mood wasn't much better than it had been when they arrived from Heathrow. "Maybe," she said, busying herself with her tote bag and purse. "So you're all dressed up for the evening. Where are we going for dinner?"

His gaze lingered on her as she moved things from her tote bag and into a small purse. She was dressed in black from head to toe; slim jeans, a semi-cropped shirt and a black sweater left unbuttoned enough to expose her tight abdomen. On her feet were black flats, making her appear shorter than her five feet four, but her demure height did nothing to detract from her magnificent figure. She was, without a doubt, the most beautiful woman Bud had ever seen and his stomach began twisting giddily as he watched her secure her purse.

"The landlady told me about a restaurant not too far from here," he said. "They play jazz and have patio dining. I thought you might enjoy it."

She slung her purse over her shoulder, smiling. "A definite change from dining in a canvas tent on lentils and pork. I hope I don't die from the shock of decent food."

He grinned. "If that's the case, then I'm sure we'll go together. Christ, Rory, do you realize we haven't eaten in a restaurant in over a year?"

She laughed as he opened the door, feeling her mood lighten just the slightest. And it felt rather good. "Welcome back to the land of the living."

THE PATIO WINE Bar and Restaurant was a lovely establishment not far from Hyde Park. The weather was surprisingly pleasant as they made the mile and a half walk to the restaurant, skirting the park and talking of small things. It was good to get back into civilization again, the smell of wet pavement and the roar of car engines. Rory took it all in, feeling her spirits perk.

Bud took her arm as they crossed the street and headed for the restaurant. When he subtly tried to take her hand, however, she pretended to dig in her purse for a tissue. Regardless of the fact that she had asked him to sleep next to her, somehow, holding his hand was more of an intimate encouragement and she wasn't ready to cross that invisible line. She felt like a hypocrite.

The restaurant was lively, a three-piece jazz band playing loudly and Rory sighed with satisfaction as the host seated them. Immediately ordering a Long Island Iced Tea, she settled back with the first alcohol she'd had in fourteen months, drinking nearly half of it before they even ordered dinner. By the time the meal arrived, she was feeling no pain and happily ordered another.

"You'd better take it easy on that stuff," Bud admonished with a smile. "If you get drunk, I'll pretend I don't know you and leave you here."

She grinned, her cheeks flushed with the liquor. "Oh, lighten up, Bud. Why aren't you drinking?"

He chuckled as she munched enthusiastically on her poached salmon. "Because alcohol makes me throw up. I used to be able to drink with the best of them, but age has inhibited my ability."

She slurped the last of her drink just as the waiter came by the table with the next round. "You're not old," she scoffed. "You're only thirty-nine. If you were really old, then that would mean I only have eight more years until I become really old, too."

He continued to grin, cutting his prime rib as Rory ate her meal with gusto. After the past several hellish days, it was good to see her smile again. When the band began to play another set and she started wriggling in her seat to the music, he simply sat back and enjoyed the view.

"Wouldn't Dave be jealous of us?" he asked, nursing his cola. "Not only does he have a passion for jazz, but he can drink beer until he drops. He loves places like this."

A mischievous gleam came to Rory's eye. "I think I'll mail him a beer bottle and the program announcing tonight's band." She suddenly put up her hand as a thought occurred to her. "Wait! I've got a better idea; I'll mail him a beer bottle, a program, and a doggy bag with a bread crust. How 'bout that?"

Bud laughed. "Put teeth marks in the bread crust and lipstick imprints on the beer bottle and he'll hate you forever."

Rory joined in his laughter, picking at the last of her herbed zucchini. "He already hates me. This will just rub it in."

Bud shook his head, motioning to the waiter for another cola. "Trust me, Rory, he doesn't hate you. In fact, if it's at all possible for David Peck to become attached to anyone, I think he's fairly attached to you."

She cocked an eyebrow, her mouth full. "You call the relationship we have an attachment? Good Lord, I'd hate to be the person he truly hated."

Bud's smile faded somewhat, turning his attention towards the band. "Everyone has different ideas of attachment. Some are just more pronounced than others."

Attachment. Somehow, the word sounded a lot like obsession. Rory's stomach suddenly twisted with thoughts of Sir Kieran once again, the once-mighty warrior destined to be buried in a family crypt without his armor, without his sword, and without the trappings of the life he had lived.

The man who would take the secret of her crown to his grave.

She set her fork down, gathering her drink and wondering if the alcohol would ease her distress. Bud noticed she had grown particularly silent, passing her a glance only to notice tears streaming down her cheeks.

"Oh... Christ," he muttered, scooting his chair around to her side of the table. There was a napkin by her plate and he snatched it, drying the tears before they fell to the swell of her breasts. "Not now, Rory. Come on, honey, there's no need. We're having a wonderful evening and you're going to make yourself sick with all of this crying."

She sobbed softly as he continued to mop up the tears. "I... I can't help it. I didn't even get to say goodbye, Bud. They just took him away like he was a piece of meat and that was the end of my beautiful knight. I'm cut off completely."

"I know," he murmured. "But you can say goodbye to him at the interment. Please don't worry so much over this."

She took the napkin from him, wiping daintily at her eyes so she wouldn't smear her heavy mascara. "I'm sorry, but I can't help myself," she whispered, feeling his arm go around her shoulders comfortingly. "Every time I think about the situation, how lovingly we worked with him and then how his family carted him away like he was a mindless, meaningless object, I just go to pieces."

He hugged her gently, kissing her forehead as she sobbed into the napkin. "You have to trust that the people his family hired are going to treat him with the same respect we did. Becker says they're some of the best in the field."

She suddenly stopped crying, the hazel eyes fixing on his suspiciously. "Becker?" she repeated. "When did you talk to him?"

He maintained an even expression. "While you were sleeping."

Her eyebrows rose in outrage. "But I wanted to talk to him, too! Why didn't you wake me?"

"Because I knew you'd fly off the deep end and probably get yourself into a heap of trouble," he said frankly. "Even if the man is your uncle, he's still your boss."

Her expression was dark and she looked away, sniffling and reaching for her drink. "He's my mother's uncle," she clarified, taking a long swallow. "And when I tell her what's happened, she'll do the yelling for me."

Bud cocked an eyebrow. "Fight your own battles, little girl. Don't pull your mother into this. Whatever problems you and Becker have, that's between the two of you."

She sniffled again, wiping her nose with the napkin. "My mother's been involved in this since the beginning," she said quietly, avoiding Bud's gaze. "How do you think I got permission from the Board of Regents to go hunting for a fabled biblical relic?"

"Your mother's on the board," Bud replied softly. "One of the three ordained ministers that voted for your funding, I believe."

She didn't say anything for a moment, trying to regain her composure. The band was playing a classically jazzy tune and the place was hopping, but Rory hardly noticed. She was still pondering their conversation.

"I'm curious. Did you ever tell Dave my connections?"

"No. He was having a hard enough time dealing with the goal of the project. If he knew you were related to both Becker and Dr. Sylvia Lunde, we probably would have lost him altogether. And I needed him."

Rory remained silent, watching a band member with three-foot-long cornrows pick at his electric guitar. "I used them, you know," she murmured. "My mother and Uncle Uriah. I used them to get my dig. I would have done anything to get it because I thoroughly believed in my goal. I was willing to do whatever I had to in order to get funding. But once I had financial support, I was positive my work would speak for itself."

"It did," he replied, the hand on her shoulder caressing it gently. "Locating the crusader was a remarkable achievement."

She snorted, pulling away from his stroking hand because it threatened to move beyond casual comfort. Leaning forward, she drained her glass. "Let's face it, Bud. It was a fluke. Now we have nothing to show for it except renewed international relations between Britain and the States." She sighed heavily. "Everything I worked for is ruined. Gone. Ka-boom. God, I hate my life."

He watched her a moment, a smirk on his lips. "Well, then, have another drink and indulge your misery. You're young, beautiful, have a doctorate in Biblical Sciences and have succeeded in locating an intact corpse on your first major dig. Christ, Rory, you really have a lot to be miserable over."

She scowled at him. "Oh... shut up, Bud. You're so damned smug."

He put his hand on her back, laughing. "A confidence that comes with age, honey."

The waiter came around again and Bud ordered dessert for the both of them whether or not Rory wanted any. On her third Long Island Iced Tea, she decided the chocolate mousse looked very good and not only ate hers, but finished Bud's as well. Sick with sweets and too much alcohol, Rory languished in her chair as Bud had the waiter take away the half-finished drink and ordered her coffee instead.

As the night moved on, the band lapsed into a cool set of songs and the restaurant packed out. Rory's lids were half-closed as she listened to the music and Bud decided it was a good time to leave. They'd had a nice, relaxing time in spite of everything and he wanted to get her back to the hotel before she collapsed completely.

Halfway home, as they strolled along the darkened edges of Hyde

Park, Rory suddenly came to a halt.

"I've decided something," she said.

He paused, looking at her and noticing she appeared amazingly lucid. "What's that?"

She took a deep breath, glancing to their surroundings as she formulated her thoughts. "I've decided I don't want to go to Sir Kieran's interment."

He was genuinely surprised. "What?"

"I said I don't want to go to his interment," she repeated patiently. "You were right when you said the last thing we need is for me to run amok at his funeral. But I've got to tell you, Bud, the way I'm feeling about this, I can't guarantee that I'll remain in control. So it's probably better if I don't go at all."

He didn't try to talk her out of her decision. Frankly, he was glad she had acknowledged her limitations. "If you say so."

Rory was still gazing at him, her brow furrowed in thought. "I do. No funeral. But I still want to say goodbye to him."

He crossed his arms against the cool breeze whipping up from the park; spending the past year in a hot, arid country, he wasn't used to the chill. "And how do you want to do that?"

"By going to the morgue."

"They probably won't let you in."

"They will if I say I'm part of the Hage family entourage."

"Don't you think they'll have a list of the individuals permitted to view the body?"

"Probably." She stepped closer to him and he was struck by the expression on her face. "But if the admitting clerk is distracted, I can slip by without being noticed."

She wasn't going to take no for an answer. He could see it in her eyes. After a moment, he sighed heavily. "Christ, Rory. You want me to cause a diversion while you sneak in?"

"I just want to say goodbye to Sir Kieran. I don't care how I get in, but I'm going to get in with or without your help."

He scratched his head and turned away, resuming their walk back to the hotel. Rory remained still, watching him fade down the sidewalk.

"Please, Bud?"

He shook his head and kept walking. Rory was about to follow him when he suddenly came to a halt.

"First you steal the knight's journal, and now you want to bust into a morgue," he said with more passion than she had seen from him in a long while. "My uncle isn't a dean at a major American university, Rory. If I get in trouble, there's no way out for me."

She stared at him, a true sadness filling her eyes. "You think I'm taking advantage of you?"

"I think you're trying to, whether or not you realize it." His tone was soft again. "You said yourself that you used your mother and your uncle to get what you want. Isn't it possible that you're doing the same thing to me? Christ, you know I'd walk through fire if you asked me to!"

She lowered her gaze guiltily. He was right; she knew he would do anything for her and, at this moment, she was willing to use his devotion to her advantage. All she wanted to do was bid Sir Kieran farewell, privately, away from the eyes of his family and away from those who didn't understand her devotion to him. Even Bud. He was so blinded by his own feelings that his jealousy was making him resentful.

"Then forget I asked," she murmured, turning away from him and heading across the street.

He followed, grabbing her roughly by the arm. "Where are you going?"

She jerked away, racing to the other curb to avoid being hit by a car. Bud came up behind her and grabbed her again.

"Answer me, Rory. Where in the hell are you going?"

She broke his grip, trying to stay away from him. "To Middlesex Hospital. If I have to beg, plead, or sleep with the admitting clerk, I'm going to see Sir Kieran."

Bud was athletic and amazingly strong for his average size. Moving up behind her, he threw both arms around her torso to halt her advance. "You're not going anywhere tonight," he growled in her ear. "You've had too much to drink and you're functioning on four hours of sleep. I'll see about gaining permission to see Sir Kieran tomorrow."

Undeterred, Rory shoved her elbow into Bud's gut, releasing his hold. He grunted, holding his ribs as she resumed her eastward march.

"Dammit, Rory!" He went after her. "Listen to me, will you? We'll go see him tomorrow!"

"I don't want to go see him tomorrow. I want to see him now!" She continued walking, feeling the familiar sting of tears. "And I don't want you to come with me!"

"Why not?" he demanded.

She whirled to him, still walking, almost tripping as she marched backward. "Because you just don't understand. You said yourself that Sir Kieran has turned me into something you don't recognize. Well, maybe I don't want you to recognize me. Maybe I don't want anything to do with you!"

She saw his face go pale in the moonlight. "What in the hell is that supposed to mean?"

Her eyes filled with tears; angry, bewildered tears. "I don't know." She turned around again, maintaining her brisk pace. "Just... leave me alone. I have to do this."

"Then I have to, too."

"No, you don't," she practically shouted. "This is my obsession, Bud. It has nothing to do with you and I don't need your constant presence confusing me even more!"

He stopped. She kept walking. "Rory?" he called after her, his voice strained. "Honey, don't walk away. Please."

She came to a halt. After a lengthy, heart-wrenching pause, she turned to Bud with tears on her face.

"I'm sorry, Bud," she whispered. "I'm sorry I don't love you. I'm sorry I've made a mess out of your life. But this is my obsession and mine alone and I refuse to allow you to involve yourself further. Please go back to the hotel and let me work this out myself."

He simply stood there, watching her with more grief than he could have possibly imagined. "I've made my own choices, Rory. If my life is ruined, it was my decision to make. And I don't consider loving you a mistake."

She sobbed openly, struggling to collect herself. After a moment, she focused on him once again.

"I think the only man I love has been dead eight hundred years," she whispered. "It's difficult to describe and even harder to explain, but I love him like I could never love you. I'm sorry, Bud. I really am. I wouldn't hurt you for the world."

He sighed slowly, struggling against his own emotional outburst. "You don't love a corpse, Rory. You love his stories of valor, the chivalry he represents. Or maybe you're infatuated with him because you think he holds the key to your crown. When you get over all of this, you'll see what I'm offering you. You'll see that no one can love you like I can."

A taxi came by and Bud hailed it. Moving to Rory, he grasped her gently by the arm and marched her over to the waiting cab. But not before he forced her to look him in the eye.

"Go to Middlesex Hospital," he whispered huskily, watching the tears stream down her face. "Say your goodbyes to Sir Kieran and get this out of your system. And when it's all over and done with, come back to the hotel and I'll be waiting. I'll wait for you as long as it takes."

He kissed her hard, knowing that, for a brief moment, she responded to him. But just as he felt her body relaxing in his embrace, he released her and practically shoved her into the cab. Handing the driver a ten pound note, he directed the man to Middlesex Hospital.

Bud watched the taxi until it disappeared from view. Heading back for the hotel, there were tears in his eyes.

CB

EVEN THOUGH VISITING hours were over, Middlesex Hospital was a busy place. Rory stumbled from the cab, hardly noticing when it pulled away as she made her way to the main entrance. It was locked but she wrestled with the doors anyway as if, somehow, they would miraculously open.

Sniffling and wiping at her perpetually running mascara, she took a deep breath and struggled to regain her composure. A clear head was the only way she was going to be able to do what needed to be done, and she squared her shoulders as she reviewed her options.

Options that included slipping in through the always-open emergency room. The waiting room was packed with football players, or Rugby as she knew it, waiting for medical attention. The nurses were focused on keeping the two teams apart, the injuries apparently the result of a nasty fight, and Rory was able to slip past with little trouble.

Losing herself in the sterile halls, she found her way to the elevators and located a hospital directory. Easily enough, the morgue was in the basement and she slipped into the next available cab.

The basement was dimly lit, smelling strangely of wet earth. Rory stepped from the elevator, her senses piqued as she emerged into the corridor. Glancing to both ends of the long hall, she could hear voices and then a door slam as someone entered an office far down to her right. Deciding to go in the opposite direction of the activity, she went to the left.

She tried not to make any noise as she moved down the corridor, her shoes making soft clicking noises against the muted tile. Walking on tiptoes, she passed a series of doors, noting they were either building maintenance or the lavatories by their sickly white plaques.

Reaching a "T" shaped intersection, she was about to take the path to her left again when something to the right caught her attention. About midway down the softly illuminated hall was a large pair of swinging doors. Even as Rory made haste to identify the doors by the sign affixed to the right panel, she could see from a distance that she had succeeded in locating the morgue.

The doors were unlocked. Rory cautiously pushed into what appeared to be a waiting room, cold and unfeeling with green vinyl chairs. There was a security door in front of her, a glass window in the top portion of the panel allowing her to see into more halls of white. To her left, the receptionist's window was locked for the night. Peering into the small office, she was met with files and a neatly-arranged desk.

Taking a deep breath, she knocked on the window. She almost expected to see one of the Israeli security guards make an appearance, but she realized bitterly that the Israelis had not accompanied Sir Kieran to protect him personally. It was his possessions they were concerned with, the priceless artifacts that had already been transferred to the University of Sussex. If the guards were anywhere, it was at the university sleeping on the floor beside Sir Kieran's assets.

Clearly, artifacts were the only thing the Hage family was interested in. Sir Kieran was to be buried in disgrace while his property was displayed by his selfish descendants. Rory realized that if she had been aware of their true motives, she would have gladly turned over the artifacts if only they would have left her the corpse. She didn't care about the valuables; she never had. All that had ever mattered to her was the knight.

She continued knocking on the window, realizing that there didn't seem to be a night attendant. Glancing about the waiting area, her gaze came to rest on a small sign located just below the receptionist's window. It was so bland and unspectacular that she hadn't noticed it before. And when she read the message, a smile of pure joy came to her lips.

Due to budget cuts, there is no staff in the morgue
between the hours of 6 p.m. and 6 a.m.
Please use the corridor phone and ring 619 for assistance.

It was too good to hope for. With renewed determination, she looked around the room for something to pry open the receptionist's window when her gaze fell on the plastic chairs against the wall. Setting her purse down, Rory collected a chair and swung it through the window with all her might.

The glass shattered. Collecting her purse, she climbed through the broken glass, cutting her hand but unconcerned with the injury. All that mattered was that she was growing closer to Sir Kieran by the minute. There was a stack of files on the desk and she leafed through them, tossing them aside in her haste and creating a mess. Unable to find any reference to Sir Kieran, she went to the filing cabinet and used a letter opener to force the weak lock.

The "H" section was devoid of a Hage file. She even looked under "K". Frustrated, she was about to forgo the file altogether when her gaze came to rest on a bank of stackable trays just to the left of the phone. Peering at the file on the very top of the tray, the name she had been searching for abruptly came into focus.

Hage, Kieran I.D. #DL4509384

Snatching the file, Rory left the shattered receptionist's office in search of her knight. She's been in a few morgues during her Pre-Med days, so she didn't find them creepy or weird. She had no idea where she might find her corpse and simply stopped at the first sterile room, checking the identification number on the first refrigerated drawer she came to. And the second. And the third.

He wasn't in the first room. Nor had he been in the second. There was an order to the numbering on the drawers but being unfamiliar with the system, she didn't want to miss him by trying to guess the sequence with the numbers. A powerful sense of urgency gripped her as she progressed, knowing it was only a matter of time before the violated office was discovered.

The next room Rory entered was larger than the other. A huge, stainless steel table was in the center of the floor with drains placed around it. Checking the first two rows of drawers with unsuccessful results, she came to the third bank. Stacked three drawers high, the top two drawers didn't match Sir Kieran's number. But the third one did.

With a gasp of relief, Rory released the bolts on either side of the drawer, yanking hard to pull it out the entire length. Grasping the sheet that covered the body, she ripped it off. But her joy turned to shock the moment she laid eyes on the corpse, a hand flying to her mouth in horror.

It was the Sir Kieran she remembered, beautiful and massive and looking as if he were sleeping. But his clothing had been removed, leaving him naked and vulnerable. Rory sighed slowly, the hand coming away from her mouth as she viewed the body. They had even taken his clothes, stripping what was left of his already-damaged dignity. But along with her mounting anger came thoughts so unexpected that she had difficulty believing their power.

He was sexy. Now she knew she was going mad for thinking a dead man to be sexy. But even though the man had been dead eight hundred years, he still possessed the most magnificent form Rory had ever seen. As the magic of his allure took hold, Rory couldn't help but reach out to touch his cold chest. It was broad and wonderful and as her gaze trailed downward, she could see the wound that had claimed his life.

Odd, she thought through her haze of fascination. Even though it was the injury that had presumably killed him, it appeared to be healed. Shiny, new-appearing scar tissue. But the skin surrounding the wound was stained brown, the passage of centuries darkening the once-red blood. Rory peered closer, thinking the appearance strange. If the wound had killed him, as his stained clothes had logically indicated, then the injury should not be covered with the scarred flesh.

Maybe that was why they took his clothes from him; to study the unusual healing that seemed to have taken place after death. But even as she pondered the dilemma of a post-mortem scar which, in any event, was impossible, she was pleased to see that his wound had prevented the Hage family's hired guns from conducting their autopsy. Maybe the doctors had been so fascinated with his outward appearance that they postponed the autopsy until they could discover a logical explanation for the occurrence. An explanation Rory herself would like to hear.

It just didn't make sense, a post-mortem scar on a dead body. But, then again, nothing about Sir Kieran Hage had made sense from the beginning. Not his grave, nor his lack of decomposition, nor the clues to her Crown of Thorns in his journal. From the very moment she had uncovered her crusader, the man had remained an enigma.

An enigma with a flaccid male member the size of small sapling. Rory tried not to stare at it, a little off-balance as her thoughts turned to the evidence of his masculinity. Embarrassed, she looked around for something to cover him with, thinking that even in death the man should be allowed some privacy from gawking female eyes. Even if the only form of privacy was a medium-sized towel she found on the counter by the autoclave.

She felt better once Sir Kieran was properly draped. He looked like a football player emerging from the showers after a game. Or a Roman soldier preparing to take his ritual bath. Shivering with the unexpected erotic thoughts, Rory struggled to focus on the purpose behind her visit. Too much alcohol and a lack of sleep were making her sick with thoughts bordering on necrophilia, and she moved away from the towel to look him in the face.

A face that haunted her dreams. Even in death, he was the most beautiful man she had ever seen and she touched his cheek gently, finding herself wondering what his voice had sounded like. Deep, masculine. Soft enough to melt a woman with passion or loud enough to bellow orders to a thousand crusaders. Rory could feel the liquor coursing through her veins, making her sleepy and emotional as she tenderly touched the knight.

"I don't have much time, Sir Kieran, so I'll make this brief," she whispered. "When I found you nearly six days ago, I hadn't been looking for you in particular. I was looking for something else, something I believe we both have an interest in. At first, I was obsessed with finding Christ's Crown of Thorns and when I read references in your journal that I thought alluded to it, I didn't know what to think. It... it was like fate had led me to you somehow. Or God, or Ottis the monk, or whatever you believe in. It was like I was supposed to find you."

The room was still and cold, filled with aura of eternal sleep. Rory listened to the echo of her own voice, the tick of the clock on the wall, realizing that what she had told Bud was true. She did love the crusader as she could never love anyone else, and whether or not it was due to a strange obsession was no longer the issue.

He was somehow a part of her, not merely because he was her first official find, but the bond she felt with him was like nothing she had ever experienced. And the fact that he apparently knew the location of her crown strengthened the bond into an unbreakable tie.

Unbreakable by the Hage family or the University of California San Marcos. Somehow, he would always be a part of her and she wondered if he would recognize her on the fields of Paradise, knowing the woman who had spent her entire life loving a man who had lived centuries before she had ever been born. Rory wondered if he would know her, and if he would call her by name.

"I'm sorry for what has become of you," she murmured, feeling the sting of the ever-present tears. "Had I known your family would do this to you, I would have left you buried in Nahariya. Please don't hate me for allowing this. I... I thought I was doing the right thing by returning you to your descendants. I thought they would love you as much as I do."

The clock continued to tick. Rory's lids grew heavier, the emotional exhaustion and physical drain of the past several days catching up. She was with her knight, finally, and nothing in her life had ever felt so right. Even if the police were to come this moment and take her to jail, still, she had accomplished what she had set out to do. To find her knight and tell him how much she loved him.

Soft, rosy lips found his cheek, kissing him tenderly. "Keep your secret of the crown, Sir Kieran," she whispered, brushing her lips over his stilled mouth. "I'll leave you the last of your secrets now that everything else has been taken from you. I wouldn't dream of taking that, too."

She laid her head on his chest, tears trickling onto the cold flesh. An alcohol-induced sleep claimed her before she could hear the first few beats of his long-dormant heart.

CHAPTER NINE

T HE SILENCE. IT was too loud. And the light; it was far too bright. The mere action of breathing was pure agony, as if a massive weight was sitting atop his chest. And movement... well, at the moment, that was simply out of the question. He had not the strength to move, considering all of his energy was centralized in his brain, trying to make sense out of what was happening. A most baffling, incredible happening.

His tongue was as thick as cowhide. He tried to lick his lips, but they were completely dry. No moisture whatsoever. After several minutes of unsteady breathing, he licked his lips again and noted there was a slight amount of wetness. Not much, but some.

Kieran had no idea how long he lay in limbo, hearing the strange silence around him and struggling to clear the cobwebs from his mind. He tried to recall his last thoughts and events, remembering that Simon had sent assassins to kill him and that he had sought the healing powers of a physic... no, not a physic, an alchemist. Aye, he remembered now. A shriveled old man who had forced bitter potions down his throat in an attempt to save his life.

Save, was it? Or had the man said... suspend? It was all becoming a bit clearer now. The alchemist had to suspend his life in order to save it. That much he could recall. And if, indeed, his life had been spared by the mysterious potions... then where, in fact, was he?

He tried to open one eye. Slowly, painfully, the lid peeled back to reveal stark white light. Quickly, Kieran squeezed his eye shut, more out of agony than out of fear for the unfamiliar surroundings. After a moment, he tried again, this time opening both eyes. Blinking rapidly in the brilliant light, he struggled to determine his whereabouts.

It was all so bright, so alien. Like nothing he had ever seen before. Walls covered with shiny, green bricks and strange sconces holding equally strange tapers. He could feel his life force growing stronger, the warmth of his newly-flowing blood coursing through his veins. He wriggled is fingers successfully, feeling brave enough to move his arms. The left one moved quite nicely. But the right one refused to budge.

The clear brown eyes blinked again, turning to focus on his right side. He seemed to be lying on the floor, or at least in a bed that was very close to the ground. When his stiff neck and muddled vision fell on his right arm, he was startled to note a body lying across it. And he saw was a naked abdomen.

Kieran swallowed hard, his confusion mounting. The naked belly was surrounded on either side by black garments, a peculiar gown that looked as if it had been ripped open to reveal another garment beneath. He couldn't tell what the woman was wearing below the waist but... aye, it was a woman. He may have been unconscious for an unknown amount of time, but Kieran still knew a woman's body when he saw it. Half-dead didn't mean that he was also robbed of his senses.

His gaze trailed up the woman's torso, noting her beautiful breasts beneath the strange black shift. It wasn't even a shift; it was far too short. He didn't know what it was. His gaze traveled upward, drinking in a thick mane of chestnut hair and he suddenly wondered if he had died and gone to Heaven. For certain, the face beneath the tousled hair was nothing short of angelic.

A beautiful, sleeping angel. Kieran could hear her snoring and he watched her for a moment, summoning both the courage and strength to rouse her. His left hand came up very slowly as massive fingers touched the arm slung across his belly.

"My lady," he whispered, the pain of speaking almost unbearable. "My lady, awaken if you would."

She ignored him, snorting in her sleep and scratching at her face. He tried again.

"My lady," he shook her arm gently. "Can you hear me? You will awaken, please. I require your… assistance."

She didn't move. Then, slowly, she yawned and an eye popped open. But she wasn't looking at him; the angle of her head had her staring at his trapped right arm and, lethargically, a pretty hand with painted nails came up to scratch her head.

"Damn." An ugly word from such luscious lips.

Kieran watched as she pushed herself to her knees, the beautiful hair mussed and odd black shadows beneath her eyes. Even so, she was incredibly lovely and he continued to watch as she studied his torso, her gaze coming to rest on his left side. After a moment, she glanced at a silver bangle around her wrist.

"Great," she muttered, pushing the hair from her eyes. "One-thirty. Bud must think I've dropped off the face of the earth."

Kieran remained still, watching the woman as she moved to straighten some piece of cloth covering his privates. He could feel the material, of course, though he had yet to see it. But it was soft and warm. Like her.

"Well, Sir Kieran, I've stayed longer than I should have." She was speaking to him as she smoothed the cloth over his thighs. "I didn't mean to fall asleep on you, but… well, it's been a difficult few days. I suppose now I should go, though. I've got a lot of explaining to…"

Rory's gaze came to rest on his face. His eyes. Her brow furrowed when she realized the lids were partially open. But she wasn't frightened, thinking that perhaps the change in climate had caused the flesh to contract. On her knees, she moved in for a closer look, peering curiously at the half-lidded orbs. She was about to touch them when they blinked.

Poised over the corpse, Rory thought her alcohol-saturated mind was playing tricks on her. Not one to easily scare, she was attempting to clinically evaluate the phenomenon when the eyes blinked again. And the lips moved, too.

Rory's mouth popped open. Astonished, she could hardly comprehend what she had witnessed simply because it wasn't possible. Dead bodies didn't move and especially bodies that had been buried for eight hundred years. More puzzled than shocked, she reached out to touch the knight's face only to realize his skin was warm.

"Oh... God," she murmured, staring into eyes that seemed to be focused on her. "What's happening?"

The lips moved again. And this time, they spoke. "I... I was hoping you could tell me, my lady."

Rory hadn't been terrified until the dry lips issued words she could barely understand and then, it was as if her entire body became a lightning rod of horror. With a shout of panic, she bolted to her feet faster than she had ever moved in her life.

Stumbling away, she smacked into the stainless steel table in the center of the room. But the setback didn't stop her; still moving, she ended up banging her head against the wall in her haste. Vision clouded by a burst of stars, her horrified gaze reverted to the squirming corpse only to discover an arm pointing in her direction.

Rory screamed. She didn't know how else to react. Kieran made a feeble attempt to calm her, struggling to sit up.

"My lady," he rasped. "Please do not..."

Rory screamed again, huddled against the wall and incapable of moving any further. Kieran managed to roll to his side, grunting and shaken, his clear brown eyes focusing on the terrified woman.

"Please," he murmured, swallowing hard. "I... I mean you no harm, I swear it. Only... only I know not where I am nor..."

Rory screamed in reply, covering her eyes. This time, Kieran frowned.

"Your screaming grows tiresome, lady," he rumbled, coughing as he struggled to steady his breathing. "Moreover, the sound threatens to pierce my brain. I would kindly ask that you stop."

Rory took her hands away from her eyes, hands that were quivering violently. Hazel eyes stared at the man wriggling on the coroner's drawer, the disbelief echoed in the pale depths bordering on madness.

"You…" she gasped, then covered her face again. "Oh, God, I must be dreaming. I know I am. Please, Lord, if you let me wake up from this I swear I'll never mix Long Island Iced Tea and chocolate mousse ever again. Please!"

"I can assure you that you are not dreaming," Kieran said, trying to prop an elbow underneath his enormous body. "Unless we are dreaming together. And you, lady, are beyond my wildest dreams."

"Stop it!" she yelled, trying to cover her ears with the same hands that were covering her eyes. "Stop talking to me!"

"How else am I to discover what has become of me?"

Rory digested his words, trying to determine if she had completely lost her mind. She could hear him breathing, grunting, as he moved about on the sterile drawer. After several moments of terror, she forced herself to uncover an eye to see if her prayers had been answered.

God was not listening, however. Sir Kieran was still animated, propped up on one elbow and his face was gray with exhaustion. Rory continued to stare at him, recognizing the face, the body, as that of the knight. Everything was in the right place and she identified him completely. But the fact that he was alive just didn't make any sense and her terror threatened to explode in all directions.

"I don't believe this," she muttered. "I just don't believe this. This can't be happening!"

"It is happening."

"But it can't!"

"Mayhap not. But it has."

She was arguing with a corpse. Closing her eyes, Rory thought she might faint. Actually, she hoped she would. "Oh, please, God. I swear, no more drinking. Just make him dead again!"

Kieran licked his dry lips. "Lady, I refuse to die simply to quell your panic. If you would only cease your prattle and come to realize that a miracle has occurred, I am sure your fright will ease considerably."

The hands came away from her face. "Miracle? What are you..." Her conversation with the dead man was continuing. But if she was going to lose what was left of her mind, then she might as well go all the way. "What damned miracle? You're supposed to be dead!"

"I realize that. But, as you can see, I am very much alive." Failing to push himself into a sitting position, he fixed her with his weary gaze. "But we shall discuss my awakening when I am feeling well enough. Unless you plan to huddle against the wall like a weakling for the rest of your life, I believe I could use your help to rise."

The mere idea was ludicrous. "Rise? You can't rise!"

He sighed, ill and disoriented. "I can and I will. It is apparent that the alchemist's potions have completed their task and I shall live to see another day."

Rory stared at him, her mind still refusing to believe but her heart strangely willing to accept it. In lieu of more full-blown panic, at the moment she settled for complete bewilderment.

"But... I don't understand." Her voice trembled. "What alchemist?"

His eyes were remarkably lucid. "An alchemist who promised to heal my wound and preserve my life. Although I will admit I did not believe in his powers, the evidence is obvious. The man and his potions have wrought a miracle."

Slowly, Rory shook her head. "I dug you up myself. You've been dead and buried for eight hundred years."

She could see the shock in his expression as he absorbed her statement. "Eight hundred years?" he repeated softly. "Do... do you mean to tell me that the alchemist's potion kept me suspended for eight hundred years?"

"Something sure did."

He continued to stare at her, his ashen face glazed with disbelief. "What year is this?"

"1996."

"And… and where am I?"

"London."

Kieran tore his gaze away, closing his eyes to the impact of her information. Feeling strangely empowered by his astonishment, Rory stood on quaking legs.

"Shocking, isn't it."

He opened his eyes, dulled with fatigue and distress. "Nay, lady, not shocking. Unbelievable."

Her gaze continued to linger on him, her composure making a slow return. "Now you know how I feel," she muttered. "I just can't believe… Good Lord, this has to be a dream. A nightmare. Corpses just don't get up and walk away!"

He sighed again, making another attempt to right himself. "I am not a corpse. I am Sir Kieran Hage of Nottingham, Viscount of Dykemoor and Sewall, and I was put to sleep by an alchemist who promised to heal my mortal wound with his magical potions."

He was really struggling. Sweat was beading on his brow as he pushed himself up, his entire body shaking with effort. Even if Rory remained terrified and confused, she simply couldn't stand by while another human being suffered so obviously. Corpse or not, Sir Kieran needed help and instinct demanded she give it.

He was about to teeter over again when she moved forward, grasping his left arm to prevent him from falling. He was incredibly solid, heavy, and she pulled hard to help him recover his balance. But he could not maintain his equilibrium without help, panting and gray, and she clutched his shoulders to steady him. Somewhere in the process, Rory wound up lodged between his tree-sized legs and before she could move to a less intimate position, Sir Kieran fell forward against her chest.

Her arms went around him automatically. Considering she was embracing a living corpse, Rory's first reaction should have been one of repulsion and she did, indeed, experience a strong surge. But she fought it, torn between the wonder of what was happening and the sensation of his living, breathing body in her arms.

"Oh, God," she moaned, feeling the stiffness of his hair scratching her chin. "I'm holding a dead man."

Kieran's swimming head was pressed to her chest, the fuzz on her sweater tickling his nose and the pounding of her heart loud in his ear. "Trust me, lady, I am not dead. But, at this moment, I surely wish that I was."

Rory closed her eyes, feeling him hard and warm in her arms and struggling to come to grips with his resurrection. The clock on the wall was ticking loudly and she glanced up; it was nearly two o'clock in the morning. She knew she couldn't stay in the morgue all night with a living corpse, but the question of what to do with him wasn't easily answered.

In fact, she was just beginning to ponder that question when she thought she heard voices. Her heart skipped a beat; senses piqued, she thought she heard more noise and, immediately, her mind went into overdrive as she realized her grace period was over. If there was ever a time to leave, it was now.

"Damn," she hissed, trying to move away from Kieran to see what was happening. He clung to her with one arm, trying to keep himself steady with the other against the sterile drawer.

"What is the matter?" he asked, looking at her with great brown eyes that seemed to worsen her shaky nerves.

Seeing that he wasn't in imminent danger of toppling, Rory remained silent as she slipped to the door leading into the hall. The receptionist's desk was several doors to her right and she swore she heard the voices again. Muttering another curse, she hastily collected her purse.

"I've got to go."

He managed to cast her a long, suspicious glance. "Go? Go where?"

"Out of here," she hissed. "Before I'm discovered. If they find me…."

She suddenly looked at him, realizing what she was saying. Kieran's brown eyes were on her, great pools of amber set in his pasty face. After a moment, she sighed. "Oh… damn. What am I going to do with you?"

He raised an eyebrow. "Do what?"

Torn, Rory simply shook her head. "I can't just leave you."

He apparently agreed. "If you go… surely I must. You seem to be the only one who can help me discover why I have finally awakened."

Her indecision was momentary and she quickly retraced her steps. "Come on," she whispered, intending that he should stand.

He looked at her doubtfully. "As you can see, lady, I am having difficulty sitting much less standing. I am not going anywhere at this moment."

Rory fixed him in the eye; whether or not he was the result of too much alcohol or a blooming insanity, she simply couldn't leave him behind. If he was discovered, he could look forward to spending time in jail for breaking into the morgue he had once been a customer of. And until this situation was settled, Rory could not, in good conscience, let him out of her sight.

"You're going to have to stand unless you want to explain your presence to the cops," she said, realizing that but for the towel, he was stark naked. "But first, I've got to find you something to wear."

As if the thought hadn't occurred to him amidst all of his other concerns, Kieran glanced down at himself to note that only a small square of cloth separated him from complete nudity.

"Where are my clothes?"

She looked at him, an expression of disgust crossing her delicate features. "Your loving family took them, I suppose. Wait here until I see what I can find."

He opened his mouth but she was gone, disappearing down the hall. Kieran sat on the metal slab, his balance returning and his strength making a weak resurgence. Slowly, with great effort, he braced his feet against the floor.

It took him three tries before he propelled himself up from the drawer. Once he was on his feet, however, the room rocked dangerously and he stumbled into the green-brick wall. The small towel protecting his privates came off in the interim and when Rory came rushing back into the room a short time later, Kieran found amusement in her startled expression.

"Oh… here." She held out an odd green garment, keeping her face turned away. "Put this on."

Kieran staggered towards her, weaving as he took the peculiar hose from her outstretched hand. "What is this?"

"Pants," she said, noting from the corner of her eye that he hadn't moved to put them on. Daring to turn her face slightly, she met his perplexed expression. "They're pants, for Heaven's sake. Put them on!"

He was still frowning when a thought suddenly occurred to her. "Hose," she clarified and she could see his features relax in understanding.

She turned her back as he pulled on the green scrub pants. When he began fumbling with the ties, Rory turned around and roughly cinched them up. Kieran grunted.

"God's Blood, lady, your touch is most genteel." He tugged at the pants where they were a bit too constricting as Rory held up the green scrub shirt.

"Put this on," she demanded.

He complied, hardly able to fit into the roomy scrubs for all of his enormous size. The only shoes she had been able to find were the protective green scrubs that covered the doctor's shoes but she had him put those on as well, unconcerned with his appearance so much as she was simply eager to get him dressed. The voices were gone for the moment but she was certain they would return, and her sense of urgency was gaining speed.

"Let's go."

"Go where?"

She didn't answer, merely grabbed him by the hand. Kieran could only move very slowly and even then it was with a good deal of effort. Like a man who hadn't used his muscles in eight hundred years. Rory felt as if she were towing a barge, slow and lethargic and awkward. They made it up the hall and to the security door leading into the waiting room. She was about to unlock the door when she saw that it had a combination release. Sighing with frustration, she directed Kieran into the receptionist's destroyed office.

"We've got to climb out," she said, pulling him towards the window. "Watch the glass; it'll slice your feet. Can you make it?"

Kieran glanced at the window, the desk, running clumsy fingers through his cropped hair. "Go first, my lady. I shall follow."

Passing him a look suggesting that she had little faith in his ability, she climbed onto the windowsill and jumped through. Just as she turned to encourage Kieran, he was already in the window, leaping to the floor with enough power to rattle the walls. Startled, not to mention strangely impressed, Rory cocked an eyebrow at him for lack of a better response.

"You move very well. For a dead man."

He sighed, his massive body sagging. But the gleam in his eyes as he focused on her was anything but weak. "I shall be far more impressive when my strength has returned fully."

Rory didn't doubt him. In fact, as the minutes passed, she found herself able to think on Kieran's resurrection without succumbing to bone-numbing shock. He had explained, briefly, and perhaps his logic had been enough support against her doubt. Even if none of it made any sense, she realized that nothing about Sir Kieran Hage had made sense from the beginning. And perhaps that was the greatest mystery of all.

The corridor was silent as Rory took Kieran's hand again. But he seemed particularly slow, even for him, and she paused with frustration.

"What's wrong?" she hissed.

He looked very serious, a bit of color returning to his cheeks. "Where is my sword, my armor? I will not leave without my possessions."

Her face softened somewhat. Where to begin? "They're not here," she whispered. "Your family took them, just like they took your clothes."

His eyes narrowed suspiciously. "My family?" he repeated. "But you said… it has been eight hundred years since…"

She nodded, glancing around nervously. "Your descendants." She pulled on him, pleading for him to follow. "Look, there will be time enough for explanations later for both our sakes. But right now, we've got to get out of here."

She started to turn away but he stopped her. "I will not go anywhere without my weapon. Where did my family take it?"

"To the University of Sussex. But unless you want to fight four Israeli guards with submachine guns to get it, you're going to have to forget about your sword."

His face hardened. "I cannot. I must have…"

She squeezed his hand to silence him, shaking her head. "Please trust me, Sir Kieran. You can't have your sword back. It's impossible."

"Why?"

"Because it's locked away in a vault. It would take an army to break into the university. Now, please, we've got go!"

She took a step forward, realizing yet again he was refusing to follow. When her anxious gaze returned to him, struggling to keep her annoyance at bay, she was struck by his puzzled, if not disappointed, expression.

"I will… trust you if you say my weapon is unreachable," he said quietly. "I have no other choice at the moment. But there is something else I must know. You mentioned something earlier, a phrase I found most strange. You said that you 'dug me up'. Why would you do this?"

"Because that's what I do. I'm an archaeo… oh, please, can't I explain this later? We don't have time for this, Sir Kieran."

Rory started to lead on but, once again, he stopped her. She was verging on an irritated response when a flicker in his brown eyes cooled her rising storm. "You have called me by name, twice," he said. "Do we have the time that I might know your name?"

"Rory," she said, feeling her cheeks flush under his close scrutiny. "Rory Osgrove."

"Rory?" he repeated with distain. "'Tis a man's name. Far too unsuitable for your beauty."

She was insulted and flattered at the same time. "It was my great-grandmother's name."

He snorted. "The fashion of names has always eluded me. I once knew a woman named Jamie. Named for her father, James. Most strange."

Rory couldn't help but smile. "Jamie is a very common female name. And so are Taylor and Mallory and Brooke."

He cocked an eyebrow. He had the most beautiful eyebrows. "How disgraceful. Women are not mean to have a man's name else God would have named Eve something as unsuitable as Jehoshaphat. What else are you called?"

Rory couldn't believe she was standing in the hallway of a London hospital debating names with an eight hundred-year-old man. "My grandfather used to call my Shorty," she said snappishly. "Is that better than Rory?"

He allowed the insolent tone to go unpunished. "It is not. And you are not short. What else?"

Rory sighed; she wanted to leave. He wanted to discuss an appropriate name. Finally, she rolled her eyes in frustration.

"I don't have any other name," she said. "My name is Rory Elizabeth Osgrove."

"Elizabeth," he repeated, rolling it off his tongue with his wonderfully strong accent. "Much more suitable for your comeliness. I believe I shall call you Elizabeth."

"Whatever." She moved him down the hall, heading for the elevator banks. Even though his balance had returned and his coordination was much better, still, he seemed to be dragging. Rory turned to see what was delaying him this time when she noticed he was peering at the lights.

"What are you doing now?" she demanded.

He pointed to a bulb, touched it, and drew his hand back sharply. "What is this device?"

She grasped him by the arm once again and pulled him along. "They're called light bulbs."

He seemed to ponder her explanation as she pushed the button for the elevator. He was about to ask her how such a miracle worked when he suddenly noticed the glowing elevator button. Rory was nearly shoved to the ground in his haste to examine it.

"How does this light?" he demanded, thumping at the plastic. "Where is the wick?"

Rory watched him, her irritation fading. Looking at the world through eyes eight hundred years old would certainly be a remarkable thing. Even though she remained confused in her own right, still, she had always possessed an open mind. Hence her devotion to biblical relics the conventional world believed to be myth. Keeping that in mind, she tried to imagine what Sir Kieran must be feeling. Thrust into a world that didn't understand him. That he didn't understand.

But maybe that was the point. Whatever the reasons for his return to life, her natural acceptance of life's unexplainable things told her that somehow, some way, her knight had, indeed, become real. It still didn't make any sense. But maybe it wasn't supposed to.

Kieran was still examining the elevator button when the doors suddenly opened. A man dressed in blue hospital scrubs almost bumped into Kieran as he emerged from the elevator, excusing himself politely. Rory grasped Kieran as he watched the man stroll down the corridor, pulling the knight into the vacated car. Kieran was still pondering the strangely-clad man when the elevator lurched.

"God's Blood," he gasped, touching the walls as the elevator rose two floors. "What is happening?"

Rory smiled faintly. "Nothing to panic over. It's an elevator. Just like stairs, only without the exertion."

He looked at her, uncertainty in his eyes, when the car came to an uneven halt. Kieran emerged from the elevator struggling with his equilibrium again as Rory directed him out the way she had come.

"I do not think I like elevators," he said frankly, rubbing his stomach.

She had him by the hand as they reached the emergency room, hardly daring to hope that they would escape unmolested. She had been positive the voices she had heard in the morgue had been employees who had discovered the break-in. But no police had been forthcoming and Rory nearly shouted with relief as they entered the large emergency ward, the wide doors to freedom straight ahead.

Until a nurse stopped them; rather, stopped Kieran. "Thank God you've come, Doctor," the woman said urgently. "We've our hands full with the football players and have hardly been able to dispense medical care because of their constant fighting!"

Rory opened her mouth before Kieran could speak. "I'm sorry," she said quickly, realizing the woman had mistaken him for a physician in his green uniform. "Dr... uh, Hage was just going home. He's been on eighteen hours. You understand, of course."

The nurse looked desperate. "Oh... I'm sorry," she said, listening to the roar of the football players grow louder. "We put out an emergency call for all available doctors in the building and I assumed... well, he's still in scrubs and I thought..."

Rory shook her head again, tightly gripping Kieran's massive arm. "I'm sorry. Dr. Hage is going home."

Suddenly, one of the football players shrieked like a wild man and leapt from his chair, rushing the man across from him. The entire waiting room erupted in turmoil and the nurse detaining Kieran turned towards the mass, pleading for calm. Rory tried to use the chaos to their advantage by pulling Kieran to the automatic doors, but he was unwilling to follow. Gently, he removed her hand from his arm.

"Remain here," he said calmly. "This will take but a moment."

Rory opened her mouth to protest but it was too late; for a man who had been moving laboriously slow not moments before, Kieran suddenly came to life. As orderlies and nurses struggled to restrain one or two men between them, Kieran began tossing men aside as if they were no match for his incredible strength. One man, two men, several ended up thrown back into their seats, dazed by the massive doctor's brutal bedside manner.

Fact was, he hardly raised a sweat. By the time he was finished, nearly two dozen men had been forcibly calmed. As Rory and a host of amazed hospital employees looked on, Kieran steadily informed the rugby players that if he was forced to return to quell the situation again, they would need more than a doctor. They would need a grave digger. There wasn't one person who didn't believe him.

Returning to his open-mouthed companion, Kieran took Rory by the hand and, for a change, pulled her towards the large double-doors. Once outside in the chill London air, she came to a stop.

"Why did you do that?" she demanded.

He faced her, feeling the brisk breeze like a rejuvenating slap in the face. His strength, his vigor was returning rapidly, and he was amazed at how well he felt. Better than he had felt in eight hundred years.

"Do what? End a minor brawl?" He shrugged. "Would you prefer that I allow it to escalate and destroy the entire room?"

She shook her head, slowly. "I... of course not. But the way you handled those men…"

He turned away from her sharply when he heard the honk of a horn. Witnessing an automobile for the very first time, his eyes widened dramatically as he pointed to the passing vehicle.

"God's Blood," he gasped. "What was that?"

"A car," she said, shaking off the visions of his amazing strength when she realized he was unconcerned with her astonishment. As if such a thing happened every day which, to him, it probably did.

"A car?" he repeated, watching as another went by, and another. "What is this car, Libby?"

"Libby?" she looked at him curiously.

He watched a bus go by, instinctively standing back to allow the vehicle a wide berth. "I told you I did not like the name Rory. Libby is a familiar of Elizabeth and I like it." He was still staring at the bus. "What was that monstrous car?"

"A bus," she replied, rubbing at her temples as the jackhammer started again. It was two o'clock in the morning and they needed to find shelter for the night. But not back at the Parkwood; Bud was waiting for her and Rory wasn't sure how she was going to explain the appearance of Sir Kieran. Until she could sit the man down and discover the reasons behind his return to life, she wasn't about to tell Bud anything. Just a phone call to let him know she was all right would have to suffice for the time being.

Kieran continued to watch cars drive by, amazed, as Rory wrapped her arms around her body to ward off the night's chill.

"Come on," she said, moving down the sidewalk. "I'm cold and I'm tired. We've got to find someplace to stay and… well, figure this out."

He trailed after her, almost stepping in front of an oncoming Jaguar until Rory pulled him back onto the sidewalk. Feeling the iciness of her hand, he was distracted from the incredible concept of cars.

"My lady is chilled," he said, holding her hand in his massive palm. "A bit of mead and a soft bed will see you warmed."

Rory looked up at him, way up, realizing that he was taller than Bud had originally estimated. She was coming to think he was closer to six feet five inches in height, although she could not be sure. All she knew was that the man in life was far larger, far more imposing, than he had ever been in death.

"I don't think they make mead anymore," she said, shivering involuntarily when his thick arm went about her shoulders. "But as for a warm bed, I'm all for it. Right after I make a call."

He pulled her against the curve of his torso; she was truly a tiny, little thing, sweet and soft and round in all of the right places. Aye, she was quite pleasing.

"Libby?"

"My name is Rory."

"And I say it is Libby. Who must you call?"

She didn't reply for a moment. "I've got to call a... friend."

"What must you call her?"

She sighed. Then she laughed. "It's easier to explain when you see what I'm talking about."

He nodded faintly, watching another car go by before returning his attention to the strange, smooth cobblestones they were walking on. "Libby?"

"My name is not... oh, hell. What?"

"Who awakened me from my suspended state?"

She shook her head. "I don't know. But I intend to find out what, exactly, is happening around here."

Kieran was silent a moment. "Did you kiss me?"

Rory paused, stopping to look at him. His arm fell away from her shoulders as they faced each other beneath the haunting moonlight. "Why... what kind of a question is that?"

"Answer me. Did you kiss me?"

She lowered her gaze, looking embarrassed and defiant at the same time. "I did. But I was saying goodbye to you. I had a good reason."

A slow smile spread across his face. Reaching out, he collected her hand in his big, warm palm. "Then it is you."

She cocked an eyebrow, warily. "What is me?"

He continued to smile, his twinkling brown eyes driving daggers of excitement deep into her heart. After a moment, he brought her hand to his lips and kissed it softly, tucking it into the crook of his elbow as they resumed their walk. Rory was still lingering on the kiss.

"Nothing, sweetheart," he murmured, gazing up at the moon, the trees. "Forget my foolish statement."

She tried. But she couldn't.

CHAPTER TEN

R ORY WAS FEELING like a criminal on the run. She and Kieran found a pub not far from the hospital, nearly void of customers, which was a good thing since Kieran was a sight in his green scrubs and seemed to have little tolerance for those who stared at him. Sitting him in a secluded booth and ordering a drink from the bartender, she found a payphone by the lavatory.

She had a bird's-eye view of Kieran as she rang the Parkwood, watching as he examined the ashtray, the table, the picture on the wall. She was so involved with her observations that she was genuinely startled when Bud's urgent voice came over the phone.

"Hi, Bud," she said. "It's me."

"Christ!" he exclaimed. "Rory, where are you?"

She paused, watching as the bartender brought their drinks. Kieran sniffed the liquor, drank it, and made a face. "I… uh, I'm all right. I guess I just lost track of time."

"Tell me where you are," he demanded. "I'm coming to get you. Hell, I knew I shouldn't have let you go alone. What happened at the hospital?"

"Something wonderful, I think," she replied, noting that Kieran had cornered the bartender and was pointing to his obviously inferior drink. "Look, I've got to go. I'll call you later, okay?"

"Like hell!" Bud exploded. "Dammit, Rory, tell me where you are!"

"I'm fine, Bud, really," she repeated. "Please don't worry."

"Don't worry?" he snorted. "It's two o'clock in the morning and you're wandering around the city alone. How can you ask me not to worry?"

"Please Bud," she whispered into the phone, using a sweet tone that could coerce him into buying her the world if she wanted it. "Please don't ask me anything else. I'll have more to tell you tomorrow. Please?"

There was a pause on the line. "Christ, Rory," he muttered. She could literally see the torn expression on his face. "For God's sake, please tell me where you are. I can't let you run around London by yourself. I'm sorry for all the things I said and I promise I won't bring it up again. Please, honey?"

She felt badly for him, knowing how worried he was. But it also reinforced her determination to keep him out of what was happening until she understood it herself. "I'm not alone, Bud. I ran into an... old friend at the hospital. We're having a nice talk and I promise I'll call you in the morning."

The chill on the line was evident. "A friend? I thought you've never been to London."

"I haven't."

The line went silent again and, over her shoulder, Rory could see that Kieran had secured a huge schooner of black liquor from the bartender. He was heading in her direction and she made haste to end the conversation.

"I have to go," she said quickly. "I'll call you tomorrow."

"A male friend, Rory?"

"I'll call you tomorrow, Bud."

She ended the conversation, hanging up the receiver just as Kieran opened the door to the phone booth. He seemed far more interested in the phone itself than in who she was talking to.

"How does this work?"

He was pressing her against the glass and she could hardly breathe with the heat and closeness of his body. Turning slightly, she indicated the coin drop.

"Here. You just put a quarter in and you can make a call." When he still appeared perplexed, she attempted to describe the telephone on his terms. "It's like… like if you wanted to send a missive. But instead of writing it down, you pick up this device and simply speak with the person you want to communicate with."

Kieran put the receiver to his ear, upside down. "I hear nothing but a strange noise."

"A dial tone." When he raised a questioning eyebrow, she simply shook her head. "I'll explain later. Let's go sit down."

Although still curious about the phone, he graciously escorted her back to the table. Rory sat on one side of the booth and Kieran pushed her over, seating his massive frame beside her. When she looked strangely at him for wanting to sit so close considering they had an entire booth to themselves, he merely smiled.

"I must be able to protect you," he explained. "A man will think twice about molesting you with my threatening presence by your side."

She cocked an eyebrow, collecting her ale. She knew she shouldn't be drinking it but, somehow, she needed it. "Look around, Sir Kieran. I would hardly call these drunks the molesting type."

"They are thinking wicked thoughts nonetheless," he said, taking a healthy quaff of his drink and smacking his lips. "Passable. Not the best, but passable."

She eyed the black lager. "What is it?"

"Something called Winter Ale. Would you care to sample the flavor?"

She did. It tasted like lighter fluid. Shuddering in disgust, it somehow made her own drink less palatable and she pushed it away as Kieran continued to down the ale. She watched him, looking entirely odd in his green scrubs, stubbled face and dirty hair. But the more she stared at him, the more amazement and wonder she felt with the entire, crazy situation.

"Now," she began. "I guess we have a few things to talk about."

He nodded in agreement, smacking his lips with the first taste of liquor in over eight centuries. "Indeed, we do. But first I must ask a question."

"What's that?"

He looked up from his dark drink, his brow furrowed with thought. "You must understand... I realize a significant amount of time has passed, but it is important that I know what happened after... after..."

"After you died?"

"Aye."

Rory pondered her reply carefully. "Acre fell and King Richard returned to England a hero."

"When did Acre fall?"

"In July 1192."

Kieran drew in a deep breath, absorbing this information. For him, the events of centuries ago had literally happened yesterday and a smile creased his lips. "Then our armies were, indeed, victorious. I had little doubt, of course. It was only a matter of time. And you say Richard returned to England?"

"He did. Well, after a few minor adventures."

"Adventures? What does this mean?"

"He was kidnapped by Henry Augustus and Duke Leopold of Austria and held for ransom. But England paid and Richard returned home, safe and sound."

Kieran's eyebrows rose in genuine outrage. "The bastards. But I am not astonished by their treachery. They envied Richard his power, his wealth. Everything he had, they wanted for themselves. And more."

Rory observed him as he pondered the events of history while he had slept. In fact, he seemed quite disturbed and she decided to veer the subject away from the pitfalls of King Richard. "As I said, he returned to England and finished his reign." She didn't dare go into the rebellion of Prince John and how the remainder of Richard's reign was spent battling his brother. "Now, I have a question for you; like, who was this alchemist and what, exactly, did he do to you?"

Kieran drained the last of his schooner in one huge swallow. Ordering another, he turned his attention to Rory.

"I do not recall his name," he said, shrugging off the outrage of Leopold and Henry. Eight hundred years later, there was little place for his fury. "I came to the man believing he was a physic. I had been wounded and…"

He suddenly began fumbling with his shirt, as if he had just remembered the wound that had nearly claimed his life. Rory watched as he revealed the puckered scar, running his fingers over it in wonder.

"I know," she murmured in response to his awed expression. "I've seen it. You should have seen the clothes we found you in. Stained brown with blood. That's why we knew this injury had killed you. Or, at least, we logically thought so."

"I thought so, too," he said, touching it even as his gaze sought Rory. "By all rights, it should have. But the alchemist… he gave me a potion that, as he explained, suspended my bodily functions. And then he gave me a series of subsequent potions he claimed would heal my wound. I did not believe him, of course. I believed I was as good as dead."

Rory was leaning on her hand, listening to him with incredulity. "Are you telling me that eight hundred years ago they possessed the technology to heal a wound without conventional skills? We don't even have that kind of knowledge today."

The bartender brought over another drink. Rory ordered coffee. When the man was gone, Kieran took another healthy swallow of his ale.

"I do not know what sort of knowledge the man possessed. Suffice it to say that he was true to his word." His gaze came up from the drink, resting on Rory. "You seemed to be remarkably receptive to my story, my lady. Do you actually believe what I am telling you?"

She smiled faintly. "I wasn't remarkably receptive at first. You seem to forget my screaming fit."

He met her smile, a delicious gesture of deep dimples and straight teeth. "I have not forgotten, I assure you. My ears are still ringing." He paused, taking another drink. "Then tell me; why were you sleeping on me?"

She lowered her gaze, her smile fading. "As for believing your story, I don't think I have much of a choice." She was obviously unwilling to answer his question. "I removed you from your grave, Sir Kieran. I saw your lifeless corpse and now I see a man who has come to life. As unbelievable as all of this is, I suppose there isn't an explanation I would find too incredible at this point. Even so, I'm still half-expecting to wake up from this tomorrow morning and discover that it was all a dream."

His gaze was soft. "You still do not believe me to be real?"

She shrugged, toying with her mug of discarded ale. "Real enough, I guess. Four hours ago you were stiff and cold and I was crying all over you because I thought I'd never seen you again. I never left that room, I never heard anyone enter or leave, and suddenly you were alive. If you're a zombie, then you're like nothing I've ever heard of." She shook her head, putting a weary hand over her eyes. "Oh, hell, maybe I am dreaming all of this. Or maybe I'm just insane."

His brow furrowed, still focused on the earlier part of her statement. "What is this zombie?"

She smirked. "Other than the worst drink you'll ever taste in your life, a zombie is a walking corpse supposedly possessed by demons."

Kieran's brow relaxed, a faint smile creasing his lips. "I am not possessed. At least, I do not believe so."

Rory studied him, their eyes meeting. She knew the man she had extracted from the earth, the lines of his face and the emotions of his heart. And this living, walking being was most definitely that man. It was the most incredible thing she'd ever witnessed and her wonder, her enchantment, was a perpetual experience.

"I don't think so, either."

His brown eyes glimmered in the weak light. "You are a sensible woman, Libby."

She laughed then. "You're the only one who thinks so. Everyone else who knows me thinks I'm a nut."

His brow furrowed again. "A nut?"

She nodded, still grinning. "A kook. You know, eccentric?"

He understood the last word. "Why would they think this?"

Rory's smile faded as the bartender brought her coffee. The drink was hot and strong and she took a large swallow. "Because I go where angels fear to tread." His liquid gaze was focused on her as she took another drink. "That's how I found you, Sir Kieran. I was looking for…"

"For what?" he asked gently.

She stared at him. Really stared at him. Careful, she thought. The man died for his beliefs and there's no telling how he'll react to your admission. But as she continued to gaze at him, she realized that her most fervent wish had come true; from the moment she had read his journal, the need to ask him what he knew of the crown had been a major yearning.

But she had also resigned herself to inevitable. That she would never know the truth. And throughout this entire happening, the thought of bombarding him with questions hadn't occurred to her until this moment. There had been too much going on for her to even think about the very relic that had brought them together.

"I was looking for something but I found you instead," she said, glancing to his empty schooner. "Would you like another ale? Or maybe you shouldn't. How about something to eat?"

He was still staring at her, deep in thought. "Mayhap later. I would like to know what you were looking for when you found me."

She refused to meet his gaze but she could sense something in his tone. The brutally honest, highly intelligent man she had come to know through the pages of his journal was demanding truths. And coming to acquaint herself with the man as she had, she had little doubt that he would not let the subject rest. If there was one thing she had learned about Sir Kieran Hage, it was that he was a determined man. And he usually got what he wanted.

And it was obvious he wanted to know what had led her to his grave. Maybe if she approached the subject carefully, she could either abandon her questioning or delve into it more deeply. But her decision would depend on his response.

She took a deep breath for courage. "When we found your grave, Sir Kieran, your possessions were buried with you."

He nodded. "As you have indicated. Somehow the alchemist must have retrieved them. I can only imagine it was he who buried me to hide the body from… well, it does not matter. Please continue."

His odd statement piqued her interest, but she ignored it for the moment as she proceeded with her own line of thought. "We found your sword, your armor, and other effects. Including your journal."

Kieran didn't change his expression. "My journal?"

Rory nodded slowly. "It was found with your purse and other items. I read the entire chronicle."

"And?"

She was encouraged by his reaction; no tense body language, no facial expressions conveying distress. In fact, he seemed unconcerned and she decided to press her point. "At the end of the journal, you wrote a small passage that caught my eye." She took another deep breath. "'Forgive me Lord Jesus that my mission in Thou's name hath been thwarted. The diadem of Thou's sacrifice entrusted into my hands is forever sealed, hidden so that no man can pilfer Its beauty or omnipotence. Until such time that I can safely transport It to the land of my birth, Its whereabouts will remain my knowledge alone.'"

She paused, gauging his reaction. There was none. After a moment, she leaned forward on the table as if to drive home her real meaning. "This diadem you spoke of. Did you really mean Christ's Crown of Thorns when he died on Mount Calvary?"

One moment he was staring at her. In the next, he was moving from the pub with such speed that Rory nearly lost him. Leaving a ten pound note on the table, she collected her purse and raced after him. Out into the cold night, she didn't have any difficulty following his bright green scrubs. Onward he marched, crossing a major street without looking and Rory narrowly avoided being hit by a car as she pursued.

He was jogging slowly by the time he reached the curb, entering a small street as Rory raced behind him, calling his name. Turning the corner, he ended up in a dead-end alley and Rory came to a stop several feet behind him, panting with anxiety and effort.

"I'm sorry," she said, gasping for air. "Please, I didn't mean anything. It's just that…"

He whirled around, upon her in two strides and Rory found herself in a grip more powerful than anything she had ever experienced.

"Did Simon send you?" he demanded through clenched teeth.

Eyes wide with fright, Rory shook her head. "No, he… ouch!" He had squeezed too hard. "Let go of me!"

His brown eyes, soft and liquid only moments earlier, were like blazing coals of fury and Rory was truly frightened. "Not until we establish something here and now," he growled. "If Simon has sent you, confess this instant and I shall be merciful. But if you intend to play me for a fool, know my punishment shall be severe. Make your choice."

Rory realized that her intention to probe him for information had backfired miserably. She should have known that a man willing to die for his cause would be more than willing to kill for it, too. And if he viewed her as a threat, she was in serious trouble.

Calm down! she told herself inwardly. Think!

"How could Simon have sent me if he died eight hundred years ago?" she asked, her voice husky with fear. "I read of him in your journal, but I don't know him nor do I care to. He sounds like a jerk."

Kieran's expression was as hard as stone. But his grip relaxed somewhat and Rory nearly collapsed with relief. But not entirely.

"He is the one who tried to kill me." His voice was equally raspy, far softer than the snarling he had been doing moments prior. "Were it not for Simon, I would have lived a long life and died within the peace of my own time."

"I realize that," she said, noticing his grip had slackened further and iron-like fingers were suddenly caressing the very spot they had bruised. "Look, Sir Kieran, I'm not a threat to your holy mission. In fact, I want to help you, but you've got to help me understand the situation. Did you really have the Crown of Thorns in your possession?"

He continued to stare at her, hesitance in his eyes. It was obvious that he was having difficulty with the concept of confessing his knowledge when it was still instinct to protect his mission. Still, he was not unreasonable. And he had no reason not to trust the oddly-speaking woman who had loved him enough to rouse him from centuries of sleep.

"I did," he whispered.

Rory nearly swallowed her tongue, struggling to respond to what she had known all along. "Where is it?"

He gazed at her, wondering why she was asking questions if she had read his journal as she had said. To a woman with her education, surely it would have been a simple thing to have deciphered the crown's location and he wondered why she had not done so. Or had been unable to do so.

Confusion deepening, he released her and ran his fingers through his hair as if debating whether to answer her question. Was there a reason why she had not decoded his script? Even if she was his only link to his resurrection, mayhap he was being foolish in trusting her without question. Trust that, at one time, had led to a sword in his gut.

"Far away," he said after a moment. "In the land of my burial."

"Nahariya?"

He nodded. "Providing it is still where I left it, I fully intend to retrieve it myself." He turned to look at her then. "You see, my lady, that is why God has permitted me to awaken from my eternal sleep. My task is not yet complete and the time has finally come for me to finish what I had started. Have no doubt that I shall retrieve the diadem, as I was always meant to do. And I shall do it alone."

Her first reaction was to argue with him, bitterly, but she bit her tongue. He was showing signs of exhaustion, the energy surge following his awakening rapidly fading. Putting their conversation aside for the moment, it was apparent that he needed to recover from his experience. And Rory was exhausted, too. In more ways than one.

"Whatever," she said quietly, turning her back on him and glancing the way they had come. She was too tired to fight about it now. "Maybe the bartender knows where we can find a room for the night. I'll go back and ask him if you want to wait here."

Behind her, Kieran sighed heavily and began to walk. Silently, they retraced their steps back to the pub.

⅓

AT PRECISELY FIVE-THIRTY in the morning, there was a knock on Bud's door. Thinking it was Rory, he flew from his chair and opened the panel. But his hopes were dashed when he found himself staring into piercing blue eyes.

Steven Corbin was less than friendly. "Where is your colleague, Dr. Dietrich?"

Bud's jaw clenched. "This is all your fault, you bastard!" he seethed. "You took Sir Kieran away and now she's running all over this city doing God only knows what. I haven't seen her in hours!"

Corbin cocked an eyebrow. "I did nothing but claim the Hage family's rightful possession. Which, in fact, now happens to be missing."

Bud scowled, punchy and exhausted from worry and the lack of sleep. "I don't know what in the hell you're talking about."

"Don't you?"

It took all of Bud's control not to slug Corbin in the mouth. "I said I didn't. So what in the hell do you want?"

"I want to talk to Dr. Osgrove," Corbin said evenly. Bud noticed two other men hanging in the hallway; the door to Rory's room was slightly ajar, but he controlled his outrage as the lawyer continued. When the man was finished, then he would slug him in the mouth. "You see, Dr. Dietrich, the morgue at Middlesex Hospital was burglarized last night and Sir Kieran's corpse was taken. Do you sincerely mean to tell me that you know nothing about this?"

Bud forgot his fury. He stared at Corbin, the color draining from his face. After a moment, he turned away and wandered towards the window. Corbin followed him into the room.

"Then you did know something," he stated.

Bud shook his head. "No, nothing about… oh, hell, she threatened to do it, but I never thought she was capable." He sat on the edge of his bed, his ice-blue eyes glazed with disbelief. "You took the corpse away so quickly that she never had a chance to say goodbye. And she was obsessed with saying goodbye. I let her go to the hospital thinking she would simply forget about the idea when she saw it was impossible to gain access to the morgue. But now you're telling me the morgue was actually broken into?"

Corbin nodded, his goons coming to stand just inside the door. "The glass was smashed and we found traces of blood. But we can't figure out how she removed the corpse. She must have had help."

Bud shut his mouth then, thinking of the phone conversation they had shared earlier. I ran into an old friend, Bud. Something wonderful has happened this evening. He closed his eyes against the shock, the pain, wondering if she had allowed her obsession to get the better of her by delving into something too bizarre to comprehend. He cursed himself for having allowed her to go to the hospital alone. This was all his fault.

He looked at his hands. "I wouldn't know anything about that. It wasn't me if that's what you're thinking."

"I wasn't thinking that at all. The landlady said you returned to your room about nine-forty and haven't left since. The police estimate the morgue was broken into after the basement floor security guard went off duty, sometime after ten o'clock."

Bud cast the man a long glance. "So now you're checking up on me, too?"

Corbin's arrogant manner didn't waver. "A very valuable piece of property has been stolen, Dr. Dietrich. It is my duty to help the police follow up any and all leads." His piercing blue eyes roved the room, coming to rest on the phone by the bed. "Have you spoken with Dr. Osgrove tonight?"

Bud looked him straight in the eye. "No."

Corbin met his gaze, knowing he was lying. The landlady had already told him that Dr. Dietrich had received a call a few hours earlier. But he would not press the point; even if Dietrich wasn't directly involved, it was obvious that he was protecting his beautiful associate. And Corbin suspected, at some point, the good doctor would go looking for her.

And Corbin would be waiting.

"If you speak to her, will you let me know?" He tossed his business card on the bed. "I promise, Dr. Dietrich, I simply want to talk to her."

Bud didn't answer, turning away as Corbin left the room with the stealth of a stalking cat. When the door closed, he went to the window facing the street, waiting a minute or so as Corbin and his henchmen climbed into a black Mercedes 500 SEL and drove off. Immediately, he went to the phone and placed an overseas call. To Nahariya, Israel.

"Hello, Dave? Brace yourself, pal; you'll never guess what's happened..."

CHAPTER ELEVEN

T HE HOTEL RECOMMENDED by the bartender was close to the British Museum. The landlord had eyed Rory and Kieran strangely at first, a very tired-looking American and a massive man in green scrubs, but Rory hastily explained that their luggage had been lost by the airline and her… uh, husband was a surgeon visiting from abroad. The story sounded weird even to her, but the landlord didn't seem overly suspicious. Having little cash, Rory charged the room on her American Express card.

It was a small room with a small window and a very large bed. As Kieran poked around, examining everything from the doorknob to the rugs, someone rapped on the door. The landlord's wife, a round woman with well-lacquered hair, held two bathrobes and a variety of personal products and Rory thanked the woman graciously.

Locking the door, she realized Kieran had discovered the tiny bathroom and the light switch all at the same time. Between the running water and the annoying on-and-off of the lights, her irritation was pushed to the limit as she snappishly pulled him from the water closet and shut the door. He appeared displeased with her behavior, but more disappointed that she had spoiled his fun.

But Rory had little concern for his discovery of the modern world. She was still lingering on the fact that he was determined to retrieve the crown alone. Embittered and exhausted, she ignored him as he opened the bathroom door again, flipping the light off and on but a good deal more discreetly. Kicking off her shoes, she fell asleep on the comforter.

When morning finally came, she awoke to Kieran's beautiful face. But he wasn't looking at her; he was peering at the hurricane lamp beside the bed. Rory stared at him a moment, viewing him in the bright morning light and realizing that she could get used to awakening to him every morning. The very real sight of her living, breathing crusader.

Her thoughts were warm as she gazed at him, but just as quickly her manner turned hard and defensive. Still angry from the previous night, she rolled away and climbed from the bed. Moving to the bathroom, he crowded in behind her before she could close the door.

"What is this room, Libby?"

His sensual voice startled her more than the presence of his massive body. He was without the scrub shirt, clad only in the green pants, and his magnificent torso was distracting her from her anger. Refusing to look him in eye, she fumbled with the faucet.

"It's called a bathroom." Her tone was decidedly unfriendly.

He was still wedged behind her, his hand coming over her shoulder to turn on the shower. Rory shrieked when the cold water sprayed her arm.

"Quit that!" she demanded, turning the knob off. "Now, go. Shoo. I need a moment of privacy."

He didn't budge. Still, she refused to look at him, gazing at the mirror only to discover that she looked terrible. Her mascara was under her eyes and her cheeks and lips were devoid of any color. Groaning, she pushed past him and went to find her purse. Returning to the bathroom, she set it on the sink.

"I asked you to leave," she said, looking at the mirror once more. His massive reflection nearly filled the glass and she tried hard not to make eye contact with him. "Will you please go?"

Instead of leaving, he crossed his arms and Rory had to close her eyes against biceps as big in circumference as her waist.

"Why are you so angry with me?"

She remained stubbornly silent, grabbing some tissue from the roll. Wetting it and using a little soap, she began to rub at the black smears under her eyes. When she didn't reply, he simply moved closer.

"You will answer me. Why are you angry?"

She could feel his heat against her buttocks, the back of her legs. Swallowing hard, she struggled to form a reply before he took her over his knee for her refusal. And from what she had witnessed at the emergency room, she had little doubt that he could, and would, do it.

"What would you have me say?" she asked after a moment, wiping at the blotched makeup.

"I would have you tell me the truth."

She paused, feeling her anger rise. So he wanted the truth, did he? She turned around, looking him in the eye for the first time that morning.

"Fine. If you want the truth, here it is. You see, Sir Kieran, I was searching for the Crown of Thorns Jesus Christ wore on Mount Calvary when I came across your grave. Ancient manuscripts I have been studying for the better part of five years pinpointed Nahariya as the location of the crown. But instead, I found a crusader with a journal indicating that he had been in possession of the precise relic I was looking for." She watched as his gaze grew guarded and it only served to fuel her fury. "I didn't want you, just that damned crown. And last night you had the audacity to tell me that you will retrieve it alone. After I risked everything to raise you from the grave, you show your thanks by shutting me out like a disinterested bystander."

His nostrils flared and she angrily tossed the tissue into the toilet, the dam of emotion bursting forth. After all, he had asked why she was angry and she would do him the courtesy of answering. Tearing off more tissue, she whirled to the mirror once more and began cleaning her eyes with a vengeance.

"Don't look so perturbed." Her tone was laced with sarcasm. "You asked why I was angry and demanded the truth. So there. Now you have it. You're acting as if you have sole claim to the crown, like it's your private possession. And it's not."

He simply stood by the door, arms crossed and brow furrowed. Rory cleaned what she could from her eyes, going to work on her cheeks.

"Who hired you to find the diadem?" he finally asked, quietly.

Rory splashed water on her face. "No one. I'm a biblical archaeologist and exposing ancient relics is my job. I told you last night that I go where angels fear to tread. Even more than conventional bone diggers, biblical archaeologists are considered dream hunters, trying to prove a correlation between the Bible and known historic periods and events." She grabbed a towel. "I took on the greatest hunt of all when I came across cryptic references to Christ's Crown of Thorns, buried somewhere along the Pilgrim Trail. Eventually, I was able to pinpoint Nahariya, which is where you came into the picture."

He didn't reply. Rory finished drying her face and dug in her purse for her makeup. She tried not to look at him as she put on a bit of concealer to cover her dark circles, or when she applied warm brown shadow and dark liner. He continued to remain silent as she brushed mascara onto her long lashes and when the silence grew particularly uncomfortable, she dared to steal a glance at him from the corner of her eye. He was watching her.

"What is an archaeologist?"

His voice was soft, without tension or strain. She sighed, wondering if he had understood even half of what she had said.

"A person who goes to school for years studying history, the knowledge of which is eventually applied to field sciences. Although my degree is in Biblical Sciences, my special area of expertise happens to be the Crusades." When he looked puzzled, she sighed again and picked up her blush compact. "In order to decipher the annals of man's history, archaeologists go out and dig up ancient cities and bodies and other stuff. We can discover how people lived and worked, and we come to understand ourselves better."

He watched her as she brushed on a pair of rosy cheeks. "And would locating Christ's diadem help you understand yourself better?"

She paused, turning to look at him with a lip pencil poised in front of her mouth. "What do you mean by that?"

He raised an eyebrow, his eyes roving her wonderful face flattered by the strange cosmetics she was applying. "What is it you seek, my lady? The crown to enhance God's glory, or do you seek it to fill a void in your own life?"

She stared at him, her anger all but vanished. Just as in the pages of his journal, the wisdom of Sir Kieran Hage was a remarkable thing. As if the gem-clear brown eyes could look deep into her soul and know everything about her. But as beautiful as the eyes were, they were unnerving as well and she returned her focus to her mirror. Lining her lips, she applied rose-tinted lipstick.

"I want to find the crown simply to lend support to biblical legends," she said quietly. "It's a marvelous piece of history revered by millions of Christians. Just like Noah's Ark, or the Holy Grail. People these days are looking for a little bit of extra faith in this crazy world."

"But faith is having belief in something you cannot see or hear or touch. It is a feeling, a matter of conviction that fulfills the soul." Kieran uncrossed his arms, leaning against the doorjamb. "If you locate the crown, you are, in essence, forcing mankind to believe in the reality of God with the tangibility of your proof. Isn't faith something that should be freely given rather than be forced upon?"

Rory put her makeup back in her purse. "I'm not forcing anyone to believe anything. And what's wrong with hard evidence to support the greatest story in the Bible?"

He gazed into her eyes, his guarded expression faded. "Look deep inside yourself, Libby. You do not seek to support the glory of Christ. You seek to fill something within yourself that you have always lacked. You seek to become whole under the pretense of doing God's work."

"I never said I was doing God's work."

"Then whose work are you doing?"

Rory lowered her gaze, bewildered by his gentle question. After a moment, she sat on the toilet lid, gazing up at his marvelous face.

"Let me ask you the same question. Whose work were you doing when you came into possession of the crown?"

"I shall answer your question if you will answer mine."

She looked thoughtful for a moment. Since there was no use in lying, she decided to be truthful. "I guess you could say I'm doing my own work for my own reasons. So why are my motives any worse than yours? Can you honestly tell me that the crown was in your possession because you sought to glorify His name like some sort of holy envoy?"

He drew in a deep breath, looking away from her and out into the small bedroom. Rory drank in his profile, thinking how completely gorgeous he was. Even dead he had been beautiful, but it was nothing compared to his living aura.

"What I did, I did for the good of thousands. My reasons were not selfish, nor were they to support God's Word. They are entirely different from your motives."

Rory observed his movements, sensing distress in his manner. She thought a moment on his journal and the words therein. Suddenly, she cast him a long, curious glance.

"A peace offering?"

He looked at her with a neutral expression she was becoming accustomed with. "What do you know of this?"

She shook her head, rising from the toilet seat and facing the mirror once more. Her hair was a disaster, limp and unruly, and she ran her fingers through it as she considered her reply.

"Nothing, really," she said. "It's just that I read something in your journal about a Christian offering of peace that I understood to be linked to the Crown of Thorns. The ink had been blurred, though, and it was difficult to read much at all. You mentioned Saladin, though, and a man named El-Hadid, I think."

"El-Hajidd," he corrected her.

Her gaze found him in the reflection of the mirror. He sensed her attention, looking up from the doorjamb he had been studying with distraction. "Why do you look at me like that?"

She appeared to be groping for words as she turned from the mirror. "I don't know," she murmured, her mouth working as she struggled to explain herself. "It's just that with everything that's happened over the past few hours, I'd nearly forgotten the very real fact that you actually fought with Richard the Lionheart. As I stand here looking at you, I can hardly believe that you were one of the thousands to have served in the great quest. I mean… my God, it's a mind-boggling concept."

He scratched his head, a modest gesture. "I do not know this 'mind-boggling', but I can guess. And as for simply fighting for our king, I was more than a soldier. I was a friend."

"That's what you said in your journal," she said, her anger with the man forgotten as the glory of his past took hold. "When I read your journal, there were so many questions I wanted to ask you. So many things I wanted to know. Now I don't even know where to begin."

He cocked an eyebrow. "You already have. With the diadem."

She smiled for the first time all morning. "Apparently, it doesn't mean the same thing to both of us. But it's no less important to me than it is to you. I want it to strengthen my profession, but you… I still don't know why you want it."

"My interest is far more significant than yours."

"Why?"

He paused a moment, deliberating just how much to tell her. But if she had read his journal as she had obviously demonstrated, then she knew a good deal already. The natural instinct to protect his mission was still a powerful force, but he realized that it was foolish to maintain his defense against her. Any threat to his task had passed into dust eight hundred years ago and the lady before him was clearly not a hazard. Selfish and demanding and petulant, but certainly no threat.

"Because," he began quietly. Still, it was difficult to form an admission. "Because you were correct when you interpreted it to mean an offering of peace."

"Peace for what?"

He snorted, pushing himself off the doorjamb and wandering into the bedroom. Rory followed.

"A truce to end the siege of Acre, of course," he said, moving to collect his giant green shirt. "El-Hajidd was an envoy representing several Muslim generals under Saladin's command. Without Saladin's knowledge, for the man was reluctant to surrender his fortress, El-Hajidd arranged a secret meeting with me and several other knights to propose a truce, extending the Crown of Thorns as a proposal of good faith. I accepted the crown by Richard's authority and gave El-Hajidd my word that our king would do everything in his power to end the siege peacefully. But I never had a chance to prove my honor."

"Why not?"

"Because several of my fellow knights turned against me, as their leader," he said quietly, fumbling with the ungainly garment. "They didn't want peace, only the satisfaction of complete victory over Saladin. Even as I carried the Muslim offering to Richard, my men were plotting against me."

The pieces of the journal were falling together and Rory was enthralled. As Kieran finished with the awkward shirt, she sat on the edge of the mussed bed, her hazel eyes wide with anticipation.

"The betrayal you wrote of?"

He nodded, scratching at his stubbled chin. "Men I trusted turned against me. Even my best... friend."

"Simon?"

Again, he nodded. "We fostered together. I thought I knew him as well as I knew myself, but I was wrong. Men from Henry Augustus' army convinced him that there would never be a peaceable surrender and persuaded him to take the crown from me and dispose of it, forever erasing all peaceful intentions the Muslims had offered."

Rory could see the heartache in his expression, coming to understand a great deal of the writings in his journal. Like pieces of a puzzle coming together. Lying on her stomach, her chin rested in her hands, she watched Kieran pace about, lost in thought. Lost in an ancient world that had betrayed his altruistic intentions those centuries ago; still, the pain of betrayal was fresh.

"Why didn't you just go to Richard with all of this?" she demanded. "He knew about the meeting in the first place, didn't he?"

He nodded weakly. "Of all of our commanders, he was the only man who had been contacted by the Muslims. The lesser of the evils, I suppose. He was wary of the enemy's intentions and sent me to discover the truth of their word. 'Twas his hope that when I returned with the diadem of Christ, he would be able to propose a truce to Henry Augustus and Barbarossa and the rest, using the peace offering as proof of Muslim honor."

Rory was stunned. "So the Muslims proposed an armistice before Acre actually fell?"

Kieran had moved to the window, gazing out over a London he no longer recognized. "You mentioned that Acre fell in July 1192. My meeting with El-Hajidd was in December of the previous year. But no one would ever know the results of our rendezvous. When I did not return, forced to flee from those I had once trusted, I am sure Richard assumed the Muslims had killed me. He never knew it was not the enemy who could not be trusted, but his own men driven to destroy the hated insurgents rather than accept a peaceful surrender."

On the mattress, Rory pondered his shocking revelation. But in the same breath, she recalled Bud theorizing nearly the same happening and realized with little surprise that he had been right. Then again, Bud was always right.

"Amazing," she said after a moment. "Think of the lives that could have been saved had the crusading armies accepted the peace proposal. And with the Christians willing to lay down their arms, there was no way Saladin could refuse to do the same if he wanted to preserve his honor. With his men literally plotting behind his back for peace, he wouldn't have had a choice."

Kieran nodded, turning to look at her. A woman he had known a matter of hours, yet a woman he felt more comfortable with than he had ever felt with anyone. And considering the betrayal he had experienced in his short life, trust was not an easy thing to come by.

"I kept the crown, of course, realizing that I would most likely not be able to make it to Richard intact, but hoping I could at least return to England." He rubbed his left side, the location of the puckered scar. "I made it as far as Nahariya. I knew Simon and his cutthroats were closing in on me so, in desperation, I hid the very object they were looking for. When the assassins finally found me, it was to my satisfaction that they did not find the crown in my possession. Fools that they were, they stabbed me before they had their answers."

Rory smiled at his cleverness. "They killed you before they discovered you didn't even have the crown. And with you dead, they would never know where you had hidden it."

"Precisely." His voice was quiet as he thought of the encoded location in his journal. Wondering if, by some stroke of magic, his enemies had managed to decipher the writing and further wondering if the crown was where he had left it. The need to know was nearly overwhelming. "I managed to kill my assassins and make my way to a man I believed to be a healer. But, as you can see, he was not a healer."

Rory raised her eyebrows in agreement. "He was some sort of miracle worker." Kieran continued to linger halfway between the bed and the window, his brow permanently furrowed. He looked rather distressed, in fact, and she sat up on the bed. "But it's all over with now. I mean, the crown is safe and you're, uh… alive. That's what matters, isn't it?"

His gem-clear eyes moved from her face, focusing once again on the world beyond the window. "I would like to think so. But now that I find the shock of my rebirth diminishing, I wonder about the world I am now a part of. Last eve, the cars, the ele… ele… the box that moved, the device that you spoke in to… I am discovering myself overcome with it all. 'Tis an amazing, alien world that I find myself in."

"And you're afraid?"

He shook his head. "Nay, lady, not afraid. But I am wary. How would you feel if you woke up in my time, alone and disoriented and misplaced?"

Rory pondered his question a moment. "I would think I was dreaming. Or crazy. And then I would be afraid."

He smiled at her honestly. "I did think I was dreaming when I awoke to a beautiful woman draped across my body. Even as you find my resurrection an event of awe and disbelief, I find it the same. And I wonder if I made the correct choice, allowing the alchemist to work his magic on a man who was meant for death."

She sat on the end of the bed. "Are you thinking you were better off left in your own time, maybe? Dying for a cause you believed in?"

He cast her a glance, his smile becoming an ironic gesture. "At least I understand my time. I do not know if I want to understand yours."

"Why not?"

He shrugged, turning away from the window. "You will not even tell me what a bathroom is. Is it so mysterious that I will not comprehend?"

She laughed. "I apologize for that. Would you like a demonstration?"

He grinned. "That, my lady, would be appreciated. And this lever that gives and takes light. You will explain that, too."

☙

BREAKFAST HAD BEEN an interesting experience. The landlord and his wife served a simple but plentiful fare, scrambled eggs with tomatoes and cheese, ham slices and toast with homemade jams. Still in his green scrubs, Kieran ignored his fork and wolfed down at least a dozen eggs with his spoon as Rory and the hotel proprietors watched in wonder. Tea was served, something Kieran was unfamiliar with, and Rory prepared it for him with milk and sugar as the English drank it.

He loved the tea. In fact, he loved everything set before him and

Rory was rather embarrassed by his enormous appetite. Considering the man hadn't eaten in eight hundred years, she suggested he go slowly but he scoffed at the idea. Her breakfast finished, she sat back with her tea and watched as Kieran polished off several slices of raisin bread, glancing about the table as if looking for more to eat.

When his searching gaze came to rest on her astonished expression, she burst into laughter and he demanded to know the source of her humor. Giving him the orange off her plate, which was also very new to him and quite delicious, he finally seemed satisfied. At least, for the moment. But she had to admit, she was dreading lunch.

The day was progressing as they went back to their room. Rory knew she had to contact Bud but was reluctant to do so considering she still wasn't sure how she was going to break the news to him. She continued to ponder the dilemma as they entered their room, moving for the phone by the bed and wondering if she was brave enough to make the call.

Seated on the edge of the mattress, she glanced at Kieran as he picked at the green scrub 'shoes' on his feet, her focus turning to the fact that the man was in a sorry state of dress. All thoughts of Bud aside, there were more pressing matters in need of attention.

"We've got to get you some clothes," she said. "You can't continue to walk around looking like the Jolly Green Giant."

He cocked an eyebrow. "The last person to call me a giant met with an unfortunate accident. My fist accidentally met with his jaw."

Rory giggled. "I meant it as a figure of speech, Sir Kieran. I wasn't openly insulting you. Although…"

He held up a warning finger. "Tread carefully, lady. My size is not to be trifled with."

She went to find her purse. "Good Lord, no," she exclaimed, removing her wallet and digging through her credit cards. "Although you must have been a sight in your day. As large as two men put together. Oh, here it is."

She pulled forth the piece of green plastic she had used to pay for their room. He peered at the shiny square with the strange writing. "I find it amazing that your small card was able to pay for our lodgings. Is it somehow like a signet ring, insuring faith that you will pay the proprietor his money at a later time?"

"Sort of." She put the card at the front of her wallet and put the wallet back in her purse. "It represents a credit account. The hotel owner bills the credit card company and they bill me. I pay them, and… oh, hell, this is confusing. But trust me, this is as good as currency."

His brow furrowed as he digested her words. "Coinage? Plate?"

"Not really. We use paper money these days. Each piece of paper represents a certain amount of hard currency. Gold. It beats having to carry around a lot of heavy coins and jewelry."

He nodded in understanding. "Indeed. Then if you have paper currency, what exactly is this American Spress Card?"

She grinned. "American Express. It's really just a credit card named after the country with the greatest debt ratio in the world."

He was back to his puzzled expression. "Since I would assume you do not mean Express, where is American?"

"America," she corrected him again. "It's where I'm from. Didn't you notice my strange accent?"

He shrugged. "I merely assumed it was another bizarre aspect of this age you live in. But I must say that sometimes you are very difficult to understand. You speak very quickly."

She laughed, turning away from him as she began planning their day. "I'll try to remember to slow down. But now, we've got to find a department store." Heading for the door, she motioned him to follow. "Well, come along. Those scrubs aren't going to stay in one piece for much longer. Besides, they make people stare at you. And we don't need to attract any more attention."

He held the door as she walked through, taking a moment to flip the light switch on and off a couple of times. He was still fascinated with light bulbs. "Where are we going?"

"Shopping." She grabbed his hand, forcing him to give up the light switch and close the door. Walking down the hall towards the stairs, Kieran enfolded her hand in his massive palm.

"Will we eat again when we are finished?"

She had to chuckle. "Yes, we will. Is that all you care about? What about the fact that you don't have any clothes to wear?"

They descended the stairs. Rory saw the landlord's wife in the den and was preparing to ask the woman the location of the nearest department store when Kieran squeezed her hand gently.

"You will take care of me, my lady," he said. "I suspect you have been doing so now for several days."

His smile melted her to the core.

FORTNUM AND MASON was a top-notch department store near Piccadilly Circus, not far from their hotel. It would have been close enough to walk but Rory wanted to get there as quickly as possible; Kieran was attracting quite a bit of attention in the daylight with his bright green clothing and Rory was desperate to get him into something less conspicuous. Taking the bus line the short jaunt, she tugged him inside the store as he gaped at everything from the bus they had ridden in to the punk rockers with bright purple hair.

Rory suspected that she was going to have quite a bill on her hands before all was said and done. Finding the men's department, she kept a tight grip on Kieran as she found a stack of jeans and began searching for what she hoped was the correct size. As Kieran touched the shirts, commenting on the terrible style and lack of quality, she found several pairs of jeans and shoved him into the nearest dressing room.

She tried to keep the salesman away from him as she went in search of a shirt. She was terrified that the man would do something in his attempt to help a man who would undoubtedly consider being cornered in a dressing room a challenge to his personal safety. So she pulled the salesman with her, asking that he help her select a few shirts for her, uh, husband. While the salesman was busy finding shirts that would complement Kieran's massive frame, Rory heard a hissing noise from the dressing room.

Kieran was waving her over, trying to hide himself in the process. Rory went to him, concern etched on her face, when he suddenly reached out and pulled her into his stall. Closing the door, he turned to face her.

The fly of his jeans was unfastened and Rory's cheeks immediately grew hot. But he didn't notice her chagrin, instead, indicating the very area she was trying to avoid.

"These hose…" He struggled with the button-down fly. "They are unlike anything I have ever seen. How do I…?"

Rory maneuvered past him, no easy feat in the tiny dressing room, and opened the door. "I'll find you ones with the zipper-front," she said, trying to note the fit of the jeans without catching sight of his bulging manhood. "Uh… how do they seem to fit?"

"Well enough." He shifted around in them; they were supposed to be relaxed fit, but his waist was so small and his legs so massive that they ended up fitting him snuggly. In fact, they looked rather good and Rory turned away, hoping her blush wasn't too obvious.

"I'll be back," she muttered as she closed the door. "And with some underwear, for Heaven's sake."

It didn't take long to collect everything she had come for; briefs, two pairs of socks, three shirts, a belt, and an expensive pair of American-made blue jeans. The sale was more than she had intended to pay. But having no choice, she charged it all on the American Express. Kieran thought his new clothes were rather nice, different than what he was used to, but nice all the same. Once he learned to work the zipper on the jeans, he didn't seem to mind the odd clothing in the least.

Finding the shoe department was the next step in her long string of excessive charges. Entering the large section that smelled of leather and new carpet, Rory knew the knight presented a strange picture; new clothes, unshaven, spikey-haired, running around in his socks. Nonetheless, the saleslady in the shoe department sold him a moderately-priced pair of work boots, of which he seemed to admire more than the new clothes. And the steel-toe in the boots had his undying admiration.

Purchases complete, they passed through the fragrance department on their way out but the lure of a free duffle bag with purchase caught Rory's attention. Charging the Italian designer aftershave, she collected her free duffle bag and struggled to get out of the store before the total on her account reached four digits. But Kieran, dressed in his jeans, a collarless shirt made of burgundy cotton, and his new work boots, stopped at every counter they passed. Perfume, jewelry, handbags… nothing escaped his curiosity.

So Rory humored him, explaining the concept of costume jewelry and glass diamonds, hosiery that was nothing like the hosiery he knew, and cash registers that beeped and printed out marvelous slips of paper. And the light bulbs, too; all of the wonderful light bulbs had him fascinated like a kid at Christmas.

She somehow managed to maneuver him away from the hanging light fixtures and towards the exit when they passed through the junior miss department. Alternately appalled and intrigued by the collection of short summer dresses on clearance, he scowled at Rory when she showed interest in a particular garment. But he quickly changed his mind when he thought of her in it.

So she bought the dress. And a few other things she didn't need, but Kieran had shown interest in them and she somehow found the will to spend the money. Besides, he looked so unbelievably great in his new clothes that she felt it necessary to keep up with him. And the fact that she wanted to please him was a contributing factor as well, whether or not she was willing to admit it.

Rory was carrying all of the packages herself by the time they reached the exit, nearly out the door when she realized she was alone. Searching frantically for Kieran, her gaze came to rest on him as he wandered among the racks of fine lingerie several feet away. With a blustery sigh, she went in pursuit.

"Now what are you doing?" she demanded quietly.

He was examining a see-through nightie closely. "What are these things, Libby?"

"It's called lingerie," she said with limited patience. "It's for women. To sleep in, to have sex in, or whatever. Now, can we go?"

He moved to the next rack in response, coming across a beautiful white nightgown with a matching robe. It was sheer, sexy, and cost eighty-five American dollars.

"Hmm. This is lovely," he commented, holding it up to gain a better look.

"Yeah," she said shortly. "Lovely and expensive. Can we please go now?"

He continued to examine the finery. "Do you have such a garment?"

There was something in his tone that cooled her irritation. As much as the man fascinated her and as much as she had professed her love for him, the thought of intimacy frightened her. Her love for him had nothing to do with sex, but more to do with emotion. Still, as the reality of Kieran's living presence deepened, it was difficult not to ponder the eventuality of physical contact.

"No," she said, turning away. "I don't have any use for something like that."

He followed her. "You will buy this."

She froze. Turning slowly, she fixed him in the eye. "I told you, I don't have any use for it. Now, come on. It's close to lunchtime. You wanted to eat, didn't you?"

"I would rather see you in this." His reply was soft.

Rory's limbs went weak. Clutching her packages with a death grip, her breathing began to come in short pants. Good Lord, she simply couldn't... could she?

"I don't have any more money," she said finally.

He didn't argue the point, but she could sense his disappointment. Putting the nightgown back, he followed her from the store and out into the brilliant sunlight.

CHAPTER TWELVE

T HE LONDON STREET was alive with people going about their business and Kieran decided, now that he had the proper shoes, that walking back to the hotel was a good idea. Moreover, it would give him a closer look at the city he had once known. The England he had risked his life for. Rory agreed, but not before she handed him the packages he had obviously considered beneath his station to carry.

While Kieran stared and pointed and asked questions, Rory was on the lookout for a tea house. Lunch wasn't a big meal in England, as she had been told, and suspected their best bet for getting something to eat would be in either a pub or a tea shop. Finding a quaint little business down the street from the department store, she sat Kieran down at a table on the fragrant patio and went inside to order tea and scones.

Knowing the appetite he had displayed earlier, Rory ordered six fruit scones, clotted cream and fruit, and a large pot of tea. Carrying it to the table on a tray, she set it down and took a seat opposite the knight. He watched her closely as she broke open the scone and spread it with cream, pouring his own tea and imitating the milk and sugar as she had done at breakfast.

Once he had a taste of the scones, however, Rory was only able to eat half of her own before he ate everything on the tray. Ordering more tea and more scones, she returned to the table only to find him staring at her.

"What's wrong?" she asked, somewhat sarcastically. "Didn't I get enough?"

He took a scone and broke it open, nearly crumbling it until Rory came to the rescue. As she salvaged the biscuit, he continued to stare at her.

"I was merely thinking," he said as she passed him his broken scone.

"About what?"

He took a bite, chewing thoughtfully. "About the future. And what is to become of me after I have completed my mission."

Rory looked up from preparing her own scone. Not an entirely odd question considering she had been pondering that very same problem only minutes earlier. "What do you mean?"

He shrugged, still eating. "Exactly that. I find myself in a world that is nothing as I ever dreamed it would be, a complete stranger in the land of my birth. Tell me, Libby; is there a knighthood today?"

She shook her head. "Not as you knew it. There are knights, but it is mostly a symbolic title. Modern-day knights are soldiers in the military, or cops on the street, but it's nothing like you knew it to be."

He pondered her statement, moving for another scone. "What are 'cops on the street'?"

"Police officers. Men and women who enforce the law of the country."

That concept wasn't entirely foreign. "I see. And this military; you speak of the king's troops?"

She smiled faintly. "The queen's troops, Sir Kieran. A woman has ruled England for forty years."

He raised an eyebrow, a look she equated with the arrogant male ego inside every man. "A woman? And what is this woman's name?"

"Elizabeth," Rory replied. "She's an extremely capable and prestigious monarch. But her children…"

She shook her head and Kieran nodded in understanding. "I see nothing changes from century to century. Do they plot against her?"

She laughed. "Not as far as I know."

"Do they vie for her power? Seek to turn the country against her rule?"

Rory continued to laugh. "No, no. They're just… colorful, that's all. They're not a vicious band of petty royals like you've come to know."

He finished his seventh scone. "All royals are petty, greedy and unscrupulous. Except for Richard, of course."

"What?" Rory scoffed in outrage. "He plotted against his father, for God's sake."

"That was different. Henry was an incompetent ruler. Unscrupulous himself."

She shook her head. "Oh, brother. I can see where this conversation is going to wind up."

He was munching on another scone. "What do you mean?"

She smirked, downing the last of her scone before he could steal it. "It means that Richard can do no wrong in your eyes no matter what history proves. You'll defend him until the end."

"He is my king," Kieran's voice was considerably softer. "'Tis right that I defend him. 'Til the death, if necessary."

The mood suddenly took a downturn. Sensing the dampened ambience, Rory watched the man as he set his half-eaten scone to the plate, drinking what was left in his cup. When he settled back against the chair and allowed his gaze to rove the small garden against the shop wall, Rory set her own cup down.

"Before we got off the subject, you asked what was going to become of you," she said, her chin resting on her palm. "All I can tell you is that I don't know. But considering I dug you up and somehow roused you from your eternal sleep, I feel responsible for you. So until the situation changes, you'll stay with me."

He looked away from the garden, his gaze drinking in the beautiful, chestnut-haired woman with the wide, hazel eyes. Not strangely, the prospect of staying with her was not an unpleasant one. Nor was it a surprising suggestion, considering it was her kiss that had roused him.

A kiss from the one who loved him best.

"You are most gracious, my lady," he said, his gem-clear eyes glittering in the soft sunlight. "I look forward to our time together."

She cocked an eyebrow, ever-prepared to take advantage of any situation to further her cause. First her mother, then with Bud, now with Kieran. She simply couldn't let the opportunity pass. "Enough to let me help you find the crown?"

He didn't grow defensive as he had done previously when the crown was mentioned. After a moment, he shrugged his shoulders. "It is the one task I must complete now that I have been awakened. My sole reason for existing on this earth. You will forgive me if I again decline."

Rory's face darkened. "Why?"

"Because it is my burden alone."

The mood that had been soft and gentle, warm and interesting was abruptly shaded with fury. Rory smacked the table with an open palm as she faced off against him. "No, it's not. I thought we discussed this earlier."

He refused to give in to her anger. "Nay, lady, you discussed it earlier. My conviction has always been the same; I will retrieve it alone and return it to England as I had intended eight hundred years ago."

She gasped in disbelief, her cheeks mottled with resentment. "Not a moment ago, you were lamenting what was to become of you, thanking me when I offered to take care of you. So you think that you'll be able to travel to Israel alone to claim your crown? Think again, buster. You can't go anywhere without me!"

An eyebrow slowly lifted at her angry tone, her unbridled words. "I can and I will."

She was on her feet, agitated and completely ignorant of the other customers in the shop. "Why? Because you don't want me sharing in your glory?"

"I thought you weren't after glory."

In an indignant huff, Rory clumsily grabbed their bags and stormed from the shop. Kieran calmly finished his tea before following. He found her about a block down the street, marching determinedly through the crowds of London shoppers. Catching up to her, he reached out to grab her arm and ended up spilling several packages to the ground.

"Let go of me!" she snarled, struggling to collect the goods as he calmly assisted her. "Just... go away and leave me alone! Go and find your damned crown and I hope the next assassin who catches up to you is successful in his endeavor!"

She tried to move away from him but he held her firm. "Enough of your impudence, lady. I have my reasons for what I must do and I am sorry if you feel excluded."

She succeeded in yanking her arm away. "And I have my reasons, too, but you seem to only care for yourself." She swallowed hard as she met his steady brown eyes, horrified to realize that tears were close to the surface. "Your motives are no more important than mine. Don't you see? If I find the crown, I'll bring the profession of Biblical Archaeology to the forefront. The university will be the recipient of grants and funding, I will have proven that I'm not just a silly young doctor with outlandish theories, and my mother will finally be proud of me."

He stared at her. "Your mother?"

Rory tried to maintain her gaze, but her features crumbled and she turned away. Kieran grabbed her arm as she struggled weakly, her hands too full to wipe her tears.

"My... mother is a Doctor of Ministry," she said, her voice trembling. "I was her only child. Ever since I was young enough to understand, I knew my mother wanted me to make something great of myself. She's such a demanding person, Kieran, never satisfied. The more I achieved, the more she wanted. So I thought... I hoped that finding the Crown of Thorns, one of the most powerful biblical relics in history, would finally make her proud of me."

He took the packages from her, holding the bags in one hand and her in the other. "So this is the void you are trying to fill with the reclamation of the diadem?" he asked. "You seek to give your mother a reason to love you?"

She shrugged, wiping at her damp eyes. "I just never lived up to her standards. I always felt like such a failure no matter what I did."

His features were soft with compassion. "Then I know your feelings well. My father was much the same." He watched her as she struggled for a Kleenex in her purse, realizing more similarities between them. A mother who was looking for reasons to be proud of her daughter and a father who had been looking for reasons to be proud of his son. A son who had risked his life in the name of peace, pride, and glory. "Do you truly believe that the recovery of the diadem will mend all wounds between you and your mother?"

She shrugged, sniffling. She couldn't believe that she had actually confessed her deepest incentive for recovering the crown, the desperate reasoning of a neglected child finding a way to buy her parent's love. But it was something that had affected Rory her entire life and she truly knew no other way; at the root of the entire situation, her schooling, her determined motives, her search for the crown, was the very basic factor of a mother's ignorance.

Pity she hadn't asked Kieran what he knew of parental neglect. He would have been able to give her a good deal of personal, if not painful, insight.

"My mother became the first woman in the university's history to sit on the Board of Regents," she explained. "She was the one who convinced the board to approve funding for my dig in Nahariya. If I fail at this, not only will she look like a fool but it'll just cement the fact that I'll never be good enough at anything to please her. I... I just couldn't face that happening. Not when I've worked so hard."

He didn't reply for a moment, studying her delicious beauty as she struggled to compose herself. She was a proud woman and he could easily imagine the turmoil of her soul. To be so close to what she sought only to be denied. Aye, he knew well how she felt. He had been very close to completing an important task once himself, only to be cast off track by forces beyond his control. He could sympathize with her completely.

He kissed her gently on the forehead in understanding, in surrender. With every moment that passed, every tear that fell, he felt himself weakening towards her plight. It was obvious they both had a good deal invested in the elusive diadem and his resistance towards her aid was dissolving. In fact, Kieran was a firm believer in the powers of Fate. If God had permitted him to awaken in this time by a woman who knew of his duty all too well, then he would be a fool to refuse her assistance. Indeed, he would be a fool not to realize that God had placed her here for his use.

"You are not a failure, Libby," he said, pondering the will of God as he was coming to perceive it. "You found me, did you not?"

It sounded like an egotistical statement, but it was the truth. "Yes, I found you." She wiped at her nose, the thrill of his tender kiss almost enough to make her forget her tears. "But no one will ever believe that you and the knight I dug up at Nahariya are one and the same."

"Aye, they will." He gave her a quick squeeze before leading her down the sidewalk. "And if they do not believe me, then I shall be forced to prove it."

She dried the last of her tears, casting him a wary look. "What does that mean?"

He simply grinned, his dimples carving a deep path into each cheek. "Why, I shall be forced to defend your word, of course. Do men fight with broadswords these days? I notice that no one carries a weapon. And I see no armor, either."

She smiled weakly. "No one carries a sword any longer. Just guns."

His brow furrowed. "What are guns? Furthermore, what is this university you spoke of earlier? And why would your mother want to sit on a board when there are finer chairs for ladies made available? These references are most confusing, Libby."

She sighed, preparing to launch into what would undoubtedly become another long, painfully detailed conversation as they made their way back to the hotel.

❧

"RORY, WHERE IN the hell are you?" Bud was trying to control himself.

Seated on the bed at the other end of the line, Rory struggled to brace herself for the ensuing conversation. But it was an increasingly difficult fight as she listened to the familiar comfort of Bud's voice. "I'm at a hotel and I'm fine. But I've got to talk to you."

Bud clapped his hand over his face in a gesture of disbelief and frustration. "Christ," he muttered. "I'll say you've got to talk to me. Tell me where in the hell you are and we'll talk in person."

"I can't, Bud. Not now. Will you please just listen to me?"

"Listen to you?" he was trying desperately not to explode. "Listen to what? More cryptic answers? Christ, I should have never let you go to the hospital alone. What in the hell was I thinking?"

"You were doing what I asked," she replied steadily. "Please calm down, Bud. I need your level head. Okay?"

He sighed heavily. What choice did he have? "All right, all right. So go ahead and tell me what happened after we parted last night."

She took a deep breath, contemplating her answer. Kieran was playing with the shower, having grown tired of the light switch. Rory watched him a moment before replying.

"I went to the morgue just like I said I was," she said. "And I... I broke into it."

On the other end of the line, Bud closed his eyes to the reality of her confession. "And then what, honey?"

There was no way to skirt the subject gracefully. Better that she simply jump into it and pray to God that he didn't think she was completely out of her mind. Her palms began to sweat as her grip on the receiver tightened.

"I only meant to say goodbye to Sir Kieran like I told you," she said quietly. "I'll admit, I'd had too much to drink and I wasn't thinking clearly. The morgue was closed for the night so I broke the receptionist's window to get in."

"And did you find him?"

"Yeah," her tone was growing increasingly soft. "He was in a drawer, naked. Can you believe that, Bud? His family even took his clothes. They took everything from him."

"I know, honey. Go on."

She swallowed, summoning the courage to continue. "So I said my goodbyes. And then I fell asleep on him because I was drunk and exhausted. And... Bud?"

"I'm here."

Oh, God. Here it comes. "When I woke up, he was moving."

There was a long, long pause on the line. "He was what?"

"Moving," she repeated, stumbling over her words. "I thought it was my imagination. At first, his eyes were open and I thought it was due to the change in climate and the deterioration of the body. But then... then he blinked. And before I realized what was happening, he spoke to me."

Bud didn't say anything. And then Rory heard what she thought was a moan.

"Rory, honey, where are you?"

He sounded exceptionally distressed and Rory felt her defenses go up. She could only imagine what he must be thinking.

"Look, Bud, I'm not insane. I'm not drunk, and I'm not imagining things. Sir Kieran wasn't dead; he's very much alive. And I'm sitting here looking at him."

Bud didn't reply. He didn't know what to say. But he had never felt so completely terrible in his entire life and before he could stop himself, his eyes began to water.

"Honey, just tell me where you are. Let me come and get you and I promise you won't be in any trouble. Please, baby. Just tell me where I can find you."

He's crying, Rory thought with anguish. The reality of Bud reduced to tears because he thought she had gone insane only set Rory into another emotional fit and she sobbed softly into the phone. "Bud, I'm not crazy. Please don't… please don't cry. I swear to you on the Holy Bible that Sir Kieran Hage wasn't dead when we found him. As he explained it, he was in some sort of stasis. Remember how beautifully preserved he was? The flexibility of his tissue, the lack of decomposition? It was because he wasn't dead at all; he was in suspended animation."

On the other end of the phone, Bud sniffled loudly, wiping at his face and struggling to maintain control. "Christ, Rory… I just can't go on with this conversation. Please, I'm begging you; tell me where you are. Let me come and get you."

She paused, noting that Kieran was watching her as she dabbed at her tears. She hadn't intended for Bud to see Kieran quite so soon, at least not before could amply prepare him, but she couldn't stand his misery. And she couldn't allow him to think that she had gone off the deep end into madness, thinking that somehow it was his fault by letting her go to the morgue alone. If seeing was believing, she would have to make Bud a believer for his own sake.

"All right," she whispered. "Go to Bloomsbury Square, near the museum. I'll meet you there in a half-hour."

She hung up the phone before she could hear any more of his sobs. When she looked up, Kieran was standing beside her.

"This Bud. Is he your husband?"

"No."

"Your lover, then."

"No," she stood up, going to get a tissue from the bathroom. "He's an archaeologist like me. And my friend. He was with me when we exposed your grave."

Kieran continued to stand beside the bed as she wiped her face, blew her nose, and repaired her damaged makeup. When she returned to the bedroom, he reached out to gently grab her arm as she passed by him.

"We are going to meet Bud?"

She nodded. "He the smartest man I know and I really think we could use his advice as to how to handle this… situation."

Kieran didn't let go of her arm. In fact, his massive fingers were caressing her flesh and Rory found herself forgetting all about Bud's misery. In truth, Kieran looked fairly miserable himself.

"What's the matter with you?"

He continued to hold her arm tenderly, somehow pulling her closer, and Rory was electrified by the sensations of his magnificent touch.

"I heard what you said," he said quietly. "Am I to understand… the place I awoke in was some sort of vault and you violated its security to see me? Is that why we left so quickly? Because you were afraid of the clops?"

"Cops," she corrected him.

He didn't acknowledge her subtle rectification, his brown gaze finding her luscious hazel eyes. "I may not be of this time, Lady Rory, but I understand a great deal. You were not supposed to be with me when I awoke, were you?"

She shook her head. "No."

"And you are in trouble because of me."

"I'm in trouble because I wanted to say goodbye to you and nothing could stand in my way, not your family or a locked morgue window."

He maintained his gaze, looking deep into her beautiful eyes. "With all else that has happened to me in the past several hours, I failed to understand the precise circumstances of my awakening. I comprehend now what you meant when you said you risked everything to raise me from the grave."

She could hardly breathe through the force of his hypnotic stare. "Only partly," she whispered. "After all, I found you and even though you officially became your family's property, I still felt attached to you. I… I just couldn't let you go that easily. I had to tell you goodbye before I left for home and never saw you again."

"Then why did my descendants take custody of me if I was your 'find', as you said?"

"I turned you over to them as a gesture of goodwill because you were their revered ancestor. And also because Bud convinced me that you would be better off in the country you had died for. It was where you belonged."

She had somehow moved closer to him, his other hand coming up to gently enclose her free arm. "Even if England is where I belong, you were reluctant to let me go."

She nodded unsteadily, feeling the heat and emotion between them like a raging vortex. "You were... mine."

He smiled faintly and her knees went weak; she literally had to catch herself from falling. All of the enchantment and wonder she had felt for him since the moment she had uncovered him was multiplying by the moment. Her respiration began to come in sharp pants, her limbs aching from the magic of his touch. When he began to gently stroke her cheek with his thumbs, she thought she might faint from pure pleasure.

"And you love me?"

She heard the question, responding before she could form a rational denial. "I do," she breathed. "God, I do. I always have."

His smile broadened. Rory hardly realized that she had been pulled against his massive body, feeling his flesh and warmth envelope her like a glove. Gone was the fear of his intimacy, the earlier thoughts of confusion and distress. In fact, she found herself wishing she had bought that over-priced negligee; never in her life had she felt more fulfilled, more satisfied, or more complete. As if, always, this was meant to be.

And then he kissed her.

But it was no ordinary kiss. It was a raging promise of passion, a silent vow of a timeless desire were she only to submit. Rory responded immediately, as if she had never known another man's kiss but his. Scorching, heated, tongues intertwining with mesmerizing power; Rory felt it all, sensed it all. When Kieran's arms wrapped around her, she knew at last she had found what she had been searching for.

She was hardly aware when he lifted her from the ground and carried her to the bed. Suddenly, she was on her back and his mouth was all over her face, her neck, suckling gently on her ears. His massive body was warm and protective and comforting and she could feel his hands moving to her breasts, touching the exposed skin of her abdomen and causing her to gasp in response. He growled low in his throat, his fingers moving underneath her shirt. And then he stopped.

"What is this?" he demanded huskily.

He was fingering her bra. Rory was about to undo the fastens when a brief flash of sanity reminded her that she had asked Bud to meet her in the square. Panting like a dog in heat, she looked to her watch and groaned.

"No, Kieran… we can't," she murmured, trying to roll away from him. "We've got to meet Bud."

He kept her on the bed, nuzzling her neck. "I would rather do this."

She was grasping for composure, sucking in her breath sharply when his hot, wet lips found her earlobe. "No," she grunted in a last show of strength. "Please, Kieran. We have to see Bud. It's important."

He raised his head to look at her, his beautiful brown eyes glazed with passion. "More important than this? It has been at least eight hundred years since I last had a woman. Would you deny me now?"

There was something in that question she didn't like. Brow furrowed, she pushed herself away from him and regained her feet. He rolled onto his side, watching her with a lazy smile.

"Look," she said pointedly. "I don't care how long it's been since you last had a woman. I'm not here to service you like some whore. I'm not obligated to relieve your needs in any way, shape or form."

He raised an eyebrow. "I never said you were. But you said you loved me and I was allowing you to demonstrate that love."

He couldn't have possibly said anything worse. Rory stared at him as if she hadn't heard correctly; then, she whirled on her heel and stormed towards the bathroom.

Kieran was on his feet before she took two steps. For as large as he was, he was as agile as a cat and Rory took a swing at him when he tried to stop her. He easily avoided the blow, grasping both of her hands to prevent from being further assaulted.

"Why are you angry with me? I simply said…"

"I heard what you said, you conceited bastard," she snarled, struggling within his grip. "How dare you twist my words? Words you coerced from me, no less."

"Hold, lady," he said with his usual composure. "I did not coerce anything from you. I merely asked a question; 'twas your choice to answer."

She was furious. Managing to yank one hand away, she struggled viciously to pull away. But he refused to let go and she tried to hit him again. Deftly, and quite calmly, he sidestepped her and spun her around all in the same gesture so that she ended up facing away from him. Wrapping his massive arms around her body, he effectively trapped her.

"Now," he breathed in her ear. "You will cease this tantrum. I did not mean to insult you with my factual words and if you were offended, I will apologize. Surely you sensed my want to exceed your own."

She calmed somewhat, her brow furrowed with the gist of his words. He had apologized in an offhanded way and she wasn't sure if she should maintain her fury or not. Taking deep breaths to steady her furor, she realized that she was no match for him physically. The deep breathing also served to ease the lust rising within her breast as a result of his lips on her ear.

"I'm still not going to sleep with you," she grumbled, knowing it was a lie. As easily as she had given in, it wouldn't take much for her to surrender a second time.

"But you slept with me last night. I was on the floor and you were…"

She shook her head in frustration. "No, I didn't mean that. I meant that… that I won't let you bed me."

He didn't say anything for a moment, his breath hot on her ear.

"But if you love me…"

Her anger was on the move again. "Just because I said I love you doesn't mean I'm willing to have sex at your beck and call. And I refuse to be taken advantage of by a man who hasn't had a woman in eight hundred years."

He let her go then and she turned to face him. To her surprise, he looked somewhat bothered. "You… you believe I would take advantage of the woman who resurrected me?"

"I think you would try if I let you," she said, eyeing him for a moment. "And who said I resurrected you? We still don't know what actually woke you up."

He turned away, running his fingers through hair that needed to be washed. "I know," he murmured. "I have always known."

All thoughts of anger vanished like a puff of smoke. Rory reached out, grabbing him by the arm for a change. "You have? Good Lord, why didn't you tell me?"

He smiled weakly. "I do not know. Mayhap the time was never right." When she looked particularly puzzled, he gently cupped her chin in one massive palm. "You awoke me with your kiss, Libby. The alchemist told me that I would only be awakened by a kiss bestowed from the one who loved me best. And that, my dear lady, was you."

She was astonished. "Then you've known all along… I mean, you've known how… how you awoke?"

He nodded. "You were right when you said that I belonged to you. I am yours in more ways than we can possibly comprehend."

Rory didn't know whether to feel exceptionally embarrassed or incredibly amazed. She continued to stare at him, speechless, when he suddenly bent down to kiss her gently.

"Come along, Libby," he said. "I suspect your Bud is waiting for us already. Oh… and Libby?"

"Hmm?" she snapped from her daze. "What?"

"The showder. I do believe it would be a good idea to bathe when we return."

Her brow furrowed a moment, accepting her purse when he hand-ed it to her. "If you are referring to the shower, who did you mean it would be a good idea to bathe; you or me?"

He grinned, moving for the door. "Considering I have not had a bath in eight hundred years, I am sure I could benefit from the use of water. And a shave, too."

She slung her purse over her shoulder, following him into the hall. "Then we'll have to stop at the drugstore and get you some shaving cream and a razor. Or I think they call it a chemist in England."

"Chemist?" he cocked an eyebrow suspiciously. "As in al-chemist?"

She laughed. "Good Lord, I hope not. It's just a place where you can buy personal products like toothpaste, hairbrushes, deodorant and... you don't understand one thing that I've said, do you?"

He shook his head ruefully. "Again, you speak too quickly and in terms I cannot comprehend. Really, Libby, you must show me more consideration."

The sunlight was bright, fading into late afternoon as they exited the hotel. Kieran took her hand, holding it tightly, and Rory smiled warmly into his beautiful, stubbled face. Odd how she didn't seem to recall the anger she had felt for him earlier, but rather the warmer emotions he so easily evoked.

"I'll try," she said.

"You are exceptionally impolite."

"I know. And you're a conceited bastard. Doesn't that somehow make us more compatible?"

He laughed. "Either that, or we shall surely kill one another."

Kissing her hand, he led her off into the sunshine.

KIERAN HAD BEEN right. Bud was already waiting at the square when they approached and Rory caught sight of him before he saw her. Seating Kieran on a bench and asking him to give her a moment before joining the conversation, she made her way through the clusters of tourists and Londoners until she came upon him. Having his back to her and his hands in his pockets as he urgently scanned the area for Rory's familiar face, her hand on his arm startled the hell out of him.

"Christ!" Bud exclaimed, immediately pulling her into a crushing embrace. "Rory, honey, are you all right?"

She let him hold her a moment before pulling away, trying to smile at his pale, shadowed face. He looked as if he hadn't slept in days.

"I'm fine," she assured him. "But you look awful."

He shrugged weakly. "I never did sleep well in a strange bed." His gaze licked her from head to toe. "Christ, I'm so glad you're here. Are you really all right? Have you eaten?"

She nodded patiently, trying to disengage his iron grip. "Yes, Bud, I'm really fine and I've eaten. God, there's so much to tell. So much to…"

He refused to release her, keeping a tight hold on her arm. "I know, honey, I know. But tell me first; where's Sir Kieran?"

She met his gaze steadily. "He'll be here in a minute. But I wanted to see you first, alone. We've got a real problem on our hands."

He shook his head slowly. "More than you know. Look, honey, Steven Corbin wants to talk to you. Just talk, okay? He came to see me this morning before I actually knew you had… oh, hell, where did you store the body?"

She frowned. "Didn't you hear one word I said, Bud? I didn't store him anywhere because he doesn't need to be stored. He's a living, breathing, walking human being and I've spent the past fifteen hours with him to verify that fact."

Bud's expression took on a look of incredible sadness, his rough hand coming up to gently touch her head. After a moment, he sighed. "Listen to me, Rory. I know how much he meant to you, but all of this stuff about him coming to life… honey, no matter how badly you wanted such a thing in order to find out what he did with your crown, it just isn't possible. Maybe those drinks last night hit you harder than you thought and you've simply been imagining the whole thing."

Her tolerance was brittle and she struggled to maintain her composure. "Bud, I swear to you, I didn't imagine anything. I thought I had at first, of course; I mean, corpses just don't come to life. It's a scientific impossibility. But Kieran explained that he wasn't actually dead, only in a suspended state because of his wound."

Bud's expression was the supreme example of skepticism. When he should have been throwing her over his shoulder and heading for the nearest shrink, he found himself willing to humor her because she seemed to truly believe what she was saying. Christ, the lengths he would go to for this woman.

"His wound?"

She nodded. "He had been mortally wounded by assassins and sought out a man he believed to be a physic. But the old guy wasn't a physic at all, but an alchemist who gave him a potion to put him in some sort of a stasis. And then the man gave him medicines that healed his wound without conventional skills. It's the most amazing thing I've ever heard."

Bud sighed heavily; Rory knew the look. He didn't believe a word she was saying and she put her hands against his chest, pleading with the man inside that was so desperately in love with her. She knew she shouldn't be cruel by encouraging that aspect of Bud's psyche, but she had to make him listen somehow. She had to make him understand.

"Please, Bud," she begged. "I'm not making this up. When you see him, you'll know I'm telling the truth."

He felt the warmth of her hands against his skin, feeling himself relenting. And the look in her eyes was enough to weaken him completely. "Oh... hell, Rory. Are you listening to yourself? How can you ask me to believe something like that?"

She sighed patiently. "Because it's true. I didn't want to believe it, either, but it's true. Bud, aren't you the least bit willing to believe that there are forces at work in the world that we can't possibly comprehend? Like ghosts and UFOs and reincarnation?"

He shook his head as if baffled by the entire conversation. "How did we get onto the subject of UFOs? I'm talking about a knight you stole and a family who wants him back. In case you haven't realized it, you're in a lot of trouble."

She looked at him. Hard. Dislodging his grip, she stood back and pondered her next move. "All right," her voice was strangely hoarse. "So if I stole the knight, then explain how I carried a two hundred pound body out of the morgue all by myself?"

"You told me that you had run into an old friend. You could have had his help."

"The old friend I was referring to was Kieran. And even if I'd had help, don't you think someone from the hospital staff would have stopped me? I mean, what would be more conspicuous than two people carrying a dead body between them?"

Bud's gaze was equally hard as he met her challenging expression. "You're very convincing, Rory. You can make anybody do anything you want if you've set your mind to it."

Her countenance softened somewhat, her eyes taking on a look of distinct hurt. "What you mean to say is I'm manipulative."

He cocked an eyebrow. "Yes, you are. But I've ignored that aspect of your personality because you have so many other good qualities."

Rory maintained his gaze a moment longer before looking away, feeling entirely rotten. After a moment, she sighed. "I'm not manipulative on purpose, Bud. I guess… I guess I have more of my mother in me that I care to admit. I see how she deals with people and I do the same thing. She's bold and aggressive, and I try to be, too."

Bud softened ever-so-slightly. "Your mother is a hard woman, Rory. I know that she's pushed you and pushed you until you'll do anything you have to simply to satisfy her. But you've got to realize, honey, that you don't have to manipulate the people who love you. They'll do anything for you simply because you're you."

She looked to him again, her gaze veiled with guilt. "Like you?"

He nodded, a smile coming to his lips. "Like me. You don't have to try and sell me this cock-and-bull story just because you want me to defend you against Sir Kieran's family. I'll defend you regardless, but you've got to tell me the truth. That's all I'll ever ask of you, honey. The truth."

She met his smile weakly, moving towards him once again. This time, she grasped his hand and squeezed it gently. "I've told you the truth. The honest-to-God truth. Sir Kieran came alive before my very eyes and he's waiting on that park bench over there to meet you."

The warmth in Bud's expression faded. "Rory…"

"Please?" she begged, tugging him with her. "Please see the reality of what I'm telling you. If I was lying, do you think I'd be so eager for you to meet him face to face?"

He let her pull him forward, across the cement and through the grass of the square. There were people milling about busily but Bud didn't notice; he was thinking what a fool he was. Humoring Rory so she wouldn't run away from him again by allowing her to carry on with this ridiculous story. He didn't think she was crazy as much as he believed she was trying to worm her way out of trouble.

And he was helping her. But as long as she remained within his custody, he almost didn't care. They would face the trouble together.

CHAPTER THIRTEEN

THERE WERE QUITE a few people in Bloomsbury Square as Rory towed Bud behind her like a reluctant child. There were so many people going about their business, in fact, that Rory didn't see the bench she'd left Kieran on until she was nearly on it. When she immediately realized it was vacant, she let go of Bud in a panic.

"Oh… no!" she began searching desperately for the knight. "He was here, Bud. Right here! I left him here!"

He wasn't really surprised that the bench was empty. In fact, it only served to reinforce his belief in the stupidity of her story. When she leapt onto the bench to gain a better view of the surrounding square, he moved up beside her and gently, but firmly, grasped her arm.

"Was he really here, Rory?" he reached up and tapped her head. "Or here? Come on and get down. We're going back to the hotel."

"No!" She struggled furiously as he pulled her from the bench. "I'm not going anywhere until I find him. Maybe… maybe he went back to the hotel. Maybe something upset him and he's gone back."

He had her with two hands, realizing they were attracting some attention. "Calm down, Rory, you're causing a scene. Let's just go back to the hotel and…"

She succeeded in pulling one hand free, trying to free the other. "I said I'm not going anywhere until I find him. Let me go, Bud!"

He was really struggling to keep a grip on her without looking as if he were trying to assault her. "Honey, just relax. Let me take you back to our hotel and we'll figure out how to deal with the Hage family. You don't have to…"

She suddenly broke free, racing towards the street. Bud followed and, having been a running back in college, was on her heels in no time. But she dashed across the asphalt before he could get to her and Bud almost got plastered by a car in his haste to pursue. Waiting for the car to pass, he continued after her at breakneck speed.

LINGERING BY THE edges of the square, a man dressed casually in slacks and a shirt hastened to a black Mercedes parked on the opposite side of the street. Leaping into the passenger side, he nodded to the man in the driver's seat.

"Follow Dietrich," he commanded. "Maybe she's heading for wherever she may be hiding out."

"Do you think she has the body with her?"

Corbin shrugged as the driver threw the car into gear and swung a wide U-turn. "Probably. But even if she doesn't, we'll find out where she's hidden it. Or Dietrich will tell us if he knows. Certainly, somebody will tell us when I use the beautiful young archaeologist as an object of discovery."

The man in the back seat with more flab than muscle chuckled sinisterly as his cohort directed the car down Bedford Place in pursuit of the Americans. "Discovery of what?"

Corbin didn't say anything for a moment, his piercing blue eyes searching for the fleeing figures. "Niles, the Hage family is paying me a good deal of money to protect their interests in Sir Kieran. Not only did I threaten an international lawsuit against Osgrove's university in order to gain the family their rightful ancestor, but now that Dr. Rory has been foolish enough to steal what no longer belongs to her, I suspect there is more behind her motive to abduct Sir Kieran Hage than Dietrich is telling us."

"You think they're hiding something?" the driver asked just as the three men caught sight of Bud disappearing into a small two-story hotel.

His driver parking the car, Corbin studied the structure a moment before turning to his associates.

"They are," he said frankly, turning to fix his colleagues with a heady gaze. "Or Sir Kieran is."

The fat man in the back seat looked particularly dubious. "What in the hell could an old corpse be hiding? We watched when he was stripped down yesterday and examined by those other doctors. There's nothing on his body at all."

Corbin shrugged. "Nothing we saw, at any rate. But remember, the Americans have had the body for several days. Maybe they've had time to discover something we haven't yet come across. Or, better still, maybe there is something actually inside the body they want to keep from us."

The driver looked interested as his counterpart shook his head. "Jesus, Steven, do you think they've smuggled something into the country inside of the knight's body? Why in the bloody hell would they do that?"

Again, Corbin shrugged and opened his door. "I don't know. But I intend to find out. Clearly, there is more to this situation than meets the eye."

IT WAS A short chase down the quiet street. Rory immediately disappeared into a small building about halfway down the block and Bud followed her into what was apparently a small hotel. Ignoring the wide-eyed woman at the desk and several people seated in a large living area to his left, he made way for the stairs directly before him and pounded to the second floor.

He caught sight of Rory just as she disappeared into a door about midway down the corridor. Before she could lock it, he was behind her, shoving it open with such force that she shrieked with surprise. The door swung open, banging against the wall, and the sight of Rory's astonished face was the last thing Bud saw before stars exploded in his head.

And then it was dark. Sort of. He thought he heard Rory's voice, her warm hands on his face. Bud blinked, thinking he must have struck his head somehow but having no idea what, exactly, he had hit. Gradually, the stars began to fade and he realized he was lying flat on his back. Shaking his head, he was about to ask what had happened when a rumbling male voice infiltrated his dazed mind.

"It was a trap, my lady," the voice said grimly. "God's Blood, I should have suspected. Are you well? Has he harmed you?"

Trying to support Bud's head, Rory frowned at Kieran. "What trap? You're not making sense, Kieran. And you didn't have to hit him."

Kieran's stubbled face was flushed with emotion, his massive hands working. "He was a threat to you. I had no choice."

"Bud is not a threat."

"But he is working with them. He must be."

"Working for who, for God's sake?"

Kieran didn't say anything, watching Bud try to blink some clarity into his vision. Swallowing hard, he went to the door and peered down the hall as if expecting someone. Rory watched him closely, noticing his whole body was taut with anticipation. As if he were preparing for a fight.

Or his death.

"Kieran," she demanded, still holding Bud. "What's wrong?"

He maintained his post by the door, his eyes riveted to the staircase at the far end of the corridor. After several tense moments, he entered the room and closed the door behind him. Throwing the bolt, he went directly to the window and peered outside. Rory continued to observe him, curious and apprehensive at the same time.

"Kieran, please," she said again. "What are you looking for? Why did you leave the square when I told you to wait for me?"

He finally looked to her, his features uncharacteristically hard. Then, he left the window only to hover over both her and Bud as if he were some sort of horrific avenging angel. Rory gazed up at him, frightened for reasons she didn't understand. But the mere expression on his face scared her to death.

"Because I saw him. I instinctively returned for my sword when I remembered I no longer had it within my possession. But you were in no danger for the moment and I was confident I could return in time to defend us both."

She was understandably puzzled. "Defend us from whom?"

His jaw ticked. "Simon."

Rory's brow furrowed. Bud was growing more lucid and struggling to sit up, so she gently pushed him into a sitting position before replying.

"Kieran, you know that's impossible. Simon has been dead for eight hundred years."

"So was I."

"But you were different, you know that." As Bud rubbed his jaw, eyes closed against the spinning room, Rory stood up. "Are you saying that somehow Simon has managed to follow you though time? The chances of your survival were astronomical, but the chances of two of you surviving through potions or magic or miracles are completely ludicrous."

His expression remained hard as he gazed at her. "I know what I saw, lady. I saw Simon lingering by the edges of the square, shielding himself behind a post of some kind. He didn't see me, however; he was looking at you. You and at your... friend."

Bud opened his eyes, still working his jaw. His ears were ringing but his head had cleared somewhat and he suddenly found himself gazing at massive leather boots. Gaze trailing up the shoes, he digested the sight of massive thighs and an equally massive chest. When his ice-blue gaze came to rest on gems of clear brown, Rory watched him closely for his reaction.

"Uh... Bud, this is Sir Kieran Hage," she said, moving to stand in front of Kieran. Obviously, the knight didn't trust Bud and she was fearful of what he still might do to him. "Sir Kieran, this is Dr. Bud Dietrich."

Bud just stared at him. Rory bent over him, her expression a mixture of anxiety and compassion.

"See, Bud? I wasn't crazy. It's really him."

Bud's eyes never left Kieran as he rose to his knees. Rory watched apprehensively as he continued to rise to unsteady feet, his face completely pale and his eyes as wide as saucers. She moved away from Kieran and gripped Bud's arm supportively.

"Are you all right?" she asked. "Speak to me, Bud. Say something."

He blinked. Then, taking a deep breath, his jaw popped open. "Christ," he hissed. "Rory, this is... this is nuts! Who is this guy?"

Kieran cocked an eyebrow, a decidedly unfriendly gesture. Rory made sure she remained between the two men.

"I told you," she said patiently. "This is Sir Kieran Hage, the knight we excavated at Nahariya. He's alive, Bud, just like I said."

Bud shook his head slowly, with disbelief. "No... no way. It just isn't possible."

Rory sighed. "Yes, it is. Like I explained to you. An alchemist put him into a trance and I woke him up last night with... well, with a kiss."

Bud seemed to snap out of his daze somewhat, eyeing Rory as if she had gone completely mad. "This isn't some damned fairy tale, Rory. I don't know who this guy is, but he's got you convinced he's... Christ, this is completely insane. What in the hell has happened to your common sense?"

Behind her, Rory heard Kieran shift uneasily and she broke away from Bud, putting both hands on Kieran to prevent him from advancing on the outraged doctor. Obviously, Bud was unwilling to believe the evidence and she furiously searched for an explanation, or demonstration, that would make some sense to him. After a lengthy, uncomfortable pause, she suddenly grasped Kieran's hands.

"Look," she said, holding them up for Bud's inspection. "Remember the knight at the dig, how large his hands were? Take a look at these babies. Large enough to handle that broadsword we weighed in at thirty-three pounds."

Bud opened his mouth to refute her but she was on the move, unbuttoning Kieran's brand new shirt. Kieran was torn between his hostility towards Bud and the erotic gesture of Rory's hands undressing him. He settled for the neutral position of watching her curiously.

"Look here." Rory opened the shirt, exposing Kieran's broad chest. Her gentle fingers began to dance across the flesh as she spoke. "Look at the scars, Bud, from practicing for years with broadswords and maces and flails. And look how broad he is, rippled with raw muscle; no steroids in this body. And here; look at this huge scar. This is where all the blood came from that had stained his tunic and hose. Remember?"

Bud's expression clouded as he studied the enormous man, unwilling to admit that he was coming to look vaguely familiar and that Rory's reasoning seemed to make a good deal of sense. Before he could respond, however, she put her hands on Kieran's face, tracing the rugged lines of his beauty.

"And look at his face, Bud," she said, turning to look into Kieran's magnificent eyes. "You know these features. You saw them, along with me and Dave, for the very first time nearly a week ago. You even said he was good-looking enough to run for Mr. America. Don't you remember? Dammit, Bud, look at him."

Face pallid with shock, Bud could only stare in amazement. Everything she said made perfect sense and the longer he gazed at the massive man, the more horrified he became by the tendrils of recognition.

"It's impossible, Rory," he finally said, his voice husky with confusion. "What you're suggesting is purely impossible."

"That may be, my lord," Kieran entered the conversation for the first time, his hostility banked for the moment. "But it is nonetheless true. I was put to sleep by an alchemist eight hundred years ago only to be awakened by the strength of pure human emotion. Apparently, the lady's attachment to me served as the catalyst for my resurrection."

Bud's mouth was hanging open again. "Christ... that accent," he muttered. "Incredible. I've never heard a British accent so... heavy."

Rory sighed thankfully, seeing that Bud was, once again, returning to the calm, reasonable archaeologist she knew. But he was brutally analytical and she was further aware that convincing him of Kieran's reality would still take a good deal of persuasion.

"That's because it's real, Bud," she smiled, one hand still on Kieran's face. "He's not an actor or anything like that. He's a knight of King Richard's realm."

Bud continued to stare, although he had closed his gaping mouth. After a moment, he scratched his head in a puzzled gesture, indicating that his shock was wearing thin and his brain was starting to work again.

Rory watched him closely as he turned away to pondering the situation. Removing her hand from Kieran's face, she batted at him when he grasped it and tried to kiss her fingers. Although the demonstration sent her heart fluttering wildly, she nonetheless shook her head in a scolding gesture and went in pursuit of Bud.

He was moving towards the window, his face ashen and his eyes somewhat glazed. "Bud?" she prodded gently. "Please tell me you're at least trying to understand this."

He cocked an eyebrow. "Understand?" then, he snorted, turning to look at Kieran as the man fumbled with the buttons of his shirt. "Christ, I have to say this for him; he certainly looks like the knight in the grave. But what makes you think that this guy hasn't been sent by the Hage family in an attempt to somehow mislead you?"

"Why would they?" she responded. "For what reason? I don't have anything they could possibly want or use. They took everything I had. And then some."

He shook his head, eyeing the massive man who seemed to be having a good deal of trouble with the buttons. Rory noticed Bud's curiosity and quickly moved to shore up the modern fastens. Kieran smiled his thanks, abruptly sending Bud's confusion sparking into a raging fire of jealousy. And the way Rory responded to him, coyly, only fanned the flames.

The control so thinly held was leaving him once again. "So just like that, you believe him," he said, shoving his hands in his pockets. "Tell me, Rory; did you actually see this miraculous resurrection? Did you see his heart began to beat again or his lungs start to breathe? Or did you just wake up from your drunken stupor to discover him alive and well?"

Rory looked at him, aware of his condescending tone. "It was just like I told you," she said quietly. "I kissed him goodbye and fell asleep on him because I was exhausted. When I awoke a few hours later, he was stirring. I think that even in a drunken sleep, I would have noticed if someone had moved the body I was lying on top of. It wasn't like I was in a coma."

Bud's gaze shifted from Rory to Kieran. The man met his gaze evenly, not as challenging or angry as it had been earlier. Hell, it looked like the same man. Even down to the shape of the lips; and Bud should know, considering he stuck his fingers in the man's mouth. But the concept of raising a man from the dead... well, it just wasn't possible.

"I'm sorry," he murmured, shaking his head and retracing his steps away from the window. "I just can't... Rory, I don't know how this guy has managed to hypnotize you, but dead bodies just don't come back to life. I need you to come back with me to the hotel. You've got a lot of explaining to do to Steven Corbin."

Her heart sank. "Oh, Bud," she whispered, feeling defeated and sickened. "Please believe me. I'm not trying to manipulate you, or lead you on a wild goose chase or anything of the sort. This really is Kieran Hage."

Bud reached out, putting a hand to her cheek and forcing her to look at him. "I know you wish he was." He looked to Kieran, his eyes roving the man suspiciously. "Look, pal, I don't know who you are or what you've done to her, but if you've got something to do with the disappearance of Sir Kieran's body, then you're in a lot of trouble, too.

Come on, Rory. We're going."

He grabbed her by the hand, intending to pull her to the door. But he hadn't taken a step when Kieran was on him, separating him from Rory with unearthly strength. Rory shrieked, pleading for Bud's safety as Kieran abruptly placed Bud in the nearest chair. It was done roughly, without particularly thought for comfort, but not a hair on Bud's head had been damaged in the process. Yet the message was obvious.

"My lord," Kieran's bass voice was even, a return to his usual calm composure. "My name is Sir Kieran Hage, Viscount of Dykemoor and Sewall, and I was born January 4, 1160 in my family's castle of South-well. I have three younger brothers and a father who still resides at Southwell. My mother died when I was eight years of age, after the birth of my youngest brother, and I have a host of other family members scattered throughout eastern England. Since you do not believe the lady, mayhap you will believe me. I am who I say I am, my lord, I assure you."

Bud stared at him, annoyed by the man's brutal action but strangely compelled by his eloquent words. Rory hovered beside the massive man, eyes wide with apprehension.

"Ask him something, Bud," she encouraged. "If you don't believe who he is, then ask him something only he would know."

Bud's eyes darted between the man and Rory. "Like what?" he demanded.

Rory glanced at Kieran's profile; he was still staring intently at Bud. Like a cat watching its prey. After a moment, she put her hand on his arm gently to ease him away from the angry man in the chair. The last thing she needed was Bud provoking Kieran into violence with his stubborn stance.

"Ask him about King Richard," she finally said. She didn't know what else to suggest.

Bud took a deep breath, muttered a curse, then fixed his ice-blue gaze on Kieran. "All right," he muttered. "If it'll help convince you that he's an imposter, then I'll do anything. You want a question, pal? Then here's a question. Rumor had it that King Richard preferred both men and women sexually and that he had a bastard son by a lesser noble-woman. What about that?"

Rory rolled her eyes in a disbelieving gesture; of all the questions to ask! Kieran, however, remained completely calm. In fact, his massive hand had found Rory's as it rested on his elbow and he began to caress her fingers gently as he spoke.

"I was aware of the rumors of his preference and a few times saw evidence of the truth," his voice was quiet. "But it was something we did not speak of. As for his bastard son, I met the boy once when I was newly knighted. Although Richard himself did not tell me the lad was his son, the resemblance was striking."

Bud cocked an eyebrow; a generic answer and not particularly con-vincing. He looked to Rory, suggesting his patience with this charade was dangerously thin, and she hastened to rectify the situation.

"The crown, Kieran," she turned to the knight, her voice as soft as Bud as ever heard it. "Tell him about the crown. Your reason for having it."

Kieran cast her a dubious look; speaking to the lady about his mis-sion was one matter, but speaking to a perfect stranger was entirely another.

"He knows all about it," Rory encouraged when she read his doubt. "In fact, he was helping me search for it when we found you. Please, Kieran, tell him about El-Hajidd. Tell him everything."

Kieran sighed; certainly, he had nothing to lose. The man with the ice-blue eyes was obvious inferior in both strength and size and there was naught the man could do against him. Even if he was in league with Simon's phantom, still, it wasn't as if he could cause more betrayal or pain than Simon already had. And it was extremely important to Rory that her friend be convinced of Kieran's authenticity for reasons Kieran was having difficulty comprehending.

So he was a friend, a fellow archaeologist who had been on hand when his grave was uncovered. But why he needed to know everything that Kieran and Rory had discussed privately was still a mystery. Nonetheless, Kieran was willing to elaborate for the lady's sake; in a country he no longer recognized, thrust into a future he didn't understand, he had little choice but to trust the kindness of strangers.

After a lengthy pause, he moved away from Bud and Rory and eased himself onto the edge of the mattress. "When our Lord Jesus Christ died on the cross at Mount Calvary, his body was taken and prepared for burial by Joseph of Arimathea among others. 'Tis said that after the resurrection, Joseph collected not only the shroud of Christ's burial, but the diadem of thorns that had been cast to the floor of the vault when our Lord's body had been wrapped." His voice was unusually gentle as he formulated his thoughts. "As you know, Jerusalem was under Roman control and no place for Christians. Especially those close to Christ. Joseph traveled north in his ministry, carrying with him the shroud and the crown. Until he came to Tyre."

Not surprisingly, Kieran's hypnotic tone had Bud and Rory listening intently. As Rory sank to her knees beside Bud, enraptured by Kieran's beautiful voice, the massive knight calmly continued.

"While in Tyre, he stayed with an innkeeper and his family. Romans abound, however, and the innkeeper saved Joseph's life against a band of particularly cruel soldiers. In thanks, Joseph gave the pious man one of the only possession of value he had. The Crown of Thorns."

"The innkeeper was a Christian?" Rory asked, her tone faint with wonder.

Kieran smiled at her. "Indeed, my lady. He accepted the crown as if it were more valuable than gold, passing it down through generations of his family. A family that eventually converted to Muslim, though the crown was still kept sacred. When the Crusades came, the patriarch of the family buried the crown to keep it from being destroyed by Allah's vengeful fanatics. Even as the family fought against the Christian knights from the west for years to come, the crown was still kept hidden. Until the coming of Guy de Lusignan and Frederick of Barbarossa."

"What happened then?" Rory was thoroughly enraptured.

Kieran was fixed on her. "The family had risen to prestige within the ranks of Saladin's warriors, including the eldest son and heir. When the collapse of Acre became apparent over three years of continuous fighting, he attempted to negotiate a truce without Saladin's knowledge or consent. Saladin, of course, was reluctant to a surrender of any kind, but El-Hajidd was convinced a peaceable treaty was necessary in order to preserve what was left of Saladin's forces. As a show of good faith, he was determined to extend a peace offering. Something the Christians would value above all else."

"The crown."

This time, it was Bud who spoke. Kieran looked to him impassively. "Aye, the crown. I was chosen the leader of a secret delegation appointed to retrieve the crown. As I explained to the lady, the other men of my delegation turned against me because they believed that God's only true victory would be in the complete destruction of Saladin. Forced to flee with the crown in my possession, I managed to hide it before assassins found me and did this," he touched his left side gingerly, rubbing the scar. "An alchemist gave me a potion to put me into a deep sleep while other potions he administered healed my wound. And in sleep I remained until the lady awoke me. But now that I have been resurrected, 'tis my destiny to return to the place where I buried the crown. I must complete what I started eight hundred years ago."

When Kieran finished speaking, the silence in the room was deafening. Rory stared at him, lingering on his story of adventure and history as Bud remained completely unmoving. He was gazing at the massive man, observing intelligent eyes of clear brown and knowing the truth, as the man believed it, was evident. And he continued to stare at the alleged knight until Rory broke into his train of thought.

"Well?" she asked. "What do you think?"

Bud released a slow sigh, tearing his eyes away from the enormous man and gazing to his enthralled colleague. "I think your Sir Kieran is a gifted storyteller," he said quietly. "And I think I need to go back to the hotel and ponder all of this for a while."

"But…" Rory's eyes were wide with surprise. How on earth could he not believe? "What about the fact that you were right about the Muslim forces extending the crown as a peace offering? I never said anything to Kieran about your theory, so how would he know what you speculated? Doesn't that mean anything?"

Bud's ice-blue eyes were steady. "He's an intelligent man, Rory. I'm sure he took the things you told him and pieced together a logical, if not somewhat involved, story."

Rory rose to her feet, her expression sorrowful. "Oh, Bud… how can you still not believe?"

Bud stood up from the chair, his attention on Rory as Kieran rose from the bed. "Look," he said. "You can't honestly expect me to believe this guy has risen from the dead. Whoever he is, he's the most gifted actor I've ever seen and I'll give him credit. But you… Rory, you were infatuated with the knight from the very moment you saw him. And you want him to come alive so badly so he can help you find your crown that you've somehow fallen prey to this… this opportunist. Honey, why can't you see the situation for what it is?"

"Why can't you?" she shot back, feeling abandoned and hurt by the man she had come to depend on so terribly. But her reasons for her dependence were different from his, one person in love with another who did not return the feelings. Bud somehow symbolized a strength and support she had never known, while he wanted to be the husband she would grow old with. It was a painful paradox for the both of them.

"Because it's not what you want it to be, no matter how hard you wish it was," he said earnestly, ignoring Kieran's massive presence lingering behind him. "This isn't a fantasy, Rory, or a movie. This is real life."

Focus on what's real in this life. Rory heard the strains of her mother's words echoed in Bud's voice and her soft demeanor, her pleading manner, vanished. So he considered her outlandish and bizarre, too. Just like her mother did. For Rory to be trying to convince Bud that Sir

Kieran was real was like calling Wolf; she had tried to convince him that the crown was real and she had failed to prove her point. And now he wasn't willing to believe the verity of her words a second time around. He wasn't about to be made a fool of twice.

"Fine," she turned away from him. "Go back to the hotel, Bud. I'm not going to bang my head against the wall any longer. If you don't believe me, then that's your problem."

"No, it's our problem," he said with growing irritation. "You stole an ancient corpse and I should have stopped you. And until you tell me where you've hidden it…"

"I didn't hide it!" she practically shouted, jabbing a finger at Kieran. "It's right there, big as life! Good Lord, Bud, if I've ever needed you to believe me, it's now. I'm not making this up!"

Bud eyed the knight, shaking his head after a moment. "No more, Rory. Come on; you're coming with me."

She balked stubbornly. "I'm a big girl, Bud. I can do what I want, when I want, or where I want. And I don't want to go back to the hotel with you."

Bud's cheeks mottled a faint pink. "So you're going to stay here with… him?"

She nodded, turning away. "Since I can't count on you to help us, I guess I'll have to figure this out by myself."

Bud's jaw ticked. "You've committed a crime, Rory. If I let you stay here, then I'm an accessory. I can't leave you…"

There was a gentle knock on the door then. Before Kieran could stop him, Bud opened the panel in a fit of irritation. Steven Corbin's piercing blue eyes filled the room.

Before another breath was drawn, Kieran was moving for the doorway like a madman. Rory gasped with fright as Corbin's two goons pushed the lawyer out of the way, propelling themselves into the room and taking out Bud with a swift blow to the jaw.

Kieran grabbed the man who had struck Bud, sending him to the floor in a burst of blood and fists. Corbin himself had moved into the room, heading for Rory, who immediately scampered away from his advance in search of a weapon. In her panic, the only thing she was able to locate was the small lamp beside the bed and she grabbed it, swinging it at Corbin with all her strength.

He grunted as she caught him in the shoulder, but it wasn't enough to deter him. The bed was behind her, a considerable obstacle that she was unable to overcome before Corbin capture her like a cornered mouse.

"Well, well, Dr. Osgrove," he grunted with exertion as she fought furiously. "We meet again under far less pleasant circumstances."

"Let me go!" She brought up her knee, catching him in the thigh and trying to shove her open palm into his nose.

But Corbin would not be dissuaded. He tightened his grip, holding her obscenely close as she wrestled with surprising strength. "Not until you tell me where Sir Kieran is. And you will furthermore tell me why he seems to interest you so."

She had no idea what he meant by the last statement and chose to ignore both questions entirely. She was still fighting him, but he was far stronger than she was and her exhaustion was rapidly growing. Just as she thought she might actually have to give up her struggle for the moment, a booming voice shook the very walls of the room.

"Simon!" Kieran roared. "Release her if you value your life!"

Chestnut hair askew, she turned in time to see Kieran stepping over the bodies of Corbin's two cohorts. Bud was twitching somewhat, trying to push himself up as Kieran's blazing eyes focused on Corbin. But the lawyer merely cast him an unwavering glance.

"I don't know who you are, but this is a legal matter and you will refrain from interfering," he turned back to Rory, flushed and panting in his grasp. "Once again, Dr. Osgrove, you will tell me what you did with Sir Kieran's body. The Hage family's patience is sorely tested with your maverick actions."

She didn't say anything, her wide-open gaze on Kieran as he approached. Kieran met her eyes momentarily, if only to soften for a brief moment at her expression of fear and anger. But just as swiftly, his gaze returned to Corbin.

"I told you to release her," he demanded hoarsely. "You came for me and I shall turn myself over to you completely. But you will let her go first."

Again, Corbin looked at him strangely. "I most certainly did not come for you. But you'll vacate this room if you know what's good for you."

Kieran sized the man up. Aye, he looked like Simon. And he spoke like Simon, too. But there was something in his harsh expression that indicated lack of recognition and Kieran was puzzled. The Simon he had once known would have dropped the woman and had a dagger to his neck by now.

But this Simon did not have any weapons. And the men who had accompanied him were not the usual cast of characters. Aye, even though the man holding Rory bore the same features of the man he had once loved and then grown to hate, there was a distinct difference that was difficult to isolate.

Nonetheless, he sensed nothing but danger from the man and quickly decided to act. Reaching out, he grasped Corbin by the neck, causing him to release his grip on his quarry. As Rory fell away, Kieran tossed Corbin against the wall like a macabre rag doll.

Rory gasped as Corbin hit the wall with a thud, knocking over the bed stand. Kieran immediately went to her, placing his big body protectively between the dazed lawyer and the frightened lady. Gaze hard as stone and body tense, he continued to watch Corbin as the man shook his head in an attempt to regain his senses.

"You stupid bastard," Corbin finally hissed, rubbing the back of his head. "Now you add assault to the list of charges."

"He was protecting me!" Rory fired back, her hands on Kieran's thick forearm. "You've got a lot of nerve breaking in here like this and beating people up!"

"And you, Dr. Osgrove, are in deep trouble for stealing what does not belong to you," he snarled, eyeing the massive man in front of her. "And your... your bodyguard here cannot protect you from jail time."

Before Rory could respond, Kieran delved into the conversation. "Damnation, Simon, how did you find me?"

Corbin's brow furrowed in puzzlement and irritation. "I told you to stay out of this. And as for..."

"Do not play games with me." Kieran's expression darkened. "I realize it's been a long time, but surely you cannot take me for such a fool. I asked how you found me and you will do me the courtesy of answering."

Corbin sighed heavily. "I have no idea what you're talking about. This matter is between the doctor and me and I cannot believe I'm debating this with you."

"We are not debating. In fact, we are scarcely communicating. But know this; even as you resort to trickery and brutality to gain your wants, I will tell you now that I do not have in my possession what you seek. You have followed me a very long way for nothing, old friend."

Corbin was thoroughly perplexed not to mention greatly annoyed. "What in the hell are you talking about? You have nothing to do with..."

His words were abruptly cut off by a loud shattering of glass and metal and wire. Rory shrieked with surprise as Bud brought a fine porcelain lamp down on Corbin's neck and head, having managed to sneak up behind the man as Kieran kept him occupied. The lawyer fell like stone, sprawled out on the floor as Rory removed herself from behind Kieran and rushed to her pale, shaken associate.

"Bud!" she cried softly, jumping aside when he tossed the base of the lamp still in his grip. "Are you all right?"

He nodded weakly, massaging the back of his neck. "Yeah, yeah," he mumbled, looking about the carnage of the room. "But we'd better get out of here before these guys come around."

Kieran knelt beside Simon, looking him over intently. "God's Blood," he muttered, rising to his feet. "Through eight centuries, he has actually found me. Strange how he didn't outright kill me, but rather resorted to covert actions to…"

"Enough," Bud reached out and grabbed Rory by the arm. His head was swimming and his stomach lurching and he simply wanted to get the hell out of there. "Come on. We'll figure out what to do next after we've collected our luggage."

"But Kieran…" Rory turned to the knight as Bud pulled her by the arm. "Hurry and get your duffle bag, Kieran. We've got to go!"

Bud didn't protest as Rory beckoned the big man to follow; he was desperate to leave and had no intention of lingering a moment longer to argue the point with his smitten colleague. There was little doubt, however, that he would get rid of the imposter at a later time. With Rory in tow, Bud stepped over the bodies of Corbin's colleagues, noticing that one man was beginning to stir.

Outside in the corridor, Rory pulled her hand free of Bud's grasp and, in turn, took Kieran's hand. Bud cast them both a long glance, feeling the embers of jealousy burn bright, once again, but put his turbulent emotions aside in lieu of getting them all out of the hotel before Corbin and his men grew lucid. Ignoring the fearful looks of the people still in the sitting area who had heard the commotion upstairs, the three of them spilled out into the late afternoon sunshine.

As Rory pondered what the total of the damaged room would come to on her already maxed-out American Express card, Bud noticed the black Mercedes parked at the curb. He recognized it as Corbin's and went to the window, peering inside. Suddenly, he jerked the door open.

"The keys are in it," he said as he motioned for Rory and Kieran to get in. "Come on! Hurry!"

Rory jumped in as Kieran fumbled around with the door latch. With a grunt of frustration, she leaped out of the car, opened the door for him, and practically shoved him inside. She plopped back into the passenger seat. Bud turned on the engine and threw it into gear as Rory took the cigarette lighter away from Kieran in the back seat. Whipping a wild U-turn, they took off in the direction of Hyde Park.

CHAPTER FOURTEEN

B UD CHECKED OUT of the Parkwood so fast that the landlady thought she had done something to offend him. He assured her that everything had been wonderful and thanked her for a lovely stay even as Kieran and Rory grabbed the luggage and threw it haphazardly into Corbin's car. Certainly not the activities of well-satisfied guests, but Bud continued to smile as he paid the bill. The poor landlady made every effort to believe him even if actions spoke louder than words.

Bud finally emerged from the hotel only to find Kieran in the passenger seat examining the dashboard as Rory explained the panel's function. Had he not been so eager to put distance between them and the hotel, he would have had little patience for the man's playacting. And Rory's willingness to go along.

All irritation aside, Bud had no idea where he was going or what they were going to do. Even though he was driving a stolen car, he assumed that Corbin had no intention of reporting it to the police; were that the case, Rory could easily press assault charges against him for breaking into her hotel room and roughing her up. And Bud had quite a bruise on his jaw, more evidence of Corbin's unethical brutality.

So at least for the moment, he was certain they were reasonably safe. Driving away from Hyde Park, Bud headed north on Edgewater Road and skirted Regent's Park, trying to find his way out of the city. He was so involved with his right-side driving that he hardly noticed

Kieran's stiff stand. Only by accident did he pass a glance at the man's ashen face.

"What's the matter with you?" he asked, trying to drive and deduce Kieran's condition at the same time.

Rory leaned forward from the back seat, concerned, as Kieran shrugged weakly. It was only then that she noticed his bug-eyed expression.

"This car… the speed at which it travels is astounding," he muttered, pounding his head on the ceiling when they hit a rut.

Rory smiled, putting her hand on Kieran's shoulder. "I usually react to Bud's driving the same way, Kieran. You're not alone."

Bud, gripping the steering wheel with two hands, cast her a threatening glance. "Instead of insulting me, you should be figuring out where we're going."

She kept her hand on Kieran's shoulder, leaning forward between the front seats. "Hey, you're the one driving like you have a plan."

Bud's ice-blue eyes were focused on the road. He swerved around a corner and Kieran grunted as he bashed into the passenger door. After a few minutes of wild driving and deliberation, Bud came up with an idea.

"All right; first thing, we've got to ditch this car," he said, abruptly pulling to the side of the road. "And look over there; the Underground. Let's get on and go as far as it'll take us. Even if Corbin finds his car and realizes we've taken the subway, there are a dozen stations we could have disembarked at. It'll take him days to pick up our trail."

If Kieran thought Bud's driving had been terrifying, the Underground was beyond comprehension. Rory sat beside him, holding his hand as he was sweating rivers and tried not to become ill. She felt sorry for him, having never experienced speed of this magnitude before. In spite of everything, he managed to maintain his composure exceptionally well. But when they disembarked at Cockfosters station, she halfexpected him to sink to his knees and kiss the ground.

But even if he didn't give thanks to the solid earth, it was obvious that he was pleased to be off the terror train. As Rory congratulated him on surviving the trip, Bud ignored the warm praise and led them away from the depot in search of lodgings. In fact, he had fairly ignored them both since entering the subway, pretending he hadn't witnessed the handholding or Rory's gentle murmurs of encouragement.

And still, as they moved along the quiet streets of the rural subdivision, Bud seemed fixed on finding them a place to hide. But Rory was acutely aware of what he must be feeling in spite of his aloof appearance; how the woman he loved was showing affection to another man.

Cockfosters was more provincial than urban London and Kieran seemed more comfortable in the rural surroundings than he had in the heart of the city. The soft green of the meadows and the smell of the air invigorated him, relaying the timeless quality of the country he had once known. Bud found a small bed and breakfast across the street from a playing field, checking them into two separate rooms and paying with travelers cheques.

Rory's room was beautiful with large French doors that opened onto a lovely garden. Kieran followed her into the room and set his black bag down, much to Bud's dismay. Handholding was one thing, but if this guy thought he was going to stay in the same room as Rory…. Setting his own luggage down in the large room with two single beds, he went back to Rory's chamber just as Kieran opened the French doors and drew in a deep breath of his beloved England.

Rory was in the bathroom. Bud could hear the water running and he eyed Kieran, moving towards the massive man as he inspected the lock on the French door. Kieran caught sight of Bud, pointing to the dead-bolt.

"This is a remarkable device," he commented, turning the key to expose the bolt. "Much more pleasing to the eye without the hindrance of ungainly external bolts. But these doors," he thumped them and the panels shuddered. "Too weak. A gaggle of children could break them to pieces."

Bud watched him, not unaware of the fact that this was the first time he had been alone with the imposter. As Rory remained behind the bathroom door, Bud found his irritation with the man returning.

"Look, pal," he said quietly. "Rory and I are in a load of trouble and we don't need to continue this stupid charade of yours. Maybe you can convince my colleague that you're her knight in shining armor, but I'm not as gullible as she is and I'm finished playing games. Now, just who in the hell are you really?"

Kieran looked up from the door, his expression customarily calm. "'Tis no charade, I assure you. I am Sir Kieran Hage."

Bud pursed his lips with frustration. "Bull. You're the best actor I've seen and you really should be in movies, but don't give me any more of your crap. I just want to know who you are."

Kieran removed his hands from the brass deadbolt, fixing Bud in the eye. "My lord, I am not a performer. I am a knight. Present me with a sword and I shall prove my point. And I shall prove it on your liver if you continue to accuse me of lies."

Before Bud could challenge Kieran's declaration, the bathroom door opened and Rory emerged, shoeless and without her sweater. Ignoring the two men, she went to her luggage and began rummaging through the case.

"Do I have time to take a shower, Bud?" she asked. "I promise I won't take long, but I'm really filthy."

The two men watched her as she drew forth clothing and other personal items. "Yeah, you've got time," Bud said, crossing his arms and lingering on his frustration. "No hurry, honey. It'll give your friend and me a chance to… talk."

She looked up from her suitcase, eyeing Bud's stiff stance and Kieran's calm expression. And as she continued to watch the two men, a thought suddenly occurred to her; clearly, Bud still didn't believe Kieran was who he said he was. Maybe if he were to spend some time with Kieran, alone, he might come to see the truth. Or maybe he would end up dead. There was only one way to find out.

"Kieran needs to take a shower, too," she said, rummaging through her overnight bag again. Drawing forth a wrapped bar of soap and a sample-size bottle of shampoo, she extended them to Bud. "He knows how a shower works, but we've never really discussed shampoo and soap and shaving cream. Can you please help him, Bud?"

Bud stared at her. "Christ, Rory…"

He was unwilling to take the offered items and Rory moved to him, shoving them into his palm. "You'll need to demonstrate how a razor works, too. And don't let him scald himself with the hot water."

Bud looked to the products in his hand, shaking his head after a moment. "Look, I think I've been a pretty good sport up until now. But I refuse to…"

"Fine," Rory extended her hand to Kieran. "Then I'll take him in the shower with me."

With a smirk on his face, Kieran was already unbuttoning his shirt. "Gladly," he murmured seductively.

"Wait a minute!" Bud put up his hands. Glaring at the big man, who merely continued to grin, he shook his head in a gesture of defeat. "All right, you win. Go take your shower and I'll… babysit him."

Rory smiled, patting Bud on the cheek. "Thanks, Bud." Casting a lingering glance at Kieran, who openly returned her gaze, she disappeared into the bathroom and closed the door.

Bud was lingering on her, too, but for a different reason. No matter how resistant he was to her foolish story and the presence of the man with the heavy accent, it would seem that he was, nonetheless, willing to accept the unacceptable. He still didn't believe their tale and knew he never would, but somehow, that didn't prevent him from doing as she had asked.

Christ, what an idiot he was.

"Come on," he growled to Kieran.

The knight followed without another word.

☙

MAYBE IT WAS a good thing that Bud saw Kieran in the shower. Maybe it was a good thing that he saw the multitude of scars, the heavily muscled legs, the calluses on the inside of his knees from hours and hours in the saddle. Furthermore, Kieran didn't have any inoculation scars and he hadn't been circumcised. And the healed wound across his left forearm was a truly impressive sight. Certainly, seeing the man nude had been an enlightening, if not odd, experience.

Bud could have attributed the scars to rugby or another sport, but they were too cleanly done. As if he had been smoothly sliced. And the thick calluses on his knees were void of hair, defying any other logical explanation than what Bud knew to be the only possibility. Even if the mystery man was an avid rider, Bud could hardly see him astride a long-legged gelding riding the hounds; he was far too large, too rugged, and just plain raw. He simply didn't fit the mold.

But he fit the mold of a man destined to spend his life on the back of a charger. Bud tried to distance himself from that idea as he watched Kieran fumble with the shampoo, getting it in his eyes. He had no idea what a washcloth was, soaping his bare skin and commenting on the smell and texture of the soap before rinsing himself and splashing water all over the floor.

Bud continued to observe, feeling like a voyeur when, in fact, he continued to stare at Kieran in an attempt to convince himself that the man was not who he said he was. For the first time since meeting the mysterious stranger, a true seed of credence had been implanted in Bud's mind and he struggled to keep it from growing out of control.

A seed, however, that would not be quashed as Kieran emerged from the shower and proceeded to shave. His fingers were so big that he had difficulty maneuvering Bud's razor, and the awkward event became a complete disaster when he squirted shaving cream all over the sink. Bud merely shrugged, wiped it up, and dispensed the cream into Kieran's hand himself. When Kieran struggled to apply it, Bud took pity on the man and smeared it on his face. Lifting the razor, he demonstrated its use.

It went slowly, but Kieran managed to come through his modern shaving experienced without a cut. He had no idea what a comb was for, having only had experience with heavy brushes, and ran his finger though his dark blond hair to dry it. When Bud proposed he brush his teeth with a spare toothbrush, Kieran raised an eyebrow and did as he was told as Bud talked him through it. He nearly choked on the strong-tasting toothpaste, but somehow managed to emerge unscathed.

Back in his new Levi's and a mustard-color mock turtleneck that emphasized his magnificent chest to the hilt, he put his boots on carefully and tied the strangest knot Bud had ever seen. The more time he spent with the man, observing his natural manner and genuine behavior, the more Bud found himself leaning towards the concept of believing his story. And the more real confusion he experienced.

Dead men don't awaken!

Rory pounded on the door as Bud was changing his shirt. Kieran opened the door for her, a bit too eagerly for Bud's taste, and she swept in to the room in the dress she had purchased at Fortnum and Mason. Kieran's eyes glittered as he drank in the sight of her beautiful naked legs, outrageously smooth, and the way the dress seemed to cling in all the right places. Her long chestnut hair was perfect, her makeup flawless, and she ate up the attention as Kieran put her hand to his lips for a gentle kiss.

"Don't you think it's a little cold to be wearing that dress?" Bud's voice was stern as he finished with the last button.

Rory shrugged faintly. "I've got a sweater." Pulling her hand from Kieran's grip when she noted Bud's expression, she moved to the window overlooking the street below. "Did you see the pub across the street? Maybe we can go there for dinner."

Bud had been looking at Kieran as she spoke, the way the man's gaze seemed to fairly reek with lust. More than his own spurned feelings for Rory, the urge to protect her against the mystery man was a powerful thing, indeed. Christ, he thought he might truly go mad were he to allow himself to linger on the fact that Rory was deeply taken with the guy, but he fought the pain, the anger, and the deep-seated anguish.

Were he to openly display his jealousy, it would only serve to drive her away from him even further. And until he could find a way to chase off the glorious imposter, a man who claimed he was a corpse returned to life, he would simply have to accept a situation he was helpless at the moment to alter. Even if it killed him.

And it just might.

"Yeah," he responded belatedly to her question, glancing at his watch. "We'll grab a bite and go to bed early."

Rory smiled happily; after fourteen months on the sands of Nahariya, she was ready for a bit of nightlife. Stopping by her room to pick up her sweater and purse, she preceded Bud and Kieran down the stairs and across the street. The pub was brightly lit, full of smoke and music. An Irish band played loudly in one corner of the establishment as the laughter and the liquor flowed freely.

There were mostly younger people, one group exhibiting a myriad of pierced body parts as Rory pushed into the place with Bud and Kieran in tow. They took seats against the windows overlooking the bed and breakfast, ordering ham steaks and French fries and beer from the limited menu. When the dark brew came, Bud ignored the fact that he couldn't drink alcohol and downed nearly the entire glass as Kieran diverted his attention from Rory long enough to study the make-up of the room.

"Why would they puncture themselves in such a manner?" he asked, pointing to the collection of youths with pierced eyebrows and noses.

Rory shrugged, tasting her drink. "Who knows? I think they like the attention of people staring at them, wondering why they would suffer the pain of piercing sensitive parts of the body."

He turned to look at her then, studying her closely. A massive hand came up, fondling her earrings. "You have punctured your ears, too. Why would you endure the pain of this for the attention it draws?"

Bud found that question funny for some reason. He snorted, drinking the rest of his beer and ordering another. But Rory simply shrugged again, relishing the sensation of Kieran touching her sensitive lobes.

"It's different with pierced ears," she said. "Almost all women pierce their ears because it's easier to keep your earrings in place. Women of your time pierced their ears, too."

He removed his fingers from her velvet ear, reluctantly. "Not many. Mostly the French and their corrupt ideas of physical beauty."

Bud was into his second glass of beer, the alcohol in his veins wreaking havoc with his composure and loosening his tongue. "What about you? You've got scars all over your body and now you have the nerve to look down your nose at people who pierce their ears?"

Kieran collected his glass for the first time, eyeing Bud as he spoke. "My scars were not by choice. I have years of fighting and tournaments to thank for my haggard appearance."

Bud rolled his eyes and looked away, draining his glass. Kieran watched him a moment, taking a swallow of his own beer and nearly choking on it. When Rory saw his reaction, she called the barmaid over and ordered him the strongest beer in the house. His tar-colored drink arrived just as the food came and Kieran delved into both with gusto.

If watching the man shower had been an interesting experience, watching him eat was a real education in Medieval manners. Bud hardly touched his food as he watched Kieran literally inhale the ham steak, chow down on the fries, and then take the liberty of finishing Rory's food before she had barely taken three bites. To top it all off, he belched loudly and called the barmaid "wench" when ordering more food. Bud was astounded.

"Jesus Christ..." he murmured as Kieran ate the lettuce-and-radish garnish while waiting for his second round of dinner.

Rory was well aware of the man's manners and merely lifted her shoulders. "You should have seen him at breakfast, Bud. Eating like he hadn't eaten in eight hundred years."

Bud shook his head, draining his drink. The table manners of the man across from him were nothing short of barbaric, something that was completely natural to him and not in the least contrived. After the experience with the shower and shaving, to observe Kieran's table manners only brought Bud closer and closer to believing his story.

As remarkable as it was, as impossible as it seemed, Bud couldn't shake the burgeoning seed of credence. Maybe Rory was right; maybe there were things in this world that were unexplainable, like UFOs and ghosts and reincarnation. And maybe the man sucking down the ham steak in three huge bites was a product of one of those unexplainable phenomena that were difficult to comprehend and even more difficult to believe.

Bud just couldn't seem to shake the growing probability.

"Kieran," he said, watching the brown eyes come up from the plate. Even Rory looked at Bud; it was the first time he had openly used the knight's name and she was understandably surprised. But Bud ignored her eager expression, singularly focused on the man that was growing in authenticity before his very eyes. "If such a thing were possible and I'm not saying it is, I want you to tell me again; precisely how did this alchemist preserve your life?"

Kieran swallowed the bite in his mouth, wiping his lips with the back of his hand. Rory, hardly daring to feel some hope in Bud's question, handed him a napkin and watched carefully as he cleaned his hand and pondered his reply.

"To be truthful, my lord, I do not know the details," he said. "I can recall drinking a series of bitter brews as the alchemist told me he had been working the majority of his life to discover an elixir for immortality. Although he claimed he could quite easily put a man to sleep and thereby preserve him forever in a suspended state, the difficulty was apparently in the awakening."

"But you awakened."

Kieran nodded. "Only by the strongest of human emotions. The lady loves me, therefore, her kiss was the catalyst needed to rouse me from my eternal sleep."

Rory blushed dully, staring at her plate. She couldn't bring herself to look at Bud. But she could feel his eyes on her nonetheless. After a moment, his fork hit the plate and he took her half-empty beer glass and drained it.

"I see," he said quietly. "But you have no idea what was in these potions you drank?"

Kieran, having no idea of the situation between Bud and Rory, was oblivious to her embarrassment and his shattered heart. In answer to Bud's question, he merely shook his head. "None. But as I was fading off into blissful unconsciousness, I seemed to recall the alchemist mentioning succotrine aloes, zedoary gentian, saffron and rhubarb. I apologize that I am unable to recollect more."

Bud was lodged in his chair, Rory's beer glass in his hand and his ice-blue eyes glittering at the man across the table. He was about to continue the conversation when someone turned on a television over the bar and Kieran's eyes widened.

"Look!" he hissed. "God's Blood, what is that?"

Rory looked up from her plate, hoping her red cheeks weren't terribly obvious in the dim lighting of the pub. "A television. It's like... like if you were going to see a play, except this machine brings the entertainment directly into your home or business. You can simply sit and enjoy it."

He stared at the American program, complete with women in red bathing suits and his eyebrows rose. "God's Blood, the women are... indecent. They are practically nude!"

Bud was observing him critically, noting his genuine awe and realizing this guy really meant what he said. Passing a glance at the TV, he caught the barmaid's attention and ordered another drink. "Yeah, they are," he sighed heavily. "This whole world is indecent. Damned confusing and indecent."

Rory looked to Bud, wanting to comfort him in the midst of his heartache and puzzlement but somehow not feeling that her consolation was appropriate. After all, she was the one who had rejected his advances when she had been cruel enough to encourage him. But she had been confused herself, wallowing in self-doubt and pity regarding the outcome of her dig and the very future itself.

Bud was a wonderful man and she loved him dearly in a companionable sort of way, and she had been somewhat willing to pursue an intimate relationship between them for her own foolish reasons. But that had been before the introduction of Sir Kieran. Now, she realized the only man she had ever loved was living and breathing before her and as much as she hated to hurt Bud, she had to remain true to her heart. No matter what the cost.

And the cost was already high. As Kieran marveled at the miracle of the television, she looked to Bud only to note he was staring at the knight. And the pain, the confusion, she saw in his eyes was unmistakable.

"Libby, how do they get the people inside the box?" Kieran broke into her train of thought. "Is your age so advanced that they can do this?"

Rory tore her eyes away from Bud, looking to the amazed knight. "The people aren't inside the box. They're on film, or at a studio, and… boy, I'm way out of my league on this one. Care to help me, Bud?"

The barmaid brought Bud's beer and Kieran's food. Bud accepted the drink, taking a long swallow before answering.

"Actually, I'm more interested in talking about Sir Kieran," he said, the alcohol in his manner growing more evident. "For example, now that he's awake, when does he plan to retrieve this crown I spent fourteen damned months of my life searching for?"

Rory well remembered only days ago when the situation had been reversed and she had been out of control with her alcohol intake. Watching Bud take another drink, she struggled to lighten the mood before it turned ugly. "Bud, didn't you tell me once that if I got drunk, then you'd pretend you didn't know me?" She grinned when he looked at her. "Besides, I thought beer made you sick."

He continued to look at her and took a deliberate drink. "I don't suppose I could feel much worse than I do now." He turned away as her cheeks mottled a fierce red once again. "What about that, Sir Kieran?

When are you going back to get your crown?"

Kieran had already finished his second round of ham and fries, his gaze moving between Rory and Bud as notes of tension passed between them. But he was his usual composed self, moving to wipe his mouth with his sleeve when he remembered the napkin Rory had given him.

"I am going back immediately," he said calmly.

"But why are you even going at all?" Bud wanted to know over the top of his glass. "I mean, you said you had a mission to complete. A peaceful mission that would bring a cessation to the siege of Acre. Well, I've got news for you, pal; Acre fell eight hundred years ago. There's no more peace mission for you to complete. It's over!"

Kieran's jaw ticked slightly but he maintained his cool. "Mayhap the siege has, indeed, ended. But my task has not. I vowed to endow the crown to England as a symbol of lasting peace, and I shall do so. I must do so." He tore his eyes away from Bud lest his anger gain strength and focused on Rory. "Since I would deduce that men do not use chargers or carriages as their primary mode of transportation these days, I suppose I should learn how to operate a car if I am to make it back to Nahariya. Although I could take the land route to Nahariya, 'twould be faster to go by boat. Are there still boats, Libby?"

Bud cut her off before she could answer. "And that's another thing. What's all this 'Libby' garbage? Her name is Rory."

Kieran met Bud's gaze again, cocking an eyebrow. "She is far too beautiful for such an unsuitable name. I have decided her name is Elizabeth."

Bud snorted, uncharacteristically animated. "Christ, you're an arrogant bastard. Just because you don't like her name, you give her another? What happens when you decide you don't like her hair color, or that she's too thin? Are you going to change that, too?"

"I would change nothing on her person. She is perfect."

Bud slammed his hands against the table, rattling the dishes. "You're damned right she's perfect. She's the most perfect woman on the face of this earth and if she's going to fall in love with you, then you'd better realize what a treasure you have." He tried to stand up, the chair falling away, but he was too drunk and he almost ended up on his bottom. When Rory reached out to steady him, he shrugged her off cruelly. "I'm going to bed now, Dr. Osgrove. Have a pleasant evening with your... knight."

Rory's eyes were bright with unshed tears. "Please, Bud," she whispered. "Let me take you back to the hotel."

He moved away from her before she could grasp him. "Forget it. I can make it. Alone. Alone like I'll be for the rest of my life."

Rory stood up but Kieran held up a hand, preventing her from following him. Bud staggered through the door, across the street, and disappeared into the bed and breakfast. Rory stood there, tears streaming down her cheeks, as Kieran gently pulled her to sit. It took her a moment to realize she was in his lap.

"He loves you a great deal, Libby," he said. "Why did you not tell me this before?"

She sniffled, wiping her nose. "I don't know... it's our own private situation, I guess. Not something I go blurting about."

He watched her as she struggled with her tears. She was so sensitive to the feelings of others, this beautiful woman with a hole in her very own heart. Mayhap that was why she was so concerned how another might feel; having been subjected to a callous mother, as callous as Kieran's father had been, she understood well what it was to be rejected. Constantly striving for approval and affection wherever she could find it.

Aye, he understood well. Mayhap he understood best of all the fact that he had accepted the secret mission to procure Christ's diadem was to somehow, someway, provide his own father with a chance to be proud. The man had fathered four sons, pitting one against the other for his affection and wealth like some demented game. Still, Kieran was competing. Going to retrieve a crown that was absolutely meaningless to the peace of England now. But eight hundred years ago, it meant a great deal.

It still meant a great deal. Rory wanted it to make her mother proud of her, and Kieran knew, deep down, that he had wanted it for the same reason. Altruistic intentions aside, the more profound meaning lingered.

Lost in thoughts of his crown, he shook himself of the involving implications and back to the world at hand. A world where Rory was weeping for Bud's spurned feelings. Feelings Kieran himself had robbed the man of, intentional or not. Gazing into Rory's sad face, he realized that he couldn't pity Bud overly when he himself was so very, very content for nearly the first time in his life.

"You care for him, do you not?" he asked, feeling her warmth and softness against his thighs. "I can sense it."

She nodded, sniffling. "Care for him, yes. But I don't love him."

Kieran sighed, pulling her close as the smoke and noise of the pub surrounded them. "To be denied a chance at true happiness is a cruel fate at best. 'Tis no wonder he resents my presence."

Rory blew her nose on a napkin. "Not only does he resent you, but he doesn't believe you either. That just makes it worse."

Kieran glanced at the band as they launched into a particularly loud set, noting the open area in the middle of the room filling with writhing people jumping in beat to the music. "He is coming to believe me, though he refuses to recognize his own weakness," he said. "You were easy to convince because you saw the transformation in a far more sensible manner. Bud refuses to acknowledge the truth because he lacks the insight to do so."

"Bud is very insightful."

"Not when it comes to you."

The dance floor was alive with revelers. Rory pondered the dilemma of Bud, still seated on Kieran's lap as they both watched the activity that Kieran would later term as "seizures". The fact that the majority of patrons seemed to be busy with the music, however, cleared up the pool table and the video games just beyond the entry. Having eaten his fill and no longer willing to linger on Dr. Dietrich's personal problems,

Kieran saw the miraculous lights of the arcade games and demanded to inspect them.

Rory reluctantly followed him through the crowd, explaining the video screen, the knobs, the electrical current that came in through the wires, and eventually the rules of the game as she could understand them. Even if her mind and body remained with Kieran as he delved into Mortal Kombat, her mind was with Bud as he wallowed in pain she could only imagine. How she wished she could offer some words of comfort to ease his ache, but she knew there was nothing she could possibly say to the man short of setting a wedding date that would end his suffering.

There just wasn't any hope for a future between them. Bud knew the situation for what it was and she hoped that, someday, he would meet another woman that would make him forget about the eccentric biblical archaeologist who broke his heart. She found herself praying that he would, for all their sakes.

They left the pub when Kieran accidentally broke a pool cue and nearly a punk rocker with it when the man laughed at him. Returning to the bed and breakfast, Bud's door was unlocked and Rory encouraged Kieran inside, insisting he take the other twin bed. Kieran tried to tell her that he feared for his safety sleeping in the same room with a jilted suitor, but she ignored his protests and bade him goodnight.

Going to her own room, she locked the door and fell asleep in her underwear. When the dreams came, not surprisingly, they were of Kieran.

RORY WASN'T SURE how long she had been shivering. It was freezing in the room and she snuggled under the fluffy comforter, trying to stay warm. But the chill didn't dissolve and she opened her eyes sleepily, thinking about asking the landlady for an electric blanket when she realized her French doors were wide open. The chiffon curtains blowing in the soft night breeze, she could make out a figure in the silver moonlight.

Kieran stood against one of the doors, his gaze lingering on the garden beyond. He was without his shirt, his massive arms folded across his chest and Rory sat up, brushing the hair from her eyes.

"Kieran?" she asked softly. "What's wrong?"

He turned to look at her, a faint smile on his lips. "I apologize, sweetheart. I did not mean to wake you."

"You didn't," she pulled the blanket around her. "But it's freezing. Close the door."

He dutifully pushed himself off the doorjamb, closing the doors and using the marvelous lock. Rory watched him as he moved to the lamp beside the bed, turning on the soft white bulb. Noting her sleepy, inquisitive gaze, his smile broadened as he sat on the edge of the bed.

"It would seem that I am unable to sleep at all," he said quietly. "I suppose eight hundred years of sleeping is enough. Moreover, I do not like the beds of this time. Far too soft. I feel as if I'm going to suffocate."

She met his smile, sleepily. "Is that why you slept on the floor last night?"

He nodded. "And because you were angry with me. I suspected that my presence beside you on the mattress would not have been well met."

She sighed and lay back down, pulling the covers up around her shoulders; it was still very cold in the room. "And you were correct." When he chucked, revealing his deliciously deep dimples, she rolled onto her side and tried to get comfortable. "So why are you here? I hope you don't think I'm going to talk to you all night just to keep you entertained."

He shrugged, his smile fading. "Nay, I do not expect you to keep me entertained. But I have been thinking heavily since we parted earlier and there are things we must discuss."

"What things?"

"The diadem. Bud's argument against the completion of my mission was solid, but I know in my heart that I must return. And he also set me to deliberating the fact that I have wasted two precious days lingering about London when I should have very well returned to

Nahariya the moment I awoke."

Rory scratched her head, trying to clear the cobwebs of sleep from her mind as she pursued his train of thought. "Kieran, I would hardly call what we've been doing 'lingering'. We've been very busy avoiding jail."

"I realize that," he said. "But my attention has been diverted by this strange new world when I should be concentrating on my chosen task. Therefore, I have come to a great many conclusions this night; you said I could not go to Nahariya without your help and you were right. I do need you, Libby. I need your knowledge and wisdom to help me retrieve the diadem."

She sat bolt upright in bed, her sleep-heavy eyes instantly wide with surprise and delight. "Do you mean it?"

"I do."

Her mouth opened with glee. Forgetting the fact that she was clad only in her bra and panties, she threw her arms around his thick neck and giggled happily with pleasure. It was only when Kieran's arms wrapped themselves tightly about her naked torso did she realize her state of dress and, by that time, it was too late. He had her.

She pulled back, still enveloped in his arms and not feeling an ounce of the chill she had been experiencing earlier. And the look in his eyes only seemed to create more heat. "Uh… what changed your mind?"

He cocked an eyebrow and she could feel his big hands caressing her. With only a bra between their respective naked chests, Rory struggled to maintain her control as his gaze seemed to drill a scorching path deep into her soul.

"I am not sure," he said. "Somehow, I've come to realize that God has led you to me. Or mayhap He had led me to you. In any event, it is obvious that we were meant to have this crown together. I need you because you can help me with the intricacies of this modern world, and you need me because I know where the crown is. One without the other will not succeed."

He was terribly close, his hot breath on her face. Rory swallowed hard, wondering if she should try to disengage herself but not wanting to relinquish him for a moment. He was so masculine, so massive, so entirely wonderful and nothing on this earth had ever made her feel more like a complete woman.

She'd known from practically the moment of discovery that Sir Kieran Hage was something beyond her wildest dreams. And the more time she spent with him, the more she came to know the collected, intelligent man behind the marvelous journal and the incredible adventures, the more she knew she was hopelessly in love with him. Like no woman had loved a man before.

"You said once that you belonged to me," she said, her voice tinged with an aching quiver. "I guess I belong to you, too."

His grip tightened. "I cannot explain it, Libby. I have known you for two days yet I feel as if I've known you a lifetime. I feel as if God had a grander scheme in mind when He allowed me to be surprised by Simon's assassins. Had I not been mortally wounded, I would have not found the alchemist. And had I not been subjected to the alchemist's potions, I would have never found you. You would have never found me."

Her limbs were beginning to quiver with a peculiar ache, her gaze raking his thoroughly marvelous face as he spoke his serious words. And he was right; the bond between them was difficult to explain and even more difficult to understand. More than words could express, it was a feeling like nothing else. A feeling that transcended time and space and the conventional boundaries of a normal relationship.

Without Kieran, Rory knew she would not be whole. He was a piece to the puzzle that completed her, solidified her, made her want for nothing. Not even the crown. As long as she had Kieran, her precious diadem ran a distant second. But because retrieving it would close a chapter in his terribly eventful life, she was willing to assist him however she could. No matter what it would take.

She was deliciously warm in his arms, a warmth that weakened her, filling her with wicked, giddy emotion. She didn't care if she would be giving herself to a man she'd known a matter of two days; emotionally, she'd known him a lifetime and the desire to feel him on her, in her, invading her body and senses, was an overwhelming need. The hands embracing his massive shoulders suddenly found their way into his hair.

"So I found you," she murmured seductively. "And I woke you from the dead. Little did I know when I petitioned for my Nahariya dig where it would lead me."

He closed his eyes as her fingernails raked his scalp. "God's Blood, Libby," he muttered. "Yesterday… when I said I hadn't had a woman in eight hundred years… I never meant that I was desperate for any woman at all. No other woman but you will do."

She smiled, her hands moving to the face she had known so well in death as well as in life. "You say that now. But at the time, you really ticked me off with your conceit."

His eyes opened, the brown orbs coming in to focus. "What is this ticked?"

Good Lord, his lips were beautiful when they moved. Impulsively, Rory caught his lower lip between her teeth and suckled gently, drawing the flesh out as she released it. "It means you made me mad," she whispered, groaning softly when he returned her gesture, suckling her lips with painful sweetness. "God, Kieran, you really drive me mad."

He grinned, his entire mouth closing down over her lips, ravishing her with his power and desire. Throwing caution to the wind, Rory came alive in his arms, responding to his passion as if she had waited for this moment all her life. They fell back on the bed together, groping and suckling and caressing and somewhere in the process, Rory's bra came off and she moaned loudly when his scalding palm closed over her bare breast.

Hot. Hot. Hot. She felt like a whore but she didn't care. All that mattered was Kieran's body against hers, his heat filling her, his delicious flesh taunting her lust. When his heated lips came to bear on a peaked nipple, she bit off her screams in the top of his hair. He suckled her faster, hotter, better than she had ever known, and when her panties were literally ripped from her body, she was unable to bite back the scream of pure ecstasy as his searching mouth invaded her private core.

The pants of her pleasure filled the room as Kieran manipulated her with reckless abandon. Sprawled out on the bed, her legs over his shoulders, Rory thought quite possibly she might die from his expert attention. Just as she felt herself building to an immediate release, he suddenly pushed himself off her and removed his Levi's in a flash. Rory watched, dazed and panting, as his massive body covered her once more. Tasting herself on his lips, she plundered his mouth with her eager tongue.

But it didn't end there. She was determined to taste him everywhere, to pleasure him as he had pleasured her. In little time she was moving down his chest, sampling his scars and biting his nipples. Kieran growled like a bear as her hot hands found his throbbing manhood, her delectable mouth plunging down on him again and again until he thought he might go mad with the rapture of it. Knowing he would not last long against her wicked skills, he pulled her up by the hair and flipped her over on her back.

He settled between her legs, bracing himself as she instinctively guided his manhood against her threshold. Lips fused with unquenchable hunger, he pushed into her slick body in one smooth thrust, burying himself as she groaned into his mouth. Coiling his tight buttocks, he drove into her again and again, pounding her with the proof of his desire. Rory grunted with every thrust, gasped with every withdrawal, tightening her sugared walls around him as if to never let him go. In a flash, she was on top of him, riding him and feeling an entirely new sensation with his member deep inside her. After a few powerful thrusts, he hit the magic spot deep in her body and everything suddenly exploded.

Rory's climax came so hard and delicious that she thought she had blacked out for a brief moment. She fell forward, her labored breathing filling the room. Kieran's arms went about her and she was under him again, feeling him driving into her love-drenched body until he groaned her name and she could feel his manhood throbbing deep inside her. The movement, the gasping, slowly faded until all she could feel, hear, or think was the rhythmic pounding of Kieran's everlasting heart.

Rory didn't know how long she lay there, sandwiched between Kieran's massive body and the soft mattress. He was holding her tightly, protectively, and she relished his embrace with all of the satisfaction of her soul. As she always knew it would be, the physical union with him had been beyond her most vivid dreams. More than that, she knew that she would never be the same again.

"God, Kieran," she murmured into his neck. "You're not too bad for an old guy."

He laughed, shifting his enormous weight and curling her into a comfortable position against his chest. "And you… you have done this before."

Rory's eyes opened, pondering the deeper issues of his statement. Women of his time were maidens until married. If they went to the marriage bed without their virginity intact, then they were usually considered a lower life form. Kieran had remained remarkably open-minded about this new world he suddenly found himself thrust in to; she hoped that his sensibility would pertain to her as well.

"Things are a little different these days," she said, her warm hand stroking his muscled shoulder. "Sex isn't like it was in your time. It's given more… freely."

"Freely?"

She didn't like the sound of that word either. "What I mean to say is that people don't consider it a forbidden happening. When a man and woman meet and there is an attraction, sex between them is considered quite common to demonstrate those feelings. And the feelings don't necessarily have to do with love."

He drew in a deep breath, pondering her words. "Love is not an issue when it comes to marriage. In my time, a man and woman physically join only in matrimony. 'Tis considered disgraceful for a woman to go to her husband deflowered."

She lifted her head, looking him in the eye. "You and I aren't married, yet you were perfectly willing to 'deflower' me. Using your logic, I would then go to my husband in disgrace."

"Untrue."

"And why not?"

"Because I will be your husband."

All of Rory's mental faculties seemed to leave her at that moment. She could only stare at him, her eyes wide with astonishment. "What?"

He put a massive arm leisurely behind his head, his expression entirely calm. "I said that you would not have gone to your husband in disgrace because I will be your husband." A brown eyebrow lifted slowly. "But I would know who has taken this virginity that belonged to me. The man must be properly dealt with."

Her mouth was still open with surprise. Abruptly, she sat up, clutching the sheet to her breast. When he reached up and seductively dislodged it, she was incapable of making a move to reclaim it.

"Kieran," she breathed. "Are you serious?"

He was greedily drinking in his fill of her beautiful breasts. "On all accounts, lady."

Through her haze of astonishment, she noticed that he was lustily distracted and she hastened to reclaim the sheet. "Look at me." When he did, she lifted her eyebrows to emphasize her point. "Are you serious about marrying me?"

His eyebrows lifted in the same gesture. "I told you I was. Why is this so surprising? You love me, and I am madly passionate about you as well. God has brought us together and we shall not question His wisdom."

She stared at him. "Do you love me?"

"I told you I was…"

"You said madly passionate. Do you love me, Kieran?"

His gaze turned uncharacteristically warm. A huge hand came up, gently tucking stray tendrils of hair behind her ear. "What is not to love about you, Lady Rory? Although I have never been in love before, I suspect these feelings I am experiencing for you can be nothing else. God has given you to me, and surely, I will never let you go."

She seemed to soften, her shock fading. "But you just said... you said that love had nothing to do with marriage. And now you tell me you love me, therefore, you will be my husband?"

He shrugged. "I said that love was not an issue when it came to matrimony. And it is not. But it is the most powerful force on this earth and I find that, in my circumstance, it links me to you as much as God and the diadem and ancient potions ever could. Truly, I cannot explain that which I feel. But I only know that you must be my wife, and I will feel for you as I do now until I die."

Rory simply stared at him, the joy of his words filling her with an oddly fluid warmth. Speechless with the power of his declaration, she attempted to lay back down beside him but he stopped her.

"And now that you know of my feelings, you will listen to me well when I repeat my demand." He held her face between his two palms, swallowing up her entire head. "You will tell me this man who has touched you before me. Where may I find him?"

She smiled, trying to kiss his hands playfully to soften his stern stance. When that failed, she sighed. "I don't know where he is. We dated in college for four years, Kieran. I thought we were going to get married when he found someone else he liked better."

"Impossible. There is no one better than you. Not only will I kill him for taking what belongs to me, but I will kill him for shaming you."

She laughed at those words, dislodging his hands and snuggling up beside him. "Don't worry about him. He's ancient history. Oh; gee, sorry. I didn't mean to cast the two of you in the same category."

He pulled her close, stroking her back and listening to her groan softly with pleasure. In fact, she sounded very much like a purring kitten. "No offense taken. But you will tell me this man's name."

"No."

"Tell me or I'll force it from you."

"You will? And how do you plan to do that?"

His stroking hands grew bolder. "Do you truly wish to know?"

She gasped as his scorching mouth bit into her delicate shoulder. "I do. Oh, God, I do."

Kieran never got his name. But in faith, he hardly cared.

THE SECOND FLOOR corridor of the bed and breakfast was dark, a single light bulb providing the only measurable light. The guests had long since gone to sleep, the only sounds filling the night those of distant crickets or an occasional car. Or, if you happened to be standing in the corridor, the pants of pleasure coming from room 2B.

A figure was hunched against the wall near the doorway leading to a world of ecstasy, the head bowed and the feet bare. The sounds of faint screams had awoken him from a dead sleep, the gasps of delight drawing him out into the corridor. The sounds had faded for a while, but now they were back with a vengeance.

Joints popped as the figure moved, turning away from the room that was alive once again with the audible cries of bliss. As Bud made his way back to his cold, dark room, he found himself wishing he had never found that corpse in the desert. With every cry, every moan, a stake was being driven deeper and deeper into his heart until he could hardly stand the pain. Pain that was his own damned fault.

He shouldn't have been so foolish. He shouldn't have fallen in love with her. He should have known that she wasn't particularly attracted to him no matter how hard he tried to sway her opinion. Back in his own bed, Bud stared at the ceiling, listening to the bed in the next room bump the wall with precise rhythm. Knowing that with every thump, his anguish grew. Knowing that now, there would never be a Dr. Rory Dietrich.

Rolling onto his side, he picked up the phone.

CHAPTER FIFTEEN

"D R. BECKER, THIS is Steven Corbin. I apologize for disturbing you, sir."

The sun was beginning to set over the wide Pacific as Uriah Becker sighed at the sound of Corbin's voice. When the man wasn't threatening an international lawsuit, he could be quite cordial. But as Becker had come to discover over the past week, any semblance of congeniality was strictly an act.

"You're not disturbing me, Mr. Corbin," he replied evenly. "In fact, I was just preparing to leave for the day. What can I do for you?"

Corbin took a long drag of his cigarette, blowing the smoke to the ceiling as he spoke. "Quite frankly, sir, I need your help. Have you been in touch with Dr. Dietrich or Dr. Osgrove recently?"

Becker glanced up at the woman seated across from him, a glass of Seagram's in her hand. If Dr. Sylvia Lunde felt the intense stare from her uncle, she didn't react. She merely took another drink.

"I... no, I haven't heard from either of them recently," he replied. "Is there a problem?"

Corbin took another drag on his cigarette. "If I might ask, when was the last time you spoke with either of them?"

Becker thought a moment. "I spoke with Bud Dietrich nearly two days ago, I suppose. After you took possession of Sir Kieran's corpse. Really, Mr. Corbin, you could have waited until they had settled themselves before demanding the return of the body. As I understand it, Dr. Osgrove was quite upset with your tactless display."

Corbin didn't reply for a moment, his piercing blue eyes glittering in the weak light of his study. "That may be, sir. But as tactless as my display was, at least it was a legal action."

Becker's brow furrowed slightly. "Yes, it was. What are you driving at, Corbin?"

Corbin took another long, enjoyable drag off his cigarette. As he suspected, Becker knew nothing of the actions of his two archaeologists and it would be Steven's pleasure to inform him that his people had run amok. A sadistic form of glee, to be sure; rubbing the man's nose in the fact that his subordinates were in serious trouble.

"I'm not driving at anything, sir. But I regret to inform you that Dr. Osgrove is the prime suspect in the disappearance of Sir Kieran's body from the morgue at Middlesex Hospital two days ago. Although Dr. Dietrich wasn't directly involved, he's protecting her from the law."

Becker's face was ashen. Having finished her drink, Sylvia was in the process of pouring herself another when she noticed her uncle's odd expression. Before she could question him, however, he swallowed hard and turned away from her.

"You're... sure she did this?"

"Fairly sure. A nurse in the emergency room placed her at the hospital around the time the morgue was broken in to. Dietrich himself said she threatened to do it, but he didn't take her seriously."

Becker rose unsteadily from his chair, scratching his head. "Dear God... what on earth is she thinking? How could she possibly..?"

"Dr. Becker, I have little time to waste. Dr. Dietrich and Dr. Osgrove are fugitives from the law and Scotland Yard is aware of the crisis. Considering the crime is involving a national treasure, I am sure you can understand the seriousness of the situation."

Becker was staring from his window, the warm rays of sunset reflecting on his pale face. "I do," he murmured, feeling sick to his stomach. "You... you mentioned you needed my help, Mr. Corbin. I'm afraid I know nothing beyond what I've told you. Dr. Dietrich has not been in contact with me for some time and…"

"I understand, sir," Corbin finished his cigarette with relish, pleased to have the upper hand in the situation. With Becker cowering like a fool in the face of a predicament that could all but ruin the university, Corbin savored his power. "At some point in time, however, I expect that Dietrich will contact you. And when he does, I would appreciate your letting me know where he and Osgrove are hiding. It would be much better for me to reach them first rather than the police, as I'm sure you will agree that perhaps I could influence them into relinquishing the body and thereby lessen the charges against them."

On the other end of the line, Becker was literally ill with the myriad of plights invading his thoughts. Never in his wildest dreams would he have imagined Rory to have gone above the law, even for an archaeological find that obviously meant a good deal to her. And the fact that Bud had failed to inform him of the course of events wasn't particularly surprising. Maybe the man was trying to resolve the issue himself without creating a publicized incident.

Still, the fact remained that Corbin was right. Rory and Bud were in a good deal of trouble and whether or not Dietrich was trying to resolve it quietly, the point had come for outside assistance. And, at the moment, Becker was without many legal options being that the infraction occurred in a foreign country. Certainly, he could send a university lawyer, but that would only serve to broadcast the entire event. And Becker, like Bud, wanted to keep it quiet as long as he was able.

After a moment, he sighed heavily into the receiver.

"Of course," he said. "I would… appreciate anything you can do for them until I arrive."

Corbin set his cigarette butt to the ashtray. "Arrive? I don't understand."

Becker turned away from the window, his gaze fixed on Sylvia as she drained her fourth glass of Seagram's. "Certainly you don't expect me to stay here, idle, while two of my associates are in a great deal of trouble. I shall be on a flight to Heathrow as soon as I am able."

Corbin fought down his rising annoyance. He didn't want Becker in England, interfering with his plans for the lovely Dr. Osgrove and her smitten colleague. It was necessary that Becker stay in the States, far away from the justice that did not directly involve him.

Corbin wanted Osgrove to tell him why she had risked her life and career for an eight hundred-year-old corpse; Dietrich was enough of an obstacle, but Becker might prove to be even worse. With the two of them protecting her and the secret of the corpse, Steven doubted he would ever know the truth.

"Your presence isn't necessary, I assure you," Corbin said calmly. "If you remain in California, Dietrich and Osgrove know where you can be reached and you are far more valuable if you stay where you are. Should you come to London, you'll simply be chasing after them like the rest of us."

Some of the color returned to Becker's cheeks as he came to grips with his shock. "Mr. Corbin, have you ever heard of an answering service? If Dietrich calls my office, I can simply retrieve his message and return his call. And I can do this from London as well as from Southern California."

Corbin knew his argument had been weak from the beginning and Becker's condescending tone only served to fuel his irritation. "As you say, Dr. Becker." Since debating the man was useless, he endeavored to return the conversation to a civil tone. "I look forward to meeting you in person. But until that time, if you hear from Dr. Dietrich, you will please let me know. The Hage family simply wants the body returned and I promise I will do all that I can to ease the charges against Dr. Osgrove."

Becker's razor-sharp mind was already thinking ahead to his trip, the course of action to take. He didn't have any more time for Corbin's blather. "I appreciate the offer, Mr. Corbin. I shall be in London within the next two days."

"A lot can happen in two days, Dr. Becker. I'll do the best I can until you arrive."

Becker paused, hating the fact that Rory and Bud's only hope would rest in the hands of a shark for the next forty-eight hours. But he had no choice. "If I hear from Dietrich, I'll let you know."

"Good." Steven couldn't help smiling. "I shall await your call, Dr. Becker. And thank you."

Staring off into the dimness of his study as he lit another cigarette, Corbin simply smiled.

BECKER DIDN'T ACKNOWLEDGE Corbin's sickeningly polite farewell; he simply hung up the phone. As Sylvia sipped her glass, he rounded the desk, his hazel eyes focused intently on the once-beautiful woman. She caught his movement, turning her attention to the aged features.

"Well?" she asked, her speech faintly slurred. "What has Rory done this time?"

Uriah's jaw ticked. "She's stolen the body of the knight she uncovered at Nahariya. The lawyer representing the Hage family says she and Bud are running from the law and are in very serious trouble." He sighed heavily, at a complete loss to understand. "We simply didn't need this. The department is already in danger of losing funding from the university and with this little escapade... Good Lord, we just didn't need this. We're going to lose everything if word gets around."

Sylvia stared at him, finally tearing her gaze from his stone-like features and taking another drink. "Damn her," she hissed. "I always knew she was irresponsible and naive, but this goes beyond what even I believed her capable of. Why would she do this?"

Becker cocked an eyebrow. "Why? Who truly knows? The only person who can tell us is Dietrich, and apparently he's running with her. He said she was upset when Corbin claimed the body from the airport and maybe she was upset enough to somehow retaliate. But until I talk to Bud, I just don't know why your daughter has become a fugitive."

Sylvia toyed with the rim of her glass, rolling it along her lower lip as she stared into the fading light of the room. "She's going to ruin everything," she muttered. "The Nahariya dig had finally become a success with the discovery of the crusader. Why would she jeopardize everything she's worked for? I simply don't understand her."

"That's the problem." Becker tapped the glass in her hand, his jaw ticking with disgust. "You never did. The harder she tried, the more pressure you put on her. You were never satisfied with her and maybe she's finally reached the point where she doesn't care any longer. Hell, Sylvia, you're not concerned with Rory. You're only concerned with the shame she'll bring down on you by her actions."

Sylvia turned to him as he walked away from her. "That's not true. Why do you think I petitioned for funding for her dig? She's brilliant and beautiful and deserves everything I can give her."

"She deserves your love." Becker paused by the desk, jabbing a finger at his niece. "You act as if she has to earn it."

Sylvia slammed the glass down to a small mahogany table. "Damn you. How dare you tell me how to respond to my own child?"

Becker shook his head, turning away from the swaying woman. "Somebody needs to. Since the day she was born you've held her illegitimacy against her like a weapon. If she didn't make anything of herself, then you could blame her for your shame. And if she did make something of her life, then you could find the false pride to overlook your own shortcomings. And all that crap about her father dying in Vietnam is the most shameful secret I've ever kept, Sylvia. Have the guts to tell the woman the truth someday if for no other reason than she deserves to know. Her father wasn't a decorated fighter pilot; he was a married Marine on leave."

Sylvia's gaze was wide with drunken emotion. She tried to respond but, in truth, there was nothing to say. Shaken and dazed, she collected her glass and drained the last few drops.

"Bud was supposed to keep an eye on her," she muttered, wandering aimlessly away from her uncle. "You said he would be perfect for her."

"Bud Dietrich is the finest field archaeologist I know," Uriah said. "A bachelor, without any family and completely dedicated to his work. When we saw how he was attracted to her, you agreed that Rory needed his experience and guidance if her project was going to be a success. And I saw a person who would finally show her the pride and compassion she needed. Even if Greek and Roman culture was Bud's specialty and not Biblical Archaeology, still, I wanted him on the dig. I wanted him with Rory."

Sylvia snorted. "I was hoping his level character would calm her eccentric nature somewhat."

"She is only eccentric because she's spent her entire life trying to capture your attention."

Sylvia looked away, refusing to be roped into the familiar argument yet again. "Do you think Dietrich suspected that we were trying to make a match?"

"Who can say? But if he's willing to protect her from the British authorities, it must mean something."

"Certainly it does." The once-beautiful woman was colored with bitterness. "It means that he's let her ruin his life just like she ruined mine thirty years ago. And now with the abduction of this... this corpse, she's trying to finish me off."

Becker sat behind his desk, ignoring his drunken niece. The story was always the same with her; over-achievement in the field of Ministry and Education to make up for the fact that she had conceived a child out of wedlock. And she fully blamed Rory for the secret of shame she had been forced to hide. Blame in the form of harsh discipline and scholastic pressure that had all but ruined a truly gifted young girl, and apparently drove her to do something rash.

As Sylvia poured herself another drink, Becker moved to pick up the phone when it suddenly rang. His eyes widened with surprise and relief as he acknowledged the caller, the conversation abruptly moving from cordial to exceptionally serious. More dialogue as Becker tried to remain calm, assessing the situation and agreeing upon an immediate course of action.

Ending the call that had come from the outskirts of London, Becker didn't even hang the receiver up before he was dialing Corbin's private number.

❧

RORY AWOKE ALONE in the large bed, snuggled under mounds of covers. The sun was up, the day bright, and she sat up in search of Kieran. But he was gone and, disappointed, she stumbled into the bathroom and turned on the shower.

Soaping her body, she could still feel his touch and found herself wishing he was in the shower with her. Her chest was tight with the warmth of happiness, her limbs languid and weak. Never in her life had she felt so much joy, so much fulfillment, as if everything in her life was finally right.

It was as if the void Kieran had described in her soul no longer existed, filled by the emotions and adoration of her knight. Smiling happily as the warm water rinsed the soap clear, she turned off the shower and dried off.

Suspecting Kieran was probably downstairs eating everything in sight, she hastened to put on her makeup and dry her hair. Donning jeans and a white, sleeveless mock-turtleneck, she was putting her shoes on when a soft knock rattled the door. Thinking it was Kieran, she threw open the door only to be confronted by Bud's grim face. And by the expression on his features, there no doubt that he knew everything.

"Uh... hi, Bud," she said, feeling extremely uncomfortable under his intense gaze. "How are you feeling?"

He pushed into the room without being invited. Rory stepped aside, raising an eyebrow when he locked the door behind him. Only then did he turn to her. "Let's get something settled right now," he said in a tone she had never heard before. "I am finished being your stooge and I'm done with your manipulative mind games. I want Sir Kieran's journal and I want to know what you've done with his body. Now!"

He had actually shouted. Rory jumped, her eyes wide with surprise and a certain measure of fear. "But... I told you what happened to Kieran. You've been with the man for over a day; can't you see the truth of what's happened?"

The veins on his temples were pulsing. "The only truth I see is that you're playing me for an idiot. Tell me what I want to know or I swear I'll call the police this minute and turn you in myself. Do you hear me?"

Rory was shocked. But she was also angry. Bud was using the situation to punish her for not returning his feelings and she resented his bitter attempts at manipulation.

"Fine," she lowered her voice, the hazel eyes sparking. "Go right ahead. But I'll tell them what I've told you; I don't have the body. The body they're looking for is alive and well. Whether or not the authorities believe me, it's the God's honest truth."

His features tensed and he brought up a hand and for a brief, horrifying moment, Rory actually thought he might strike her. But that didn't fit the character of the man she knew so well. Still, she was relieved when the raised hand moved to his head and scratched at his scalp in a frustrated gesture.

"I'm not going to listen to any more of this," he said, his tone suddenly hoarse with emotion. "I thought we had more respect between us to continue this lie. But I guess I was wrong. About a lot of things."

She refused to allow him to use guilt against her. "Bud, you're my dearest friend, but we can't plan who we're going to fall in love with. You didn't plan to fall in love with me, and I didn't plan to fall in love with Kieran. But I did and I'm sorry if you're hurt."

"Hurt?" he snorted, an odd smile coming to his lips. "Hell, Rory, you pulled me into bed with you the night we arrived declaring that you needed my comfort. And then you spend all last night hitting the sheets with your... friend. What is it with you? Do you have to control all the men around you like some sort of sick game?"

Her cheeks flushed and she took a deep breath to steady herself. "I'm not trying to control anyone. When I asked you to sleep with me, I really did need the warmth and comfort of another human being. You even asked me if I was trying to seduce you and I told you that I wasn't. I apologize if I led you on, Bud; I didn't mean to. I really don't know what I was thinking at the time."

"And you don't know what you're thinking now," he fired back. "God only knows how that guy has managed to bewitch you, but it's got to stop. For your own sake, this has all got to stop."

"And who's going to stop it? You?" she shook her head. "Will calling the police on me somehow give you the revenge you need against my spurning your feelings?"

He stared at her, the rage in his eyes cooling somewhat. "It has nothing to do with that."

"Bull."

"Damn you, Rory. Why do you think everything has to revolve around my feelings for you?"

"Because it does. Everything you've ever done since the moment we met has revolved around your attraction to me. It started the day you agreed to the dig, placing your reputation on the line for a woman determined to chase biblical myths."

His fury continued to ease, the truth of her words weighing heavily on his heart. After a moment, he sighed and looked away. Rory relaxed slightly, feeling his pain and again so very sorry that she had caused it.

"Kieran and I are returning to Nahariya for the crown, Bud," she said. "I would like you to come with us."

He snorted. "I don't think so. I'm finished with all of this, Rory."

"But I need you."

"No, you don't. You have your Kieran. Or whoever in the hell he really is."

Rory watched his slowing movements, seeing his anguish reflected in every muscle, every limb. Moving to him, she gently placed her hand on his arm. "If you go with us and he leads us straight to the crown, won't it prove to you that he is who he says he is?"

He glanced at her, his ice-blue eyes laced with defeat. After a lengthy pause, he simply shook his head. "Look, even if he managed to completely convince me, I'm not the real problem. Do you realize what would happen if the authorities got their hands on a living, breathing corpse?" When she shook her head unsteadily, he continued. "Think about it, Rory. Suppose you actually manage to convince the world who Kieran really is; the man has been in a catatonic state for eight hundred years. Once Science gets hold of him, he can look forward to a life of experiments and needles and testing to determine the secret to his immortality. Is that what you want for him?"

Her face fell. "Of course not," she replied, the distress in her expression evident. "I just want him to be able to live peacefully, admired and respected for his what he truly is. He's lived so much, Bud. He deserves the best this life has to offer."

He cocked an eyebrow. "If it's proven he's actually a resurrected Medieval knight, he can expect a life as a sideshow freak. Or he'll simply disappear from sight altogether. Do you really think the world is ready for the concept of an eight hundred-year-old man?"

Rory held his gaze a moment longer before looking away, feeling sickened and stunned. Being so close to the situation, she'd never truly given the negative aspects of Kieran's resurrection much thought. Once again, Bud was right; he was always right.

But it didn't change the facts. Kieran was determined to return for the crown and Rory was going with him. Beyond the actual retrieval, she refused to ponder the future. If they ended up living in a mud shack in the middle of the Serengeti Desert, hiding out from the long arm of the law, then that would suit her just fine. As long as they remained together, she trusted that the strength of their bond would see them through the worst this life had to offer.

"We're going back for the crown," she finally murmured. "After that, I suppose we'll just have to take one day at a time."

Bud continued to stare at her, not knowing what to say. She was determined to return to Nahariya and the thought that she was slipping further and further away from him was nearly more than he could bear. But all reality of his anguish aside, he knew, for her own protection, that he simply couldn't let her go.

"Rory, you're not going anywhere right now."

She looked up from the floor. "What do you mean?"

He took a deep breath, feeling completely evil for what he was about to say. But he also knew in his heart that he only had her best interests in mind and, perhaps, just a small amount of the revenge she had accused him of. When dealing with matters of the heart, it was difficult to think clearly. But he was trying to do just that, praying she wouldn't hate him overly for what he felt he had to do.

"What I mean is that I called Becker last night. He's on his way to London and I've been told to keep you here until he arrives."

Rory's eyes widened. "You what? Damn it, Bud, how could you do this?"

"It's for your own good. You're in a lot of trouble and we've got to prevent it from getting out of control more than it already is."

Instantly inflamed and terrified by his treachery, Rory's body began to quake with emotion. "So you turned me in just like a damned traitor!" she seethed. Then, her expression suddenly slackened. "Oh, God. Bud, what have you done with Kieran?"

"Nothing," he replied evenly. "When I left him, he was trying to shave. And when he comes knocking on the door to take you to breakfast, you're going to tell him to go ahead without you."

She was so shaken even her lips were trembling. "And then what?"

"And while he's occupied with his meal, we're checking out and moving to another hotel."

"No!" she shouted. "You can't do this!"

"I can and I will. If you value your job, your reputation, and your freedom, you'll do as I say."

Rory was livid. "You bastard! I thought you were my friend, Bud. I trusted you!"

"And I thought you were my friend, too. But friends don't lie to other friends. And they don't treat them like idiots."

Her cheeks were mottled a bright red. "I never treated you like an idiot and I've never lied to you. And if you weren't blinded by your own jealousy, then you'd understand what I'm telling you."

Bud's jaw ticked but he remained calm. "I understand completely. But you've got to understand that I'm doing this for your own good. And as for Sir Kieran's corpse, if you won't tell me where you've hidden it, then I guess we'll have to tell Becker that you destroyed it somehow."

"I didn't destroy it!"

"Then where is it?"

She let out a hissing curse, turning away from him in a fit of frustration. "You've been talking to it for the past twenty-four hours!" she exploded, nearing the edge of insanity with the repeated argument. "And I slept with it last night and can tell you for a fact that Sir Kieran Hage is alive and well and more of a man than any living male on the face of this earth!"

Bud blanched, struggling to maintain his composure. "Christ, you love throwing that in my face, don't you?"

She stopped in the middle of her rage, tears of distress and emotion filling her hazel eyes. "No, Bud, I don't. But I love the man and he loves me and I'm sorry if I've destroyed your world. But I can't help what I feel and I won't let you separate us. I swear to God you'll be sorry if you try."

Bud raked his fingers through his short hair, turning away from her thoroughly disturbing expression. "I've got to do what I know is right. And what's right is getting you away from that… that man so you can start thinking clearly again."

Rory stared at him, feeling so terribly defeated. Her rage was fading, her emotions brimming, and she collapsed on the edge of the bed in exhaustion. "I am thinking clearly," she murmured, watching him pace about in agitation. "Don't you even believe me just a little, Bud? Just a tiny bit?"

He came to a halt, pondering her words for a moment. As Rory watched him closely, he finally gave her the signal she'd been waiting two days for. A small, nearly imperceptible nod.

"Maybe," he muttered, his tone scarcely audible. "All I know is your Sir Kieran is unlike anything I've ever seen before. From head to toe, that man is an anomaly. Christ, Rory, I just don't know what to think anymore."

"Don't think," she whispered. "Believe."

Ice-blue eyes turned in her direction, seeing the woman he loved so much and feeling the familiar weakness sweep him. But it wasn't enough to overcome his doubt.

"Rory... I just can't."

"Can't or won't?"

Bud never had the chance to reply. The locked bedroom door suddenly exploded, drawing a scream of fright from Rory and sending Bud ducking for cover. When the noise ended and the pieces of wood cluttered to the fine flooring, their startled gazes fell on a man of enormous size and strength lodged in the doorway.

"Kieran!" Rory gasped. "Why did you do that?"

He stepped into the room, kicking aside a heavy piece of panel as if it were nothing. His jaw ticked as he looked directly at Bud.

"The door was locked and I heard your urgent voice," he said, his voice a growl. "I will not be locked away from you. Not even for a moment."

He was still looking at Bud. Rory leapt up from the mattress, moving to intercept him before he could do to Bud what he had done to the door.

"Bud wasn't locking me away from you," she said, putting her hands on his thick arm. "We were... talking."

Kieran cocked an eyebrow. "I would hardly call words such as 'bastard' and 'traitor' mere talk. What has he done that has angered you so?"

Rory swallowed, looking at Bud. Surprisingly, the man's expression was without fear and Rory returned her attention to Kieran, hoping she could delicately explain the situation.

"Bud spoke to our superior last night and was instructed to keep me in his company until the authorities from the university can arrive." She didn't want to make Bud out to be the bad guy, even if he had gone behind her back. "Obviously, I don't want to remain. I want to go to Israel with you."

"And you shall," Kieran said firmly, looking to Bud once more. "I would assume the lady told you of her plans to accompany me to Nahariya. We will not deviate from these plans."

Bud took a deep, long breath. "Look, pal, Rory is facing serious charges. You know this. Why don't you just make it easy on her and let me do what needs to be done? She can't go to Nahariya with you now, if ever."

Kieran remained calm. In fact, he was inordinately good at calming his fierce temper once aroused. Taking Rory's hand in his large, warm palm, he kissed it gently before returning his attention to Bud.

"The only thing Rory is guilty of is loving a dead man," he said quietly. "You see, we are linked by this crown somehow, a passion and devotion that has brought us together and refuses to let go. I need the lady if I am going to complete my mission, and she needs me if she is going to find this diadem she has spent a great deal of time searching for. We are two pieces of a puzzle, Bud, finally made whole. One without the other is incomplete, but the two of us combined are invincible."

Bud's gaze held steady, his ice-blue eyes lined with fatigue and emotion. He looked to Rory, so incredible at peace within the grasp of the gentle knight, more content than he had ever known her to be. True, Bud loved her terribly; but he also loved her enough that he simply wanted her to be happy with whomever she chose. And if it wasn't him, then he would have to accept it. But his rejected devotion still didn't erase the fact that she was in trouble. Meeting Rory's gaze, his focus was intense. "I can deal with this in time," he said finally. "If you really love him, then that's the way it's got to be. But the fact remains that Becker is coming to London to save you from British justice. He can probably get you absolved from the charges of breaking and entering, but stealing a national treasure is another matter. If this man before me is the living corpse of Sir Kieran Hage, then we really do have a problem on our hands. Just what in the hell am I supposed to tell Becker?"

"Tell him I ditched you," she said quietly. "Tell him that I snuck out in the middle of the night and you don't know where I am. For God's sake, tell him anything."

Bud continued to stare at her, finally turning away and dragging a hand over his weary face. "All right. So let's say I give Becker a contrived story while you and Kieran return for the crown. Then what? Do you think that returning the crown to England will solve all of your troubles and the charges against you will be miraculously dropped? You'll still be in the same predicament, Rory, only worse because you fled the country." He gestured weakly at Kieran. "And what about him? When all of this is over and he announces his true identity, he'll either be thrown into a science laboratory or into an insane asylum. Don't you see where this is leading, honey?"

Rory held Kieran's hand tightly, hearing the truth of Bud's words and growing more distressed by the moment. "I do," she whispered. "But we don't have a choice. We have to go, Bud, can't you see? Kieran must retrieve the crown and I'm the only one who can help him. It's like… like this was meant to happen. I can't retrieve it without him and he can't retrieve it without me. But even more than that, it's as if we truly belong together just like Kieran said. Even if we were born eight hundred years apart, he fills in me something I never realized I lacked. He makes me whole, Bud, like I've never been in my life."

Bud's eyes glimmered with the force of his emotion. "I'd always hoped to hear you say those words where they pertained to me." He smiled weakly, feeling weary and defeated and completely resigned to the inevitable. He didn't want to fight her anymore, or to resist her determination. Whether or not it ruined him professionally, he was already ruined emotionally and he found himself, once again, willing to do her bidding. "All right, then. So you're going back to Nahariya. Back to the grave site, I take it?"

Rory looked at Kieran, who met her gaze with a shrug. "I am afraid I cannot elaborate on that aspect, considering I do not know where I was buried."

"We found you in the ruins of an ancient Grecian temple where the Muslims buried their trash," Rory told him. "It sits on a rise above the city and you can see the Mediterranean in the distance. Do you know the place I'm talking about?"

He thought a moment, his brow furrowed. Then, realization dawned; his brown eyes suddenly took on a marvelous twinkle and he grinned at the wide-eyed lady by his side. "Is that where you were looking for the diadem?"

She nodded. "All of the ancient manuscripts pointed to it as the location of an ancient Muslim temple. A temple where the diadem of Christ would be found."

He shook his head in confusion. "What ancient manuscripts do you speak of? You have mentioned them before."

"Fourteenth century manuscripts written by a Byzantine monk named Ottis. I don't know where he received his information, but he was quite specific with his description. I came across the scripts in Rome when I was doing my post-graduate work."

Again, Kieran's brow furrowed and he released Rory's hand, pacing absently across the room. "I do not know how he came to know. Unless..." he held up a finger, looking to both Bud and Rory. "You informed me that I was buried with all of my possessions, including my journal?"

Bud was the first to answer. "Everything. It was laid on top of the corp... uh, you in layers. First your mail, then your sword, then the rest of your personal effects."

Kieran digested the information intently. "After the assassins wounded me in my room at the inn, there was little time to collect my property before going in search of a healer. Which can only mean…" he suddenly slapped his open palm against his thigh. "God's Blood! It has to be!"

Bud and Rory looked at each other curiously. "Be what?" Rory asked timidly.

Kieran looked to her, understanding written all over his face. "The alchemist mentioned that he knew Hut, the owner of the hostel where I was staying and the same man who referred me to him after I was wounded. I can only assume that it was Hut who collected my possessions for burial and somewhere in the process…" he tapped his head in a thoughtful gesture. "Somewhere in the process, his insatiable curiosity caused him to read my journal."

"And?" Rory lifted her eyebrows encouragingly.

He looked surprised that she hadn't followed his train of thought. "You read my journal, Libby. I have never understood why you were unable to decipher the location of the diadem as well. Certainly you are much smarter than Hut."

Her mouth opened with shock. "The location?" she repeated. "I didn't come across any type of description pinpointing the location of the crown. But much of the latter part of your pages were muddle with age and…"

She suddenly broke away, rushing to her overnight bag and tossing the thing onto the bed. Very, very carefully, she extracted the familiar leather-bound cover and Kieran's features softened as he beheld the chronicles he hadn't seen in over eight centuries. When she extended the book, he accepted with the utmost reverence.

"Oh, Libby," he murmured. "You have it."

"Of course I have it." She couldn't help but smile as he touched the vellum, weakened with age. Even Bud was becoming enthralled with Kieran's obvious worship for the ancient book, watching as the man inspected it over carefully before opening the heavy cover.

The yellowed pages turned, one at a time, as Kieran scanned the contents of his journal. Rory hung over his shoulder, crown forgotten for a brief moment as she pointed out the more legible passages and even questioning him about the incident with Al-eb-Alil. He modestly shrugged off the heroic circumstance as she knew he would; any virtuous knight would have done the same, he said. He had simply been closer to the situation and far better equipped; therefore, it was logical that he should be the one to engage the general.

Bud stood by, listening to him speak as if the incidents had happened only yesterday and coming to believe that the man did, indeed, know what he was talking about. No actor could have conveyed such casual flair when speaking of a brawl at an inn in Joppa, or paying five thousand dinars for a beautiful Arabian stallion that had been shipped home to Southwell for breeding purposes. The more Bud listened, the more he found himself believing. And the more his resistance began to fade.

Maybe dead men do walk.

"You knew King Richard personally?" he heard himself asking. He couldn't help it. And he almost looked around to see where the eager schoolboy had come from.

Kieran looked up from the faded pages. "Indeed. A man of average height, reddish hair, and a sadistic sense of humor. Actually, you remind me of him somewhat. Both of you are extremely stubborn."

Bud cocked an eyebrow, not sure whether or not he had been insulted. "But you knew Henry Augustus? And Conrad of Montferrat, too?"

Kieran's warm expression faded. "You would not like to hear my opinions of them."

"Like hell!" Bud said, moving for the chair by the long French doors and preparing to take a seat. "Christ, do you realize... My God, you're a walking history lesson, an archaeologist's dream! Not only for your knowledge of the Crusades, but for your knowledge of life in Medieval Europe. And... Christ, the fact that you've been in stasis for centuries is beyond our medical science today. When I think..."

"Bud?" Rory interrupted him, a smile on her lips. "Are you trying to say that you finally believe what we've been telling you?"

He lowered himself on the chair, taking a long, heavy sigh. "I guess I've just resigned myself to the inevitable. I know I shouldn't give credence to the impossible, but the more I hear him speak and act and... hell, exist, the more I just can't deny the evidence. And I've got to tell you; this whole thing has got me verging on a thrill of discovery like I've never experienced in my life. I told you once we weren't living a movie, Rory; well, maybe I was wrong. Maybe we're living something better."

Rory's smile broadened and she went to him, bending down to kiss him on the cheek. "Now you know how I've been feeling." He still looked skeptical; excited, but skeptical, and she returned her attention to Kieran. "Get to the part where you describe the location of the diadem. I've been through that entire journal and I swear I haven't come across it."

Kieran immediately flipped to the very last page, careful of the brittle parchment. His brow furrowed as he searched the wording, smeared and stained with age. Slowly, still fixed to the vellum, he moved towards Bud and Rory.

"Here," he said softly, trying to decipher his own writing. "I wrote it here, as I was bleeding to death. I never gave the exact location, mind you, but a cryptic description written in Hebrew. But now the ink has been ruined and the writing is illegible. God's Blood, no wonder you were unable to decipher it."

Rory looked over the top of the book at the familiar last page. "Hebrew? You can write Hebrew?"

He nodded. "There was little more to do during the time between battles for Acre than sit. Since Jerusalem is the heart of the Hebrew nation, I put my time to good use and studied the language. Fortunately, it eventually came of some use to me."

Rory looked up from the page, gazing at his beautiful profile. "So you used your knowledge and wrote the location of the diadem in a language your fellow Englishmen would not understand?"

"No one in Nahariya spoke Hebrew, but Arabic. Even if my enemies found the journal, I was willing to have faith in the fact that they would have been unable to find someone to decipher the writing. Unless they found an orthodox rabbi, who would, mayhap, have thought twice before divulging the information to a band of English cutthroats."

Rory smiled. She couldn't help it. "So you wrote it in a language only a Jew or perhaps another devout Christian such as yourself could decipher?"

"Deciphered by those who were worthy enough to know." He continued to stare at the faded pages. "But the page was not like this when I finished; the writing was quite clear. Clear enough for Hut to read it, I am positive."

Rory cocked an eyebrow. "The innkeeper? Do you think he could read Hebrew?"

Kieran looked up from the ruined writing, his eyes locking with her beautiful gaze. "Hut told me that he was originally from Jerusalem, forced to flee with his family when the Muslims took occupation. The man was a Jew, Lib. I have no doubt that he read my journal and either told another or wrote it down himself. Information that somehow found its way to your Byzantine monk."

Rory stared at him. Behind her, she could feel Bud rise from the chair. "Then Ottis knew what he was talking about?" Rory murmured, feeling the heady grasp of excitement embrace her heart. "Was he right, Kieran? Is the crown in a Muslim mosque?"

Kieran looked to her, her glittering eyes, her eager face, and smiled. Closing the book, he touched her silken cheek gently. "Indeed it is, my lady. I hid it in the last possible place my traitorous Christian brothers would look."

Rory's eyes widened, a marvelous smile coming to her lips. Giving a crow of pure triumph, she turned to Bud. "Did you hear him? I was right all along! It really is buried in a Muslim mosque!"

Bud couldn't help but smile in response to her excitement. Excitement he hadn't seen from her since the commencement of their dig fourteen months ago. "Ok, so you were right. But where is this mosque? As we found out, our dig site was an ancient Grecian temple."

"If you are referring to the ancient temple of Bacchus, I know its location well." Kieran was focused on Bud, drawing Rory against his torso. "Your position is only slightly awry. The mosque you seek is down the hill, about three hundred paces."

Rory's blissful smile faded as she gazed up at him. It was difficult not to keep the astonishment from her face. "But... but there's no structure there. That's where our workers' camp is."

He met her gaze, raising an eyebrow confidently. "Then your camp is sitting right on top of it."

Bud could hardly believe what he was hearing. As Rory continued to wallow in astonishment, he let out an ironic snort and ran his fingers through his cropped hair. "Christ... do you mean to say we've been close to it the entire time and never knew? Dave's going to lose his mind when I tell him!"

Kieran set the journal carefully to the table beside the French doors. "Who is Dave?"

"Another colleague," Rory said huskily, still consumed with the revelation of Kieran's words. "He was with us when we found you. In fact, he fell in love with your broadsword."

"A wise man," Kieran replied, watching Bud move for the phone. Rory saw him moving, too, struggling to digest the stunning information and return to the serious world at hand.

"What are you doing, Bud?"

Bud glanced over his shoulder. "Calling Dave, of course. We can't close the dig down now, not when we're so damned close."

As Bud picked up the phone, Rory turned to Kieran. He smiled faintly and reached out a hand; putting both her hands in his massive grip, she met his warm expression as the shock of his revelation faded.

"I'm just a little curious," she said as Bud conversed with the overseas operator. "You were so adamant about protecting the crown when we first met, so determined that you would retrieve it alone."

"As if it were my own personal possession?" His smile broadened as he repeated her words.

She gave him a lopsided grin. "Exactly. If you were so protective about it, why did you write its location in your journal?"

Bud was waiting for the connection to go through, listening to their muted conversation and wondering much the same thing. Why would a man who had died for a brittle wreath of vines have given away the location of the very object he was trying to protect to those intelligent enough to decipher his writing?

Kieran continued to gaze at Rory, knowing Bud was listening. After a moment, he shrugged weakly. "In faith, my lady, I do not know what possessed me to divulge the location. I only know that as I sat dying in my rented room, a powerful urge compelled me to lend clue and conscience to what I had done. As if… as if a voice inside me demanded I describe the location for future reference."

Rory's brow furrowed. "But you said, and I quote, 'Forgive me Lord Jesus that my mission in Thou's Name hath been thwarted. The diadem of Thou's sacrifice entrusted into my hands is forever sealed, hidden…'" she paused for a moment.

Kieran continued for her. "…so that no man can pilfer Its beauty or omnipotence. Until such time that I can safely transport It to the land of my birth, Its whereabouts will remain my knowledge alone." Kieran smiled, touching her velvety cheek. "I know well what I wrote, my lady. I vowed that no man would ever pilfer its beauty. But I never referred to a woman in the same negative context."

Rory's brow furrowed. "I don't understand."

He chuckled softly. "Nor do I. Only that by writing the cryptic location of the crown as I was immediately unable to complete my task, I hoped that someday an educated man would learn the secret and come to my aid. When, in fact, the educated man was in actuality an educated woman."

"But I never read your description."

"Nay, you did not. Someone read it for you and made sure you understood its worth."

Rory shook her head, finding herself pulled into his warm embrace. "Your answers are as cryptic as the writing in your journal. Are you saying that you wrote the description specifically for me?"

His big shoulders lifted lazily, a warm expression on his face. "Who can say? But it was as if... as if, indeed, I wrote it specifically for you. Knowing you would come along eight centuries later to help me complete my task."

"Then you never truly believed you were dead?"

"I did, indeed. But there was always hope for a miracle."

Bud continued to observe as Rory and Kieran gave into sweet, delicious kisses and he was forced to turn away as his stomach twisted with anguish. But as he did so, something beyond the short garden walls of the bed and breakfast suddenly caught his attention and the receiver clattered to the bed beside him.

"Damn!" he hissed, racing to the cracked French doors and peering outside.

Kieran was immediately by his side, the brown eyes alert. Rory joined them, wedging herself between the two men and unable to hold off a small cry of fright as her eyes drank in a vision she had never expected to see again. At least, not this soon.

"Corbin!" she gasped.

Kieran whirled away from the doors, already on the move. Bud, thoroughly startled and struggling to keep his own fear at bay, watched as the lawyer and two men he didn't recognize disappear from view. Undoubtedly heading for the entrance to the hostel, as indicated by the direction they were walking, and Bud threw open the French doors.

"Come on." Bud noted Kieran was shoving his journal into his duffle bag as Rory groped for her purse. "They're coming in the front; you can slip out through the garden while I hold them off."

Rory froze, purse in her shaking hands. "But... Bud! You've got to come, too!"

He shook his head, grasping her by the arms and trying to direct her to the open doors. "I can't, honey. Someone has got to stall for time while you two make an escape." He gestured towards her suitcase sitting against the wall. "Look; leave your suitcase here. I'll tell him that you've just gone out and I'm expecting you to return soon. That should keep him here for an hour or two, enough time for you and Kieran to make it to safety somewhere."

Rory was beside herself. "But I just can't leave you here!"

"You've got to," Bud insisted softly. "Those men with Corbin are probably detectives from Scotland Yard. The man's coming for us and he's not going to take any chances the second time around. If I run with you, they'll be on our tail in no time."

Rory swallowed hard, torn and frightened and confused. "Oh, God… how did they find us? No one knew we were here!"

"Except Becker," Bud said quietly, zipping her purse when she seemed unable to finish the task and completely disturbed by the implications of Becker's involvement. When he looked up and saw tears in her eyes, he shook his head briskly and kissed her on the cheek. "No tears, honey. Go on; get the hell out of here. I'll stall as best I can."

As Rory struggled to come to grips with the sharp turn of events, Kieran understood the circumstance well; aye, he was quite used to fleeing like a criminal, when one's life depended upon the ability to think and react quickly. He'd spent time doing just that as he evaded Simon and his cutthroats. And it would seem he was destined to continue the tradition in the wake of Bud's selfless sacrifice.

"Thank you, Dr. Dietrich," he said quietly, grabbing Rory's hand and moving for the ajar panels. "Your sacrifice is appreciated and we shall delay no further."

Bud met Kieran's gaze, a thousand words demanding to be expressed. But he hardly had the time. "Look, I know we've had our differences. Just… take good care of her. All I've ever wanted is for her to be happy."

Kieran met his expression strongly, with the greatest sincerity. In spite of everything they'd been through, the bitterness and tension, he was willing to pretend none of it had ever existed. Everything that had been said or done had been in Rory's best interests and Kieran could hardly fault the man his loyalties. "Have no doubt, my lord. I swear on my oath that I shall make you proud."

Rory found herself being pulled along, out into the garden. But not before she gave Bud one last try; she simply couldn't imagine being without him in the final throes of the most important task of her life. Now that he and Kieran were finally coming to terms with one another, she was more desperate than ever for Bud's wise, level-headed company.

"Please, Bud! Please come with us!"

His gaze was soft, her pleas weakening him. The thought of separation, perhaps never to see her again, tore at him and he reached out his hand, brushing her outstretched fingers one last time. Feeling her warmth touch him, the golden magic it had always provoked. But she had made her choice and he wasn't a part of it; there was no use in torturing himself. But, Christ, with every step she took, the knife of anguish plunged deeper and deeper into his already-battered heart.

"I can't," he said hoarsely. "Go on, honey. Do what you have to do."

Bud slammed the French doors and locked them before she could argue further. Kieran was tugging her gently and she followed him dumbly, wishing there was time to tell Bud how much he had meant to her. How much he would always mean to her in spite of the fact that she wasn't in love with him. But the look in his eyes as he gazed at her through the glass, the final expression on his face before Kieran whisked her through the sweet English foliage, spoke volumes that reached her very soul. Whether or not she had been able to verbalize her feelings, he seemed to know. He seemed to sense it.

You're really not such a bad guy, after all.

CHAPTER SIXTEEN

THE PICCADILLY LINE from Cockfosters ran all the way to Heathrow. Having nowhere else to go, Rory decided to head directly to the airport and make plans once they arrived. Kieran was more comfortable with the Underground the second time around and showed little of the fear he had displayed previously. As he observed the people, the passing sights, and even tried to comprehend a modern-day newspaper, Rory wrestled with the guilt of having left Bud behind.

But all thoughts of Bud's jeopardy aside, a very real problem remained; getting Kieran to Israel. The man obviously had no birth certificate and no identification whatsoever, which made applying for a passport rather difficult. Short of smuggling him on the plane, she was at a loss as to what to do and her distress increased the closer they drew to the airport.

Kieran, of course, had no idea what a passport was. And the first time he saw an airplane take off, Rory thought he was going to burst a vein; his eyes widened as the roar of engines shook the terminal and he grabbed hold of her, refusing to let go. Not for his own protection, as he pointed out, but for hers. Rory thought there might be a little bit of falsehood to his statement, but she didn't let on. If he wanted to protect her from the overwhelming concept of an airplane, then she would go along.

As Kieran continued to marvel at the jets, Rory was determined to organize their priorities. Providing Bud could hold off Corbin and Scotland Yard for any amount of time, the need to leave England was, nonetheless, pressing. Moving to the big display screens that announced arriving and departing flights, it took Rory nearly forty minutes to locate a flight leaving for the Middle East.

Another few minutes and she succeeded in finding a TWA flight that departed for Israel, but it was scheduled to leave in less than two hours. Checking with the TWA representative, she discovered that the next flight from Heathrow to Tel Aviv wasn't until the next day. Not wanting to wait that long, it was essential that she figure out how to get Kieran a passport. And she had an hour and forty-seven minutes in which to do it.

The terminals at Heathrow were spotted with bars and restaurants designed for the weary and nervous travelers. With Kieran clinging to her like an over-sized coat, his eyes glued to the windows as the planes took off, she directed him into a dimly-lit bar. Seating him along the windows where he could continue to watch the great flying vehicles, she ordered two very stiff drinks.

Kieran downed his in one swallow, smacking his lips with satisfaction. In fact, the quality of the alcohol was enough to distract him from the airplanes. "What is this liquor, Libby?"

She toyed with the rim of her glass, lost in thought. "Bacardi One-Fifty-One. It's rum."

He raised an eyebrow. "Pleasing."

She looked up at him and couldn't help but laugh. "Kieran, this stuff is designed to burn a hole in your stomach."

He smiled as she laughed, motioning the bartender for another. "'Tis the only drink I've had since my awakening that hasn't possessed the taste and consistency of water. I rather like this... this... what did you call it?"

"Gasoline."

He scowled weakly as she continued to giggle. "Insolent wench," he growled, taking her hand and playing with her fingers. "But at least you are smiling. I have not seen you smile all day."

The bartender brought Kieran's drink. Kieran told the man to bring the bottle, which wasn't a particularly strange request in an airport. Rory watched as the swarthy-skinned bartender returned to his cabinet of alcohol.

"Good Lord," she sighed, her humor fading. "I just can't figure how to get you to Israel."

He downed his drink. "Because I do not have a pass-a-port?"

"Passport," she said softly, hardly looking up when three loud men entered the bar and sat at the counter. She had explained the concept of passports while they were on the subway and he thought the whole idea ridiculous. "Without a birth certificate, you can't get one. And I wouldn't know where to go to get an illegal passport. Besides, even if I did, we don't have time. We need one now."

Kieran cocked an eyebrow in thought as the bartender put the bottle of Bacardi on the table. Presenting Rory with the check, she begrudgingly paid.

"And that's another thing," she muttered. "I'm almost out of money and my credit card is maxed out."

He watched her as she struggled to sort out their problems, wishing he could do more to help. "I used to have a good deal of money at my disposal," he said, caressing her hand. "But you took it from me when you uncovered my grave."

She looked up from her glass, smiling ironically. "I know. And now I'm sorry I didn't keep your coinage like I kept your journal."

He met her smile, kissing her fingers as the rowdy group at the bar began toasting one other. Rory looked up as Kieran downed another shot of rum, watching the three men and deducing from their broken accents that they were returning to their native country. One man was particularly large with light brown hair and a flashing smile. His English was broken as he spoke to his friends. As Rory watched, the origins of an idea suddenly took hold.

"Kieran," she squeezed his hand. "Do you see that guy over there?

The one in the blue shirt?"

He glanced over with the customary haughty expression that men use when inspecting one another. "What of him?"

She squeezed his hand again as her plan began to take shape. "I said I didn't have time to get you an illegal passport, which is the only way you'll be able to get one." She looked at him, her hazel eyes glittering. "But we've got time to steal one."

He raised an eyebrow. "Steal one?"

She nodded firmly. "Look at that guy," she whispered, leaning closer to him. "He's about your size and coloring, and he looks a little bit like you, too. Not enough of a difference on a passport photo, I'd guess. Especially if we scuff up the print quality a little bit, just enough to muddle it."

Kieran appeared very interested. "Indeed," he mumbled, stroking his chin. "And just how do we steal his pass-a-port?"

Rory's mind was working furiously. After a moment, she dug into her purse and withdrew her compact. Freshening her makeup, she took out a little bottle of expensive designer perfume and sprayed it on her neck. Kieran continued to watch her, curiously, until he began to suspect what she was up to.

"Nay, lady," he suddenly said firmly, grabbing her hand when she tried to stand up. "I will not allow this."

She made sure her back was turned to the counter as she faced him. "We don't have much of a choice. Look, I'll get him drunk and try to get his identification off him. You just sit here in the shadows and keep quiet."

She tried to move away but he had a firm hold on her. "I told you that I will not permit you to… to prostitute yourself in this manner," he said, his tone deadly serious. "I will not permit my wife to display herself as a common whore, no matter what the motive."

"I'm not your wife yet." She yanked her hand away and he stood up, towering over her. In lieu of becoming upswept in a physical confrontation, since her plan was the only solid scheme she had managed to come up with, she put her hands on his chest to soothe him. "Please, baby, please. Just sit down and let me do this. I promise I won't let it get out of hand. Please?"

He cocked an eyebrow, thoroughly resistant. "There must be another way, Libby. Mayhap we can purchase his pass-a-port from him?"

"With what?" she shot back quietly. "I've got about thirty pounds on me, Kieran. After we steal his passport, we're going to have to rob a bank to pay for our airline tickets."

His face was molded in a permanent frown. She had sacrificed so much for him and he was only being difficult; certainly, he had trusted her implicitly since the moment of his awakening. He would simply have to keep trusting her, no matter how ridiculous the scheme. No matter how badly he wished he could simply take the man into a darkened alley and steal his passport the proper way.

… proper way?

"Lib," he said softly, a plot of his own taking hold. "I will agree to this scheme under one condition; that you allow me to steal the pass-a-port. Buy him all of the liquor he can drink and when he moves to relieve himself, I shall take care of him."

Rory looked thoughtfully at the counter, noting that the lavatories were across the wide hall directly in her line of sight. Since she wasn't a particularly accomplished pickpocket, the thought of Kieran manhandling the victim was somewhat appealing. At least Kieran would have a better chance.

"All right," she agreed. "I'll get him drunk and you can take the passport when he goes to the bathroom. They're over there, across the hall. See the sign?"

"I do."

"And don't kill him. We just need his passport, not his blood."

He nodded faintly, feeling more in control of the situation now that he was a viable player. Kissing Rory on the forehead, he moved past her and slipped by the counter without being noticed. Rory watched as he moved across the hall, pausing to linger by the large lavatory sign. With a deep breath for courage, she moved to the bar and took a seat next to her unsuspecting victim.

He was Swedish. Iarn, a name she could scarcely pronounce, was leaving England after a brief holiday with his brother's family. When his two friends saw that their companion had found more attractive company, they said their farewells and quit the bar. Trapped in the intense gaze of the large Swede, Rory struggled to maintain her poise while dodging his amorous hands.

She was glad that Kieran couldn't see what was happening, for he certainly would have recanted his pledge not to kill the man. Iarn's hands were on Rory's knees, moving up her thighs, when, suddenly, they'd be on her shoulder and into her hair. She bought him several drinks under the weak pretense of celebrating the end of their respective holidays and he drank heartily of the dark, high alcohol content ale.

Ale that was making him quite drunk. He was actually a nice man, a bit too aggressive, and Rory was caught off guard when he suddenly grabbed her and planted a big, wet kiss right on her lips. Over Iarn's shoulder, she caught Kieran's expression and suddenly he was moving across the wide corridor towards them. In a panic, she told Iarn she had to use the Ladies' Room and seductively asked that he wait for her. She hoped it would be enough of an incentive to make him stay.

But her bigger concern at the moment was heading off Kieran's offensive. No sooner did she leave the bar than she ran headlong into him, throwing her arms around him to halt his advance. Her frantic pleas somehow broke through his haze of fury and she managed to turn him around before Iarn caught sight of them both. Dragging him behind a bank of telephones, she pulled him into a small alcove partially hidden from the rest of the terminal.

"Calm down, baby," she murmured, her lips against his cheek. "He's just drunk. You really can't blame him."

Kieran crushed her in his massive embrace, smelling her perfume and feeling her delicious warmth against him. "Bastard," he muttered, still not entirely composed. "To steal a kiss is surely…"

She kissed him once, twice, smiling gently when he responded. "There," she whispered, kissing him again. "You've erased him. Now, will you please go back to your post? I think he's about to break."

"Not before I break him first," Kieran growled, giving in to her kisses and plunging his tongue deep into her mouth. Rory gasped softly, feeling his rock-hard arousal against her thigh already.

"Kieran, please." She tried to avoid his seeking mouth, putting her hand over his lips. "Not now. There's no time. We've got to get Iarn's passport."

"I would rather have you," he muttered against her open palm.

She grinned. "Be a good boy and get the passport. There will be time enough for our pleasures later."

He sighed, displeased and eager to be done with it all. "Very well." He lowered her to the ground. "But this had better be finished soon. The more I watch him touch you, the more I want to snap his neck."

She raised an eyebrow. "You promised you wouldn't kill him and I'll hold you to it. Killing a man is much more serious these days than it was in your time. If you think I'm in trouble for breaking into a morgue and stealing a body, that's nothing compared to murder."

He matched her raised eyebrow. "Then you had better hurry with your plot to separate the man from his pass-a-port. I cannot guarantee my control much longer."

"You have to," she whispered, touching his cheek seriously. "No matter what he does, you have to stay calm. If we're going to get back to Nahariya, this is the only way."

He didn't look happy. Rory pecked him on the cheek before peering around the corner of the small alcove, making sure the coast was clear. Noting all was calm, she emerged from the alcove and returned to the bar as Kieran resumed his position near the lavatories.

Iarn was extremely pleased to see her again. Rory spent the remainder of her money on more beer, struggling to keep his happy hands from groping her. Intermittently, she would glance at Kieran only to note he seemed to be more displeased by the minute. When someone put a quarter in the jukebox and a romantic melody began to play, Iarn decided he wanted to dance and pulled Rory off her barstool.

She had been positive Kieran would come storming into the bar only to remove Iarn's head from his shoulders and was quite surprised when no violence was forthcoming. When Iarn's dancing feet moved aside to allow her a clear view of Kieran still by the lavatories, she could see plainly that the knight's face was red. She'd never seen him red before.

The color of his cheeks was a supreme indication of his level of emotion and Rory was proud that he had held his anger in check so well. When the music stopped and Iarn released her, Rory quickly decided to cut her charade short for if only for Kieran's sake.

Since the inebriated Swede could hold a gallon of liquor before relieving his bladder, she was forced to consider an alternative plan. Thinking quickly, she collected her half-empty drink and "accidentally" sloshed it all over the front of his expensive shirt.

"Oh!" she gasped with mock surprise. "I'm so sorry, Iarn. If you go and rinse the stains with water immediately, they should wash out."

He stared at his shirt, unconcerned. "No matter. I am only going home soon."

She wouldn't let him reclaim his seat, pushing the uncooperative victim in the direction of the restrooms. "But this ale stains terribly. And it stinks. You don't want to go around smelling like a brewery, do you?"

He shrugged, completely sotted. "I do already."

"But this makes it worse." Pushing this guy was like trying to move a wall. In fact, it was very much like trying to move Kieran. "Please go and rinse out the stains. I'll wait for you."

He let her shove him out into the terminal hall, waving at her when she smiled sweetly. Staggering, sweating and all, he wobbled his way across the corridor and nearly bumped into Kieran as the man stood beside the lavatory door. Rory watched, heart in her throat, as Kieran ducked into the lavatory behind him.

Immediately, her smile faded and she hurried to collect her purse and Kieran's duffle bag. Her chest was twisting with nerves as she left the bar, eyes glued to the door of the lavatory as she leaned against the wall on the opposite side of the corridor.

Rory lost track of time waiting for Kieran to appear. It seemed to take forever when, in fact, it had only been a matter of minutes. A few men went into the lavatory, all of them reemerging a respectable amount of time later, but still no Kieran. Rory paced, chewed her nails, and wondered if she shouldn't go in. Just as she was feeling particularly panicky, Kieran suddenly exited the blue lavatory door and headed directly for her.

Rory could barely contain her anxiety. "Well?" she hissed. "What happened?"

From the pocket of his new flannel shirt purchased at Fortnum and Mason, he pulled out a small black billfold. Rory almost collapsed; snatching it from his awkward hands, she studied the contents.

"Thank God," she murmured. "His name is Iarn Solv Britson. Twenty-nine years old, six feet four inches and two hundred and twenty pounds. Brown hair, hazel eyes... Good Lord, Kieran, this is perfect!"

He smiled, looking down at the strange plastic card. "Indeed," he replied, rubbing the knuckles of his right hand. "A pleasant enough man, actually. I rather enjoyed speaking with him."

She looked at him, an eyebrow cocked. "You spoke with him? About what?"

He grinned. "You, of course. He was quite smitten with you and I told him he was wasting his time. We conversed as I was helping him clean his shirt."

"You helped him clean his shirt?"

"I had to do something while the privy was occupied by a collection of potential witnesses."

"And after they left?"

He put his arm around her shoulders, pulling her away from the wall and heading back towards the ticket counters. "I subdued him, of course." He reached into his pocket again. "And took this as well."

Rory looked at the brown leather wallet. Casting a long glance at Kieran, she opened the billfold and counted the money inside. "It's not enough," she said. "I know you were only trying to help by stealing his wallet, but I really wouldn't feel right taking it."

He raised an eyebrow. "Why not? You felt right enough stealing his pass-a-port."

"That's different." She looked away, staring at the two wallets in her hand and wondering if she was really destined for a life of crime. "We needed his passport because there wasn't any alternative. But his money… I have other ways of getting it, and not illegal ones. Good Lord, I'm starting to feel like Bonnie and Clyde."

His brow furrowed as they began to pass through the crowd of people waiting in line for the ticket counter. "Who are Bonnie and Clyde?"

She shook her head. Making sure no one was watching, she casually moved to the nearest trash can and dumped Iarn's wallet into the mess below. Clutching his passport with photo I.D. and Stockholm driver's license, she put them in her purse.

"They were a famous pair of criminals," she muttered, her gaze searching for a phone. "Which is exactly what we're turning in to. By the way; what did you do with Iarn?"

Kieran looked down at her, his manner cool and confident. "Knocked him in the jaw, pulled his breeches down around his ankles and set him on the porcelain bowl," he said smoothly. "Locking the door from the inside, I left him in the stall. It will appear to anyone looking at his feet that he is simply relieving himself."

She had to smile. "You even think like a criminal, you naught boy."

He put both arms around her affectionately as Rory spied a bank of phones. "Ah, lady, you've yet to see just how naughty I am."

She giggled as he nipped at her ear, her lightening mood indicative of the fact that her plan seemed to be working thus far. Comfortable that no one would discover poor Iarn until the man awoke from unconsciousness, by which time she and Kieran would hopefully be on a plane to Tel Aviv, she was able to shake some of the doom and gloom of their predicament. Just one final step in her master scheme was all that need be accomplished. But it was a final step that she was dreading more than any other.

The phones were somewhat private as Kieran took the small stool and settled her on his lap. Rory dug about in her wallet for her calling card as he watched.

"What are you going to do now?"

She picked up the receiver. "Get money for our tickets."

He watched her punch in the code. "How?"

Finished dialing, she turned to look at him, the warmth of her expression fading. "By begging."

DR. SYLVIA LUNDE picked up the brass and porcelain phone in her small office. "Hello?"

"Hi, Mother. It's me."

Sylvia didn't say anything for a moment, stunned. "Rory?" she finally gasped. "For Heaven's sake… Rory, where are you? What's going on?"

On Kieran's lap, Rory felt like she was five years old again. Neglected, ashamed, prepared for the verbal lashing that was sure to come. Her mother always had that effect on her.

"In London," she said. "I need your help."

Ever-present liquor on her desk, Sylvia poured from a Tupperware bottle and into a dainty tea cup. "Uncle Uriah's on his way, Rory. I can't help you. Maybe he can."

"No, Mother, not like that," Rory was struggling with her courage. "I need you to send me some money."

"Money?"

"About two thousand dollars."

Sylvia almost spilled the liquor in her cup. "Two thousand dollars!

For what?"

Rory sighed, feeling her bravery wan. Kieran was gazing at her with concern, kissing her shoulder when she appeared to falter. "Please, Mother, don't ask any questions," she said with quiet urgency. "Just wire me the money. I swear I'll never ask for anything else ever again."

"Never ask for anything ever again?" Sylvia repeated incredulously. "My God, Rory, you've already asked for quite a bit in your lifetime, countless favors and demands that have constantly taxed my patience. And now you have the nerve to demand money when you're in trouble with the law?"

Rory began to shake, feeling belittled and humiliated. "So… what? You're telling me that if I don't pay you back for everything I've ever asked for, you're not going to help me now when I really need it the most?"

Sylvia took a drink from her cup. "I didn't say that," she muttered. The cup smacked the delicate saucer as she set it down heavily. "Look, little girl. You're in a lot of trouble and I'm not going to help you out one bit. You got yourself into this and you're just going to have to get yourself out. What's the money for, anyway? Bail?"

Rory was verging on tears. Not unusual when it came to her mother's cold manner. She remained silent a moment, pondering her mother's words and knowing the woman meant what she said. And she knew without a doubt that she couldn't tell her the truth.

"Yeah," she said after a moment. "It's for bail. Can you please wire it to me?"

On the other end of the line, Sylvia poured herself another drink. "For Heaven's sake, Rory," she grumbled into the phone, taking a healthy swig. "How on earth do you get yourself into these messes?"

Rory blinked back her tears of frustration. "I'll explain later. I know it wouldn't do any good to tell you that my motives were true, because you wouldn't believe me. Just… please send me the money, Mother. I'll spend the rest of my life making it up to you, I swear."

Sylvia felt the liquor in her veins, the familiar warmth and comfort.

A warmth and comfort that only served to fuel her disgust in her only child. "We're beyond that, I think," she said quietly. "We went well beyond amends when you embarrassed me by abducting an ancient corpse. Just tell me one thing; what in the hell were you thinking?"

Rory could feel Kieran's hand on her back, stroking her gently. Feeling more love and tenderness from a man she had known less than a week than from her own mother. A woman who had never loved her, who had used her as a whipping post for her own alcoholism and personal failure.

"I guess I was thinking that no matter what I do, no matter what I've ever done, I can never be the daughter you've always wanted me to be." Her voice was quaking. "Good grades didn't do it. Gifts I made for you in Girl Scouts didn't do it. I even offered my thanks to you in my high school Valedictorian speech, but that didn't do it either. The only time I ever saw an inkling of respect in your eyes is when I went before the Board of Regents and proposed my dig. And even then, it was short-lived. The only respect you ever had for me was in knowing what I could do for your career if my archaeological site was successful."

On the other end of the receiver, Sylvia took another long, healthy swallow. "You want me to send you money and resort to insults to get it? That's just like you, Rory. The tactics of an idiot."

Rory closed her eyes, fighting off a harsh retort. Instead, she took a deep breath and struggled for composure. "I'm sorry if I've offended you, Mother," she spoke through clenched teeth. "Will you please send me the money now, before we start saying things we'll both regret?"

"I've never regretted anything I've said to you." Sylvia took another drink. "You never heard me, anyway."

"I always tried to."

Sylvia took a deep breath, glancing at the clock and realizing she had a speech to deliver at a breakfast meeting in a couple of hours. Enough time to get the smell of liquor off her breath and recover from her daughter's phone call. But the more she pondered Rory's behavior, the more sickened she became.

"Damn you," she finally hissed. "How could you do this to me, Rory? How?"

Rory sighed, a catch in her breath as she wrestled against the tears. "What do you want me to say? That I'm sorry, that I'll swear before the entire university board that you had nothing to do with my actions? What do you want me to tell you, Mother?"

Sylvia's temples were pounding. "Tell me why you did it!"

Rory clenched her teeth, her chest exploding with emotional rage. "Why?" she repeated. "All right, Mother. I'll tell you. It was because the corpse I dug up was my find, my property. Uncle Uriah and Bud practically forced me to turn it over to the proper English authorities when what I really wanted to do was keep it. So I did. I kept it."

"Is Dietrich in on this wild plot?"

"Not at all. This is all my doing, Mother. My blame. And yours."

Sylvia's brow furrowed deeply. "My blame? How can you say that?"

Rory's jaw ticked as she formed her careful reply. "Because I received more satisfaction and warmth from this corpse than I ever got from you." Her voice was scarcely above a snarl. "Now wire me my damned money and I swear you'll never hear from me again."

Sylvia tried to drink from her cup and ended up dropping it on the desk. Infuriated, she hurled the saucer across the room and smashed it against the wall. "I've waited thirty years to hear you say that!" she shouted into the phone, scrambling for a pen and a piece of paper, her hands shaking with too much alcohol and a myriad of wild emotions. "Tell me where you are and I'll send it to you. Consider it my last payment to your cause, Rory Osgrove. After this, we're finished."

Rory was beginning to crumble in spite of Kieran's reassuring embrace. Wondering if her mother knew what she was saying and truthfully not caring; she didn't need the woman any longer. Thirty years of torture had finally come to a head and Rory was willing to wipe her hands of the woman who had raised her as a duty, not as a pleasure.

"Send the money to the Western Union office at Heathrow Airport." Her whispered voice was quaking. "I'll have someone pick it up."

Sylvia scribbled the information, her sharp actions knocking her Tupperware decanter onto the carpet. Groaning at yet another disaster, she clutched the paper in her hand. "Two thousand dollars, Rory, and not another penny. You've embarrassed me for the last time."

"I hope so," she said as the tears spilled down Rory's face. "Thank you for the money, Mother."

On the receiving end of the gratitude, Sylvia's emotional state was gaining momentum. "You're welcome to it if it will sever all ties between us," she rasped. Then, abruptly, she seemed to slide into an eerie calm as she collected her spilled decanter. "By the way, Rory. Since this is the end of our association, I have a confession to make. I lied to you."

More tears spilled down Rory's face, faster than Kieran could wipe them away. "What about?"

"When you were born." Sylvia was weaving unsteadily, grasping her desk for support. "Your father wasn't a naval pilot as I've told you all these years. He was a drunken Marine sergeant with four children and a pregnant wife. He bought me a round of drinks in a bar in San Diego and we made love all night, resulting in you. I don't know what was worse; sleeping with a married man or having his baby. You don't know how many times I wished you had never been born."

Rory closed her eyes, struggling to keep rein on her sobs. Kieran simply held her closer. "His name was Clarence Lucas. He found me two years ago through a private detective and we had dinner together. A nice man, Mother. You really should have contemplated the fact that he might try to find me someday, considering you told him you were pregnant."

Rory tried to slam the phone into the cradle but missed. Sylvia heard the sobs on the other end of the line as her daughter wept loudly. Rory didn't hear the sobs from America as her mother wept loudly, too.

CHAPTER SEVENTEEN

"**D**R. DIETRICH, SURELY you realize you are in a good deal of trouble. If you'll simply tell us where Dr. Osgrove is, I am certain we can ease any accessory implications against you."

Bud continued to sit in the chair by the French doors, his ice-blue eyes steady as he faced off against Corbin and two detectives from Scotland Yard. The detectives were well-groomed men, college-educated and polite, but Bud wouldn't give them the time of day. They seemed to spend the majority of their time staring at each other, each man waiting for the other to blink. So far, no one had.

"As I told you when you arrived, Dr. Osgrove has gone out for the morning," Bud said to the young detective with receding blond hair. He had introduced himself as Larry Wolfe. "Look, she left her suitcase here. You don't think she would have taken off without her suitcase, do you?"

"It's been over two hours," replied the other detective, a handsome man by the name of Turner. He was chewing on a toothpick. "Where has she been for two hours?"

Bud cocked an eyebrow. "You aren't married, are you?"

Turner crossed his arms. "I am. But I keep my wife under a tight rein, Dr. Dietrich. She doesn't go anywhere for two hours without me."

Bud snorted. "Then you must have one hell of a leash, Turner. As for Rory Osgrove, consider the fact that the woman has spent over one year on the bleak sands of Israel. She's like a kid in a candy store with all of these western shops. Hell, I wouldn't be surprised if she's gone all day and has spent the better part of her savings by the time she returns."

Standing in a casual position by the door, Corbin lit a cigarette. "Then why didn't you go with her to prevent her from doing such a thing?" He tucked his lighter back into his pocket. "After all, the two of you are exceptionally close, aren't you? Protecting her from the law and all that."

Bud couldn't very well lie in front of the detectives any more than he was already doing, especially when Corbin was stating already-establish facts. Staring at Corbin with his ice-cold gaze, he simply shrugged. "She's a big girl, Corbin. She doesn't need me to chaperone or protect her."

Corbin met Bud's gaze, feeling the same strength from the man that he had when they'd met on the tarmac at Heathrow. Like a cornered tiger. "But that's what you've been doing, isn't it? Certainly she's told you where she's hidden the body."

Bud raised an eyebrow. "It's not hidden anywhere. If you hadn't knocked me out yesterday when you broke into Rory's hotel room, maybe you would have had some answers. But you created so much panic with your strong-arm tactics that we had no choice but to get away from you." He leaned on one arm, his eyes narrowing. "Now I'm curious; did you bring Scotland Yard in on your loose-cannon plans thinking I'd talk to them when all you have succeeded in doing is creating an even bigger mess?"

"And I'm curious, Dr. Dietrich," Corbin countered with a puff of his cigarette. "Why did Dr. Osgrove want an ancient corpse so badly that she would risk her entire future to steal it?"

Bud seemed to dull somewhat. "I never said she stole it. Even if she had, I can only guess her motives."

"And what would your guess be?"

Bud sighed heavily, looking to the garden beyond the French doors and remembering Rory as she passed among the flowers two hours earlier. The expression on her face was one he would never forget. "She felt that it belonged to her," he muttered, feeling stupid even as he said it.

"What's that?" Corbin moved away from the wall, his ear cocked. "Did you say it belonged to her? What, exactly, belonged to her?"

Bud looked at him. "I told you. She feels the corpse belongs to her since she was the one who found it. And I should have never agreed to turn it over to you."

Corbin cocked an eyebrow. "I see," he said. "Then she feels the corpse belongs to her. Or, perhaps, could it be the contents of the corpse that is her actual source of interest?"

Bud's brow furrowed deeply. "Contents? What in the hell does that mean?"

Corbin smiled thinly. Putting out his cigarette, he moved to light another. Certainly, with the police present, he had nothing to lose by continuing his provocative line of thought. In fact, the presence of the law might provoke Dietrich into a confession. "I have a theory, Dr. Dietrich, and please correct me if I'm wrong. I'm willing to wager that the actual corpse of Sir Kieran Hage isn't what interests Dr. Osgrove at all. But an ancient corpse could contain within its hollowed body cavity a collection of priceless artifacts a cunning archaeologist would be attempting to hide from the rightful owners."

Bud rose from his chair, his face a mask of disbelief. "What in the hell are you suggesting?"

Corbin was wise enough to sense Bud's hostility, moving to where the detectives were standing to put distance between them. "It's only a theory, really. But it wouldn't be difficult to smuggle artifacts in the capsule of an ancient corpse. The fact that Dr. Osgrove was adamant that no autopsy be performed only supports my theory. You two had planned to take the body to Oxford for further tests. Plenty of time to remove your ill-gotten stash before turning Sir Kieran over to his family."

Bud's jaw dropped; he couldn't help it. "Christ," he hissed. "You think that the reason Rory stole the corpse is because we're smuggling grave artifacts inside it? That's the craziest thing I've ever heard!"

"Not really." Corbin was cool. "After all, you Americans made the initial find. And even though you have turned over the contents of the grave, how do we know it's everything? How do we know you didn't withhold some things for display in your university museum? Or, worse yet, to sell on the black market to raise funds for your floundering Archaeology Department?"

"Floundering?" Bud was outraged. "The University of California San Marcos has an excellent Archaeology Department!"

Corbin examined his nails, his cigarette. "Agreed. When I meant floundering, I meant financially. I've received information that the university is suffering from a few bad investments and that the Archaeology Department is in danger of losing funding. And with the closure of the Nahariya dig, future projects are in question. Selling a few valuable artifacts would certainly help the situation, wouldn't it?"

Bud's cheeks were mottled red as he struggled to maintain his composure. "I'm an archaeologist, Mr. Corbin, not a thief. What you're suggesting is nothing short of slanderous and I refuse to dignify your theory with any sort of rebuttal."

Detective Wolfe intervened before Bud and Corbin came to blows. "I've no interest in this smuggling theory at the moment, gentlemen. The fact remains that Dr. Osgrove is wanted for questioning for the break in at the morgue and the subsequent abduction of Sir Kieran Hage's corpse. In fact, up until this point, nothing's been proven against her. We've no eyewitness that saw her break in, and we certainly have yet to find anyone that saw her lugging an ancient corpse from the hospital. It's purely circumstantial, but we still need to talk to her." He looked at Bud. "Do you understand me, Dr. Dietrich? We just need to speak with your colleague at this point."

Corbin frowned. "A nurse at the hospital saw her there around the time of the break in. How can you disregard that testimony?"

Wolfe sighed patiently. "Because the nurse said she saw Dr. Os-grove with a man. A living man. If you recall, Corbin, we're looking for an eight hundred-year-old corpse. Had the nurse told us that she saw Dr. Osgrove wheeling a loaded gurney, I might be more suspicious."

Corbin sighed in exasperation. "We've all but got a confession, for Christ's sake! Even Dietrich said she threatened to do it!"

"But he didn't see her do it." Wolfe cast a long glance at the lawyer before returning his attention to Bud. "Is Dr. Osgrove really coming back, Dr. Dietrich? Or are we wasting our time?"

Bud looked at Corbin. The detective was calm and logical but, still, he had promised to buy Rory and Kieran enough to time reach safety. And two hours, in his opinion, was not enough time to reach safety from Corbin. No matter what the cops said, he knew the Hage family lawyer wouldn't rest until he found her. And the shocking fact that he believed Rory to be a smuggler only fueled his determination to protect her.

Weakly, he gestured at the suitcase. "Her luggage is still here," he said quietly. "I…"

The piercing ring of Corbin's cell phone abruptly filled the air. The lawyer ripped it from his pocket, answering it harshly. But the moment the caller identified himself, Corbin's eyes were glued to Bud like a cat watching a mouse. Bud returned the man's gaze, wondering who was on the other end of the phone and knowing, without a doubt, it had something to do with Rory. By the time Corbin ended the call, Bud was ready to explode with apprehension.

"That was Dr. Osgrove's uncle." Corbin turned to the detectives. "She's apparently at Heathrow. Her mother received a call about a half-hour ago requesting that money be wired to her there."

Wolfe and Turner looked at Dietrich. "Where is she going, Dr. Dietrich?" Wolfe asked, perturbed with the evasiveness that had caused them to waste two precious hours. "If you know, you'd better tell us or so help me I'll throw you in jail for conspiracy."

Bud heard the threat but, at the moment, his attention was focused on Corbin. "Becker!" he rasped. "He's been helping you all along?"

Corbin put the cell phone in his pocket smugly. "Of course," he replied with a faint smirk. "You really should have told him about his niece's trouble yourself, Dietrich. He was quite surprised by the news of her crime spree and when I offered my services to aid the poor girl, he was more than willing to agree."

Bud's cheeks were mottling again. "You dirty bastard. He thinks you're trying to help her when you really want to see her hang for this!"

Corbin opened the door leading into the hall. "I simply want to see justice served, Dr. Dietrich. Now answer the detective's question; where is she going?"

Bud clamped his mouth shut. "You're so damned smart, you figure it out."

Corbin's smile faded. "I already have. And I would suspect that she's going back to the scene of the crime. Am I correct?"

Bud didn't reply. Wolfe and Turner, apparently unwilling to follow through on their threat of throwing Bud in jail, quit the room with Corbin close behind.

Bud listened to their footfalls fading down the hall, his entire body shaking with emotion as he picked up the phone and placed a call to the airlines. Not wanting to wait for the flight to Tel Aviv the next day, he booked himself on a flight to Istanbul that departed in six hours. From there, he would find his way to Nahariya.

Hanging up on the airlines, he immediately placed an overseas call. If he couldn't make it in time to save Rory and Kieran from Corbin's pursuit, then he would make sure David did.

 C3

KIERAN'S FIRST EXPERIENCE on an airplane was even worse than the Underground. Plastered against his seat, he refused to move from the time the plane took off until the moment it set down. The man didn't possess a cowardly bone in his body, but he was having a difficult time adjusting to something Rory took for granted.

The overhead reading light seemed to be the only gadget she could divert his attention with, but even then he hardly paid attention to it. When the plane landed in Rome for a short stopover and took off again, Rory gave up on the light and squeezed his hand the entire flight to Tel Aviv.

It had been an exhausting flight. Kieran was stiff as he disembarked the plane, looking back at the phallic-shaped monster as if scarcely believing he had survived the trip. But a journey that had taken months in his time had taken less than a day and he couldn't decide if his amazement was stronger than his airsickness.

The miracle of modern travel aside, the real magic was yet to come. Rory was shaking with apprehension as she went through customs, passing easily. Directly behind her, Kieran handed the customs worker his passport, looking straight at the man as the information was reviewed. As Rory bit her lip and struggled not to collapse, the customs official hardly glanced at Kieran as he asked of his business in Israel. When Kieran repeated his well-rehearsed reply, that he was on his honeymoon, the man routinely stamped the passport and welcomed him to Tel Aviv.

And that was it. No blood, no sweat, little hassle. Kieran smiled at a shaken Rory, collecting his bag and kissing her hand as they moved through the terminal. Bouncing back from their chaotic flight experience, they emerged into the bright Israeli day and went in search of a taxi. But their search abruptly ended when a familiar voice called to Rory from the curb and she looked over, only to come face to face with the familiar features of David Peck.

"Dave!" she squealed with delight, racing towards him and throwing herself into his arms. "What are you doing here?"

Peck was grinning from ear to ear, unusual for the normally taciturn man. "Bud called," he said, holding her back to get a good look at her. His smile faded. "He said you might be coming here and I called the airlines to see when the flights were arriving from England. Jesus Christ, Rory, what in the hell has been going on? Bud sounds like he's ready to collapse."

Rory knew Kieran was directly behind her, undoubtedly sizing David up. She smiled weakly at her colleague. "I don't even know where to begin, Dave. But I think I'd better start by introducing you to Sir Kieran Hage."

Pulling away from Peck, she grasped Kieran by the arm. Her eyes never left David's face, expecting the same reaction from him that she had received from Bud. Disbelief. Skepticism. Of everything David was, his logical character to his surly tendencies, she was prepared to accept the brunt of it.

Which was why she was completely surprised when he did nothing she had expected. Eyes behind the thin wire rims wide with shock, David took a step back as if witnessing something from a Boris Karloff movie.

"My God!" he gasped. "It… it's him!"

Rory was surprised by David's reaction. Without a word of persuasion or assurance, the man knew Kieran on sight. The man he had raised from the grave. As the knight gazed down at David with his usual even expression, Rory reached out a hand to steady the startled archaeologist.

"Dave, it's all right," she said soothingly. The man looked like he was going to faint. "We can explain, really. He's not a zombie."

"But…" Dave was still pointing at him. "He's alive!"

She let go of Kieran, patting David's arm comfortingly. "Yes, Dave, he's alive. But there's a logical explanation for it. You're not looking at a ghost."

David was white. Kieran cocked an eyebrow and shook his head. He'd almost rather have Bud's blatant disbelief than the naked fear of a coward.

"Jesus Ch…" David swallowed, turning to look at Rory as she continued to pat his arm. "Bud told me to expect the two of you, but I had no idea he meant… well, hell, this is just crazy!"

Rory shook her head patiently. "No, it's not. Dave, listen to me; Sir

Kieran wasn't dead when we found him. He was in a form of stasis brought on by an alchemist's potion."

"A potion?" David looked dazed. "Are you trying to tell me that some sort of elixir did… this?"

"It did," Rory maintained her calm voice. "Remember when I told you the knight's journal referred to the Crown of Thorns? Well, I was right. It really did. Sir Kieran was mortally wounded by assassins who wanted to get their hands on it and an alchemist put him to sleep in the hope of saving his life. Now that Sir Kieran is awake, he's determined to finish what he started."

"Started what?"

"The crown, Dave," Rory repeated. "That's why we've returned. He's going to show us where he hid the crown."

David simply shook his head, his entire expression awash with astonishment. "Bud said… he told me not to shut down the dig just yet. Christ, is this what he meant?"

Rory nodded. "Exactly. You see, I…oh, hell, we really don't have time for this right now. Are you well enough to drive?"

David nodded weakly. The Jeep was in the yellow zone next to the curb and Rory shoved him towards the vehicle, practically lifting him into the driver's seat. But David only seemed capable of staring at Kieran and, with a frustrated grunt, Rory pushed him into the passenger seat and took the wheel herself. Throwing the Jeep into gear, they left the airport.

The arid climate of Israel was as enticing as a warm caress as they headed out of the city. Nahariya was a solid two hours away as they traveled over lands Kieran had known well eight hundred years ago. But the knight was distracted from his view of the Holy Land by David's continuous staring. Unsure if the man's dazed expression was a challenge, Kieran stared back.

"Start explaining, Rory." David sounded calmer once they were on the highway.

She took a deep breath and launched into her story. Every detail, every move they made. Well, almost every move. When she elaborated on the part where Bud was only just coming to believe in Kieran's existence, David merely shook his head.

"How could he not believe?" he muttered, still gazing at the man in the back seat as if envisioning the Holy Grail. "I mean, look at him. We studied that body from head to toe and there's no doubt in my mind that this is the man we excavated. And all that stuff about the alchemist... well, I've heard some pretty strange things in my time. Thought your story about the Crown of Thorns was the strangest until now."

Rory grinned, glancing at him as the desert breeze whipped her hair about. "Dave, you were the last person I expected to come around so quickly. What about all your speeches about hard fact and evidence and myth-chasing?"

He shrugged, studying the scars on Kieran's hands. "This is the hardest evidence of all, Rory. I can't dispute a living, breathing man."

Rory shook her head in disbelief; gladness, but disbelief all the same. "You never truly believed in my crown. But you believe in a walking corpse?"

"Your crown isn't solid in my hands," David said, meeting Kieran's brown eyes. "Hell, if this isn't the damnedest thing I've ever seen."

Kieran cocked an eyebrow. "Is that good?"

Rory and David laughed. "Listen to that accent!" David crowed as if it were the most marvelous thing in the world. "Christ, there are a million things I want to ask him and I don't even know where to start."

Kieran, seeing that David was accepting the situation as well as or better than Rory had initially, stretched his long legs out over the back seat. "Your colleague has spent the better part of the past several days wringing forth information. Certainly she knows more than I do by now."

David hung over the seat, watching Kieran get comfortable in the tiny back seat. "I have no doubt about that," he said, the awe in his voice evident. "To get firsthand knowledge from someone who lived and breathed during the time of the Lionheart... Christ, I just can't believe this. It's amazing!"

"That may be, my lord, but the logical circumstance has been explained to you."

David grinned like a fool. "He called me 'my lord'," he snorted. "Well, hell, where to begin? How about your childhood?"

Rory's brow furrowed. "Childhood?"

David nodded eagerly. "You know, how he lived, when he fostered, the process leading up to knighthood. And I had a friend once who did his entire doctoral thesis on the sporting events of Medieval Europe. He claimed they played baseball centuries before Abner Doubleday supposedly invented it. Now I can actually find out."

Rory shook her head, looking at Kieran through the rearview mirror. "I'm sorry about him. Now that the shock is wearing off, he's only interested in your mind."

Kieran shrugged, grinning. "I would rather answer his eager questions that experience more of Bud's hostility."

David cocked an eyebrow, glancing to Rory. "Bud was hostile? What in the hell… oh. I get it."

Rory raised her own eyebrow, nodding faintly. "I'll tell you about it later but, please, don't ever ask him. Having the woman you love stolen by a corpse is not exactly something you want to shout to the world."

David nodded solemnly, his normal demeanor returning as the Jeep bumped over the highway. Truthfully, he didn't know why he had accepted Kieran's resurrection as easily as he had; but as he had always told Rory, hard evidence was the greatest persuader of all. And the fact that jealously wasn't clouding his opinion was a contributor as well.

Gazing at the weary face in the back seat, he knew the features all too well. He had sketched them for documentation as well as taken up an entire roll of film. Sure… he knew the face. And he accepted it for what it was, impossible or not. He would have been fool not to.

"All right," he said quietly, settling down for the long ride back to Nahariya and glad that Rory was driving. "So let's start from the beginning. Like your birth. Where were you born and did your mother use a birthing stool or a bed?"

Rory groaned. The stunningly blunt character of Dr. David Peck had returned with a vengeance.

CB

THE SITE WAS exactly as she had left it. It was nearly night by the time the Jeep rolled to a stop and Rory engaged the parking brake, smiling at the workers who were waving at her. David was already out of the car, having spent the past two hours in heavy conversation with Kieran and still lingering on some of the aspects of their dialogue.

Kieran bailed from the Jeep with his usual agility, duffle bag on one hand as he looked over the landscape. The Syrian foreman greeted Rory amicably, glancing strangely at Kieran but refraining from comment. Rory immediately informed the foreman that they would be digging into the night and asked him to crank up the generator.

As the camp began to move with purpose thanks to the shouts of the foreman, Rory turned to Kieran. He was still standing by the Jeep, his eyes roving the gentle slope and distant city. Quietly, she moved up beside him and slipped her hand into his massive palm.

"What are you thinking?" she asked.

He smiled at her, squeezing her hand. "I am not for certain." His bass-toned voice was equally quiet. "The smell… it is the same as it was in my time."

She leaned against his arm, the hazel eyes licking the familiar sights. "Then it smelled terrible. What else are you thinking?"

He didn't reply for a moment, his eyes riveted to the scenery. "It feels odd to be here. Strange. A timeless quality to the land and people that has not changed in centuries."

She glanced up at him, her brow furrowed. "I don't understand."

He continued to stare, trying to shrug off the peculiar sensation he was experiencing. After a moment, he squeezed her hand again and his smile returned. "Nor do I, sweetheart. Come, let us begin. If you'll show me where you found me, I can gain my bearings and…"

She laughed, pulling him towards a wide, familiar tent. "In a minute. Let's get settled and maybe change clothes. My tent is over here."

He followed, struggling against the odd hollowness that seemed to fill his stomach, spreading to his limbs. "Libby, we've no time to waste. I would suspect Simon... or the man who calls himself Corbin has managed to wrest our destination from Bud. We must hurry."

Rory pulled him into the tent, moving to light the old Coleman lantern. In spite of the sunlight, the tent was dim. "Bud didn't know our destination, remember? Maybe he still thinks were in England. He knows you didn't have a passport."

"But he knows we were destined for Nahariya." He set his duffle bag on the floor. "In fact, 'twould not astonish me if the man showed himself shortly."

The lantern cast a soft glow and Rory scratched her scalp wearily, wanting to change out of her crumpled clothes and into her customary digging attire. Kieran watched her as she fumbled with the small traveling case beside her bed, his attention momentarily diverted by the amazing lantern as she rummaged through her clothes.

"He'll be here," she said finally, drawing forth khaki-colored jeans and a t-shirt. "After he gives Corbin the slip, he'll come and help us."

Kieran heard the tone of her voice, knowing she did not believe what she was saying. Her fear that Bud had ended up in deep trouble distressed her, but she could not give up hope that he had somehow managed to slip free of Corbin's clutches. Kieran gave up fooling with the lamp and gave her his full attention as she stripped off the stained white shirt.

"Bud is a wise man, Lib," he said. "You must trust that he will come through unscathed."

She cast him a long glance. "You and Bud haven't exactly been the best of friends. And you still think he's wise?"

He nodded. "I cannot say that if our roles were reversed, my reaction to him would have been different. And just because he is resistant to the event of a miracle does not mean he is a fool." Kieran's eyes glittered in the weak light. "Moreover, he loves you, does he not? I cannot fault the man his choice of perfection."

She flushed, removing her shoes and tossing them to the floor. "I don't even know why he even bothers," she said. "He's done so much for me and all I've ever given him is heartache."

He watched her as she pulled off her pants, clad only in her bra and panties. Certainly they had no time to waste, but the more he watched her beautiful body in the weak lamplight, the more his desire threatened to outweigh his reason.

"He is a grown man," he said quietly, moving towards her. "And he has made his own choices. Whatever he has done for you has been of his own free will. Sometimes love itself is the greatest sacrifice of all."

She fumbled with her t-shirt, looking up at him and noticing he was nearly on top of her. "What does that mean?"

He smiled, a massive hand reaching out and embedding itself in her hair. "It means that you have done so much for me and all I have ever given you is heartache. Do you hate me overly?"

She tried to shake her head, unable to move when a second hand lost itself in her hair. "Of course not," she breathed, feeling the heat of sensuality ignite. "I'd do anything for you."

He pulled her against his chest as her tapered fingers went to work on the buttons of his shirt. "As Bud would do anything for you. As I would do anything for you. The joy, my dearest Rory, is in the doing. In this time or in mine. Regrets are useless."

She whimpered softly when his lips found her eager mouth, the fire of passion finding fuel. Tongues touched, tasted, and plundered as they lost themselves in a timeless desire; one loving kiss, one delicate touch, for every star in the bright Israeli sky.

☙

DAVID WAS WAITING for them near the gravesite when Kieran and Rory arrived an hour later. Signature baseball cap on his receding brown-haired head, he had difficulty looking Rory in the eye and she knew it was because he had heard their lovemaking. Fighting off a grin as David proceeded to explain the grave to Kieran, she let the smile break through when he finally met her gaze. Blushing profusely, David struggled not to appear too embarrassed.

Kieran, however, was tactfully obvious to David's chagrin and Rory's seeming nonchalance. He listened carefully to Dr. Peck's assessment of his grave, having great difficulty with the New York accent. If listening to Rory butcher the English language had been tough, deciphering David Peck was a nightmare. But he managed to catch the gist of the explanation, understanding that he had been buried in what was apparently the center of the temple. When David quieted, Kieran began to pace the gridded floor.

"In my time there was a good deal more to this structure," he said, trying to gain his bearings. Turning to Rory and David, he gestured behind them. "There were columns here at one time, thick marble pillars that had been left over when the Muslims finished building their mosque. Hypocrites that they were, they believed the Greeks to be pagans but it did not prevent them from stealing the fine stone from the Greek temples to build their own houses of worship."

Rory was fixed on Kieran as he moved about the careful grids. "We're facing west, Kieran. Were it not so dark, you could see the Mediterranean in the distance. Where was the mosque from here?"

He immediately turned and pointed down the hill. "Down there, where your camp is."

He began to walk in that direction. On his heels, Rory and David followed like eager puppies, a palpable sense of excitement filling them. They were closer to the crown than they had been in fourteen months and their enthusiasm was a powerful motivator. Kieran's long strides thundered down the hill, treading along the edge of the encampment. As Rory and David fell in behind him, David's cell phone rang.

It was a SkyPhone, a very expensive cellular phone that was linked to a satellite. If David was in the middle of the Arctic, he could still be reached. Whipping the phone from his pocket, he answered.

"Yeah?" a slight pause and then his face lit up. "Bud!"

Rory came to a halt, turning anxious eyes to David. "It's Bud? How is he?"

Even Kieran stopped as David held up a quieting hand, listening to Bud speak. After a minute, he nodded. "Yeah, she's come just like you suspected. No, I don't know how she got Sir Kieran out of the country. And by the way, it was nice of you to tell me about Sir Kieran's... yeah, but you could have tried. Not only that, but... all right, all right, hang on." He handed the phone to Rory. "He wants to talk to you."

Rory snatched the phone. "Bud? How are you? What's happening?"

On the other end of the line, Bud sighed with relief. And exhaustion. And every other emotion he could possibly feel. "Rory, how in the hell did you get Kieran out of England?"

She glanced at the massive knight, outlined by the mercury vapor lamps. "We stole a passport. Worked like a charm." She didn't really want to elaborate further on her crime spree. "We've been here for a few hours. What's going on with you? What happened with Corbin?"

Bud was calling from the ancient Turkish city of Tarsus. The bus from Istanbul had stopped there for refueling and he could hardly stand the thought that he wouldn't be in Nahariya for another four hours. And it was very, very important that Rory understand what was happening.

"Rory, listen to me," he said quickly, quietly. "Corbin is on his way to Nahariya. Hell, he's probably there by now. I tried to hold him off, but Becker called and tipped him off."

Beneath the silver moonlight, Rory went pale. "Becker? He's in on this?"

"I don't think he knows exactly what's happening," Bud said gently. "He thinks Corbin is trying to help you. When you called your mother to ask for money, Becker relayed the information that you were at Heathrow. He thinks you're running from the law, which you are. But what Corbin thinks is even worse."

Rory swallowed hard, feeling the familiar tightening of anxiety grab her. "What's that?"

Bud paused a moment. "He thinks you stole Sir Kieran's body because you were smuggling artifacts inside the corpse. The police aren't buying it as far as I can tell, but Corbin is convinced you're hiding something."

Rory closed her eyes to the horrifying new dimension of the situation. "And he's coming here to find out?"

"He's coming to get you."

Her nostrils flared with emotion. "No!" she almost shouted. "We're within striking distance of the crown and I refuse to… oh, Bud, what are we going to do? If Corbin gets here before…"

"I'm about four hours away, maybe more," Bud said, feeling her panic through the phone. "But I'll be there, honey, I swear it."

Rory was genuinely surprised. "You're… coming?" she said in awe. "You're already here? But, Bud, I thought you were still in England. You said you were finished with this!"

Bud drew in a deep breath. How many times had he resisted her pleas, denied her requests, only to give in? Christ, he was such a weakling. A weakling for the woman he would always love. "I never could stay away from you no matter what," he muttered, feeling like an idiot. "Give the phone to Dave so I can tell him what's happening. Until I can get there, he's the line of defense between you and Corbin."

A faint smile creased her lips, feeling the warmth and devotion from Bud as she always had. "Thanks, Bud," she murmured. "You're really not such a bad guy, after all."

After the phone call that would cost him a small fortune was complete, David put the phone back into his pocket as Rory and Kieran conversed quietly. No doubt pondering the current situation from the expression on Kieran's face.

"So this Corbin guy," David began, displeased with the idea of the man in pursuit of Rory. Kieran, too. "Bud says he's a mean bastard. A lawyer, huh?"

Rory nodded, her expression tense. "A shark, Dave. Unscrupulous as they come."

Next to her, Kieran sighed heavily, his square jaw ticking. "Simon was never particularly unscrupulous until Henry's men convinced him that utter victory over Saladin was the only honorable ending," he murmured, looking to Rory and David. "'Tis not only the reincarnation of Simon that follows me, but his very soul. Whereas God is working on our side, my lady, I am afraid that Lucifer is working for Simon. He is coming and he will not stop until he has me."

"Simon?" David repeated, remembering what Kieran had told him on the ride from Tel Aviv. "The guy who tried to kill you?"

Rory ignored David's question, staring at Kieran as tears stung her eyes. "He's not going to get you," she said firmly. "We'll find the crown and return to England and face up to whatever consequences there are. David and Bud will help us, Kieran. You must believe that."

"I do," he said, reaching out to touch her beloved face. "But I feel strangely now, as I have since our arrival. A sensation of foreboding and emptiness that I can scarcely comprehend. And my wound… it pains me oddly."

Rory frowned, untucking his shirt from his pants and gasping when she gazed upon the swollen, throbbing scar. Bewildered and frightened, she met Kieran's gaze.

"What's wrong?" she hissed, fighting off the tears. "Why is it acting up?"

He shook his head, retucking his shirt because the sight of his injury upset her so. "I do not know," he murmured, pulling her into his arms. "But I feel… I feel as I did the night Simon came for me at the inn. A powerful sensation of evil pursuing me, closing in on me no matter where I go. And my wound… mayhap it is reminding me that my task is not over yet. I must complete it before Simon finds me. Again."

Clouds were gathering overhead, the wind picking up. Her chest constricted with fear, Rory struggled to overcome the foreboding she, too, was feeling. The evil that Kieran had described.

With Rory in his grasp, Kieran didn't waste any time in continuing his task. Pacing off the perimeter of the Muslim mosque, he struggled to maintain a clear focus as to what he must do. The sense of urgency was greater now than ever before.

Simon was closing in.

CHAPTER EIGHTEEN

T HE FLIGHT FROM London had been exceedingly turbulent. The moment Steven Corbin disembarked at Tel Aviv, he realized he was glad to be off the plane. Gazing over the dusky landscape of Israel, the smile on his face had nothing to do with the end of his flight. Osgrove was close. Very close.

The flight he had assumed her to be on was held over in Rome. His flight had gone straight through. Even if he was trailing her, he wasn't far behind and he swore that he would have her by morning. And find out for himself why men had been willing to fight, lie and steal to protect her and an ancient corpse.

A corpse that was still missing. Even more than discovering what she had done with it, the desire to know the secret she was hiding was overpowering. And frankly, he detested mysteries. With a bruised and battered Neddy by his side, he would find out the truth of the matter. Dietrich was nowhere to be found and unable to protect her from the wrath preparing to fall.

Except for the massive bodyguard that was apparently traveling with her. Simon, the man had called him. So positive that Corbin had been this Simon that he had been willing to surrender himself in order to save Osgrove, arguing about some ridiculous subject Corbin could hardly understand. As baffling as the encounter was, he hadn't thought on it overly with all of the other pressing problems until he'd had a chance to reflect on the plane. And that's when it occurred to him.

Somehow... he knew this man. Or, at least, he thought he might have met him once. There was such a familiarity about him that he couldn't begin to describe it. Still, the persistent déjà vu plagued him. And the bodyguard undoubtedly felt the same, otherwise he would not have spoken to him with such recognition. Such anger.

Such pain.

Jolted from his train of thought as they reached the noisy luggage claim, Corbin and Neddy were immediately approached by a small man in a suit and several soldiers in fatigues. Embassy men, he correctly assumed, as the suited man extended his hand in greeting.

"Mr. Corbin?" he asked politely. "I'm Justin Darlow from the embassy. We received your wire, sir, and are prepared to assist."

Corbin shook the man's hand. "Thank you for your assistance. Since Scotland Yard only considers Dr. Osgrove a suspect, they have left it up to me to bring her back. Somehow, they still have difficulty believing she was capable of removing a body twice her size from a morgue." He eyed Neddy as the man collected the luggage a few feet away. "Did she come through customs?"

Darlow nodded. "We checked the manifest. She came through with a man by the name of Britson. Ring a bell?"

"Not really. But I was told by the ticket agent at Heathrow that she was traveling with a man. A very large man whom I've had the misfortune to meet. Disabled one of my men so severely that he's still in the hospital. And you can see Neddy's wounds for yourself."

Darlow nodded, sensing nothing but coldness from the piercing-eyed lawyer. He had been briefed on the history of Osgrove's crimes, remembering the beautiful woman from the Nahariya site and hardly believing she was capable of such lawbreaking. But the evidence, from what he had been told, was strong and the fact that she had returned to the dig must mean something significant. But Darlow couldn't imagine what, exactly. Still, he had been asked to help. And help he would.

"Very well." Darlow turned away from Corbin and gestured to the

Marines. "We've a convoy ready to take us to Nahariya if you'll collect your luggage. Dr. Osgrove has a several hour head start on us."

Corbin followed Darlow into the waning Israeli sunshine where three Rovers wait in a line at the curb. He and Darlow and a Marine took the first cruiser while Neddy and the rest of the Marines disbursed themselves between the remaining two. Three vehicles with twelve men among them pulled away from the curb and headed away from the airport.

"I take it that Osgrove is in a lot of trouble," Darlow said from the front seat as they headed out onto the highway.

In the backseat, Corbin nodded. "Quite a bit."

Darlow shook his head. "She seemed like a rather nice young woman. A bit emotional, but pleasant enough. I simply cannot believe she would do something as bizarre as stealing a corpse."

Corbin looked at the embassy aide, a thought coming to mind. "Did you ever see the body, Mr. Darlow?"

"Absolutely. A magnificent find."

Corbin cocked an eyebrow. "Did you examine it thoroughly?"

"Of course not. I'm not a scientist."

"Then you simply viewed it after the Americans had tampered with it?"

Darlow turned to look at him. "Tampered? What do you mean?"

Corbin was silent a minute, picking at his nails. "Nothing, I suppose. But I take it Dr. Osgrove was resistant to the idea of returning it to England?"

"Terribly. She carried on as if I had suggested giving her own child up for adoption."

"Then she was attached to the corpse even then."

"I suppose so. She wouldn't even let me take pictures of it. A pity, really. Sir Kieran was a very handsome man. A square jaw, even-featured from what I could tell, and exceedingly large."

Something about that statement made Corbin look up from his nails. "Large, did you say?"

Darlow nodded. "Massive. She said the man was six feet three or four and weighed well over two hundred pounds in his prime."

Corbin thought it strange that Darlow had just described Osgrove's bodyguard perfectly. But he shrugged it off, knowing the notion was impossible. As the Rovers sped over miles of Israeli highway, Corbin's thoughts returned to the beautiful young doctor who was in a great deal of trouble. And with every mile that passed, he was coming closer and closer to her dark, little secret.

Bodyguard or no, he would have his answers. He would know.

ભ

IT WASN'T EASY picking up where he had left off eight hundred years ago. As Kieran paced off the perimeter of the mosque, he realized quite a few things had changed since his day. Not merely the obvious.

There had been a wide avenue flanking the mosque, filled with shops and vendors. He could still smell the dung from the pack animals as his new boots, now covered with dust, plodded in what he hoped was the right direction. With barely a sliver moon and a gathering of clouds impeding his view, his return for the crown was more difficult than he had hoped.

Finally, he gave up in his attempt to use his sight. His only hope of regaining his bearings would be to return to the place and time that was most familiar to him. Rory and David had long since given up following him about and simply stood by, watching him work out the logistics of the situation. And they continued to watch as he turned away from the camp and faced in the direction of the Mediterranean. Closing his eyes, he took a cleansing breath and dreamed of a time long, long ago.

"What's he doing?" David whispered to Rory.

She shook her head, watching as Kieran seemed to slip into a trance. He was so terribly still. Seconds stretched into minutes as he continued to concentrate, his breathing even and his body relaxed. The Syrian foreman came to stand beside Rory, his young face inquisitive and a shovel in his hand. The three of them waited silently as the knight from the shallow grave drew closer to the object of his quest.

Just when the pause grew oppressive, Kieran suddenly opened his eyes. Blinking as if emerging from a deep sleep, he whirled in the direction of the camp and immediately put his hands up in a descriptive gesture.

"There was an avenue here, packed with straw and animal dung." He suddenly took two large steps forward, causing both Rory and David to start. They could sense his excitement. "The door to the mosque should have been here, whitewashed and bright. And the walls…"

He stepped forward again, moving towards the mess tent. When the canvas wall got in his way, he simply lifted it up and went under. Rory, David, the foreman and now a few workers followed.

"The walls were thick, mud bricks that were able to maintain a cool temperature in the hottest of days." His voice had quieted, his eyes seeing walls that no one else could. "They were quite tall, the Moorish influence evident in their design."

He was moving along the side of the tent, not bothering to use the designated exit when he reached the end. He lifted up the side and walked beneath it. His entourage followed closely, picking up more and more people as they went.

They were in a small clearing as Kieran continued to describe the structure contained in his mind. "I had come to the mosque early in the day, wrapped in the traditional white garments that the Muslims favored to conceal my identity," he said. "I had witnessed Simon and his outlaws the previous eve and knew it would only be a matter of time before they found me. My charger went lame and short of fleeing on foot, I had no choice but to hide. I knew I would be no match for them without my steed."

Rory was directly behind him, her hand on his perspiring back. "So you disguised yourself and hid the crown?"

He nodded faintly, his brown eyes focused on the dirt. They were moving away from the vapor lamps now and the foreman produced a

Maglite, shining it on Kieran's feet.

"I entered right after the morning prayer." He suddenly came to a halt. Looking around, he turned to the right at a slower pace. "The mosque was vacant and I attracted no attention. But concealed within my garments was a sturdy box, and contained within that box was the diadem. Since I did not want to bury it under the feet of worshiping Muslims, I chose a location well away from their prayer floor."

He came to another halt, pondering the dirt. Then, as a host of curious people followed, he began to move forward again. Had Rory not been so involved in his expression as well as his story, she would have noticed they were heading directly for her tent.

"There was a small alcove on the east side of the structure," Kieran said, looking up for the first time and noting the familiar opening of Rory's tent. Smiling faintly, he peeled back the tarp and peered inside. "In fact, I do believe I've found it."

Rory looked up, too, her eyes widening. "I don't believe it," she hissed, her mouth agape as she gazed into the darkness of her tent. "It... it's here? It's been right beneath my feet all along?"

Kieran continued to smile, retrieving the shovel from the foreman. "You have more than likely been sleeping on it."

He ducked into the shelter with David on his heels. Rory was so astonished that she could only stand in the doorway, watching as Kieran counted off five steps directly ahead. Rory's bed stood in his way and he moved it aside, driving the shovel into the packed sand where the frame had formerly rested.

"Fifty paces along the wall from the entrance, forty paces to the right, and five paces east," he turned to Rory, his smile widening. "Dig the length of my arm and you shall find your crown."

David didn't hesitate. Snatching the shovel, he jabbered orders to the foreman in Arabic and sent the man into a frenzy. Kieran pushed Rory out of the way as her tent was hastily dismantled in order to clear the field of excavation. Even as David dug furiously, with more energy than Rory had ever seen from the man, the only action she was capable of was simply remaining erect while it all went on around her.

"It was here all the time," she murmured, feeling Kieran's arm around her. "Good Lord... it was beneath me all the time!"

He nodded, watching David throw away shovels of earth as the foreman struggled to clear Rory's possessions. "All the time, Libby. You were always protecting it."

She turned to look at him, noticing how tired he appeared. Elated, but tired. In spite of her astonishment, she couldn't help the smile that creased her lips. "Protecting it for your return?"

He met her smile, wearily. "For our return, sweetheart. Certainly I could not have completed my mission without you."

She sighed heavily, attempting to shake off the amazing turn of events. Leaning against him, she was startled by a warm, wet stain on the left side of his shirt. Pulling her hand away, it was colored crimson.

"Oh, God." She forgot all about the crown as she yanked his shirt up to reveal the large, oozing wound. "What in the... Kieran, we've got to get you to a hospital!"

He shook his head in a quieting gesture. "That is not necessary, sweet. I've simply overextended myself, 'tis all."

"But..." the injury was truly hideous and she couldn't help the expression of disgust on her face. "You're bleeding again. You need medical attention!"

He tried to put his shirt down but she refused to let him. "A physic is unnecessary. It will heal. I simply need to... rest."

Rory was beside herself, ignoring the chaotic digging going on. Her immediate concern was Kieran's health. "You need more than rest, Kieran," she argued hotly. "You need to see a doctor. Immediately."

He looked away from her, gazing at David as the hole he was digging grew deeper. "Not until the diadem is uncovered," he said quietly, his features drawn. "I will not leave until I see it again."

Rory shook her head with disbelief, hardly able to argue with him. He had come so far and she certainly couldn't demand he abandon everything he had worked for. Everything he had died for. "If you won't go see a doctor, then will you at least let me wrap it?" she demanded.

He nodded in agreement, kissing her hand. Shaken and weary, Rory left him standing in what had once been the entrance to her tent and went to David's shelter to find the first aid kit. Bringing the entire bulky case, she proceeded to put antibiotic ointment on Kieran's wound and pack it with a huge wad of gauze. Using an elastic athletic wrap, she bound his torso tightly.

"There," she said, closing the first aid kit and setting it at their feet. "That should help for now. Until we can get you to a doctor."

He put his arm around her as she rose and Rory realized it was not only an affectionate gesture, but a necessary one; he was using her for support. Her panic surged but she fought it, knowing it would be of no use to argue with him. Until the crown was recovered, he wasn't leaving. And neither was she.

David and the foreman dug steadily into the night, their work illuminated by the big, portable lights. The workers cleared away the sand as Rory and Kieran stood silently by, holding one another and waiting with anticipation. Kieran's weight on Rory grew steadily, as if her petite stature could support his massive frame. But she never said a word, praying in one breath that his reopened wound wasn't serious and praying in the next that the crown would soon be found. The wait, for all of them, was frazzling.

And it grew worse as the night progressed. Kieran had begun to shake and Rory had to bite her tongue to keep from screaming. He needed to see a doctor or, at the very least, sit down, but he refused to move. He continued to hold her tightly, his brown eyes riveted to the digging and never once uttering a word of discomfort. But Rory could literally feel his distress and, unable to control herself any longer, let tears of frustration fall. Then, and only then, did he agree to the idea of a chair.

Midnight came and went. Kieran remained seated, his face pale and his hands clammy. Rory was torn between her anticipation of the crown and his deteriorating health, eyeing him intermittently only to be met by an encouraging smile. He was so terribly brave, so strong, and her heart ached for the pain of his reopened wound. She simply couldn't imagine how he had done it, considering it had been healed for centuries. But even though she had wrapped it hours ago, she could still see fresh blood oozing through the bandages.

And the reality made her sick. Literally sick. Fighting off tears and nausea, she didn't protest when he pulled her onto his lap. His blood stained her t-shirt as she snuggled against him, her arms around his neck and her head on his shoulder. Together, they watched David and the foreman continue the dig for a crown more men had lived and died for than any other crown in history.

Past two o'clock, David and the foreman had managed to dig nearly four feet, through a hard-packed mud that David assumed to be the mosque flooring and then several more feet of debris and sand. Rory continued to sit in Kieran's lap, deriving a great deal of comfort from his warmth and steady breathing.

But the extreme hour and her exhaustion were taking their toll. As she waited, as they all waited, Rory realized that, in spite of everything, she could hardly keep her eyes open. After a long, weary struggle, she allowed herself to close them for a brief moment. But the second she did so, David suddenly let out a whoop of surprise.

"I've found something!" he announced, tossing the spade aside. "Kieran! Look here!"

Kieran was on his feet, wavering dangerously as he rushed to David's side. Rory was with him and, together, they dropped to their knees, peering down into the hole.

It was a small wooden box. Plain and unassuming. Kieran took one look and nodded firmly. "That is the box," he said, his voice strangely weak. "Give it to me."

David obeyed without reserve. For a man who had been documenting finds the better part of his adult life, his professional training should have prevented him from handling an eight hundred-year-old box without first carefully recording the discovery. But he seemed to have forgotten his training as he lifted out the brittle box. Placing it in front of Kieran, he leaped out of the hole.

Rory's breath caught in her throat as she watched Kieran carefully examine the small chest. In fact, all activity surrounding the dig had come to a halt as the eyes of the weary and the anxious focused on the object of a year-long search. The only sound evident among dozens of people was the hum of the gas generator; not a breath or a movement to upset the magic of the moment.

A magic that was warm with the emotion of discovery. Rory could literally feel it. A timid hand reached out, touching the lid of the box as Kieran blew softly at the dusty coating. Casting Rory a glance that suggesting nothing other than pure triumph, he slowly removed the cover.

Brittle, yellowed linen greeted her. Eight hundred-year-old linen. Rory was about to comment on it when Kieran suddenly reached down, removing the linen without thought. Before Rory could chastise him, the object of years of research, of time and pain, was abruptly revealed.

Time stilled for a moment. Rory found herself gazing at a rather pathetic bundle of vines, faded and hardly spectacular. Long thorns that looked more like small branches adorned the circlet, some of them having broken off during the passage of time. But the aura radiating from the ancient wreath reached out to grab her like a vise and she gasped softly, moving in for a better look.

"Oh… Kieran," she murmured, bending low until she was nearly level with the box. "It's… wonderful!"

He smiled faintly. "Indeed, my lady. More than you know."

David was staring at the vines, actually speechless. As if he could hardly believe Rory's dig had finally produced what she had promised. In all honesty, it looked like a simple circlet of wood; no glowing light to indicate the holy stature, no voice from God announcing its identity. But David knew, without the fanfare, that it was exactly what Kieran and Rory said it was. If seeing was believing, he could hardly refute the evidence.

"I'm sorry for ever doubting you, Rory," he said, accepting the camera from the foreman. Lifting it to his eye, he focused on the small box. "You said it was here. And you were right."

Rory was practically lying on her side, gazing at the crown through eyes of wonder. "You know, even though I insisted it was here, I suppose I always had a shadow of doubt. You were right when you said I was chasing myths, Dave. I was. But it was a myth I wanted to believe in."

Kieran was seated on his rump, his arm resting on a propped knee. He continued to stare at the crown, eight centuries of a mission unfulfilled finally coming to a close. In a sense, he felt a tremendous sense of loss now that it was over. All he had lived and died for, the determination to recover what had been entrusted to him, was now ended and he realized that his desire to complete his task had been a matter of pride more than a need. England was at peace, the diadem no longer needed to cement a truce. But the fact that he was a man unwilling to let his sworn duty go unfinished had been the most powerful factor of all.

His gaze moved from the crown to Rory, completely enthralled by the brittle wreath. Darkly, he pondered what his pride had brought her; trouble, heartache, poverty and strife. She had been determined to recover the crown as well and he had used her devotion to his advantage.

Aye, he loved her; he couldn't remember when he hadn't. But he had used that love more than he was willing to admit. And if it took him the rest of his life, he would make amends for what he considered his manipulative actions.

Rory was touching the crumbled linen when Kieran reached down, lifting the crown from its cradle much to the dismay of both Rory and David. When both archaeologists turned to protest his actions, they were shocked to see the knight's eyes brimming with emotion. The conclusion of an eight hundred-year-old quest evident on the surface.

"Kieran?" Rory whispered, gently touching his arm. "Babe, what's wrong?"

He shook his head, his face pale and his hands shaking as he examined the diadem. "I do not know," he murmured. "I... I can scarcely believe I finally have it. I have it and there is nothing left for me to do with it. Bud was correct when he said it was unnecessary to retrieve the crown; my mission is over. It has been over for eight centuries."

"That's not true," Rory said. "This is a remarkable object with worldwide significance. You can't possibly imagine what sort of value this will have on the archaeological community and religion in general."

He tore his eyes away from the crown, meeting her wide-eyed gaze. "And you?" he asked, his voice hoarse. "What of you? Does this finally fill the void within your soul?"

She shook her head. "You've already done that."

"But what of your mother?"

"She doesn't matter anymore. Only you."

He sighed, his hands trembling as he set the crown back to the box. "I find this recovery rather anti-climactic," he said softly. "I had always believed that the moment I gazed upon the diadem again, unimaginable glory and honor would be mine. But now I realize that this crown cannot bring me the glory I seek. Only my heart can do that."

She put her arms around him, holding him tightly. "You're so wise in the ways of others, Kieran. But you're obviously not so wise when it comes to yourself."

His massive embrace threatened to crush her, his face in her shoulder. "I relied on this crown to bring me a sense of completion to my life, of honor and family pride. I had hoped that it would place me on a pedestal of glory for my father and Richard to worship." He pulled his head from her neck, gazing deeply into her eyes. "I have been such a fool, Libby. I thought this crown could provide me with all I had sought, fulfillment through the adoration of others. But I see now that I was wrong. My soul was complete the moment I met you, only I was too blinded by my sense of duty to realize it. And now see what I have done; you have risked everything for me. I have ruined you."

Rory's brow furrowed. "No, you haven't," she put her hand to his pale cheek. "I wanted this as badly as you did. I needed this. We needed this. Maybe if only to see how foolish our blind ambitions were and that the true meaning of life is where you least expect to find it."

He raised an eyebrow. "You are too wise, lady. Mayhap your wisdom will allow you to forgive the jeopardy I have caused you. For using your love to gain my own ends."

"Just like I used you?" She shook her head in disagreement. "I thought we agreed on this. We needed each other; one without the other could not complete the task. There is equal blame and there is no blame. It's what we both had to do."

He continued to gaze into her face, kissing her sweetly as David pretended to ignore the exchange by finishing off the roll of film. But David realized one thing very clearly; Rory's obsession for the knight in the grave had brought about a miracle. A love only dreamed of in fairy tales had come to life and if David lived for eternity, he could never hope to understand what had happened this day. But even if he never understood, he would always believe.

A strong faith that held firm as he finished with the camera and asked the foreman to videotape the find. Taking samples from the wreath and placing them in sealed tubes, he handed them over to a clerk who would forward the specimens to the laboratory facilities in Tel Aviv.

It didn't matter that it was the middle of the night. There was work to be done and David intended to see it through. But his focus didn't prevent him from noticing just how exhausted Kieran was, his shirt damp with blood as Rory cradled his great head against her breast. He went so far as to suggest that now would be a good time to seek medical attention and Rory almost had Kieran convinced when headlights on the distant road captured David's attention.

He rose, peering down the hill and to the long road beyond. There were three cars, from what he could see, and he knew their time had run out.

"Rory!" he hissed. "Cars are coming. It's probably that Corbin guy."

Kieran was on his feet before Rory could rise, his eyes sharp in spite of his pale features. Rory stood beside him, her expression laced with fear.

"Oh, God," she muttered, looking to David in panic. "We've got to get out of here. Back to the airport and head for England."

"Go back to England?" David repeated. "But you're a criminal there. You and Kieran need to fly back to the States!"

"No, David!" Rory snapped, rushing to collect the treasure that had cost so very much to retrieve. "Don't you understand? Kieran has got to take the crown back to England as he promised. And I've got to return to face up to the charges. I can't spend the rest of my life running."

"Lib." Kieran's expression was uncharacteristically gentle. "Mayhap we should remain. If it is Corbin…"

"If it is Corbin, then there's no way in hell I'm letting him have you or the crown. He tried to kill you once and there's no telling what he'll do given a second chance." She looked to David. "We've got to go back, Dave. I'll need the Jeep."

"I'll drive you." David was already moving.

"No!" Rory stopped him firmly. "I don't want you to be implicated for aiding a criminal any more than you already are. Kieran and I have got to do this alone."

Before David could protest, Rory had Kieran by the hand and the two of them were racing towards the Jeep as fast as Kieran was able. Handing him the box, Rory helped him into the passenger seat and jumped into the driver's side. Casting David a final, heartfelt expression, she threw the car into drive and headed down the back road of the dig.

David watched them go, apprehension filling him. Turning to the oncoming line of cars, he was not surprised when they veered in pursuit of the fleeing Jeep. Muttering a curse, he raced to a second Jeep they hardly ever used because the transmission was bad.

With the help of the foreman, David tore the protective tarp from the vehicle and tried to start it. When it wouldn't turn over, the foreman popped the hood and he and David struggled to find the problem like a pair of Keystone Cops.

Praying for a miracle in the meantime.

CHAPTER NINETEEN

I T WAS DIFFICULT to see the road in the dead of night. The headlights of the Jeep barely pierced the veil of darkness as Rory and Kieran sped south, away from the pursuing Land Rovers. To make matters worse, more clouds were gathering and the wind had picked up. Having spent more than a year in Nahariya, Rory knew a storm was approaching.

In more ways than one. Kieran sat in the passenger seat, his left hand over his bandaged wound, taking a pounding as the vehicle lurched over rough road. Rory knew the area well and knew that she was putting more distance between Kieran and the small hospital in the city, torn between the need to seek medical attention and the desire to be free of Corbin.

Her first instinct was to head back into Nahariya for the hospital. But Kieran wouldn't hear of it, directing her quite firmly to return to Tel Aviv where they could catch a flight back to England. He would be fine, he insisted, once he was allowed to rest. But Rory didn't believe him and tears stung her eyes as she struggled to steer in the darkness. To come so far and then risk losing him to an eight hundred-year-old wound was almost more than she could bear.

An apprehension made worse as Corbin's fleet closed in on the old Jeep with their newer cars. Rory was doing an admirable job driving over the bumpy road that wound its way around Nahariya and eventually ended up along the coast, but the pack of jackals was closing in and she knew she couldn't go much faster. If she was bordering on panic, she never let on. In fact, she almost found herself wishing Corbin would catch up. At least then, Kieran might agree to medical attention before the police locked them up and threw away the key.

Twisting their way around the hills, they emerged onto a flat stretch of land and the weak glitter of the ocean could be seen in the distance. The clouds were thickening, the smell of rain pervasive and, amidst her other troubles, Rory knew the wipers of the Jeep didn't work. In the arid lands of Israel, Bud had never given the broken blades much thought. But Rory was certainly thinking of them now. Lurching over a particularly bad bump, she gripped the old steering wheel too tightly and came away with a nasty blister.

The road sloped downward, heading for the Mediterranean. Corbin's cars were coming closer, like dogs nipping at her heel, and Rory spent a good deal of time watching the rearview mirror as the bright lights advanced. She was so involved with the approaching high beams that Kieran's warm, damp hand on her thigh startled her.

"Sweetheart," he murmured. "Mayhap you should stop the car. I do not believe it wise to run any longer."

She turned to him, noting how terribly pale he was. In fact, he looked very much as he had when she had first seen him in the grave; pallid. Refusing to fight her terror down any longer, she couldn't help the anguish in her voice.

"Oh, Kieran," she moaned. "We've got to find you a doctor. To hell with Corbin and his henchmen!"

He shook his head feebly, his bloodstained hand on her leg. "Libby, I've been running from Simon for eight hundred years. Mayhap I was not meant to elude him. Mayhap I should simply succumb to the inevitable."

"No!" she sobbed, the tears coming. "I won't let you! We've come too far for it to end like this!"

He smiled, touching her cheek and leaving a crimson streak. "It will never end between us, Lib. You and I are a part of one another, in this time or any other. We have accomplished our task and now we are finished. Mayhap it is time to allow history to fulfill its destiny."

She ran cold. "What does that mean?"

He sighed, the oozing wound draining his energy. "It means that eight hundred years ago, I defied death with the magic of an alchemist's potion. I cheated the natural course of life so that I could finish my sworn task. Now that my duty is complete, mayhap death is attempting to claim me as it should have those centuries ago. The closer Simon looms, the more my wound bleeds. I cannot believe it to be coincidence. The man was meant to kill me."

Rory sobbed, shaking her head. "You're not going to die," she whispered. "I won't let you. I'll get you far away from Corbin and we'll find a doctor who can heal you."

"There is no one who can heal me."

"Don't say that!" She slammed her hands against the steering wheel, almost losing control when it leaped over a series of harsh bumps. Gripping the steering column tightly, she wrestled for control in more ways than one. "Kieran, you're a part of me. We're incomplete without each other. If you die, I will, too!"

He touched her face again, his expression serious. Thick fingers wiped at the tears as she struggled to concentration on her driving. "Oh, Lib," he murmured. "Time could not keep us apart. Certainly death cannot either. I shall be waiting for you when you cross the threshold of Paradise, have no doubt. We shall spend eternity together, you and I."

She sobbed openly, losing focus of the road. "No, Kieran," she sputtered. "I don't want you to die. I want you to live. I want us to get married and have children and grow old together. I don't want you to leave me!"

He leaned over, grunting with pain and exertion, and lay his head on her shoulder. "I will never leave you, sweetheart. I love you with all that I am, all that I will ever be. Know this to be true, for all time."

She tried to touch him but the road was too rough and she couldn't risk letting go of the steering wheel. They were nearing the beach now, far away from Nahariya and entering Syrian territory.

The mob of Land Rovers wasn't far behind, their headlights casting flickering light on the sloping landscape of the sea. Sobbing as Kieran weakly comforted her, Rory took a turn too sharply and the Jeep nearly went over. Overcorrecting, she heard something snap and grind and the car suddenly came to a halt.

"Damn!" she screamed, beating at the steering wheel as if it would correct the problem. "Kieran, the car's busted. We can't…"

He smiled at her, so very weakly, his brown eyes filled with emotion. "I know we cannot run any longer. I am not meant to run any longer." When she started to sob again, he simply collected her hand, the crown, and opened the door. "Come along, Lib. I would show you something."

She let him pull her from the car. The Land Rovers were just coming over the rise in the near distance as Kieran staggered across the sandy soil, heading for the ocean. His wound was bleeding profusely, trailing down the leg of his new Levi's and staining his boots. Boots he had been so very proud of. Rory sputtered and wept, following him, having no idea where they were going. But Kieran knew.

He knew now.

The clouds overhead were beginning to rumble and a light rain fell as they neared the shore. Behind them, the Land Rovers came to a halt and soldiers in fatigues spilled forth, followed by two men in suits. But Kieran and Rory ignored the cluster of antagonists, heading for an outcropping of rock overlooking the turbulent swells.

His voice was soft as he spoke, the clear brown gaze moving across the dark waters. "Eight hundred years ago, I came ashore on a beach not dissimilar to this one," he grunted with strain as he mounted the rocks. "Hundreds of men and horses bound for the Holy Land, intending to rid God's country of the Muslim insurgents. I was one of those men and I wore the banner of England proudly."

Rory held on to him tightly as they moved to the top of the outcropping, falling into his embrace as he sank to his knees. She was weeping so heavily she could hardly hear him, and he stroked her tenderly. His heart aching for what he knew had to be.

"It was an awesome sight," he murmured, his cheek against the top of her head as he focused on the rolling sea. "I came on the quest because I believed in my king, in my father, and I was determined to make both of them proud. And by accepting the mission that would eventually end my life, I knew there was nothing more worthwhile I could ever do with my mortal existence. At least, that is what I believed until I met you. You and I are incredibly similar, Libby. Each wrought with determination, each aching deeply to find fulfillment. And each willing to jeopardize our destiny for what we believe in."

Rory wept into his shirt as the rain grew heavier and the army of men drew closer. She could see their features now as they crossed the sand, singling out Corbin immediately. He held out his hand to the group, silently ordering them to wait as he continued forward. A bolt of lightning lit up the sky, illuminating his evil face, and Rory raised her head from Kieran's shoulder in fury.

"Go away!" she shouted. "Go away and leave us alone!"

Corbin came to a halt several yards away. "I've come a very, very long way for you, Dr. Osgrove. I won't leave without you."

She shook her head, lying on Kieran's shoulder. "I'm staying with him."

Corbin shoved his hands into his pockets as the weather worsened. "You're both coming with me, I'm afraid. You've got a good deal of explaining to do."

Kieran heard him, the familiar voice of a man who had trailed him for centuries. But he ignored him for the moment, focused on the delicious warmth of Rory in his arms. Warmth, he suspected, he would not be experiencing much longer.

"The night I sought the alchemist, there was a storm very much like this one," he said softly, feeling Rory's grip on him tighten. "An angry storm, cursing the fact that I was intent to defy death. Not strange that a storm has gathered here tonight to witness what I evaded those centuries ago."

Rory tore her gaze away from Corbin, focusing on the ashen features of her beloved knight. Tears were still pouring but the sobs had faded. In fact, she seemed to be calming in spite of everything and she forced a smile, kissing him with a painful sweetness.

"If you go, I go with you," she said in a voice he dare not contradict. "If death is going to take you, then it is going to take me, too. You said yourself that God brought us together and I just can't believe that He would allow us to be separated after everything we've been through."

A shaking hand touched her face. Kieran's normally even expression was laced with emotion. "My sweet Rory," he murmured. "I do not want to leave you now, not even for a moment. But I cannot deny the wound steadily draining my life, nor the odd hollowness that has plagued me since my return to Nahariya. I suspect that the two are linked, announcing the onset of my true destiny. Now that the crown has been found, there is no longer any reason for me to live. But there is every reason for you to live. You must live. You must pay tribute to this love and duty that we have shared."

She shook her head, her composure making a weak return. "I will pay tribute by being at your side, for always. Don't deny me my true fulfillment, Kieran. I am nothing without you."

He didn't have the energy to argue. The rain was coming down in sheets, lightning filling the sky. He began to kiss her, tenderly at first, but with growing passion as if knowing this would be the last he tasted of her in this world.

Corbin and his men watched, so involved with the scene before them that they failed to notice a rickety old Jeep cresting the distant rise. One headlight was out, but the wipers were working. The vehicle loomed closer, eventually coming to a halt behind the cluster of Land Rovers.

"Don't go any closer, Corbin!"

Bud was out of the car before it came to a complete stop. He and

David raced across the wet sand, pelted by the driving rain. The lawyer heard the shout, turning to the source of the voice and muttering a silent curse. Bud continued to move towards him, aided by David when the man threw a punch at an intrusive Marine and sent the soldier sprawling.

"Do you hear me?" Bud shouted above the wind and rain. "Leave her alone. Leave them both alone!"

"Dr. Dietrich," Corbin said slowly. "I am not surprised to find you here. But you must know you cannot help her any longer. I've come for your associate and I demand to know what has become of the corpse she stole. What secret did it possess that she insisted on breaking the law to obtain it?"

Bud paused several feet before him, the rain lashing his face. After a moment, he gestured to the huddled pair on the rocks. "You want to know what secret it possessed?" his voice was steady. "Take a good look at that man in Rory's arms. There's your secret, Corbin. The living corpse of Sir Kieran Hage."

Corbin cocked an eyebrow, water dripping from his eyelashes. "Bloody Hell, Dietrich. Do you take me for a fool? Surely you don't think I'd be stupid enough to believe such an idiotic story!"

Bud shrugged. "Foolish or not, it's the truth. No one saw Rory carry a corpse from the hospital because Sir Kieran Hage walked out of that morgue. Remember what the nurse said? That she saw Rory in the company of a very large man." When Corbin shook his head, refusing to believe, Bud moved closer. "Think about it; if Rory was hiding a corpse, just how in the hell did she do it? Where did she do it? If she was so attached to the body like we've said all along, don't you think she would have kept it with her constantly?"

Corbin continued shaking his head, holding up a sharp hand. "Ridiculous, Dietrich. I will not listen to any more of this!"

"Would you listen to me, then?"

A soft voice floated up beside him. Corbin glanced over to see Darlow looking rather stunned. After a moment, the embassy aide fixed

Corbin in the eye. "I told you I saw the corpse. And that man on the rocks resembles the knight I saw most definitely. It's... it's truly amazing."

Corbin stared at Darlow, noting the sincerity in his voice. Sincere or not, however, it didn't erase the fact that two grown men were trying to convince him to believe in a fairy tale and his jaw ticked with irritation as he returned his attention to Bud.

"I will not listen to this any longer," he growled. "Dr. Osgrove is coming with me and her monstrous bodyguard will be placed in the custody of the Marines."

On the rocks, Rory and Kieran were listening to the exchange. Kieran was failing, his grip on Rory loosening as she embraced him tightly. On her knees with Kieran's head clasped to her breast, her anguished gaze locked onto Bud as another bolt of lightning streaked across the sky.

"Bud!" she cried. "Kieran's dying. We need to get him to a doctor immediately!"

Bud's brow furrowed as he took a couple of steps towards the rain-slicked rocks. "What happened to him?"

Rory started to cry again, the tears falling so easily these days. "His wound," she sobbed. "He reopened it somehow. He thinks Simon's appearance has something to do with it."

Bud was on the rocks before he could blink, almost slipping but managing to keep his footing. He was suddenly beside the two lovers, separating them gently and groaning softly when he saw Kieran's blood-soaked shirt.

"Oh... Christ," he muttered. "He's bleeding all over the damned place, Rory."

She sniffled in response as Bud noticed the bloodstained box between them. Kieran was holding it tightly and Bud found he couldn't take his eyes off it.

"Rory," he nodded his head at the small, wooden case. "Dave told me about the crown. Is... is that it?"

She gazed sadly at the box. "Yes," she blinked, tears splattering with the rain. "But I swear I'd give it back if it would make Kieran well again. It's just not worth the heartache it's caused, Bud."

"There was a man who thought differently, once," Kieran's voice was faint. "He believed it worth dying for."

"Well, I don't," Rory snapped at him. "It's not worth your life. God, I wish you'd never found the thing!"

Bud put his hand on her shoulder in a gesture of comfort and also to prevent her from flying out of control. Now was not the time for hysterics with Kieran bleeding to death before their eyes. Tearing his gaze away from the holy treasure he had spent over a year of his life searching for, his ice-blue eyes focused on the dying man.

"How ya doin', pal?" he asked, a ridiculous question, considering. "Looks like we've got to get you to a hospital."

The knight shook his head weakly. "'Tis of no use, my lord. Now that my task is complete, I am to die as I should have eight centuries ago."

Bud fixed Kieran in the eye, a man he should hate for stealing Rory but a man he found he could not hate. There was something in the man's nature that provoked Bud's respect in spite of everything. A determination and a sense of duty that Bud himself would have liked to possess.

"A doctor can help you, but we've got to go now," he said, feeling his desperation when Kieran, once again, shook his head. He didn't have time to argue with the man. "Look, Kieran; Rory means a great deal to me. Far too much to see her so miserable. If you die… she'll never be the same. I'll never be the same. No matter what we've been through, our differences and competition, in the end, all that matters is that the woman we both love is happy. Right?"

Kieran raised an eyebrow slowly, rain coating his ashen face. "Another selfless gesture, my lord. Pity I am unworthy of such respect for the misery I have caused you both."

"That's not true," Bud disagreed, casting the man a somewhat selfish glance. "Besides, I haven't finished pumping you for information. I haven't found out a damned thing!"

"David has served well in your stead," Kieran murmured, licking his wet lips. "The man is as persistent as a gnat."

Bud grinned. Even Rory grinned in spite of her tears. Bud held Kieran's gaze a moment longer before looking to his miserable colleague.

"We've got to get to a hospital," he said, wondering if it wasn't already too late. "Let me talk to Corbin and see what I can do."

He turned away from the drenched pair, sliding down the rocks until he reached the soaking sand. Shuffling across the grit, he focused on Corbin's haughty glare.

"Look," he said firmly. "Kieran is very sick. He's probably dying. We've got to get him to a hospital immediately."

Corbin drew in a deep breath. "Fine. I shall take them both in my custody now and will be more than happy to have the bodyguard escorted to a hospital." Suddenly, his right hand emerged from his pocket gripping a Beretta 9mm handgun. A porcelain gun manufactured in Germany that he had managed to get past the security checkpoints in both airports. Bud's eyes widened.

"What in the hell are you doing?" he hissed. "Put that damned thing away!"

Corbin aimed the gun directly at Bud's heart. "Not a chance, Dr. Dietrich. You and your associates are far too slippery for me to take any chances." He turned to the men behind him, keeping the gun aimed at Bud. "Take them. The bodyguard goes to the nearest hospital and the woman goes with me."

"No!" Rory shrieked, clutching Kieran tightly. "I must stay with him! I won't let you separate us!"

Corbin turned his attention to Rory, preparing to reply. Just as he did so, Bud saw his chance and lunged for the gun, immediately receiving a butt in the face. As he landed heavily in the sand, a Marine trained his own rifle on David before the man could move forward in his colleague's stead. With Bud wallowing just above unconsciousness and David effectively stopped, there was nothing left between Corbin and Rory.

Except Kieran.

He knew he was dying. He had nothing left to lose by protecting the woman he loved. Somehow finding the strength to disengage himself from her tight embrace, he rose to one knee and faced the man who had plagued him like an evil curse for centuries. The one man who was responsible for all of his misery.

"You will not separate us, Simon," he said weakly, feeling Rory's hands on his shoulders. "The lady will come with me."

Corbin stared at him, the odd sense of déjà vu plaguing him again. "Don't be a hero," he snarled. "From the look of you, you couldn't take a bullet wound."

Kieran cocked an eyebrow, holding out his arms as if to embrace the world. "Is that what you wish? To kill me as you once attempted eight hundred years ago?" He shrugged his massive shoulders. "Then complete your task. Complete what you started. But know this; I have what I came for. I have the crown and my lady will see that is returned to England, as I vowed. There is nothing more you can do to me to cause me any greater pain, Simon. But you can cause the lady great pain and I will not permit it. If I am to go to this hospital, then she will go with me. And you cannot stop her."

Corbin aimed the gun at Kieran's head. "You have interfered for the last time," he said with malice. "I don't know who you are and I've no idea why you insist on calling me Simon. But if killing you is what it takes to accomplish my goal, then I shall. Now, I will ask this only once; will you go peaceably?"

"With the lady at my side?"

"No."

"Then you have your answer."

Corbin cocked an eyebrow. "Very well, hero. Have it your way."

A gun went off. Rory screamed and screamed, her voice echoing off the rocks, the sky. But even as she continued screaming, she realized that Kieran had not been shot. He was still on one knee, his arms outstretched, watching Corbin fall face-first into the sand. Bud, David, Kieran and Rory all stared in astonishment as Justin Darlow, standing just behind Corbin, lowered the small caliber revolver in his left hand.

Darlow felt the stunned gazes as he continued to look upon the man he had just killed. When he did look up, his attention was directed at Rory.

"A man like Corbin only understands violence. I've known enough Corbins in my lifetime to know that. And I simply couldn't let him kill your knight in cold blood." His gaze found Kieran. Weakly, he shook his head. "I don't know why I believe you are who they say you are. But I do. How did you come back to life?"

Kieran wavered dangerously, falling on his rump as Rory dropped to his side, supporting him. The disbelief, the disorientation glazing his expression, was blatant.

"Through the miracle of love," he murmured, barely heard above the driving rain. "My... my lady and I will not be separated. I thank you for your assistance."

Darlow simply nodded. The gun dropped in the sand beside Corbin as if Darlow no longer possessed the strength to hold it. Being a law-abiding man, he couldn't understand what had provoked him into murder. Only that he feared for Kieran's and Rory's lives, for all their lives. Knowing that the evil that filled Corbin would never stop until someone stopped it. Until someone stopped him.

"You killed him." David's voice was filled with awe. And perhaps a bit of jealously. "By damn, Darlow, you killed him!"

Darlow turned to him. "I realize that and I don't particularly care. I was protecting the knight from Corbin's crazed assault and I am confident any jury will find that I did it to protect us all." He glanced over his shoulder at the lady and her knight, once again in a tight embrace as rain and lightning exploded around them. "He's a madman, you know. I just couldn't stand by and allow him to commit coldblooded murder. And he would have, too. Can't you see that the lady and her knight cannot be separated?"

"What about that speech you gave Rory about the purity of English heritage and all that?" Bud was on his feet, a huge bruise on his cheek. "Now you're saying that she and Kieran belong together?"

Darlow nodded faintly. "You know they do, too."

Bud simply stared at the man who had been willing to kill for the power of love. Odd how Sir Kieran Hage seemed to provoke the strongest of emotions wherever he went. Glancing to the sand where Corbin lay, he realized that it was finally over with the man. But the fact remained that Kieran was very ill and the need to get him to a hospital took precedence over all other thoughts at the moment.

"Come on." He motioned to Darlow and to the soldiers who had, thus far, stood silent and basically unmoving. Even the Marine who had been aiming his weapon at David had lowered it. "We've got to get him to a doctor. There's a small hospital not too far from here, about an hour up…"

Bud never finished his sentence. A huge burst of lightning suddenly lit up the sky, a jagged bolt crashing down on the outcropping of rocks where Kieran and Rory were huddled. Chunks of rock went flying and even as Bud screamed Rory's name, trying to protect himself from the white-hot projectiles, he knew his cries were in vain. He knew, before the smoke even settled, that she never heard him.

If you go, I go with you.

She had.

EPILOGUE

B UD HAD NEVER seen such opulence. David, either. As the two men stood in the foyer of Southwell, they could hardly believe the history and wealth surrounding them. Dressed in suits that hadn't seen the light of day in well over a year, they felt sorely out of place among the finery.

"Where's Becker?" David growled as he glanced about.

"He said he'd meet us here," Bud replied. In his hands, he clutched an object of particular significance and, glancing down for the thousandth time, roved the familiar lines of Sir Kieran's journal.

David tore his eyes away from a thirteenth century goblet displayed in its own case, watching Bud as he gazed at the leather-bound book. His expression softened. "Be brave, Bud," he said quietly. "You know this is where it belongs. Rory would want it here."

Bud struggled with his emotions, tears of anguish he had been wrestling with for over a week, ever since he witnessed Rory's death. There were times, still, when he simply sat and stared at the journal, the tears falling, wondering what he was going to do without her. Feeling like the journal was his last link to her and hardly wanting to relinquish it.

But relinquish it he must. Since returning to England, the journal had been the primary topic of any communication from the Hage family. Nothing about Kieran or Rory, simply the journal. Bud had to wire them the severely-altered version of what had become of Sir Kieran's corpse, just as he had been forced to wire Becker and Lunde of Rory's death. He had spent a day trying to get a call through but because of a downed satellite, it had been necessary to send a telegram. Odd, he'd never even received a reply. He was coming to wonder if they had even received it.

Becker had called him three times at the hotel, leaving messages all three times. And the last message instructed him to bring the journal to the Hage estate of Southwell just north of Nottingham. Becker was waiting and Bud and David rushed to make their designated appointment. They didn't want to anger the already-slighted family even more with their tardy arrival.

Which was why Bud couldn't believe they had been left waiting in the foyer of the manse by an arrogant butler, waiting for Becker and a representative of the Hage family as if they were waiting for the other shoe to drop. Bud continued to clutch the journal as David found enough courage to mull around, studying priceless heirlooms. Walking out in to the middle of the soaring entrance, he turned around to look at the wall over Bud's head.

"Hey, Bud," he gestured the man forward. "Look at this tapestry. Incredible!"

Bud went to stand beside his colleague, gazing up at the massive tapestry exhibited beautifully over one entire wall.

"Wow," he raised his eyebrows with as much excitement as he could muster. "Look at that detail."

David nodded. Then, his eyes narrowed as he looked closely at the scene depicted. "Do you see that knight – over there, on the right hand side? Hell, Bud, what's he holding?"

"The diadem of Christ," came the satisfied announcement.

Both Bud and David turned sharply to see a man descending the stairs. And by his side was none other than Uriah Becker, his hazel eyes alive with delight at the sight of his two archaeologists.

"Doctors Dietrich and Peck!" he greeted amicably. "Ah, the finest diggers in the world. Did you have any trouble finding Southwell, gentlemen?"

Bud looked rather stumped. Considering he himself was in a good deal of trouble with everything from aiding Rory's crime spree to witnessing her death, he could hardly understand the man's jovial attitude. He glanced at David before replying.

"Uh… no trouble at all, Dr. Becker," he said as if he didn't know how else to reply.

Becker and the man were at the bottom of the stairs. Becker shook Bud's hand happily before moving to David.

"Gentlemen, this is Sir Trevor Hage," he introduced the older man with clear brown eyes. "He is the patriarch of the Hage family. Lord Hage, I would like you to meet Dr. Frederick Dietrich and Dr. David Peck."

Lord Hage shook their hands congenially before gesturing to the tapestry above their heads. "I notice you were admiring the artwork." When Bud and David nodded with varied degrees of hesitance, he smiled. "As you well should. Considering you discovered the journal of the man it represents."

Bud suddenly remembered what he was holding. Without hesitation, he extended the carefully wrapped journal.

"Here it is, sir," he said quietly. "It's in fine shape, considering."

Lord Hage accepted the parcel, his expression creased with pleasure and reverence. "Considering it has been buried for eight hundred years? I am pleased to hear that. And I thank you deeply for returning it to Sir Kieran's devoted family."

"My pleasure," Bud mumbled. A lie, but he had no choice.

Becker was grinning like a kid at Christmas as he watched Lord Hage unwrap the journal. "A most delightful find, Bud. Based on your discovery, the Hage Family has graciously donated $100,000 to the university's archaeological fund. Isn't that marvelous?"

Bud stared at the man, hardly believing that he had yet to mention Rory. Instead of sensing sorrow or grief or even anger, all he could sense was joy and it puzzled him greatly.

"Terrific," he said, wondering if his bitterness was evident.

He and David continued to pass disbelieving glances as Becker and Lord Hage admired the journal. The tension in Bud's chest was swelling to the point of explosion when Lord Hage suddenly glanced up as if realizing he was being a terrible host.

"I do apologize for my bad manners," he said, glancing up at the tapestry again. "But this journal is… well, it's just marvelous. You cannot know how valuable this is to my family. But we were speaking of the tapestry, were we not?"

David nodded grimly. "What did you mean when you said the knight was holding the diadem of Christ?"

Lord Hage looked surprised. "Why, precisely that, of course. The knight in the picture is Sir Kieran Hage, returning from the Third Crusade with the diadem of Christ in his possession. History tells us that he ended the siege to Acre in January 1192 during what was considered some of the most…"

"January 1192?" David blurted, interrupting the man. "I beg to differ, Lord Hage, but the siege of Acre ended in July of 1192."

Hage laughed, looking at Becker. "Is that the sort of rubbish American education teaches its students?"

Becker cast David an odd glance. "David, you know better than that. How dare you embarrass me with your incorrect facts?"

David raised his eyebrows. Bud looked completely baffled. "But he's right, Dr. Becker. The siege of Acre ended…"

"It ended when Sir Kieran Hage presented the diadem of Christ to the collective Christian commanders and they agreed to a truce." Lord Hage was gazing up at the tapestry again. "A remarkable achievement for which my family is immensely proud. And, as you can see by the tapestry, he is presenting the diadem to the Bishop of Ely upon his return home."

Bud's mouth was hanging open, a creeping sense of bafflement making him uncomfortable. David was staring up at the tapestry, his brown eyes wide and his face unusually pale.

"He returned?" Bud muttered. "How… how is that possible?"

Lord Hage cocked an eyebrow. "Surely you know something of the man whose relics you've spent the better part of a year excavating." The curiosity in his tone was evident. "Although Sir Kieran was gravely injured on the Crusade, he nonetheless managed to return at the head of Richard's armies. The Diadem of Acre, as the crown is commonly known, was accepted by the bishop and placed under lock and key. Just like the Shroud of Turin, we English are only able to gaze upon the crown of Christ every 10 years or so when the church is gracious enough to allow us the privilege."

David tore his eyes away from the brilliant artwork, meeting Bud's stunned gaze. The odd sensation of disorientation enveloped them both until they could hardly make sense of the situation.

"A pity, really," Lord Hage continued. "Even though Sir Kieran returned to England what is considered to be the Holy Grail of all relics, mankind still refuses to pay the crown its heed. As with the Shroud, skeptics recant the truth of the matter. As if the faith of the entire Christian nation simply isn't enough."

"Faith," Bud murmured, still staring at David as if they were sharing a private conversation. "Sound familiar?"

David cocked an eyebrow, his bafflement gaining new heights. Lord Hage glanced at the two Americans, ignorant of their mutual confusion but noting their strange behavior all the same. Jetlag, he assumed. "And I must say, Dr. Peck, that your theory to match any DNA that might remain on the crown with swatches of DNA from the Shroud of Turin to be an amazing concept." He was sincere as he fixed David in the eye. "My niece, who just received her Master's in Medieval History, is working diligently to arrange such a test. It will take time, but you were correct when you told Dr. Becker that it would bring the human race one step closer to believing the truth of Christ. We are most eager to aid in the endeavor."

David looked as if he had been struck. It had been Rory's theory to match DNA swatches, not his. But, at this moment, he had no idea how to refute the man's statement. Lord Hage and Dr. Becker seemed so confident with the bizarre twisting of events that the more David stared at the brown-eyed lord, the more speechless he became. What in the hell was going on here, anyway?

Lord Hage, however, remained unaware of the man's shock. He was simply eager to speak on a subject that was of great interest to them all. "Forgive me for moving off the subject yet again. But I find your DNA theory absolutely fascinating." He turned away from David, pointing up to the left hand side of the tapestry. "Let us return to Sir Kieran's triumph. You will notice the woman dressed in royal purple; that is his wife, probably the single most influential person in his life. I am constantly amazed how this work is able to capture the expression of pride on her face as she observes him relinquish the diadem. Such marvelous skill."

Bud did look to the tapestry, then. He had to. And what he witnessed jolted him so strongly that he couldn't conceal his naked response.

"My God," he breathed. "Dave, do you see..?"

"I see," David said before he could finish his sentence. "Jesus Christ, I see... her!"

As the archaeologists struggled with their awe, Lord Hage beamed at the depiction of a beautiful woman swathed in finery. "The Lady Laura Elizabeth Hage. A truly gifted woman who seemed to have rather modern ideas for a proper Medieval wife. She was a great advocate for health care, education for women, and so on. Well ahead of her time, actually."

David's mouth was hanging open, staring at the tapestry as if he were seeing a ghost. Bud, his puzzlement knowing little restraint, turned to Becker with an expression of such astonishment that the older man thought his subordinate was becoming ill.

"Bud?" he asked with concern. "Are you well?"

Bud shook his head. Then he nodded. Swallowing hard, he put a hand on Becker's arm. "Christ… what's going on here? What's Rory doing on that tapestry?"

"Rory?" Becker's brow furrowed. "Who's Rory?"

Bud blinked as if he hadn't heard correctly. "Who's Rory…? She's your grandniece, Dr. Becker. The one who instigated the Nahariya dig, the one who found Sir Kieran's corpse. The one who… oh, Christ, you're not understanding any of this, are you?"

Becker's brow was furrowed, gazing at Bud as if the man had completely lost his mind. "Bud, I don't have a grandniece. My only living niece is a church secretary in San Diego and… are you sure you're feeling well?"

Bud's eyes were as wide as saucers. "No," he said frankly, looking at David and seeing his own astonishment mirrored in the man's features. After a moment, he returned his attention to Becker. "I don't think I'm well at all. In fact, I think I'm going crazy. So you're telling me that you don't have a niece named Rory?"

Becker shook his head. "I do not."

"And there's no Sylvia Lunde on the Board of Regents?"

"My niece's name is Sylvia. But how did you know that Lunde is her maiden name?"

Bud's expression tightened and he scratched his head in a baffled gesture. "I knew because…hell, this is just nuts. If you don't know who Rory is and your niece isn't a Doctor of Ministry, then tell me what you know about me? Aren't I in trouble for aiding someone suspected of stealing a corpse?"

Becker raised an eyebrow. "Not as far as I know. What corpse are you speaking of, Bud?"

Bud just stared at him, trying to comprehend what was happening and hardly caring that he was coming across as a total lunatic. He just didn't know how else to react. "All right." His voice was soft as he struggled to compose himself. "So you don't know anything about me, Rory or anything else that has happened over the past two weeks. Then what about Corbin?"

Lord Hage intervened at that point. "I must apologize for Steven Corbin, Dr. Dietrich. I never gave him permission to go to Nahariya and to steal the journal from you."

"Steal?" Bud repeated blankly. "But... but what about Darlow? He's facing murder charges, isn't he?"

"He was protecting you and Dr. Peck from Corbin's murderous rage." Lord Hage shook his head sadly. "I've known Steven Corbin for years and I will admit he was something of an aggressive man. But trying to kill you for the journal just to eliminate any competition for its priceless significance... I simply don't understand what possessed him. Thank God the embassy had sent Darlow to mediate the transfer of antiquities. Had he not been there, I would most likely be attending your funeral at this moment. And Corbin would have gotten away with murder."

Just like he did eight centuries ago. Bud couldn't bring himself to reply, his ice-blue gaze moving between Becker and Lord Hage. Nothing was as it should be in a world just slightly out of the norm. From the course of history to the relations of Becker's family, nothing was as Bud had left it when he had departed England for Nahariya a week ago. A slight alteration, a curious twist of events... nothing was the same. Nothing was as he remembered it.

And it all stemmed from the tapestry. He could feel the hazel eyes blazing at him and he looked up, staring at a face he knew very, very well. It was the most peculiar sensation he had ever experienced, yet at the same time he couldn't help the burst of understanding that enveloped him. As if the longer he stared at the lovely features, the more comprehension and joy they conveyed.

Swallowing away the last remnants of confusion, he gestured weakly at the tapestry. "Sir Kieran's wife... tell me about her."

Lord Hage moved up beside him, his brown gaze lingering on the beautiful young woman. "Not much to tell, actually. Sir Kieran brought her back from the Crusades, but she wasn't Muslim. As you can see, she was very fair and quite beautiful. There had been speculation that she was an Irish heiress, but that was never substantiated. They had ten children – eight sons, Frederick, David, William, Christopher, Gaston, Christian, Beckett, Konnor, and two daughters, Britton and Jordan. Nine of their children survived into adulthood, including all eight sons. Quite remarkable, really. Their firstborn, Sir Frederick Hage, was a brilliant and powerful knight who married a niece of King Henry III." Lord Hage's gaze moved from the tapestry, focusing on Bud. "You weren't, perchance, named for the knight, were you?"

Bud couldn't manage to tear his gaze away from Rory's face, his head slowly moving back and forth. "Why do you ask?"

"Because his nickname was Bud," Lord Hage said softly. "Since I heard Dr. Becker address you by the same term, I thought the coincidence quite striking."

Bud was still staring at the tapestry, his eyes stinging with tears of understanding. He knew without a doubt that Rory had not perished on the rocks of the distant Israeli beach. And he also knew, doubtlessly, that the strike of lightning meant to end Rory and Kieran's lives had, instead, been a beginning. Like the hand of time reaching down to claim her misplaced children, taking them back to where they belonged.

He finally removed his gaze from the display, looking at David. And from the expression on the man's face, it was apparent that he understood, too. Bud couldn't keep the smile from his face.

"But she lived a long and healthy life?" he asked.

Lord Hage nodded. "Sir Kieran preceded her in death by six months, dying at the ripe old age of seventy-three. In those days, their collective longevity was astounding. Would you like to see the crypt?"

Bud looked at the man, off-balance by the unexpected question. "W-What?"

Lord Hage raised his eyebrows in a patient gesture, as one does when dealing with an idiot. "I asked if you would like to see the crypt. They are buried together, you know. Sir Kieran is said to be embracing his beloved wife for all time."

The tears that were stinging Bud's eyes broke through. He simply couldn't help it. Hastily, feeling like a fool, he wiped at them and nodded his head. "I'd like that," he whispered. "He... he must have loved her a great deal."

Lord Hage snorted. "In a day when love was a rare thing, indeed, Sir Kieran and his Libby were an anomaly. He loved her a great deal."

"And she was happy?"

"As far as the family chronicles tell us. Something of a spirited woman, too. Sir Kieran himself wrote that he was forced to spank her once when she flagrantly disobeyed him, although the exact nature of the infraction was not recorded."

Bud had to laugh. It sounded so much like Rory. Looking at David, he wasn't surprised to notice a similar grin; indeed, they knew her well. Taking a deep breath, Bud suddenly felt as if the weight of the world had been lifted from his shoulders. A strange miracle of fate that had brought lives about full circle and he turned again, gazing at Rory's beautiful face one last time. He simply couldn't help himself.

"So that's what happened to you," he whispered. "I told you to be happy, honey. I guess you finally were."

David heard him, pretending there was something in his eye when what he really wanted to do was burst into tears. It was all so over-whelming and for a man unused to believing in myths, the past week had seen a remarkable change of opinion. Were the Loch Ness monster to swim into his bathtub, he would have believed without hesitation.

Dr. Becker and Lord Hage, however, were gazing at the two archae-ologists and wondering if fourteen months in the heat hadn't cooked their brains beyond repair. To say the men had reacted strangely to the tapestry would have been a gross understatement. In fact, Lord Hage was about to suggest they all retire to his study for a hefty shot of bourbon when faint footfalls caught his attention. Glancing to the wide doorway just off of the main hall, he smiled pleasantly at the emerging figure.

"Ah," he said, grasping the woman by the hand. "Gentlemen, I would like you to meet my niece, Laura Hage. Laura, these are the men who found Sir Kieran's journal."

Bud heard David give a sort of strangled sound. Looking away from the tapestry, he suddenly found himself staring into hazel eyes and a face that was familiar in more ways than one.

"You must be Dr. Dietrich," Christ, even her voice sounded familiar. "I'm so pleased to meet you."

Slammed with a second shock in less than five minutes, Bud moved woodenly to shake the hand of a woman who looked suspiciously like...

"My pleasure, Ms. Hage." He nearly choked on his words, feeling the heat of recognition embrace him.

Laura held his hand a moment; Dear God, but the man was strikingly handsome. Bud Dietrich was a man she had wanted to meet since she had heard of his discovery. And now that they had finally been introduced, she hardly knew what to say, only knowing that she wanted to know him better. Beyond the prestige of his find, she was curious about the man with the ice-blue eyes who gazed at her with a warmth that touched her very soul.

"Laura," Lord Hage broke into her train of thought. "Dr. Dietrich and Dr. Peck would like to see Sir Kieran's crypt. Do you mind?"

"Not at all." Laura smiled, nearly sending Bud to his knees with the beauty of the gesture. "I'd be happy to. In fact, it will give us some time to talk about my progress on the DNA tests and all the bloody red tape I've run in to. If you will follow me, gentlemen."

She was still holding Bud's hand. Or perhaps he was still holding hers. Whatever the case, Bud would remember that magnetic moment for the rest of his life. And Laura would, too, going so far as to reminisce about their first meeting on the eve of their wedding.

She couldn't have explained the feeling if she'd tried, Laura told a host of gleeful guests. One look into Bud's eyes and she knew she had found what she had been looking for. Lifting her glass to toast her new groom, she thanked her ancestor, Sir Kieran Hage, for bringing them together.

Bud thanked him as well. And Rory, too.

You're not such a bad guy, after all.

Remember that, honey. When the time comes, you'll know.

❧ THE END ❧

The Crusader Series includes the House of Hage, and includes the following novels:

Kingdom Come

Of note: The House of Hage has the distinction of being the only house with two characters – one hero and one popular secondary character – of the same name yet they are not the same man. It gets confusing, so let's explain:

Kieran Hage #1 is the hero from THE CRUSADER and KINGDOM COME. If you recall in KINGDOM COME, which is a time-travel novel dealing with Rory and Kieran being back in Medieval times, there's a big twist at the end of the book. I don't want to blow this twist for those of you who haven't read it (and you MUST read it because it's a killer twist), Kieran "disappears" from Medieval England at that point. He leaves behind his young son, Tevin, who was named after Tevin du Reims of WHILE ANGELS SLEPT, who was his mother's father (Kieran's grandfather). If you recall, Tevin from WHILE ANGELS SLEPT was the UNCLE of Christopher de Lohr because Tevin's sister,

Val, married Myles de Lohr, a knight. These two became parents to Christopher and David de Lohr, making Christopher and David distantly related to both Kieran Hages.

Kieran Hage #1, having left Medieval England at the end of KINGDOM COME, left behind his son, Tevin, who his brother Sean raised as his own. Tevin Hage was a great man, a powerful knight, and he was told that his father, Kieran, had been killed, as had his mother. Both of his parents are gone. Therefore, he knew his father was Kieran #1 and that Sean, even though he raised him, was his uncle. Sean then had three sons of his own that were younger than his nephew, Tevin, and it was Sean's youngest son, Jeffrey (named for Kieran #1 and Sean's father) who had Kieran #2, named for Kieran #1. Kieran #2 is the Kieran who appears in The Wolfe and Serpent.

Therefore – Kieran #2 from THE WOLFE is Kieran #1's great-nephew.

Kevin Hage's father is Kieran Hage from The Wolfe.

The Wolfe

Kevin Hage also appears in Serpent.

Serpent

While Angels Slept

For more information on other series and family groups, as well as a list of all of Kathryn's novels, please visit her website at www.kathrynleveque.com.

ABOUT KATHRYN LE VEQUE

Medieval Just Got Real.

KATHRYN LE VEQUE is a USA TODAY Bestselling author, an Amazon All-Star author, and a #1 bestselling, award-winning, multi-published author in Medieval Historical Romance and Historical Fiction. She has been featured in the NEW YORK TIMES and on USA TODAY's HEA blog. In March 2015, Kathryn was the featured cover story for the March issue of InD'Tale Magazine, the premier Indie author magazine. She was also a quadruple nominee (a record!) for the prestigious RONE awards for 2015.

Kathryn's Medieval Romance novels have been called 'detailed', 'highly romantic', and 'character-rich'. She crafts great adventures of love, battles, passion, and romance in the High Middle Ages. More than that, she writes for both women AND men – an unusual crossover for a romance author – and Kathryn has many male readers who enjoy her stories because of the male perspective, the action, and the adventure.

On October 29, 2015, Amazon launched Kathryn's Kindle Worlds Fan Fiction site WORLD OF DE WOLFE PACK. Please visit Kindle Worlds for Kathryn Le Veque's World of de Wolfe Pack and find many action-packed adventures written by some of the top authors in their genre using Kathryn's characters from the de Wolfe Pack series. As Kindle World's FIRST Historical Romance fan fiction world, Kathryn Le Veque's World of de Wolfe Pack will contain all of the great story-telling you have come to expect.

Kathryn loves to hear from her readers. Please find Kathryn on Facebook at Kathryn Le Veque, Author, or join her on Twitter @kathrynleveque, and don't forget to visit her website and sign up for her blog at www.kathrynleveque.com.

CPSIA information can be obtained
at www.ICGtesting.com
Printed in the USA
BVHW041728030521
606361BV00006B/88